Pat

The Lure of the Phantom's Call

Dax, too, was caught in its web, the man in him struggling, fighting hard to warn her away. Every muscle roared for release, to be able to move, to speak, to somehow save her. A few more steps and she'd be close enough to his image...close enough to the swirling mass of dark magic that had created that image. Soon the illusion of him would ripple with a cresting energy. She would hear his voice in her head, huskier this time, a heady seduction. She'd see him extend one arm, offering her his hand, and she wouldn't be able to deny him. The Phantom would reach for her, all might and magic and murderous mystery—and her soul would be smuggled right out of her, nothing left but the shell of her body.

Dax couldn't let that happen. *He wouldn't.*

But even as the thought coalesced in his brain, he heard his Phantom call to her. He felt the lift of his arm...watched as his hand stretched out...and saw his fingers curl back in an age-old gesture that meant one thing: *Come. Come to me.*

And she came. God. She came to him.

Phantom

Lindsay Randall

LOVE SPELL NEW YORK CITY

For Cheryl Bazzoui.
You inspire me, my friend.

LOVE SPELL®

June 2008

Published by

Dorchester Publishing Co., Inc.
200 Madison Avenue
New York, NY 10016

ISBN 10: 0-505-52765-0
ISBN 13: 978-0-505-52765-3

The name "Love Spell" and its logo are trademarks of Dorchester Publishing Co., Inc.

Printed in the United States of America.

10 9 8 7 6 5 4 3 2 1

Visit us on the web at www.dorchesterpub.com.

Acknowledgments

Huge thanks to Wendy Lindstrom, Ann McCauley and Lauren Nichols for critiquing the early chapters of this work, and to my family—especially Randy and Jason—for their unwavering support.

Phantom

BOOK ONE

The Betrothed

Chapter One

The Boy and his Phantom Riders

Along the Sussex Coast of England
April 1803

A cold wind swept inland from the Channel, bringing with it freezing rain that would soon turn to snow and coat the night in white. A young boy framed in the small-paned window of a chilled and tiny seaside cottage stared out at a deserted stretch of road gradually being covered by chunks of hail. He could perceive the clatter of an approaching carriage, and beyond that the ominous sound of rapid hoofbeats. He stretched his thoughts past the unexpected coach, focusing on what followed: riders, three of them, a few leagues distant and coming fast. Coming for him.

He'd first felt their presence in France four months ago, when the man his father had hired to protect him had whisked him through the winter-bare province where his mother had been born. It was as if his brief time there had brought something dormant to life, something evil stirred by his nearness and now determined to find him. Every day since then he'd felt whoever or whatever it was pressing closer.

He'd not shared any of this with his guardian, Sir Dysart Carlyle, for to do so would have meant having to explain his suddenly heightened sense of hearing and sight. It would have meant trying to explain the constant chill in his body, the urge to roam that invaded him every time night cloaked the land, and the fact that he no longer needed more than an hour's sleep. But worst of all, it would mean revealing the terrifying wisdom that had crushed his innocence, filled him with a knowledge too burdensome for a boy of twelve.

For weeks he'd wished the riders would catch up to him and end this odd existence into which he'd been thrust. Now they nearly had. By dawn, he'd either be damned . . . or dead.

He shifted his focus. From the corner of the room behind him he could hear the whispered exchange of Sir Dysart and the mysterious woman who'd come to meet them at this desolate place. They thought he couldn't make out their hushed words. They were wrong. He heard sounds other humans couldn't, perceived images others never would, and felt things he wished to God he didn't.

"You have watched him?" the woman asked Sir Dysart.

"I have. Constantly."

"And?"

"Nothing. He shows no signs of being . . . like them."

A breath of relief escaped her. "Perhaps that means we have been wrong."

"Perhaps," Sir Dysart murmured. "Still, I don't think it is wise to introduce him to the girl. Not yet, not until we're certain."

"I disagree," the woman said. "I believe my niece holds far more gifts than her mother and I combined. Meeting her will give the boy hope, a glimpse at what his future can hold if only he and she—"

The woman immediately fell silent, leaving the sentence unfinished as she finally heard the approaching carriage come rattling down the pitted, icy road and haul to a stop.

"Dax," Sir Dysart called.

Dax, eyes narrowing at the words the two had shared and thought he couldn't hear, turned slowly about. He watched as the woman drew up the hood of her cloak, cast him a warm smile, then quickly headed outside.

"Step away from the window, my boy," Sir Dysart gently coaxed. "We don't want anyone seeing your face."

Irritation bolted through him. "You have brought me to what looks like the edge of the world, sir. Who is there to see me?" he demanded.

Sir Dysart frowned wearily. "One can never be certain, Dax. Surely I have taught you that much."

Dax. How he hated the name that wasn't his own. He was so much more: the son of a titled Englishman and Parisian-born mother. But Dax was what he would be called once he and Sir Dysart left Sussex and continued on the too-familiar journey of finding a safe haven for him.

In the past, he'd been given other names, on other continents. Robert, John, Michael . . . The list was unpleasantly long. It shouldn't have mattered to be given yet another new name. Not after so many years of being bustled about, hidden, kept "safe." Not when the riders trailing him were nearly upon him.

But that's precisely why it *did* matter. He felt suddenly as if he would never reach the edge of another morning, felt as if something sinister would snare him this night.

He was tired of running, of not knowing why he'd been forced to leave home. His life should have been different. His father should be here to protect him, his mother to comfort him. But his father feared him, and his mother was dead—her soft, white throat cut by a knife-wielding thief who had lunged into their coach one evening. The clearest memory he carried from his past was the moment when he was five and his mother had been murdered. The small, crescent-shaped scar just beneath the outer corner of his left eye reminded him how miserably he'd failed to defend her. Held tight in that memory was how his father, bereft yet coldly stern, had forced him from home in the days following.

"Do not call me Dax," he suddenly blasted. "It's not my name. I am—"

"No," Sir Dysart cut in. "You are Dax, born in some hap-

less village, orphaned, and unable to recall your earliest years. Is that clear?"

He didn't reply.

"God's teeth, lad! For the sake of your father and your own life, *you can be nothing more*, do you hear?"

Dax turned to the window again, hating the flat, ugly reality of his life. "I hear you," he muttered. B'god, he heard everything. But he didn't understand a bloody thing about his luckless past . . . and wondered if he ever would.

Silence then. Nothing but the wind blasting against the aged slats of the cottage, the hail pounding down . . . and the far-off thundering of hoofbeats as the relentless riders cut through the ice-ridden night in search of him.

Dax stared out at the frozen world. For seven long years Sir Dysart had kept him secluded from all others, tutoring him, pushing him through countless hours of study as they journeyed far from England. It had always been just the two of them. Now they'd returned to English soil and Sir Dysart had brought this woman to see him, with another carriage in her wake. It made no sense.

Dax watched the driver of the coach let down the steps and pop open the door. A young girl emerged. The running lamps of the coach caught and held in her gaze, and for the flash of a moment Dax could see clearly that she had the most stunning violet eyes. The woman had whispered to Sir Dysart that the girl possessed "gifts." Dax wondered what those gifts might be in one so young. Fist-fat, dark curls framed her face, which was couched in an ermine-trimmed hood. Huddling against the wind and hail, the girl eagerly reached out a gloved hand to the woman and hurried for the door of the cottage with her.

The chill that swept inside with them matched the ever-present cold in Dax's bones. "Who are they?" he demanded of his guardian. "Why have they come?"

Sir Dysart frowned. "Where are you manners, lad?"

"I have none," he shot back. "I am Dax, remember? Orphaned, luckless, with a past not worth recalling."

"Young man, my patience with you this day is wearing thin. You will introduce yourself to the ladies and—"

"Dysart," the woman interrupted, her gaze not leaving Dax, "do not scold. He has a right to ask questions." Her eyes warmed. "I am Lady Amelia Archer, and I'd like for you to call me Amy. I am your godmother, and your sweet, lovely mother was my closest friend."

Heat streaked through Dax's chilled body, searing his chest, the pain twisting his heart. He couldn't remember his mother's face. Only the scent of rosewater and the softness of her hands remained vivid in his memory.

"Has anyone ever told you that you've eyelashes very much like hers, long and curling at the ends . . . and that you've also her height and grace of form?"

Dax shook his head, choked by the huge lump forming in his throat.

"Well, you do," Amelia said, "and it is a shame you haven't been told as much by now. But I am here to change all of that." She tilted her head to one side, her gaze soft. "Though I can see your mother in you, I can also see the stamp of your father. I see him in the way you boldly stand and how you tip your chin up, just so, as if questioning everything, trusting nothing."

Dax felt a tug deep inside his soul. "You . . . know my father?"

Amelia nodded. "It is the reason Sir Dysart has brought you here, so that I can tell you about your parents—and also for you to meet Robyn." Amelia glanced down at the girl by her side. "This is my niece—Lady Robyn Sophia Amelia Sinclair, daughter of Lord and Lady Chelsea. I call her Robbie."

Dax's gaze slid to the girl who couldn't have been more than six or seven years old.

Lady Robyn sent him a shy smile as she clutched her aunt's arm, pressing her cheek against it. "Hullo," she said, though fabric and her fear of him muffled the word.

Even so, the sound of her voice was like a warm blanket fluttering down over the coldness in Dax.

"Robyn is your betrothed," Amelia said quietly.

His world slammed to a stop.

"Your parents chose her on the day of her christening to be your wife, and Lord and Lady Chelsea agreed . . . or rather, the Countess of Chelsea, my sister, agreed." Amelia waited a moment, then added, "I thought, given all the years you and Sir Dysart have been on the road, that you needed to know this."

Emotion bloomed hard inside of Dax. He felt the prick of tears, but blinked them away. It was difficult to believe there existed in this bitter world someone with whom he was destined to share a life, to create a home, a *family*. How he ached to be part of a family.

"Well?" Amelia whispered. "What do you think of all this?"

What did he think? He thought her too young and shy, but mostly he thought of his parents and how much he missed them. "Perhaps my father does not hate and fear me as much as I have believed all these years," Dax whispered, his voice rough with feeling.

"Of course he doesn't."

"Then why did he order me taken from him? Why does he not allow me to come home? It is because he believes I am the reason my mother died, isn't it? He cannot stand the sight of me or the memory of what I caused . . . and he lives in fear of what I—I may still cause. That's it, isn't it?"

"No," Amelia said, and then, more softly added, "You are not the reason your mother died, and your father does not fear you. He fears *for* you. He keeps you hidden because he wants to keep you safe." She let out a soft breath and glanced briefly at Sir Dysart, then back at Dax. "It's time you were told, my sweet, that your father has a very powerful enemy. We believe they are responsible for your mother's death. They've been trying to ruin your father

by casting doubt on his allegiance to England. And we also believe they will harm you if they ever find you."

Dax could scarcely believe all he was hearing . . . about a hidden enemy and whispers of treason. Anger churned inside him at all that he'd lost. "But why come after us? What did we do?" he cried in frustration.

"If we knew the 'why,' it would be much easier to find the 'who,'" Sir Dysart said. "I'm sorry, lad, but right now this is the best way to keep you safe."

"Sometimes," Dax muttered, "I feel as though I have come from nothing and—and am headed for nothing. It is as though I have no past and will never have a future."

"But you do have a future," Amelia said. "That is why I've brought Robyn here to meet you, so that you can have a glimpse of that future." She smiled down at her niece, who was still half hiding in the fold of her cloak. "Robyn has a gift for you. It is something that has been handed down through our family for years and is filled with goodness, isn't it, Robbie?"

Robyn nodded. At her aunt's urging, the girl stepped forward and held out her left hand, which was fisted around the secret treasure. "Aunt Amy says this will keep you safe," Robyn said, turning her gloved hand palm down and then opening her fingers as Dax reached out.

It was a hammered piece of old silver worn smooth, heavy and heart-shaped and threaded to a hair ribbon as red as a valentine.

A necklace. "Um, thanks," Dax said.

He heard the wind moan outside—and more: the hoof-beats again, closer this time, too close. How had he let himself forget about the riders? He should have told Sir Dysart and Amelia before now. He should have told them when Amelia first entered the cottage. Now Robyn was at risk—all of them were.

Suddenly, there came a loud knock at the cottage door. Sir Dysart glanced out one window and then opened the door, asking for a report from the breathless man who stood there.

"Riders, sir," the man answered gravely, casting a glance in Dax's direction.

"How many?"

"Three. Spotted to the west and coming fast."

"You know what to do, Harry," Sir Dysart said.

"I am being followed, aren't I?" Dax demanded.

Amelia's mouth thinned into a straight line. "Yes, but you've not yet been found," she said firmly, not giving Dax a chance to explain that he'd known of the riders for months. "I've planned for this." She looked at her niece. "Robbie, my love, I'm sorry, but you'll have to head back to Land's End. You'll go in one carriage." Her gaze slid to Dax. "You, Sir Dysart, and I will head south in the other. We must all move quickly. Everything will be all right."

Dax didn't believe her. Nothing would be all right, he knew, until he faced the riders from his mother's birthplace and met whatever terror they held. "No," he said. "The rest of you go." They wanted him.

Amelia wasn't listening. Neither was Sir Dysart.

Amelia kissed Robyn on the forehead, then moved to whisper with Sir Dysart at the opposite side of the room. Dax would have focused on their hushed words, but Robyn, her very nearness, drew his attention solely to her.

He stared hard at the slip of a girl who had made him think about his past and had allowed him to dare to dream of a future. "Do you have gifts?" he asked, the question just tumbling out, his need to know strong.

"You mean presents?"

"No. I mean . . . like magic."

"Oh," Robyn said, and then shook her head. "My mama does . . . and Aunt Amy. They say I will, too. Someday."

Dax said nothing, only listened.

"Mama says that all my magic is in my heart."

Dax tightened his fist around the hammered silver, wanting to believe.

Sir Dysart called out, telling Dax it was time to leave.

Robyn's gaze remained locked on him. "My mama tells me to breathe when I am afraid."

She breathed.

And Dax breathed.

He sucked in a breath so hard it caused the scent of Robyn to whisper deep inside of him. Though it was winter, she smelled of warm, dreamy days—the kind he'd once known—and of hope. She smelled deeply of hope.

He didn't want to leave her. Not now. Not ever. Wanting desperately for Robyn to remember him, Dax pulled the lone plume from his hat. "Will you do one thing for me?" he asked.

Robyn, eyes going wide, nodded shyly.

"Take this," he said, handing the feather to her. "Let it be a wing for your every dream. Will you do this for me— for always?"

"Why?" she whispered.

Dax blinked back his tears and every one of his fears. "Because I don't think I'm going to have any of my own dreams come true. It will make me happy to know that all of yours will."

Long after Robyn was put into one carriage and he into another, Dax thought about that moment, about what he'd said. *Always* had never been a concept he could grasp . . . not until he'd met Robyn.

The mysterious riders overtook them an hour before dawn as their carriage raced fast along a lonely stretch of road. There came a shot of gunfire, then another and another. The lead horse crumpled in a hideous flailing of limbs. The driver was cut down on his seat, and Sir Dysart, bravely trying to climb out onto the box, was shot in the chest as he opened the carriage door, his body falling lifelessly away.

Dax cried out, his mind tumbling with stark terror and disbelief.

It was Amelia who kept a cool head. She pulled from her pocket a small, loaded derringer and pressed it into Dax's shaking hands even as the two of them were tossed about the inside of the vehicle. She managed to haul Dax up by his coat collar and then steady both herself and him near the door.

"You have to jump!" she told him.

Dax shook his head.

Amelia stared him straight in the eyes, willing him to be brave. "Once you hit the ground," she yelled over the wild wind and the mad creaking of the carriage, "you must get to your feet and start running and not stop. Do you hear me, Dax? *Do not stop*. Not for anything."

"But what about you?" he yelled.

"I'll follow if I can."

"And if you can't?" He suddenly sensed they wouldn't end the jump together.

"You keep going. Don't let them catch you. Do what you must to save yourself."

Dax, feeling the small pistol in his hands, knew what she meant. "I—I don't want to do this. I don't want to leave you!"

"You must."

Dax thought again of that final carriage ride when his mother had been killed. He couldn't allow the same to happen to Amelia.

Holding tight to the handle of the derringer, Dax turned to face the open door. He slammed his eyes shut against the driving, icy rain, against the blur of land whizzing past . . . and jumped.

He hit the hard earth, bounced and rolled and bounced again and again. He felt the bone of his nose crack, felt his shoulder jam into his back. His face was soon covered with blood and his left eye was stinging mightily. The ground was hard and wet, coated with icy snow. Down and down he rolled, thrust forward by a momentum he couldn't control . . . until finally he stopped, his head ramming hard

into a tree trunk just as the derringer fired in his fist and
the world went black.

Snow fell softly in huge, white flakes. Flat on his back, his
face to a leaden gray sky, he held perfectly still. A roar of
sound engulfed him; he heard *everything*, the air shifting
across the land, critters burrowing in the ground—even
the falling snow had a sound. His body ached, his nose
felt broken and swollen, and his chest burned as if there
were a gaping hole in it.

He wondered where he was and what had happened,
but his mind was blank. Empty. Swiping one hand across
his numb face, he saw the crimson smear of his own blood.

The sight of it, and the fact that he had no clear thoughts,
caused bile to bubble up his throat, the stuff burning as it
washed against the back of his tongue. Rolling to one side,
he spit it out, gagging as he sucked hard for air.

It hurt to breathe. It hurt even more to think. Forcing
himself to sit, he tried hard to remember what had happened, where he was . . . *who* he was.

Somewhere to his right, above and behind him, he
heard the sounds of frozen twigs snapping and the snort
of a horse. Fear gripping him, he jerked around, catching
sight of a giant of a man on horseback coming down the
incline toward him.

"Ho!" the stranger called out. "Y' be lookin' like y' could
use some help."

He hunkered down, staring up at the stranger.

Couched in thick, much-mended outerwear, the man
looked like a beast astride. His hair was long and shaggy
and of an indecipherable hue, given its filth and the snow
that clung to it. His teeth were rotted, his eyes an unearthly shade of green, and his meaty, ruddy face a mask
of scars and hard living. The only remarkable thing about
him was the horse he sat so well—pricey, well-bred . . . and
obviously stolen.

Drawing the beast to a halt, the man asked, "What's yer name, boy?"

A simple enough question, and yet he had no answer.

"Are y' daft? Y' got a name, don't y'?"

Did he? He couldn't remember, he—"Dax," he suddenly ground out in a heave of breath, "my name is Dax." It seemed that if he didn't say the name fast enough it might somehow escape him, as every other thought had.

"Dax, huh? Y' don't look so certain-sure o' that, boy."

He sat up straighter, angry to be questioned, angry because . . . because *why?* For the life of him, he couldn't remember. "I am Dax," he said again, louder this time.

The man leaned forward in his saddle. "Whut happened t' y', boy?"

"I . . . can't remember."

The man glanced at the tree near them, then back at Dax. "By the size of the chunk you took out o' that tree, I'd say y' broke yer neck."

"I didn't break my neck, you fool," Dax muttered, running one hand along the back of it. But as he drew that same hand down near his chest, he stopped cold.

His coat was soaked in blood and flesh, a hole burned through it. He looked up at the man, a sickening sense of disbelief washing through him. "I think I . . . I *shot myself.*"

"Aye, that y' did, clean through the heart, and broke yer neck t' boot."

Dax's head spun, his mind racing. He jumped to his feet amazed that he could even do so. He heard the distant sound of hooves. The ominous tattoo against the ground reminded him of . . .

He couldn't remember, only knew it was something sinister, something evil.

"What's happened to me?" he blasted. "And who the devil are you?"

A look of pity seeped into the man's green eyes. "My name be Jemmy," he said quietly. "As fer whut's happened t' y', well . . . I s'pect that be a story yer not yet ready t' hear, let alone believe. The same happened t' me once, and t' a few others I know."

Dax gaped at the man. "You shot yourself?"

Jemmy shook his dirty head. "It wuz a rope fer me, boy. Got strung up from a tree limb fer stealin' this horse."

Dax staggered back a step, horrified. "You were *hanged*?"

"Fer a day an' a night. Buried, too. But I came awake, just like y'. Thought I wuz livin' a nightmare."

"And then?" Dax demanded, scarcely able to believe this mad conversation.

Jemmy's eyes narrowed. "Then I realized the nightmare wuz no dream, that riders were chasin' me . . . the same that be trackin' y', boy. C'mon," he said, stretching out one beefy arm. "Climb up in the saddle. Jemmy here be the one t' teach y' how t' get by. We be two o' a kind, Dax—dead but not dead, both o' us just a green-eyed shadow of a soul."

"My eyes are blue."

Jemmy shook his head. "Not anymore, boy."

Chapter Two

Sixteen years later

"Luck is a fickle partner, Chelsea, wouldn't you agree?" drawled Lord Reginald Morely. Atop the baize of the hazard table that was situated in a crowded, smoky room of one of London's more nefarious gaming hells, lay the litter of Morely's winnings, bled from the pockets of those foolish enough to join him in game after game of hazard.

For the past four hours, the Earl of Chelsea had done just that. And lost.

"Ruined," muttered Chelsea, face pale, his eyes glazed with horror and disbelief. "You have ruined me."

Morely arched one colorless brow, taking in the sight of the many empty claret bottles strewn about Chelsea's side of the table. If anything would ruin the man it would be his own penchant for self-destruction. It was no secret to members of England's ton that Chelsea was on a low road. Dissolute, his every moment drenched in depravity, he was but a shadow of the man he'd once been, apparently having buried his good sense along with his beautiful but mysterious wife.

Morely knew what it was to lose the only woman he'd ever loved, but that had been a long time ago—a lifetime ago. Since then, he'd become as absent of emotion as his body was of color, all feeling in him leached out. Once a man of many desires, he now harbored only one. He eased back in his chair, slowly fingering the dice in one hand. "What would you say, Chelsea," Morely asked, "if I gave you the chance to retake what I've won?"

Chelsea blew out a drunken, defeated breath. "And with what am I to wager?" he demanded, bleary-eyed. "You've taken nearly all that I have, save my title and my town house. Since you've no need of my title, is it the last of my property you want?"

"Ah, no," Morely said, smiling, shaking his head. After a pause, he murmured, "It is your daughter, Lady Robyn Sinclair."

Gasps of astonishment rippled through the cluster of gentlemen surrounding the table as Chelsea went perfectly still.

"Well?" Morely asked him. "Shall we try one more game? If I lose, you leave here with what I've taken from you."

Chelsea stared at the pile of pounds and vowels in front of Morely, a battle of demons in his gaze. "And if you win?"

"Then I'll exchange my winnings . . . for Lady Robyn's hand in marriage."

Astonishment turned to outrage among the spectators, for though the Earl of Chelsea was on the road to moral ruin, the older and decidedly more jaded Morely had reached that particular destination years ago.

"You go too far, Morely," one of them blasted.

" 'Tis obscene, this wager you propose!" cried another.

Morely ignored the lot of them, pleased to see Chelsea actually consider the idea.

"For the love of God, man," muttered another spectator, reaching out and offering Chelsea a hand. "Gather your senses, get to your feet, and get out of here."

Chelsea batted away the man's assistance. "Leave me be," he muttered. "It is my fortune sitting on this table, not yours."

"But it is your daughter's future with which you play so fast and loose!"

Something in Chelsea snapped. "That's right, *my* daughter," he rasped, "whose luckless legacy has become my bane." In a sudden fury he swiped one arm across the table, clearing it of the empty bottles in front of him as if he yearned to wipe away more than just the litter of his drunkenness.

The bottles clattered to the floor, one breaking on impact. The sound of it exploding was like gunfire splitting the heavy, tobacco-filled air. The gentlemen surrounding the table broke rank. Stepping clear of the spray of glass they watched in horror as Chelsea, a savage self-loathing in his gaze, nodded to Morely. "I accept your bloody wager," he said.

Several minutes later, the crowd parted once again, people shaking their heads as Chelsea staggered out of the gaming hell, his fortune intact . . . his daughter's future gambled away.

Five nights later

"Pssst. Robbie, are you in here?"

A second of silence swelled within the dimly lit room and then, "If I say I am not, does that mean you will go away?"

"Hardly, and shame on you for even considering the possibility." Lily, muttering lovingly about cousins who couldn't be counted on, swished shut the doors of the small study and then navigated her way through the dim, firelit room. She stopped near the hearth, in front of the chair where Robyn sat, put her hands on the slim hips so many dandies dreamt about, and gave Robyn a moue of a frown. "Have you no care that I've spent the past hour fending off a herd of shepherds at this bore of a masquerade while *you* managed to slip away and remain blissfully unnoticed? It isn't fair, Robbie, not at all."

"Not much is," Robyn whispered, mostly to herself.

"What's that, coz?"

Robyn scooted her body up in the chair. "Nothing, Lil, other than me woolgathering. I'm sorry I deserted you when the shepherds descended, but I couldn't resist. This room seemed to be calling my name."

"The only thing this room is calling is the *cursed*." Lily wrinkled her very pert and pretty nose. "The place is dark as a crypt and just as cold."

"The darkness here is nice," Robyn said. "In fact, it suits my mood." And the temperature in the room matched that of her bruised heart.

"I think you're hiding, coz. Not only that, I think you've some plan afoot."

Robyn knew the arrow of discovery when it pierced her. "True enough. I am hiding." As for having a plan in motion, that was true too—but Robyn wasn't about to share that bit of information. Not even with Lily, her favorite cousin, or Lily's brother, Alexander, whom the family called Sandy.

Lily made a huff of sound deep in her throat. "Hide anymore and you'll become a dusty relic on that shelf you're so determined to fashion for yourself. La, Robbie, but you've already missed an entire Season due to your mother's passing. You should be mingling, before all the eligible gentlemen forget your face, let alone your name. Trust me, there's a house full of trousers out there. You ought to take a look and settle on a set for yourself."

As usual, Lily was dressed to be noticed by anything in breeches. Her gown was a delectable creation of shimmering silver, her blond hair swept into an elaborate knot from which cascaded several fat coils with sprays of tiny stars. With a white face mask gilded in the same and covering just her eyes, Lily looked the perfect belle. Having just turned eight-and-ten, being gorgeous and a precocious flirt, this masked soiree was exactly the type of gathering Lily loved best, though she'd never admit it. Lily liked to feign boredom as much as Robyn, three years older, sought solace from the crowds.

Robyn didn't bother to point out to her cousin that the only person she could imagine ever loving until the end of her days was the lad with whom she had been betrothed from the cradle, but he had been snatched away at a young age, and a tender part of Robyn had died with him. Now, given her father's foolishness at the gaming table days ago, Robyn had true trouble in her lap: another betrothal, one she could never abide.

"I prefer the darkness to having my pick of men," she said to Lily.

Her cousin, though, wasn't about to leave her be. "You're going to have to face your father sooner or later, Robbie."

"Later sounds lovely. I'll take that."

Lily harrumphed noisily, moved to the hearth, picked up the poker, and then jabbed at the dying embers as if she were stirring a pot, which was precisely what she did best: stir things up.

The fire got a second wind, giving off a blaze of color that slashed across Robyn. She slit her eyes at the brightness of it. "I'm guessing your presence in this room means my father has arrived."

"Not to worry. He came and went, deep into his cups as usual."

"Which is exactly why I'm sitting here in the dark and brooding, Lil. So leave me to it, won't you?"

"No, I won't." Lily turned to face her. "I can't. I want you to cast off this melancholy that has surrounded you since you were a girl—the very one that you've tried hard to keep from the family but haven't, at least not from me or from Sandy—and come join the living again. And whatever plan you have in motion for this night, I want you to put a stop to it, do you hear?"

Robyn was about to tell Lily she had no plan, but couldn't form the words. Of all her cousins—and Robyn had many—Lily and Sandy knew best what lurked within Robyn's heart. Robyn could no more hide her true feelings from them than she could coax the moon down out of the sky.

"As for Uncle Marcus, I lied to him," Lily continued. "I told your father you'd headed home, pleading a headache. Though what I should have said is that it was a heartache you have and that he's the one who gave it to you."

"I think he knows."

"Of course he knows. That's why he's so foxed."

No, Robyn thought, *he's drunk because my mother is dead and I'm not.*

Her heart squeezed tight at thought of her mother, a terrible ache echoing through her. She missed the Countess of Chelsea more than words could ever capture.

Robyn had grown up watching her mother utilize a special gift for healing and comforting others—yet there had been no one, not even Aunt Amy, who could comfort or even heal the countess after she had been struck down by a wagon and its team in a crowded lane near the wharves. She had died instantly, which should have been a consolation but wasn't, because all of Robyn's life she had been told that she also possessed a special talent for healing—a gift every generation of females in her family had known, but one that Robyn had yet to realize.

Both her mother and aunt assured Robyn that she would discover her own talent once she was older and had come into possession of at least two of a trio of heart-shaped talismans handed down through her family. She'd inherited one of the talismans in the days following her mother's burial. After the death of the countess, the earl had forbidden Robyn the company of her aunt, fearing Amelia Archer would lead Robyn to the same end her mother had met, and so Robyn had yet to talk with her aunt about the talisman.

"And Lord Morely's watchdog?" Robyn asked, trying hard to keep her voice steady. "Has he come to haunt me yet?"

Lily rolled her shoulders, heaving a sigh, which was her

dramatic way of saying *how should I know*? "I can't say since I've never met the man, Robbie."

"You'll know him when you see him. His is a pretty face, far too handsome for one so absent of soul." Robyn shivered at the mere memory of the man, knowing he'd find her this night, precisely at midnight. He always did.

Ever since her father had gambled Robyn away like so much horseflesh five nights ago, Lord Morely's right-hand man, Falconer, who somehow held entry into the best of homes, had trailed her like a hound on the hunt. He'd dogged her from party to party as if he had a right to watch over her, to see that she didn't align herself with another man, try to slip away . . . or slit her wrists.

Blast the lot of them, Robyn thought. She had no intention of marrying Lord Morely. She had told her father and Falconer as much. Falconer had acted as though she'd not even spoken, leaving her to believe he was as void of a heart as Morely appeared to be. As for her father, the Earl of Chelsea had turned a deaf ear to her protests, telling her she didn't have a choice, *he* didn't have a choice. If she didn't marry the man then he was ruined, he'd said.

Robyn foolishly had pointed out to her father that he was already ruined. And that's when it happened—he'd physically lashed out at her. Robyn could still feel the sting on her cheek.

The only thing that had hurt more was the deep wound her father had cut into her heart at that moment, which was stupid of her to feel, really, considering all that had happened between them.

Lord Chelsea was but a shell of the hearty man who had once laughed with Robyn and doted on her. On the day the body of her mother had been laid to rest January last, Robyn knew in her soul that she'd buried not one parent, but two. Her father's slap shouldn't have surprised her, let alone hurt her. But it had. It still did.

"Let's talk of something else," Robyn said. "Something

that has nothing to do with fathers who fail or daughters who disappoint."

"Oh, Robbie," Lily said, "I'm worried about you. Please, promise me you'll do nothing foolish this night or any other. Once Sandy returns home and learns of this nightmare, he'll make things right."

Robyn glanced at the fire atop the grate, the last brightness of its stirred embers hurting her eyes. Not even Sandy could help her now. Robyn knew she must do what she could to get herself out of this mess and so had laid the foul plan for doing so. But telling Lily the truth would result in a long conversation about right and wrong and a lady's only asset. It would mean admitting to Lily that Robyn was willing to shred her reputation with one single act this night.

"I simply want to sit here alone for a while longer, Lil, just until after midnight. I'm in no mood to be unveiled by someone looking for kisses or courtship."

"Truly?" Lily asked, only half believing her. "Is that what all this is about, you only wanting to be alone?"

Alone, yes, but not for long. Robyn forced herself to meet Lily's gaze. Lying had never been her strong suit. "Yes," she said simply, and hoped the lie couldn't be seen in the depths of her gaze.

It was enough, thankfully. Lily nodded, smiled. "Very well, then. I'll leave you alone, coz. But I warn you now: I expect to see you at my side, in the main drawing room with all the others, a few minutes after the hour."

Robyn gave a quick nod in answer, and with that small assurance Lily headed for the doors of the study.

Only when she was once again alone did Robyn get to her feet, pull the folds of her cloak about her, and begin pacing, her mind a riot of thoughts. The porcelain clock on the mantel struck the quarter hour. Her heart began to pound, her skin rising to gooseflesh on her arms. What she was about to do was madness.

No. It was worse. It was sinful.

But the path she'd chosen was the only avenue left to

her. Morely, Falconer, and her father were about to learn that she had a mind of her own. Robyn had hired a man—a stranger, sight unseen—to meet her in this very room. Come midnight, she intended for Falconer to find her in a very compromising position.

Before this night was through, she would have Falconer believing that she was damaged goods and more trouble than Morely would want. It was the choice she'd made. The only choice she had left.

Robyn glanced again at the ticking clock on the mantel. And then waited.

Like the thief he'd been trained to be and the ghoul he'd become, Dax silently eased through the locked back gate of the town house and stole inside its fog-shrouded rose garden.

He carried no embossed invitation to the exclusive gathering of London's elite tucked inside the house and adorned in costume for a modest masked soiree. At the height of the social season, members of the haute monde were busily attending one party after another in a mad swirl of seeing and being seen, but Dax hadn't come to be seen this night. In fact, the near-midnight hour that fast approached suited both his purpose and his mood.

He'd come here for one reason only: to get an up-close view of the female who had once been promised to him. What he would do once he got near her, how he would react, he had no clue. He wasn't certain if the smuggler in him would take from her, the monster he'd become would roar out, or if the lonely lad he'd once been would emerge.

Soon, he'd have his answer.

The garden was small, intimate. No one sat on the two lone benches in the garden's small enclave, mist threading about their bases.

Stealthily, he maneuvered past them, making his way closer to the shadowy back of the house where muted sounds of laughter and voices floated outside.

A patch of light laid itself on the ground before him, spilling through the tall windows, lighting the knee-high mist to white, eerie puffs. Inside, the soiree was at full swing. Masked guests sipped from tall, fluted crystal, chatting with each other, laughing.

Dax, his senses heightened by the night, ignored the clutter of the scene. He could not care less about the titled and their empty chatter. He'd come only for the one person who mattered to him. Closing his eyes, commanding every facet of his God-cursed legacy, he mentally searched for her. She was here, in this house. He could feel it. From the moment his feet had touched England's soil after years of absence he'd been drawn here, as though she'd beckoned with a need not even she realized.

A voice came to him. Soft. Sweet.

Hers.

Dax opened his eyes. Any other man would have seen only a wall, but Dax was like no ordinary man, hadn't been since a young age and maybe not even then. He saw far more . . . he found and saw his once-upon-a-too-long-ago-time betrothed. *Robyn.*

Dax felt his head grow light at the sight, could sense his blood stirring, his pulse pick up pace. Years and tears and so much more simply melted away.

Her eyes, beneath her gilded half mask, were as violet and as beautiful as he remembered, dark as the cusp of dusk on the far side of daylight. Such mystery they held, and more—things he'd never wanted to see in her . . . like fear, worry, dread. B'god, but whoever had dared set such a tumult to rage inside of her would have him to deal with.

He longed to be near her, wanted to smell her scent once more, to feel the warmth of her, if only for a moment. And he could, he knew. He could use his Curse to go inside the town house, to be next to her, and she wouldn't even know it. But would the faceless riders that trailed him know? Would use of his legacy bring them to this place . . . to Robyn?

Indecision ripped through him. He should leave. He should—

No, he thought savagely. He strongly sensed Robyn's need. It's what had led him to this stately town house, from the moment his ship had berthed along the Thames. That Robyn needed him—or rather, needed someone or something this night—was reason enough to cast caution aside. No matter what came of his choice, he'd protect her. He'd shield her from every fiend that trailed him, protect her from whatever coil she'd managed to ensnare herself within. He would do at least that much for the girl she had been, the one who'd stolen his heart and had gifted him with her own.

Wrapped tight in the night's mist and darkness, Dax waited, watched, felt a volley of emotions surge through him . . . and then moved forward, right through walls and corridors and into the room where she restlessly paced.

Robyn sensed suddenly that she wasn't alone in the study. Though she'd not heard the doors open or close, she knew someone was with her.

The man she had hired had finally arrived. That he was nearly thirty minutes late annoyed her. That she must now put her plan into action terrified her.

Still facing the hearth and that blasted tick-tocky clock, Robyn breathed deep. She felt the man as though her every nerve ending was uncannily attuned to his overpowering, but unseen presence. Bracing herself for whatever might come, turning to face him fully, she watched as he moved out of the shadows and into the dull light spilling from the hearth behind her.

He was taller, larger than she'd expected. Garbed completely in black, he wore a coachman's many-caped coat and a dark, full-face mask that hid the color of his eyes and concealed his features. Features, she suspected, that would be hard and calculating once unveiled, for Robyn decided instantly this man was no untried youth. There was something in his stance—black, booted feet planted slightly apart, strong arms held loosely at his sides—that hinted at untold power and hard-won worldliness.

Robyn swallowed, fighting the urge to tell him she'd changed her mind. Now wasn't the time to lose her nerve. She sternly reminded herself of what she must accomplish this night, and this man appeared to be exactly what she needed: a bold, daring stranger unafraid to take her in his arms and do exactly as she asked. Do *anything* she asked. And what she intended to ask, God forgive her, was a lot.

Gathering her courage, damning her unease, Robyn moved directly to the enigmatic man and announced crisply, "You're late."

In Dax's estimation, he was years too late. But Robyn didn't know that. She didn't know they had once been betrothed, while she was still in the cradle and he just a mere slip of a boy. She obviously didn't know he'd once been the lad to whom she'd gifted her heart. She didn't know he'd just crossed bodies of water returning to the country of his birth to uncover the age-old enemy who had ruined his family . . . and she didn't know he'd used unworldly powers to shimmer himself into this room just to be near her.

That she could see him amazed and alarmed Dax, but the knowledge pleased him, too, on some deeper level. Nobody, at least no one untouched by the same dark legacy as Dax, had ever been able to perceive his presence when he'd gone Phantom as he'd done just now in projecting his body through brick and mortar and too much wood. Did that mean his betrothal to Robyn so many years ago had formed some sort of bond from which neither of them could hide? Or was it the talisman she'd gifted him with, the same he still wore looped about his neck and always dangling close to his heart that made him visible in the flesh to her?

Dax had no idea. Whatever the reason, he was glad Robyn could see him—or could see as much as he allowed, anyway, thankful for the full mask he'd donned, the one that made his existence a bit more bearable to the rest of the world. Had he not put on the mask Robyn would have been truly terrified, for there were things about the Phantom that weren't pretty, his uncovered face at night being one of them. She was the last person he wanted to terrify. For years the essence of her had dwelled in his mind. When he'd lost everyone and everything—mentor, father, home, his very name—thoughts of Robyn had kept Dax from drowning in despair.

"You should have been here a half hour ago," Robyn said, cutting into his thoughts, her tone as cool as the air that enveloped them. "It is now nearly midnight."

"My apologies," he murmured, realizing she'd mistaken him for another, which was a good thing, the *safest* thing for her. Dangerous though it was, Dax decided to play along and let her believe what she would. "I am here now."

She did not seem pleased. Her gaze swept over him, a frown tugging at her lips. "I distinctly remember my note instructing you to dress as a knight in full armor, not as a highwayman."

"Does it matter?"

"Yes. There are three others in the main drawing room dressed as knights, but none as highwaymen."

So, she wished her companion to be incognito and possibly confused for another. Dax wondered what else she desired of the man, and he felt a jealous, territorial knot clench tight in his gut. "You needn't worry. My face is covered. No one will know who I am . . . that *is* what you want, that my identity remains a mystery?"

She nodded, a visible shiver coursing through her. "That is exactly what I want. We shall not even exchange names. It's best for me that you don't know mine . . . and I—I don't care to know yours."

Dax wondered if it was the coolness of the air that made Robyn shiver, or fear of whatever reckless plot she'd placed in motion. She nervously clenched and then unclenched her white-gloved hands, glancing once over his shoulder toward the doors of the study. Confident they weren't about to be discovered, she returned her gaze to his. "I know that my note to you was vague. You're no doubt wondering why I asked you here."

"I am," said Dax, hoping she didn't make a habit of meeting strangers in dark, secluded rooms. "What is it you want me to do?"

"Had you arrived at the expected time, I could have explained things fully," Robyn went on, purposely reminding him of what she imagined to be tardiness on his part. "As it is, I must now give you the abbreviated version."

"I'm listening," Dax said. He caught a whiff of her scent carried to him on a swirl of air. Like so many years ago when he'd been near her, Robyn smelled deeply of hope . . . but this time she smelled of something more, something wholly female that beckoned to the man he'd grown to be, causing a shot of arousal through him that spread and bloomed and made him hard.

"I am in need of you to play a certain part this night," Robyn said, unaware of the effect she had on him. "I believed that a man of the stage, such as you are, was a natural choice."

So, she'd wanted an actor. Instead, she'd gotten a thief . . . and a phantom at that. "And what part am I to play?" Dax asked quietly.

With swift determination, as though she might lose her nerve, Robyn bluntly whispered, "The part of my lover."

The last word hung heavy between them as Dax's brain tried to work through whatever perilous game Robyn sought to play with some actor she'd plucked from the streets. "Go on," he ordered, "tell me more."

Robyn let out an annoyed breath. Clearly, she didn't like to be ordered. "You have been hired to help me create the illusion of a liaison," she explained, obviously deciding to just out with it. "You are an actor. I am told you are very good at what you do. Tonight, you've been hired to act as my lover."

The power of the Phantom shimmered hard through Dax. Did the young lady always offer herself so carelessly? Dax hated that there was so much he didn't know about this woman who had once been his. What he hated even more was the possibility that Robyn may already have known a lover . . . or two. Another surge of jealousy vaulted through him, and he couldn't stop himself from asking, "Why the need to hire a man? Surely a woman as beautiful as you has many suitors . . . possibly even one who would—"

"My reasons don't concern you," Robyn cut in, her violet eyes sparking beneath her half mask at his mention of suitors. "We have exactly three minutes before we must get started. Now tell me, are you willing or not?"

A moment passed. "Willing," Dax said, feeling nothing like the caring lad he'd once been and wholly like the Phantom he'd come to be.

"Very well then." She stared straight at him, breathed, then said, "Let's get started, shall we?"

Dax nodded, once, their pact complete . . . and suddenly, in the deepest depths of his soul, in that space he never dared dwell too long, that place he didn't even want to acknowledge, the Phantom stirred. Dax wondered if he—or she—would come to rue this night.

Chapter Three

Dax studied the room, knowing that in just a few seconds he'd be hard-pressed to remember anything at all. But he needed to keep his wits about him. It was, after all, nearly midnight, and every midnight since that moment when he'd lost his innocence, faceless riders had trailed him. When they came for him this night, as he knew they would, he'd have to fight them off not only for his own soul, but for Robyn's as well.

The only light in the study was a low-burning fire in the grate of a hearth across the room. A large, gilt-framed mirror hung above the mantel. The curtains of the two tall windows had been pulled shut against the night. A huge wing chair sat near the hearth. Banks of filled bookcases loomed large in the shadows.

"We haven't much time," Robyn was saying.

Dax acclimated himself to the lay of the area and the soft, shadowy light of the room. "Much time for what?"

She glanced at him from the corners of her mask. "In a few minutes, these doors will open. I want the person who opens them to discover us—" She hesitated, groping for words—or perhaps the nerve to say those words.

"The two of us acting as lovers would act?" Dax suggested.

Robyn nodded. "That's why I chose you. I believed that you could draw on your acting talents, that you could make your actions appear natural, based in true feelings. Do you think . . . can you do this for me?"

Her question made his heart ache and the tiny bit of soul left to him squeeze tight. For half his childhood and all his adult life, Dax had wanted to find her again, wanted to do for Robyn, for his betrothed, what no other could. "Aye," he murmured, his voice just a husk of a sound. "I can." He *would*.

The tiniest of tremors rippled through Robyn with his words, as though the force of them, the heat of them, unsettled her even more than her own scandalous intentions.

She moved toward the hearth. Facing the low-burning flames in the grate, she lifted her face and peered at Dax's reflection in the mirror above the mantel, as though she found it easier to gaze at his image than his true self.

"I think it best that we stand here," she said, indicating that he should join her.

Without a sound, Dax moved forward.

"The light of the fire will illuminate us," she continued, her gaze beneath her half mask watching him as he moved directly behind her. "While I want you to remain cloaked in mystery, there should be no question of my own identity."

She reached up and undid the clasp of her cloak, hands trembling as she pushed the garment from her shoulders. Dax watched as the velvety folds of material slid provocatively down her arms, pooling in the curves of her elbows and looking like the wash of a dark wave against the frothy white of her gloves.

Robyn wore little more than a sheath of white satin, caught at each shoulder with a gilded leaf of purest gold. She'd gowned herself in a costume reminiscent of a Grecian goddess. A gold-colored rope with tassels at each end cinched her svelte waist, and her hair, a rich cascade of midnight-dark curls, was caught up to one side in the Grecian mode. It was a costume intended to seduce.

For Dax, it set his blood stirring even more. He let his gaze rove over her, imprinting to memory the gentle curve of her back, the tiny mole at the nape of her neck, the soft sheen of firelight against her naked shoulders.

With gloved hands that ached to touch her, Dax reached up, his fingers curling around the edges of the cloak, his eyes behind the slits of his mask steady on her own gaze. He felt his loins tighten as she straightened her arms, allowing him to slowly ease the garment from her body. He tossed it atop the chair.

"What do you want me to do now?" he asked thickly, bloodlust pounding through his veins.

A tiny shiver, fully felt by him, whispered through Robyn's body. "You—you should probably place your hands on me . . . as—as a lover would do."

Dax wanted to ask if she'd known many lovers—if she'd known *any* lover—but he stilled his tongue, put a check on the jealousy teeming through him, and focused on the nape of her neck, bare and luminous, beckoning his mouth to taste her. Greedy for the feel of her, he stripped off his gloves, shoved them deep into the pockets of his greatcoat, then laid his palms upon her bared shoulders.

"Will you trust me?" he whispered.

She nodded, mute at his touch, as though what she truly didn't trust was her voice to speak.

Her skin was incredibly warm and soft. The lick of firelight cast exotic shadows over her naked upper arms, and in the mirror's reflection Dax could see her nipples crest as he touched her. Firm, tight buds pressed against the satin that had but the thinnest of linings.

Dax fanned his fingers wide, gently massaging her. "And now?" he whispered.

Robyn drew in a soft whoosh of breath as his fingers stroked her. Clearly, she hadn't expected her own reactions to his touch. She closed her eyes for a moment, as though trying hard to gain composure. Opening them once again, she looked directly into his reflection. "You tell me. Were we to play this moment on the stage . . . h-how would it progress?"

So she wanted an actor's opinion of the mechanics of the moment. Dax could offer her far more than that, no acting involved. "I can show you," he murmured.

Silence slid around them, broken only by the crackle of the fire's final flames. With a barely audible whisper, she said, "All right . . . show me."

In the mirror, their reflections were as opposing as night and day: Robyn bathed by the dying light of the fire, her dress as bright as starlight; Dax cast in shadow, a Phantom-masked presence looming behind her.

"First," he whispered, "I would touch you, would learn the feel of you. . . ." He let his hands smooth from her shoulders down the length of her bare upper arms, felt gooseflesh cresting on her skin as he did so. He ran his hands down over her gloves, to the very tips of each of her fingers, then very lightly settled his own fingers over hers. Applying a gentle pressure, he stroked the backs of her fingers, up to the knuckles, then down again.

"I would learn your every hollow . . . your every curve . . . every indentation," Dax said, drawing his hands back up and whispering his fingers atop the sensitive skin at the insides of her elbows, just where her gloves ended. As he stroked her there, he brought his head near to the right side of her face and drew in a breath.

"I would learn the scent of you." He let his breath out in a soft curl of air that swirled against the shell of her ear. "I would come to know the taste of you." With the barest of touches, Dax pressed his mouth against her earlobe, his tongue tasting the delicate skin there.

Robyn drew in a rasp of air, her body held infinitely still, her pulse quick and light beneath his mouth.

Dax cradled her face with his right hand. Lord, but he'd dreamt of this moment—of touching her—for so many heart-hardening years that the reality of it took his breath away.

Lifting his head, he peered at her reflection in the mirror. Beneath her mask, her eyes had turned dark with passion. How many other men had known such a look from her? No matter the answer, Dax yearned to wipe the memory of them from her mind, wanted to erase every trace of them from her body if indeed any had ever touched her. Consumed with his own keen need, Dax fanned his fingers, his thumb teasing the soft corner of her mouth, his fingertips brushing her left temple and the soft skin beneath her earlobe.

"And after I learned the taste of you?" he murmured into her reflection, "I would then learn your every want, your every desire . . . and I would make them a reality."

Robyn gazed at him, as though transfixed. He could feel the pulse at her temple quickening. Against the pad of his thumb, her breath passed in quick, crazed wisps. Was she a seasoned seductress, or a young woman sliding for the first time into seduction's hot heat with his touch?

Dax felt again the snake of jealousy slither through him and couldn't help wondering how many others had made her react like this. "Tell me," he urged, having to tamp down the Phantom within, "why do you need to hire a man to playact as your lover? Surely there is someone you trust—"

"No. There is no one."

"You want someone to find us. Who?" Dax pressed. "A real lover, perhaps? Is that whom you want to stumble upon us?"

"You ask too many questions."

"Will you answer them?"

"No."

"Then tell me one thing. What *had* you in mind for this night?" Dax asked, wanting some answers, wanting to know just how far she was willing to take this sensual playacting with a stranger.

Robyn drew in a breath, then let it out, her words coming in one long rush. "Me, in your arms, even partially unclothed—that is . . . if—if you dare."

Bloody hell. Of course he dared. She was the brightest part of his ill-fated past, the hope of his future—and God, but he was hungry for her, ravenous.

"I dare," Dax rasped.

As he said the words, he realized that the gentle lad he'd once been was thoroughly lost to him this night. Suddenly, uncoiling inside of him was the hard-edged part of his character, the one born on the roughest of England's roads, schooled in the arts of a thief, and taught to smuggle. Worse was the Phantom in him, the soulless fiend clamoring to be unleashed . . . the being that was never far from the surface and that, when freed, took whatever the hell it pleased.

And what would please Dax right now was having Robyn, all of her. What he wanted most was to have what had been denied him for too many God-cursed years to count. His gaze fell to the gold-leaf enclosures holding up her gown. He could have them undone in a second. He could . . .

Dax reached for the clasps, his fingers making quick work of the enclosures.

Robyn was breathing faster now, her chest rising and falling. Dax pushed the gold clasps and material down, baring Robyn's upper back to his gaze.

She had an exquisite back: skin unblemished and white as a moon-bathed froth of ocean water, two dimples, down low, just above her sweetly curved buttocks, which remained hidden beneath her gown. The small of her back beckoned to him. Dax wanted to kiss her there, wanted to taste the salt of her skin, to tease his tongue into each dimple. Someday, he promised himself, he would.

Moving his gaze back to her reflection in the mirror, Dax reached up and gently pushed at the material remaining atop Robyn's shoulders. She shivered as the wispy fabric slithered downward, and he could see, in the deep violet of her eyes, a spark of passion igniting. His gaze dipped lower, watching as the material receded like a wave of satin over the crests of her breasts, then fluttered in two long strips of white down over the corded belt of rope, her upper body fully bared to him.

Full, high breasts with tight dusky nipples met his gaze. Beautiful. Better than anything he'd imagined. His heart hammered hard in his chest. He wanted to touch those perfect globes, wanted to fasten his mouth over each taut nipple and suck and tease and caress.

But he held himself in check.

"If we were on stage, I would kiss you," he murmured, voice heady with wild desire.

Robyn drew in a shaky breath. "Yes . . . a kiss would be good," she said in a barely audible whisper.

He *should* kiss her, *all of her*. But his mask was in the way, as was hers. With a whispering softness, he lifted his right hand, brushing the back of his fingers against the long length of her throat. Up and up he moved, past her jawbone, then her cheek, until his fingers touched the base of her mask.

Robyn's mouth parted slightly.

Dax lifted the stiff, diamond-studded mask, tossing it on her cloak, his gaze never leaving her reflection. He hadn't realized until now the true depths of violet in her eyes, or how high her cheekbones were. While she'd looked to be a young princess in the cabin where he'd first met her, she now appeared a temptress in the study's firelight. His insides burned with a wild want. He leaned his head closer, brushing his masked lips against her right ear, and felt tiny tremors ripple through her body as he did so.

Robyn tilted her head into his nuzzling, trembling slightly, then turned so that Dax no longer had his masked mouth against her ear, but near her lips.

"Perhaps I should remove my own mask," he muttered. That he even considered the notion proved how far gone he was, how drunk with passion for her.

Robyn lifted one white-gloved hand, pressing her index

finger against his mouth. "No," she murmured, urgency in her tone. "The color of your hair, your eyes, must remain hidden."

Dax thought he'd go mad with wanting her. He caught the tip of her finger between his lips, and then pulled it into his mouth, suckling her, wetting her glove, unable to stop himself.

Robyn drew in a sudden, short breath at his boldness, but didn't pull away.

"Tear it," Dax whispered around her finger. "Tear my mask so that my mouth can cover yours."

Robyn, her breath coming in soft gasps, drew her finger from his lips, slipped it inside the slit his mask offered for his mouth, and then tugged. The fabric ripped. His mouth was freed. She dropped her hand, as though amazed at her own boldness.

A low scrape of a sound escaped Dax. He'd been waiting years for this moment; he could take no more. Cupping his hands more fully atop her bared shoulders, he drew Robyn's body flush against him, lowered his head, and brought his lips down over hers in a kiss meant to capture all the past they'd been denied.

Breasts to chest with him, steeped in his warmth, Robyn felt swept away as the man's kiss imprinted itself on her very soul. Powerful, hungry, indescribably wild, it was the kiss of a man who knew exactly what he was doing.

Sweet heavens, he was a talented thespian, igniting passion within her with but a touch, making her feel as though he'd yearned to kiss her since the beginning of time.

And his *hands* . . . His large, strong hands were now feathering down her bared back, his fingers caressing her spine, causing sparks of feeling to ripple through her. His hips—hard, firm, pure male—pressed against hers, making her body feel like candle wax melting down and around a hard taper that held a hot lick of flame at its tip. She could feel the hardness of him and . . . *oh*, the feel of him against her aroused a passion she'd not known before. It kicked to life a sensual curiosity that was all new, all exciting, and sent a pinch of fear—a fear of the sultry unknown—through her.

Robyn's mind turned fuzzy, need and desire blossoming over that fear, the world somehow receding. Without even thinking, she curled her arms about his neck. He was so very strong and solid, and her body leaned into his granite hardness as though made to do so. Was every man of the stage so finely honed? Her hired stranger was long and lean, broad at the shoulders and narrow at the hips, and he had the hard thighs of a man who was no stranger to long hours in a saddle. His coat and mask smelled of cedar and salt spray . . . and his lips tasted of a manly spice she'd never known.

Robyn heard herself emit a small moan against his mouth, taken aback by her own startling reaction to him and the fact that she'd allowed him to half undress her. Though she had intended to fall from grace this night, she had fallen under this man's spell far too gracelessly.

"It's all right," he whispered, as though reading her thoughts. He drew his hands forward, fitting them perfectly about her waist. His fingers splayed. Gently, he caressed her, sending more of those soft sparks of feeling coursing through her. "Trust me," he murmured.

His voice—rich, heady, edgy with desire—clouded Robyn's brain. *Trust him?* She didn't even know him. But she wanted him. She wanted more of what he'd done to her this night, wanted to experience all that he'd murmured into her ear.

While she'd thought only to hire a stranger for the evening to help her weave a plot of deceit, she never, not even once, considered she might *react* to the man. How wanton she'd become in just the course of, what, minutes? Always, Robyn had been in control. Always, she'd fought hard to maintain herself in any situation.

But not now. Not here. Not with this man. He undid her.

Robyn didn't even know his name, but she felt, ridiculously enough, as though she knew *him*. In some inexplicable way, he was familiar to her, like a dream she'd had more than once in her life, or like the fragrance of something precious from her past.

"If you want to stop . . . if you want *me* to stop, just say the word," he murmured against her mouth. "If this frightens you—"

"No . . . please . . . d-don't stop."

Terrified of how he made her feel, and just as afraid that she might never know a moment like this again, Robyn closed her eyes and leaned deeper into his embrace, all thought evaporating.

She felt his lips meld with hers and the slide of his tongue as he tasted her, teased her, and then slid inside of her. She allowed it, a rush of heat sweeping through her. His tongue licked gently against hers . . . and then she was lost as he explored and excited her. She didn't know where she ended and he began. Liquid heat gathered between her thighs and her heart slammed against her breasts . . . just as the doors opened behind them.

Falconer.

For the briefest of moments Robyn had forgotten the threat that hung above her like the blade of a guillotine. She remembered now—Falconer's presence bringing it all back with crashing clarity. She heard him give a low chuckle, one intended to undermine the scene she'd so carefully orchestrated.

The stranger in whose arms Robyn was held stiffened imperceptibly. His tongue receded from her mouth as his right hand abandoned her waist in search of her own, gloved one. She knew what he intended—to draw her behind him in a protective gesture as he turned to face the intruder. While the innate reaction served to endear the man to her, it was one she did not want.

"No," she whispered against his lips. "You are my lover, remember?"

Reluctantly, he took her cue, fastening his mouth once again over hers, as though the very taste of her fueled him. His right arm snaked around her waist. His large hand, palm open, pressed hard and hot against the naked small of her back, guiding her body more tightly against his.

A breath of panic tinged with excitement bubbled up in Robyn's throat as her breasts, nipples taut and aching for his touch, were crushed against his powerful chest. Her tall, daring stranger swallowed that breath into his own mouth, his tongue searching for and then tangling with hers in a devouring kiss that became a mindless moment out of time. Though they had an audience, it seemed to Robyn there was only the two of them, their lips searching and tasting, their bodies locked tight.

Falconer lingered, letting Robyn know he hadn't missed the intensified kiss. He spoke just before he pulled the doors shut. "Don't think this changes anything," he warned. "It doesn't."

Robyn felt her insides churn as the doors clicked into place, and she and her stranger stood alone in the room once again. She must have sagged slightly into him for he whispered against her lips, "Are you all right?"

No, she wanted to sob; her life was chaos—and that man, along with Morely and her father had created the upheaval. The three of them had pushed her hand, forcing her to take this scandalous path. Clearly, though, it hadn't mattered at all to Falconer to find her half naked in another man's arms.

"I—I'm fine," Robyn insisted, the lie coming easily to her lips. How many times had she uttered those words in the last few days?

Instead of pulling away, the stranger drew closer, his kiss turning from hard and hungry to soft and feathery, as though he understood the fragility of her emotions. If possible, this kiss was far gentler than the last.

"If that man poses a threat to you, if you want me to go

after him, challenge him, I will," he said against her mouth. "Just say the word and I'll—"

"No," Robyn cut in, a shiver of fear coursing through her. Falconer wouldn't be daunted by an actor coming after him in a show of chivalry. If anything, he'd merely see her hired stranger clapped into irons.

At the fringes of her brain Robyn heard the muffled yet unmistakable clatter of carriage wheels on the pavement outside the windows. In another few moments it would be midnight and the guests of her host and hostess, after unmasking themselves, would be heading out for yet another gathering, their night of party-going still in its infancy. Soon, she'd be expected to depart herself.

Robyn ended the contact. She stepped back from the man, hastily snatched up the strips of satin that hung down over her belt, her face burning crimson that she'd actually been so bold as to let him uncover her. Her hands trembled uncontrollably as she clutched the material to her breasts, but try as she might she could not reach the gold-leaf enclosures and the material that dangled down her backside. Embarrassment engulfed her.

Without a word, her hired stranger drew his arms around her, pulled up the gold-leaf clasps and dangling material, then gently reaffixed her gown.

Robyn drew in a shaky breath at his tenderness. She trained her gaze on his mask—only to see the place where she'd torn it, showing fully his handsome, sensual mouth. The sight of the torn fabric was decadent. *Had she actually done that?*

Firelight caressed the divot of his upper lip that appeared oddly light colored in the darkness of the room. Robyn could feel again the excitement of his mouth fastened over hers, the remembered heat of his hard, lean body and rigid erection.

Robyn tamped down hard on her rioting thoughts, knowing she must end this mad, wild moment. Her plan to thwart Falconer, Morely, and her father had failed. It was time to bid her hired stranger good-bye before she found herself in even more dangerous waters.

"You need to leave. Now."

He didn't budge. "If there's something more I can do for you this night, name it," he urged.

"There's nothing more," she said, though it was on the tip of her tongue to beg him to whisk her away, to take her with him, to take her far from the troubles that plagued her.

Robyn reminded herself that her life was no fairy tale and this man was not some knight-errant who'd come riding to her rescue. "What I want is for you to go," she said, and turned for the door. "Your work here is finished. You did what I asked, and I—I thank you for that. But it's nearly midnight, so please, before you—we—are discovered by the others, *you must leave.*"

As though she'd splashed a bucket of icy water in his face, he drew back, his dark-hooded head nodding. Without a word, he turned, scooped up her discarded mask and cloak, and followed her soundlessly to the study's doors.

She led him to the back of the town house, voices and laughter chasing them. They remained undiscovered, thankfully, as all the guests were gathered in the front rooms of the house, anticipating the unmasking at midnight.

Without being asked, the man settled her cloak about her shoulders, then reaffixed Robyn's mask. Did she imagine it, or did his hands linger overly long on her? Before Robyn could decide, he reached for the latch of the door leading to the garden, opened it, and then slid outside, turning to look at her one last time. "Tell me you'll be all right," he said. "Promise me."

The urgency, the sheer feeling of his words startled her. "I'm always all right. Now go, please."

He turned to leave just as Robyn remembered that she hadn't paid him.

"Wait," she called. "I—your payment . . ." She reached

into one pocket of her cloak, pulling out a wad of pound notes she'd thrust there earlier as somewhere beyond and behind her a clock struck the midnight hour. *One . . . two chimes . . .*

He looked at her over one broad shoulder as he moved with swift ease off the step and into the garden. *Five . . . six chimes . . .* His right hand lifted and pressed against his chest, just over his heart, as if he searched for something that lay beneath layers of clothing. He shot her a smile that lingered somewhere between harmless and hellion. *Nine . . . ten chimes . . .* Green eyes suddenly aglimmer, the white of his teeth near dazzling, and the sensuousness of his odd-colored mouth unnerving her, he said, "Keep it. Your kiss is a treasure beyond value." And with that, he disappeared, shimmering into nothingness, seemingly swallowed up by mist and shadow as the faraway clock chimed one last time.

Robyn stared into the foggy night, wondering if she'd imagined the man. The hammering of her heart and the tingling of her body told her she hadn't; his sultry kisses and heated touch were very real. So why hadn't he taken the money he'd earned? Though he'd been hired to do a job— and had done his task more readily, and with far more fervor than she'd expected—*he'd not taken his payment.*

Why?

Doubts and worry suddenly crowded into her brain like a flock of birds settling down to pick at a fertile field. Could it be that the man she'd hired this night had been won over by an even larger purse paid to him by Morely, her father, or even Falconer? Could they have known her intent and used her own plot against her? Was *that* why Falconer had seemed so carelessly amused by her staged display?

A groan of despair hitched up Robyn's throat just as a thin, not-so-very-tall man appeared before her in the foggy garden, his costume of slipshod armor clanging loudly.

"Apologies for my lateness," he said, drawing the helmet from his head and sketching a hasty bow, "but it's a deuced foggy night. Got lost twice, I did. Are you the one I am to meet?"

Robyn gaped at him. "*You* are the man to whom I sent the note?"

"Ah, then you are the one," he said, answering his own question, "and yes, I did indeed receive your note. Why else would I be tripping through a garden dressed in full armor at midnight? Not for applause, I tell you. Good gawd, but I nearly impaled myself getting over that gate. You might have *unlocked* the thing."

Fury and fear swept through Robyn. If this was the man she'd hired . . . then who had kissed her, touched her, and half undressed her so artfully?

If she didn't soon hurry after the enigmatic stranger, she'd never know the truth. Thrusting the pound notes at the thespian trapped in armor, Robyn said, "I'm sorry for all of your trouble this night. Please, consider this payment for services I no longer need."

The man frowned. "But I thought I was to meet you in the study. I thought—"

"Forget what you thought," Robyn said, already in a mad dash for the back gate. Over her shoulder, she called, "Simply head inside that door, wend your way to the front, and then leave. Look at no one, speak to no one, and your work here is finished."

"That's it?" he called. "That's all?"

"Yes," Robyn cried, glad to see him turn and head for the door. She thought of him no more as she raced for the back gate, which was indeed locked tight. She managed to throw the bolt and whip open the gate all in the same instant . . . just in time to step out into the mews and see her masked stranger heading fast away atop a pitch-black steed. He held a bow in one hand and had a packet of arrows strapped across his back, while all about him wisps of fog curled tight.

Angry, intrigued, and breathless all at the same time, Robyn yelled, "Stop!"

The man who had kissed her as if she was the most precious find of his life immediately reined in his mount and whirled the beast around in a half circle. He tamed the animal to just a claw of impatient hooves on the cobblestones, and then, miraculously enough, waited to hear whatever it was she wanted to say.

Robyn sucked in a breath at the sight of him. He'd removed his mask, leaving his face bare, but for the life of her all she could see was the weald green of his eyes. Beautiful eyes he had, but all else was shimmering whiteness—the color of a full, turbulent moon. Surely it was the fog, Robyn told herself. It played tricks. Painted a phantom where there was a man. "Who are you?" she called out, needing to know. "Why did you come here? Why did you play me for a—a fool?"

"Ah, lass, I don't think you a fool." His voice slid through the night, sounding like a heady whisper in her ear even though he was far away. While she had to yell to be heard, he seemed only to have to whisper and she heard. "Never that."

And then his gaze went beyond her, and she saw those beryl-colored eyes of his slit hard, like something demonic had just reared itself in the man's very soul. She pivoted— and that's when she saw them: three hooded riders, gleaming a ghostly white and pounding through the misty mews straight for them. One moment she was standing frozen in disbelief, and the next she heard a wild shriek as the first rider, pierced by a well-aimed arrow from the man behind her, disintegrated into nothingness, horse and all. Another arrow winged through the fog, and a second rider and its beast instantly vanished.

"Go," she heard the man who'd kissed her into oblivion command. "Run. *Now.*"

Robyn ran, right back into the garden, with no time to slam the gate shut, a scream of panic catching in her throat. She stumbled once, righted herself, then hitched up her skirts and darted forward just as the third of the faceless riders thundered through the opened gate, hot on her heels. Terror hollowed her gut as she collided with one of the benches. She felt her shins slam into the thing, and then her body was vaulting forward, her face hitting and then scraping hard earth in a bone-jarring thud. Robyn pressed her eyes shut tight, felt her gloves rip and the skin of her jaw break open as she toppled to the ground and her mask went flying into the air from the force of her hit. Instinctively, she rolled to her back . . . and saw doom.

The faceless rider meant to crush her with his horse's hooves, and would have, if not for her now-unmasked stranger, who vaulted his own animal over the gate of the garden. At the same instant, he sent an arrow to burrow into the back of the man's head, the tip jutting through the left eyehole. Instantly, rider and horse vanished into nothing but a fine dust that mixed with droplets of fog, all of it showering down toward Robyn.

Swallowing another scream, Robyn did a crazed crab walk backward on her palms and feet, stark terror engulfing her as the man who'd kissed her so thoroughly in the study loomed above. She understood nothing of what she'd just witnessed. Feared everything. Most of all him.

The horse he rode pranced anxiously around her, steam coming from its nostrils, becoming part of the fog, as the man clearly fought an internal battle of deciding whether to gather her up from the ground or not touch her at all. The fog, knee-deep when she'd first entered the garden, seemed now to swallow them whole. All Robyn could see clearly was the emerald fire of the man's eyes, his gaze filled with a tumult of warring emotion—as though something dark and sinister ate at his insides, clawing to be freed.

"You're bleeding. You need help." While his words indicated tenderness, his voice did not.

Robyn violently shook her head. *"No,"* she ground out, scooting backward some more. "D-Do not touch me. Come no closer!"

"You fear me." It was a statement, not a question. Another rise of wild emotion crested in his gaze. "Very well. I'll do this for you instead: Come morning, you will remember nothing of tonight."

"Impossible!" Robyn shot back, her mind frantic with fear.

"Not for me it isn't," he muttered, and his words lingered like a dark enchantment as he turned and rode away as fast and as silently as he'd come, nothing but the earth's white breath stirring in his wake.

Chapter Four

In the hours following midnight, he trailed her. From the town house where he'd tasted her, to the dark coolness of the carriage that whisked her home, to the bedchamber where a single flame flickered in wait for her, he followed—not with his body, but with a thread of thought fashioned from the Phantom, a mind-sway he radiated outward and moved with dark magic through the night.

He knew the moment it reached her, the instant it touched her.

Just as the moon could pull the tide, the Phantom in him could sway the thoughts of others. No matter if that person was miles away or a moment away, so long as they were mortal and he'd recently touched them Dax could slide their thoughts from one reality to another. It was the Curse that gave him such a talent.

It had taken Dax years to learn how to control even the slightest of his dark gifts, and it had taken even longer to remember the tiniest pieces of his true past. But no matter how far he'd come in remembering everything about the life he once knew, and no matter how hard he tried to deny the life he now had, he couldn't stop the Phantom from rising like a tide in him each night.

From the cusp of midnight to the break of dawn, Dax

became fully Phantom. Though he could utilize pieces of the Phantom at will and at any time—as he had tonight in shimmering into the town house to find Robyn—after midnight the Phantom claimed *him*, leaving little of his own will to surface.

It was during those desperate hours before dawn that Dax hungered most to let loose the gravest of his powers. While the Curse afforded him talents such as mind-sway, Dax also possessed the darkest power of all . . . the power to harvest the soul of another.

Dax was caught now in the grip of that biting hunger— the evil in him wanting to crest and to capture Robyn's soul, the man in him determined to protect her. The moment midnight marked the hour, it had taken every ounce of will in him to move off that step and shimmer away. Another moment and he'd have lost all ability to control what little clear sense he possessed. In the garden where Robyn had fallen, he'd had to fight hard not to possess her then and there. He hadn't even dared to help her off the ground, for to touch her would have been to take her.

Now, hours later and miles away from her, in a third-floor flat he hadn't occupied since his youth, Dax anxiously waited for dawn to edge the darkness so that the evilness in him would ebb. Until then, he was glad the fiend in him had settled on stealing Robyn's memories of the night instead of her soul. Dax knew Robyn would be far safer and less distressed if she had no recollection of what she'd witnessed earlier.

Like an opiate breathed in by her skin, he sent his dark charm whispering into the deepest depths of her. He laced her thoughts with forgetfulness, spun the memory of a night unstained by a Curse that brought riders from another realm . . . and though he hated to do it, he cast the kisses they'd shared into nothing more than dream wishes that would drift away upon her awakening.

But instead of his mind-sway causing a current of serenity to flow outward from her, there was a surge of fierce energy, *hers*, pushing back—and then . . . nothing. It was as if he'd hit a wall of stone.

Irritation bit at the beast in him, until the man was on the move with his mind, projecting his masked image, and Dax saw himself standing just beyond the wrought-iron gate of her father's front door, his body nothing more than an illusory essence in the fog-washed night. The damned dawn was further away from Dax than the evil inside. Unable to stop, he sent out another sway of thought, moving it like a whisper on the wind: *Come to me. Know that I want you.*

He felt Robyn stir, felt her try to fight the dark magic that swirled around her and pulled her like a strong current from her bedchamber, to the hall, down the stairs, and out the front door.

He could hear the mad beating of her heart, could taste the fear that bubbled up from the pit of her belly. The wispy white of her nightdress mixed with the mist as she slipped out the front gate, her bare feet nearly slipping on the wet cobbles. Her hair was a wild cloud of dark tresses framing her wide-eyed face. Her breath came in fast gasps. Terror and the cool dampness made her shudder. However she'd fought the call of his dark curse earlier, she was now fully ensnared by it.

Dax, too, was caught in its web, the man in him struggling, fighting hard to warn her away. Every muscle roared for release, to be able to move, to speak, to somehow save her. A few more steps and she'd be close enough to his image . . . close enough to the swirling mass of dark magic that had created that image. Soon the illusion of him would ripple with a cresting energy. She would hear his voice in her head, huskier this time, a heady seduction. She'd see him extend one arm, offering her his hand, and she wouldn't be able to deny him. The Phantom would reach for her, all might and magic and murderous mystery— and her soul would be smuggled right out of her, leaving nothing but the shell of her body.

Dax couldn't let that happen. *He wouldn't.*

But even as the thought coalesced in his brain, he heard his Phantom call to her. He felt the lift of his arm . . . watched as his hand stretched out . . . and saw his fingers curl back in an age-old gesture that meant one thing: *Come. Come to me.*

And she came. God. She came to him.

The mist formed beads on her skin, on her eyelashes. The pulsating energy that was his image flickered and reflected in her violet eyes. He felt that energy build, knew that it would soon smite the ground as it coiled tight and then swirled high in a violent rush as it sucked around her . . . and then—*no.* He would not let it happen.

He had one moment, one chance to save her and it was now.

Just as Robyn stepped forward to reach for the hand of his image, just as the force began to spiral around them, Dax centered all the God-cursed energies left to him into one thought, which he threw wide, like a net, hoping to capture what he could.

Amazingly enough, he caught something.

There.

To the left.

He heard movement . . . hooves hitting stone . . .

Even at this predawn hour, others stirred—a horse and its rider, the nightwatch for this wealthy area of the city.

Dax, from his place in the third-floor flat far away, wrapped a tight thread of thought around the mind of the man—and then, fast as a hangman manages the noose, he pulled that thread taut, sending rider and horse straight at his image . . . straight *through* his image.

The commotion was enough. It blasted apart the growing vortex of the Phantom, kicking it into chaos as the watchman and his horse kept on going, oblivious to Robyn and off on some imagined mission lanes away. Robyn, suddenly freed from the acute mind-sway, stumbled back, falling, and caught herself with her palms on the cobbles. She blinked, righted herself . . . then fled back into the house. Or at least Dax thought she had. He couldn't be certain. Something suddenly had him by the chest. Like the fox that would chew the shackled leg from its body, the Phantom in Dax clawed at his heart, wanting to squeeze the life's blood from the organ that had trembled and nearly broken at what had been Robyn's imminent demise.

Dax sucked hard for air, tearing at his clothing, fighting to free his neck, his chest. His skin poured sweat. His throat constricted. God, he was dying. Suffocating. And that's when he realized, dully, that he was back in the flat and the moments outside with Robyn were done, a thing of the past. He hadn't murdered her, hadn't smuggled her soul. She was safe, *safe from him*—and he was . . .

. . . flat on his back and beneath the hard, muscled body of Gideon Dance, the one person in this world Dax knew for certain had no soul but walked the earth as if he did.

The rage in him boiling harder, the beast angry at being pinned down, Dax felt his eyes slit hard as he growled, "Get. Off."

"Not bloody likely. Not until you're sane again." Gideon, his lip split and his jaw beginning to swell from Dax's fist, nodded toward the window—to the dawn that was slowly staining the sky a pale shade of pearl.

Meager light leached into the flat, crept across the floor planking, and touched the tips of Dax's boots. As if on cue, the Phantom's presence in him decreased, sliding back into the darkest spaces of him.

Dax shuddered and then fell back, his body spent. He sucked in a long, precious breath as Gideon eased sideways off him and sank to the floor beside him.

"I nearly snatched her soul," Dax rasped. "The one person I promised myself I'd never hurt."

"It wasn't you," Gideon reminded him. "It was the damned Curse. It makes us do all manner of messy things."

"I should have been in control."

Dax scraped one palm across his forehead. He opened

his eyes. Gideon suffered just as much from the Curse as he did, maybe even more. It was different for the two of them: The things they endured . . . *did* . . . due to the Curse weren't the same.

Dax had met Gideon in the West Indies years before Dax had fully remembered his past and years after Gideon had been forced from his mother's homeland of Arabia. Eyes, skin, and hair exotically dark, Gideon had the stamp of his mother's people. In fact, the only things he'd inherited from his English father were a title, a temper . . . and the Curse.

Dax and Gideon had become wary friends. They still were. Dax knew Gideon had no soul . . . and Gideon knew—though it wasn't Dax who had done the deed—that Dax was similar to the very thing that had smuggled the soul right out of him.

Dax suspected that Gideon preferred death to a soulless existence, but the Curse didn't offer choices. And it was never the same from one person to another; the vagaries of the Phantom were as wide as they were frightening. Though Gideon no longer understood human emotion, there existed somewhere in his brain—or perhaps in his heart—some memory of a moral . . . or two. Which was why Gideon was helping Dax now.

Neither Dax nor Gideon knew from one minute to the next whether Gideon could be trusted. A Cursed man with no soul was difficult terrain to navigate, but just as thieves and pirates and others who carved out an existence on the underbelly side of life held their own codes of honor, so did the Cursed—they would band together when they could . . . and steer clear of each other when they had to.

"I let my Phantom follow her," Dax said into the stillness, pushing himself up to a sitting position as disgust and self-loathing pumped through him. "I wasn't strong enough to stop the beast from trailing her."

"But in the end you saved her, yes?"

"For now." But it wasn't enough. It would never be enough.

"It's enough," Gideon assured him, picking up on his thoughts.

The two leaned back against the wall as dawn continued to push pale fingers of light into the flat, sending the beams higher and wider, until they were drowned in a sea of light.

The time it took the Phantom to recede and the man to return was swift once the sun rose. It was the calming of his mind that took a bit longer for Dax. So he spent the time reacquainting himself with the small flat he'd once shared with Sir Dysart, remembering the countless hours of study his guardian had pushed him through.

From the time Dax was six years old until he was ten and two, Sir Dysart had kept Dax protected and on the move. Back then, Dax had only had a dull suspicion that he was somehow different. It was only when his guardian had taken him through the French province where his mother had been born that Dax had felt the beginnings of the Curse stir to life inside of him—and had begun to sense the riders that had trailed him every midnight since.

Dax and Sir Dysart had lived in this tiny flat for seven months—the longest of any place they had stayed—and had only left it for the provinces of France one bitter winter morning a few weeks before Dax's twelfth birthday.

Dax looked around the place, remembering how eager he'd been back then to learn and to grow . . . to get back home to his father and make him proud. Shelves of books lined the main area as well as the mezzanine, where a single bed took up whatever room the books didn't swallow. Within this small space, Dax had labored to learn every line constructed by Shakespeare, to pick apart all things Greek and Roman, and to read—when Sir Dysart wasn't looking—every bawdy poem of Rochester.

As he stood before the cold hearth of the main room,

Dax mulled over those memorized words of so long ago and the events of last night. He couldn't erase the memory of the kisses he'd shared with Robyn in the study. He could still taste her on his lips, could perceive the scent of her clinging to him, and every bit of it reminded him of the poetry of John Wilmot, Second Earl of Rochester—a man who had hotly argued that passion had a consequence, and who had sworn that he was willing to risk all consequence to live by passion instead of reason.

God help him, but Dax felt the same as he remembered clearly the feel of Robyn pressed against him, the soft fullness of her breasts, the sweet small of her back beneath his hands. Even now, unquenched arousal continued to roll through him as he relived every detail of their time together. Ah, but he knew a keen urge to risk all consequence and live by passion instead of reason—with Robyn.

Gripping the mantel, Dax lowered his head and blew out a frustrated sigh. He hated having been so close to Robyn yet unable to reveal the truth of their shared past, and it nettled him to wonder what had happened to make her hire a man to playact as her lover. A lady's reputation was her most guarded asset, and yet Robyn had dared to play loose with hers last night. *Why?* And who was the stranger who'd discovered them in the study?

Dax would have enjoyed letting his Phantom deal with the man. Hell, he'd have loved to slam his fist into the man's face. But Robyn had stilled Dax's innate reactions with her words and her mouth—a mouth, alas, that had been created to undo him. Even now, he felt himself go hard at the memory of his lips covering hers, of Robyn's tongue curiously colliding with his own . . . of her body blossoming at his touch—

Bloody hell.

Reason, Dax reminded himself, *focus on reason and not passion.* It did no good to think about Robyn. He'd been a fool even to go to that town house last night. The fiends that rose up to trail him every midnight—the ones that could only be annihilated by the slice of an arrow through the left socket of where an eye should be—might actually be cognizant enough to realize that Robyn was Dax's one weak spot. Being as close to her as he had been last night could very well have brought permanent danger into her world.

Too bad his first mind-sway to alter her perception of the night had gone awry. Either she was too damned stubborn and strong . . . or there had been other powers at work. That she'd seen him when he'd gone full Phantom told Dax she wasn't like other people; that she had fought off the power of his first mind-sway proved it. And that the beast in him had been determined to have her, told Dax he couldn't risk getting near Robyn again. He had to protect her by staying away.

Dax had returned to England to uncover the unknown enemy who had ruined his life. Until he laid bare all of the evil from his past—until he cut down whoever had destroyed his parents, and until he learned how and why he had been crippled with this blasted Curse—he would have no rest. He could be nothing other than the thief, smuggler, the very Phantom he'd become, for it would take a fiend to defeat a fiend.

A single rap sounded at the door. "Ho, are you ready?" a man called quietly, popping open the door.

Dax lifted his head, glancing over one shoulder as Randolph entered the flat. "Aye," he replied, pushing thoughts of Robyn, of his past, from his mind. "We're ready."

Randolph, tall, blond, brawny, and five years younger than Dax, was the truest friend Dax had ever known. Fully mortal, he knew of Dax's dark legacy and had a suspicion about Gideon's. While he made certain to keep a distance from Dax between the hours of midnight and dawn, he made just as certain to stick close to him at all other times. He possessed a swift fist and a huge heart, and he had deemed himself Dax's protector. As such, Randolph wasn't one to mince words and didn't bother to do so now.

"You don't look ready," he said. "In fact, the two of you look like hell."

Gideon, standing near the front window, glanced up and grinned. "No doubt we do," he said. "It was a long night—more so for Dax than for me, if you can believe it." With his right hand he rubbed lightly at his jaw that now sported the hue of a bruise.

"You fought each other?"

"No," Gideon said. "Dax fought himself. I just managed to get in the way."

Randolph's blue eyes narrowed. "Oh?" he said, glancing from Gideon to Dax. "Does that mean you saw her, or that you tried to find her and couldn't?"

"I saw her."

"And then some," Gideon added.

Randolph blew a soft whistle through his teeth. "Disaster."

"Nearly," Dax admitted, and that was all he would say about last night's misadventures with Robyn. Both Randolph and Gideon knew that Robyn was the one bright spot of his past, the hope of his future. What they didn't know was that Dax suspected there was something even more special about her, something that the evilness in him coveted. He dragged one hand through his unruly black hair as he met his friend's blue gaze. "Nothing's changed. We leave London this morning as planned."

With a nod, Randolph asked, "And Lady Archer?"

Amelia . . . Amy . . . Robyn's cherished aunt . . . his mother's bosom friend . . . his father's staunchest ally, and his own godmother—gad, but she held so many connections to the people who mattered in his life. She'd been wildly brave in that carriage just before Dax had "died" as a lad. Amy knew things about his past, secrets she'd intended to share with him all those years ago when she first introduced him to Robyn, but she'd never had the chance.

It was only recently that Dax had reconnected with her, via two letters: one she'd sent to him, and his reply—neither missive long or involved. That he'd received her letter at all amazed him, making him marvel anew at her many contacts in life. His time now in England should have been a reunion—*would be*, he promised himself. Amy had written she would meet him at the flat if possible, and if not there, then at Land's End, at her home in Sussex. She knew about the thief in him . . . and Dax suspected she knew even more about the Phantom. It was past time *he* learned the full, hideous tale. Plus he ached to know more about Robyn—to know everything.

"She was here," Dax said, "though I'm not certain when. Most likely just before our ship docked. Had we fair weather, we'd have met her." He motioned toward the small table in front of the sofa. "She left me a gift from my past." He nodded to the piles of vellum littering the table-top, each page containing long passages written in a bold, decisive script—every word of which Dax had read when he'd arrived at the flat after leaving Robyn in the fog-washed garden.

"What is it?" Randolph asked.

"A journal. It was kept by my guardian during the years he shuffled me from place to place, attempting to keep me hidden from whoever had murdered my mother." Dax's green eyes clouded. "It was meant for my father, intended to let him know of his son's small triumphs during those years, to give him some bit of comfort until we were reunited . . . but we—I never saw him again. My father was branded a traitor to England, charged with having republican sympathies simply because he saved my mother's French family from starvation. He was stripped of his holdings and hanged alongside murderers and thieves." Bitterness tinged his words. B'god, but whoever ruined his family would soon know the bite of his vengeance, the full immortal fury of his Phantom self.

"Amy—Lady Archer—must have kept up the rent on this flat after I disappeared," Dax went on, pushing through the pain of remembering his father, of how his life had ended. "She probably hoped I'd have some spark of memory and return to the places of my past. That she's continued to search for me all these years . . ." He gave a small shake of his head. "If anyone can help me understand my past, it's Amy."

"I'll help you, too," Randolph said. "However I can, I'll help you right the past."

Gideon, arms folded across his chest, turned his black-eyed gaze once again to the window and the busyness of street below, saying nothing.

Dax knew what Gideon was thinking: There *was* no righting the past, at least not for Dax and Gideon. There was only an endless march of nights that had no end, fears that unfurled, and phantoms that rose and rose and rose.

Dax nodded his thanks to Randolph all the same. But he knew, just as Gideon did, that he'd never make use of the younger man's offer. When it came time to face whatever had brought the Curse into their lives, Dax and Gideon had some sixth sense that made them believe they would each face that moment alone. Dax and Gideon had spent long hours talking about the Curse. They had come to the conclusion that they had each been born Cursed . . . but how the Curse manifested within each of them had been different. For Dax, it had been the blast of a gun and the snap of his neck against that tree in Sussex when he was a lad of twelve that had marked the beginning of his hell. For Gideon, it had been a space of doom in the desert, on a cold, windless night, when he had realized his life was not charmed . . . but Cursed. The one thing they shared was their eagerness to end it all.

Dax moved to retrieve his saddlebags, packed and at the ready atop a chair in a corner of the room. Though he was anxious to meet with Amy, he hated leaving Robyn behind. She'd told him at the town house that she would be all right, and for now Dax had to believe her. Only after he sifted through the rot of his past and did away with his Curse—if, indeed, he ever would—could he go in search of her once more. There was no way he wanted to repeat last night. He couldn't risk allowing the riders to veer off their course and chase her again, and never, ever, did he want the Phantom to coax her from her bed as it had last night. The farther away from Robyn Dax got, the better for her.

The best he could do for now, was to allow a whisper of thought to linger near her, as protection. Should she be in true need, Dax would know instantly.

Meanwhile, he would keep to his plan to rendezvous with Amy at Land's End. Immediately following that meeting, he and Randolph and another of his men that Dax would bring along as lookout would head back to their camp along the coast. Dax would then oversee a shipment of goods that would never be found in any ledger. Not only was he a smuggler of souls, but a smuggler of goods as well. Barring inclement weather, Dax figured he and the rough lot he commanded could begin unloading the smallboats hours after he met with Amy. In the depths of night he could have the goods stuffed safely into the warren of caves he knew too well.

As always, a world of danger stood between Dax and the one thing he wanted most: Robyn.

Nearly twenty-four hours after Robyn's reckless plot had brought a masked stranger into her life whose touch made her weak and whose hot mouth made her wanton, Robyn was plotting again, this time determined to get out of the city.

What she'd felt in the darkness of the study last night and then later witnessed in the foggy garden and beyond her father's front door told Robyn that the man was someone—some*thing*—she shouldn't tangle with ever again. His promise of making her forget the events of the night had nearly come true . . . but Robyn had fought hard against the heady mindlessness that beckoned her. She had felt his dark enchantment pour through her with pure persuasion. How easy it would have been to succumb—an erotic pleasure, actually. It had taken every ounce of will not to do so. But even so, the pull to leave her bedchamber, to go outside, to walk right into the man's embrace, had been too much. Whatever had broken the spell hadn't come a moment too soon. Once back in her bedchamber she hadn't fallen asleep. Instead, she'd spent the remainder of the predawn hours fearing that the image of him would shimmer to life at the foot of her bed, or that faceless riders would come charging through the hallway.

But somehow, as the darkness slid away to daylight, Robyn went from fearing the man to replaying in her mind every moment spent in his embrace. Though she flipped one way in her bed and then the other, she couldn't find a position that eased her troubled mind or settled the desires his heated touch and seductive kisses had stirred to life in her.

Could he truly have been a pawn of her father, Lord Morely, and Falconer? Some magic-wielding miscreant for hire? But how could they have known of her plans to stage a pretend seduction in the study? She'd told no one.

So if not that, then what? A fellow guest of the soiree who'd stumbled upon her and decided to merrily play along with her you're-my-lover-for-the-night charade? Robyn's face grew warm as she remembered how masterfully he'd done just that.

Though he'd kissed her in the study as though she were the most precious find of his life, Robyn willed herself to remember how the man, and the riders that trailed him, terrified her. She'd never seen the like of what had pounded after him on horseback. And she'd never felt such a pull within her mind—not when trying to fight off his promise to make her forget what had happened, and not when he'd drawn her out into the night and nearly into his arms. Though his touch and his kiss were all man, there was a part of him that was danger and demon and dark desire all mixed together. Being near him was like stepping into a realm she'd never known before. That he'd coaxed her from her own bed made Robyn realize no place was safe.

Combining all of that with the threat of her betrothal to Lord Morely, Robyn knew she must act and do so quickly. She couldn't risk another moment spent in London—especially not after facing her father's wrath earlier today.

He'd come blazing with a fury into the breakfast parlor, reeking of drink and smoke, smelling of something living that was slowly being eaten away. Face haggard, eyes wild, cravat and coat rumpled, the Earl of Chelsea had appeared a horrid sight.

"What the devil were you about last night?" he'd demanded, his voice rife with anger as he moved directly toward Robyn. "Do you think to play Morely and Falconer for fools? Do you think to play *me* for one?"

Robyn, unable to help herself, had jerked. So, Falconer had told her father what he'd seen in the study, as she knew he would.

"Answer me!" the earl had thundered, hovering above her.

Robyn, forcing herself to lift her face to her father's furious glare, had tried hard to keep her tone steady. "No, of course I didn't intend to make a fool of you. I told you before, Father, I do not wish to marry Lord Morely, nor will I. I—I've my own plans for my life. They don't include that man."

"What man *do* they include?" he'd demanded. "In whose arms were you held when Falconer found you?"

"He—he is no one of your acquaintance."

"I shall decide that. Now tell me his name!"

Rebellion had sparked within Robyn. She hated when her father bellowed at her—and unfortunately, he yelled far too much lately. Even if she'd known the name of the man who'd held her with such care and kissed her with such passion, she'd not have shared it. "He doesn't move in your circles, Father. I'm certain he neither drinks to excess nor gambles away the flesh of his own blood. In fact, he is most likely a man far above the lowly machinations of you, Lord Morely, and Morely's watchdog."

Those had been the wrong words to fling at the earl. In a fury, he'd reached out, dragged Robyn's chair away from the table, and grasped her hard by the shoulders, yanking her to the edge of her seat. "You dare question my ability to find you a suitable husband?"

Robyn, devastated by her father's harshness, had begged him to stop his tirade, had told him he was hurting her.

"And what do you think your actions of last night have done to *me*?" he'd railed. "Do you think I enjoyed hearing Falconer tell me what he found in that study last night? Do you think it made me proud to hear that my daughter behaved as nothing more than a lightskirt?"

The encounter turned uglier then, becoming a moment Robyn wanted to forget. That she carried no bruise upon her cheek amazed her; that she still cared for her father amazed her even more.

But though she loved him, Robyn knew she could no longer remain beneath his roof—which was why she had to leave, *now*, this very night, while her father was out gaming and Lord Morely and Falconer believed she was securely abed.

After peeking outside her window to be certain no handsome phantasm stood staring up at her from the pavement below and no fiends on horseback were circling the perimeter, Robyn hurried to wake her maid.

BOOK TWO

The Bedeviled

Chapter Five

Robyn had run away twice in her life; this was the second time. The first had been when she was just a girl, and Aunt Amy had come into her room at Land's End late in the night with bruises and a broken wrist and had wept as she told Robyn of a carriage accident. The blue-eyed boy Robyn had met—her betrothed, to whom she'd given her hammered heart—was *gone*.

Robyn had run away that day, while Aunt Amy, forced into taking medicine by the physician someone had summoned, slept fitfully, fully upright in the chair beside Robyn's bed. Robyn had run all the way back to that lone cottage on the hill—on that patch of flint-strewn grassland, perched atop the chalky cliffs—where just the night before she had met the lad who was to have been her future.

Snow had swirled, while far below the water raged in waves that fell, over and over. It had seemed to Robyn as if everything was falling—the snow, her tears, her very self.

On her knees in the snow, a young Robyn had held on to the only thing she could. With both hands, she'd gripped tight to the feather he'd given her.

He had said it was to be a wing for her every dream. Robyn had closed her eyes . . . and dreamt . . . of him, safe and alive, and somehow, someday, coming back for her.

He'd never returned, of course, his body believed to have been lost to the rocks and restless waves of the Channel, the same that had claimed the runaway carriage. Now, ages older and far wiser, Robyn was heading back to the one place she loved best—her aunt's sprawling estate, known as Land's End to the family, which was situated deep in the South Downs of Sussex, with that lone, battered cottage still standing atop the hill.

But after hours on the road, Robyn was no closer to feeling calm. In fact, she felt chased. She felt as if not one person was in pursuit of her, but many. Fear of Lord Morely, Falconer, and her father marred the daylight hours, while at night the man who'd kissed her so thoroughly in the study and whose shimmering image had coaxed her out of her father's home haunted Robyn's every moment.

He slipped inside her mind, not as pervasive as before, but a presence nonetheless—as if he were a thought in the air around her, keeping watch over her from afar.

A ridiculous notion, surely, Robyn thought, now staring out the window of her father's traveling carriage, her maid, Mattie, sitting opposite her.

But even though she tried, there was no way she could forget the man. He terrified her just as much as he intrigued her . . . and his touch had set her on fire. Whatever he was—man, sorcerer, phantasm—he was dangerous. He held the power to push his way into her thoughts, to pull her out into the dark night, to haunt her still . . . and he'd held the knowledge to annihilate whatever those things were that had chased them.

As if the turmoil raging inside of her weren't enough, there was a storm on the way. The wind had picked up. Gray clouds skirted inland from the Channel, blotting out the weak sunshine, and the light ash trees lining the road swayed at their highest tips, leaves fluttering in the ever-shifting wind. A shiver of agitation coursed through Robyn.

"Coo, m'lady, have y' caught a chill?" asked Mattie.

Robyn shook her head. "No, I'm just thinking is all."

She glanced over at her abigail, noting the faint mauve shadows beneath the girl's green eyes. She felt another twinge of guilt at having forced her, as well as Tom Coachman and her father's footman Benjamin, to hastily prepare and then embark on such an unexpected journey, all without the blessing of her father.

Both the coachman and footman were fretting over Robyn's safety—no doubt worrying about what the earl would say to them upon their return—and poor Mattie had had to quickly pack all of the necessities Robyn would need for an indefinite stay at Aunt Amy's.

"You're not too tired, are you?" Robyn asked. "I know how you hate to travel, and our pace has been relentless, to say the least."

Mattie waved away Robyn's worries. "La, m'lady, 'tis my task t' worry over y', not the other way round. But no, I not be too tired."

From the moment of her birth, every servant in Lord Chelsea's employ had doted on Robyn. They had indulged her even more following the death of her mother. That three of them had willingly left London with her in a carriage not her own was but more proof of their fierce protectiveness and of their staunch loyalty to her mother's memory.

Robyn turned her gaze once again to the carriage window and the world that whizzed past outside. She wondered how long it would be before whoever trailed her caught up to the carriage. Her mother had known there was more to the world than any person could ever imagine. All of her life, whenever Robyn had had a "feeling" about something, her mother would tell her to trust her senses, to be still inside, to listen to what her surroundings were sharing with her.

Hurry. That's what her surroundings were saying now. *Hurry, hurry, hurry.* She had a phantasm haunting her thoughts, Falconer and her father no doubt trailing after her, and a storm stirring. And something else . . . some other something stirring as well—but Robyn didn't know what, couldn't sense anything other than a restless agitation within herself.

For perhaps the hundredth time since leaving the city she longed to be free of the carriage, of *anything* that reminded her of her father and his devious plot.

And she would, she promised herself. Soon she'd leave it all behind. She was as familiar with these lands as she was with the back of her hand. Just the sight of them gave her a feeling of much-needed peace.

"Look, Mattie," Robyn said, pointing out the window. "Those trees mark the western borders of my aunt's lands. We're only an hour away by carriage, closer by horseback. Up ahead, there's a path that veers off the road and cuts straight through the woods of Land's End, eventually giving way to the lawns surrounding the main house."

Mattie moved forward on the cushions. "Ooh, m'lady, but it be lookin' ever so dark behind them trees. Dangerous even."

"It isn't dangerous, Mattie," Robyn said as she got to her feet and rapped against the trapdoor above. "In fact, I intend to take that trail."

"Oh, la." Mattie sat back, alarm flitting across her freckled features. "I s'pose this be why y' had me unpack yer ridin' habit and gloves for y' this morn, and why y' hired them hacks at the last inn?"

Robyn nodded, casting her maid a smile of reassurance. The inn where she had requested the horses wasn't far behind. In fact, it was closer than the darkness that would soon fall. If she insisted, Tom Coachman could have the carriage back there and tucked away from sight within the hour, and he and the others could stay at that inn until morning. If anyone had followed Robyn, those who had aided her in leaving town would be safe from reach.

"But it be lookin' like rain comin' soon, m'lady. If y' stay in the carriage, y' won't get wet or—"

"Mattie," Robyn cut in gently. "I'm not staying in the carriage. I'm sending it back."

The girl's green eyes grew wide as the coachman lifted the trapdoor and Robyn asked that he stop the coach.

"But whut o' yer things, m'lady?" Mattie asked.

"There will be everything I need at Aunt Amy's."

"But whut o' Tom Coachman? And Benjamin?"

"They'll be glad to turn around and head back, I'm sure. I should never have involved them."

"But . . . whut o' *me*, m'lady?"

"Or you, Mattie. I shouldn't have involved any of you." Robyn glanced down at the girl and felt her heart squeeze tight. "I can't ask you to come with me. I don't even know what my plans are. . . . I only know I have no plans to return to my father's house."

"Then I don't either."

"Don't be silly, Mattie. Your place is back there, not here. I'll send you to my cousins' home. Miss Lily is always in need of a maid."

"I be followin' y', m'lady."

Robyn dropped back down onto the seat, blowing out a breath as the carriage soon ground to a stop and Benjamin, who'd been riding his mount behind the carriage, came alongside and opened the door.

"Lady Robyn?" he asked.

"She be sendin' y' and Tom Coachman back t' town, trunks and all," Mattie blurted, "while she and I take them hacks and head fer the main house." Before Robyn even had a chance to speak, Mattie shared Robyn's plans of riding astride the last miles to Land's End.

Benjamin, clearly alarmed, glanced from Mattie to Robyn. "Forgive me, but do you think that is wise?" he asked. "I shouldn't let you go alone into those woods, my lady."

"Mattie and I will be fine. Truly," Robyn said to Benjamin, and then asked that he and Tom Coachman turn about, head back to the inn, and take up room for the night, tucking the carriage out of sight.

A reluctant Benjamin finally said he would do all that she asked, though clearly he wasn't pleased with her decision. As he turned his horse about and headed to the task of readying the extra horses, Mattie smiled at her.

"Thank y', m'lady."

Well, at least one person was happy. Robyn returned the smile, but felt a strong wash of foreboding whirl through her, as if she'd just sealed not only her fate, but Mattie's as well.

Shaking off her worries, Robyn reached for the hooded cloak that lay beside her on the cushions. Aunt Amy had given the garment to Robyn in the hours following the death of Robyn's mother, whispering that she should keep it close. It was the same cloak Robyn had worn the night of the soiree—the night she'd so willingly stepped into the arms of the masked stranger and all but begged him to play the part of her lover. Just touching it made her remember every moment, every touch, every—

Robyn clamped down tight on her thoughts. The man was something odd and dangerous. Remembering him did her no good. The phantasmlike scoundrel had obviously made an opportune moment out of a chance meeting. Though he'd done all that she'd asked—and more—he'd taken advantage of her. And somehow, in some way, the essence of him still lingered about her, or so it seemed.

His was a haunting magic Robyn could do without.

She swiped up the cloak. The color of a deep, bluish midnight, with a quilted stand-up collar and a deep hood lined in snow white satin, the garment had come to represent a sort of seal of freedom to Robyn. Her aunt had led an unfettered life and Robyn desperately yearned to do the same. Donning the cloak always made her feel as though she might be able to do just that—which was the reason she'd worn it the night of the masked soiree. Needing to feel such freedom now, she put the thing on and stepped out of the carriage.

Minutes later, Robyn was astride a nervy mount and

charging along a path she'd ridden through the years, Mattie trying to keep pace from behind. A cool wind in her face, Robyn allowed the energetic horse its head. The trees towering above created a dark canopy that made the forest floor seem like a blurred carpet of deep green and earthy black, and for the first time in a long while Robyn felt as though she were as free as the wind that coated her body.

The moment was short-lived.

Just as Robyn leaned down to pass beneath a low-hanging branch and move into a wide clearing, she felt a stinging blow to her shoulders, one that knocked her sideways off her saddle. The hard ground came up like a shot of lead fired from a gun barrel. A gasp of astonishment curled up and out of her just as something huge and unforgiving fell down on top of her, forcing the remaining breath from her lungs.

It was a man, Robyn realized dully. Her riding hat was torn free of its pins as a savage hand yanked hard at her hair, hauling her face upward.

"Blast it all, Ned!" her assailant cried. "This ain't who we be hopin' ta find! Look at her, young she be!" The man hauled Robyn to her feet, shoving her hard toward another man who seemingly materialized out of nowhere.

The man was all filth and grime. "She got the right color cloak, *but she ain't the one.*" He swiped the back of one hand against his sweaty upper lip, eyeing Robyn more closely. "Mebbe we should just take the cloak and still get our pay. After all, blue is blue and ain't nobody gonna fault us fer pickin' the wrong gel with the right color cloak. Besides, she probably gots some baubles on her, too, eh Bart?" He pressed one meaty hand against the bottom of Robyn's chin, forcing her head up and back as he smiled an ugly smear of a grin at her.

Robyn tried to jerk away, but Mattie came tearing down the path then, and Ned, hearing the maid before he saw her, was quick to turn about and make ready for her.

"No," Robyn yelled. *"Turn back."*

Her call of alarm came too late. Ned hefted a fallen, sturdy limb, neatly clipping poor Mattie off her saddle just as she unsteadily broke free of the thicket.

"Mattie," Robyn cried.

The girl was knocked out long before she hit the earth. Robyn would have rushed to her side, but Bart clamped his filthy hands on her shoulders, holding tight. Robyn twisted, trying to fight him, but was cruelly pinned against the trunk of a light ash. The man reached for the cords of her cloak, trying to yank the thing from her body. Robyn, terrified and furious, batted his hands away.

"Won't let the cloak go yet? All right then, how 'bout yer baubles, have any of those?"

The folds of her cloak were roughly shoved back, her spencer and the blouse beneath ripped open at the throat as Bart groped for jewelry. With one cruel swipe, he broke the clasp of the gold locket about her neck, but thankfully ignored the long and worn red ribbon, with its ancient heart of hammered silver dangling deep from the end of it. He pocketed the gold, then grabbed her hands and stripped off her fawn-colored gloves. He pocketed those as well, plus the two rings she wore.

Robyn's head swam. Who'd have thought *thieves* would attack on her aunt's lands? She forced herself not to give in to the panic threatening to overwhelm her, but if not for the tree behind her, Robyn knew she would have slid to the ground.

It was then the very earth shuddered and shook.

"Riders," Bart muttered.

"It be too soon fer our own boys," Ned said, dread in his eyes.

Events happened with lightning speed after that first shake of the ground. One minute Robyn was being accosted, and in the next she heard the hushed *zing* of an arrow let forth from its bow, another following.

Bart was the first to fall away, an arrow piercing his thigh and causing blood to flow. Ned staggered away next as another arrow slammed into the back of his right shoulder.

Robyn didn't waste time worrying over them. She pushed away from the tree and would have raced toward Mattie had she had the chance.

But the thundering sound continued. Suddenly a man appeared, charging into the clearing atop a very spirited—very familiar—horse. He had a bow, he had arrows, and he had Robyn's full attention.

She clutched at her cloak, wondering if she'd conjured the image of him, as he brought his horse to a dirt-spewing halt near her. The green of his eyes matched the forest . . . and her memory.

"It *is* you," she gasped, taking a huge step back even as she drank in the sight of his uncovered face—a countenance that stirred something deep inside of her. There was no shimmer of whiteness coating him now; instead, he was a vivid slash of dark brilliance against the shades of the forest. Coatless, shirt open at the throat and exposing his sun-burnished skin, he looked a mix of mystery, predatory instinct, and raw, undeniable power. His hair was night black, his nose near perfect. She noted a faint crescent scar beneath his left eye, the expressive sweep of his dark brows, and the sensuous bow of his lips—lips with a divot she remembered only too well. Even now, she could recall their texture, taste, and feel.

There came another pounding of sound, and suddenly two more riders appeared. The man, obviously their leader, motioned wordlessly to them. Barely slowing, the two riders broke apart. One of them veered straight for Ned and Bart, and seemed the sort who would have no trouble dealing with the duo. The other, brawny, with fair hair and memorable blue eyes, headed for Mattie, who lay far too still on the ground.

Everything happened with a rapid-fire pace after that. Robyn heard the howls of protest and then of fear as Ned and Bart met the swift punishment of the rider who charged at them. At the same time, she looked quickly to Mattie, fearing her maid would be equally harmed, but the other rider had merely jumped down off his mount and appeared to be checking Mattie for signs of life. He pressed his ear close to her mouth, and then called to his leader, "She's breathing!"

Robyn released a breath of her own.

Just when she would have demanded to know what the man and his friends were doing here on her aunt's lands, there erupted a shift of violent movement beyond them. Robyn whipped about just as Ned, fighting to be free, pulled a small pistol out of the lip of his boot and fired—missing his mark, but hitting her.

Robyn staggered back a step, feeling the bite of lead as it grazed her right shoulder. Stunned, a sudden flow of blood blooming, she wasn't certain she wouldn't fall to the ground in a dead faint. It was the stranger who held her upright, reaching down for her with swift strength. His eyes flickered with a terrible green flame as he motioned for his men to deal with the brigands. By the set of his jaw, Robyn guessed her rescuer wanted to deal with them himself; she sensed, though, that he wouldn't . . . that she was his first worry.

There came then the pounding thunder of more hooves. It sounded as though an entire mounted army were charging toward them.

"Who now?" Robyn gasped, confused by the whirl of events, her head strangely light. Terrified, she glanced up. "Friends of yours?"

"No," he said, sharp, and she realized that he had no fear, only fury. She could sense a growing rage in him, a wild, untamed force that threatened to spill up and out. He was furious that she'd been harmed. A dangerous, unholy light flickered hard in his gaze as he reached down and offered Robyn his hand. "Come," he ordered.

Robyn shook her head, remembering the shimmering

unearthliness of him the other night. "No. I don't want your help. I—I have my own horse. I—"

"You're white as a sheet. In another second, you're going to faint."

"I won't." She willed herself to stay upright.

He could haul her up onto the saddle if he wanted—he could do anything, he was that powerful. He knew it. She knew it. But something in him fought the awful force straining to be free. He clearly wanted Robyn to make the choice to go with him.

Again, he beckoned her with his hand. "Do you trust me?"

Robyn, her mind foggy, her body feeling odd, gaped at him. He'd asked her that in the study the other night, hadn't he? She couldn't remember, couldn't think straight. "Trust you? I—I don't even know you."

He leaned low toward her. "You knew me once, lass."

There it was again, just like the other night—that word, *lass*—uttered from him as if his every emotion was packed into it. Robyn blinked, trying to clear her brain, sensing strongly that he wasn't meaning just that night in town, but something more, something deeper. *Had* she known him? She didn't know, couldn't be certain of anything other than the searing pain in her shoulder and her raw fear of the towering power in this man, a strength he obviously tried hard to keep leashed.

The pounding of hooves drew closer. The wind whipped. The sky, visible only through the treetops, grew ominously dark. The world had become a dangerous, dark place, and Robyn, feeling odd and light-headed, didn't know what or whom to trust.

The stranger yelled to the man with the blond hair and blue eyes to see that Mattie was gathered up from the ground, and then he returned his attention to Robyn. "Take my hand, lass. Do it. Come with me."

The wild wind whipped her hair into her face. Robyn scraped the tendrils away, felt the burn in her arm, and

knew she would pass out soon. She made a fast decision—
she clutched at his hand.

He was warm. God, he was warm. And strong. Power
rippled through his arm, pulsated from his palm. Robyn
felt his fingers curl tight around her, and then, suddenly,
she was on the saddle in front of him. He'd drawn her up
and to him as though she weighed no more than a feather,
and now he drew her tight against him, shielding her with
his body. He gave a signal to his horse with just a touch of
his legs, and the huge animal leapt forward, tearing off
along a rarely used path through the trees. They went
winging through the woods then, his companions behind
them and an unconscious Mattie held tight by the sandy-
haired man.

Robyn gripped the horn of the saddle, her mind whirling. The only thing keeping her astride was the man's muscled arm snaked about her waist. He held her tight. She
felt her breasts being bunched upward, felt his long, strong
fingers splayed at her waist . . . and for the briefest of seconds, she could smell him.

He smelled of cedar and the ocean's salt. He smelled,
God help her, of hot, stolen kisses in a study lit only by
firelight. And he smelled of something more . . . faint but
familiar, something she couldn't puzzle out.

Had he wrapped another sway of thought about her?
Was that why his scent called to the deepest reaches of her
mind? Robyn felt her heart slam hard against her ribs at
the possibility. She knew nothing about this man other
than that his kiss and his touch could shatter her senses . . .
and that the beastly power in him could terrify.

He turned a sharp bend in the thicket, cutting a new
path where there was none. His horse didn't even balk but
merely plunged onward, totally trusting its master's lead.
Brambles snapped and caught along the trailing ends of
Robyn's cloak, tiny vines whipping against her legs and
bared hands. The scratches, immediately beading with

blood, were nothing compared to the burning of her shoulder and the rising crest of unbelievable fear. The press of the wind grew stronger now, even amid the trees, and it held the heavy scent of approaching rain.

"Where are we heading?" Robyn yelled. "If you turn back, there is a manse not far from here! I want to go there. Nowhere else!"

"No." The single word beat out of him, as though he understood her need but must deny it no matter the cost. "Your manse is far enough—and between us and it are those riders behind us. I can't fend them off and take care of you at the same time."

"But you're heading toward the water, and the storm is—"

"Nearly above us," he finished for her as they tore free of the line of trees and he urged his mount to an even faster pace. "Like it or not, we're heading to my camp."

"Stop," she yelled, "I won't go with you." The horse thundered on. "Stop. Now! Do you hear?"

A moment swelled between them before the man muttered, "I hear you, lass, but I'm not about to let you go. I can't. So hush, will you? Like it or not, I'm taking you to my camp where you'll be safe from those men and sheltered from the storm."

His words were a dark promise filled with hard will. Robyn knew then he meant what he said, that he wouldn't be swayed—not by anything or anyone. Against her back, through the material of their clothing, through even the wild beating of her own heart, Robyn felt the strong pulse of the man, felt his iron resolve. And beneath it all, deep within him, she sensed the ever-present battering of a beastly nature fighting hard to be free.

As they raced fast for the lip of rocky land jutting out to the water's edge, Robyn wondered what would keep her safe from him and his beast within.

Chapter Six

Dax urged his horse to a bone-jarring pace, watching as the darkness of the woodland gave way to a sweep of rugged terrain, beyond which lay the churning waters of the Channel. Bolts of lightning flickered in the distance, while out on the water could be seen a leaden curtain of drenching rain headed straight for them.

Dax, frowning at the sight, felt a tempest of a different kind brewing inside of him. He could feel the Phantom biting to be released. Though it wasn't midnight, bits and pieces of the evil that churned in him could manifest in various ways, none of them good. Seeing Robyn shot had enraged Dax and made his inner beast shimmer with fury. It had taken every ounce of his control to keep the fierce power within him contained. He could have annihilated everything—man, animal, leagues of forest and villages—when he realized Robyn had been shot. That she was now bleeding and frightened infuriated him like nothing else. He had to fight to keep tethered the ungodly force that threatened to engulf him.

Having sent a whisper of his magic to linger about Robyn, Dax had sensed her inner turmoil, but it wasn't until today that her emotions had turned to pure terror. He'd felt her presence the moment she'd entered Amy's lands—and he'd known the very instant another man un-related to her had laid hands on her. *Mine.* The Phantom had put wind beneath his horse's hooves, and he'd raced hard to reach Robyn, gladly letting his arrows fly.

What was she doing in the South Downs? And what in hell had brought her into contact with those men? Dax didn't doubt that her plot of hiring some stranger to play-act as her lover was somehow part of the reason for her presence on Amy's lands. He was beginning to realize that the precious girl of his past had grown into a strong-willed woman—one whose life was not at all the halcyon exis-tence he'd imagined it to be.

Did the men who'd attacked Robyn have something to do with Amy missing their rendezvous? She'd never ar-rived at the cottage where he'd first met her, though he'd waited for hours. Dax sensed something was in motion—something that reached far wider than Robyn fleeing London and Amy being absent from a meeting she'd not have missed. It was as if his past, present, and future had collided the moment he'd stepped foot on English soil.

Dax urged Robyn to lean low over his horse's neck as he gave the animal its head and it fairly flew over the ter-rain. If he had thought they could make it to Land's End, he'd have tried. But the odds were against that. Though he and his men proved match enough for the riders be-hind them, he wouldn't risk putting Robyn in further jeopardy. Her wound needed immediate attention, and the storm promised to be a mighty one. He had no choice but to take her to his camp.

Sight of the path that eventually led to the water's edge snapped Dax out of his wandering thoughts. It was then the rain came. Hard, stinging, pinlike drops that nearly blotted out what little could be discerned of the steep, narrow path that led to the water and was breached by hard-edged rocks. The storm in full force, there came the crashing sounds of breakers hitting the farthest rocks, the snap of lightning above and beyond them, and the ever-present screech of wind gone wild.

Dax, feeling the stinging needles of water biting into his skin, tried to draw Robyn's body closer to his own in an attempt to shelter what part of her he could. But she stiffened on the saddle before him, body rigid. Before them lay a gray, blocky shape of jagged rock, with an opening like a yawning, black-filled mouth leading into the earth's belly.

"The caves?" she yelled, realization dawning on her as the wind tore at her sodden tresses and snatched her words away. Having spent a great deal of time at her aunt's home in her early years, she was clearly familiar with the dark and treacherous caves that dotted the edges of Sussex. "What manner of men make camp in caves?" she demanded, though he suspected she knew the answer.

What kind of men? Thieves. Smugglers. Those with no hope and fewer prospects. *Phantoms like me*, Dax thought. He said nothing, though, because he had no words to soothe her terror, especially since he was leading her into danger of a different kind than that of those men back there.

A jagged streak of lightning flashed directly overhead just as they entered the gloomy mouth of the cave. The crack of booming thunder that followed echoed like a monster's howl, reverberating through the blackened tunnel of rock. Dax felt Robyn's body jerk and then tremble, but still she kept her spine stiff, her gaze trained straight ahead. Only once did she move, and that was to push the wet hair from her face. She didn't look at him, didn't speak, and he knew she was damning him for bringing her into whatever hell awaited her here.

A minute later they entered into a huge, domed area, beyond which was a higher ledge of stone accessible only by a slab of rock that had been smoothed by years of seawater washing over it. A few torches were lit, sputtering in crude holders alongside the walls. A trio of his men—Bones,

John, and Blade—sat hunkered down near a low-burning fire. Beyond them stood Gideon Dance, a dark menace in the shadows.

Bones, wiry and as thin as his name implied, got to his feet first, a grin of relief flashing across his face at sight of Dax. "Glad I am t' see y', boss," he said. "I wuz gettin' worried whut w' the storm and all." Bones reached up for Dax's reins, glancing only briefly at Robyn. "Sam and Randolph?" he asked.

"Right behind us." Dax swung down off the saddle, drawing Robyn with him in one fluid motion. As soon as her feet touched the ground she backed away from him. Dax let her go, watching as her violet, fear-filled gaze took in every detail of the huge area. She noted the bedrolls laid out near the fire, noted Dax's men staring at her with curiosity—Blade with contempt—noted the extra horses in the far-off corner . . . and the wagons, small but sturdy, empty but ready for loading. By the time she swung her gaze back to him the fear in her eyes had turned to loathing. Dax had expected as much, but even that didn't lessen the sting of regret that sliced through him.

Randolph and Sam rode into the area then, Randolph holding the red-haired girl in his arms.

"*Mattie,*" Robyn breathed, moving past Dax and hurrying toward Randolph's horse.

"She's still unconscious, mistress," Randolph said as Robyn reached up to touch the girl's cheek, "though I do think she'll be coming 'round soon."

Dax, seeing Robyn's features twist with worry, motioned for John to help get the girl off the saddle. He noted how Robyn reached for the young woman—as if Robyn believed her touch could soothe the maid. "Put her near the fire," he said, "where she can get warm and dry."

John moved to do just that, while Blade—mean looking, with coarse features and a patch over his left eye, and who had earned his name from his unerring skill with a knife—muttered in dissent as he slowly got to his feet and left the fire's side. "What the hell is this?" he demanded of Dax, hooking one dirty thumb toward the women. "You be risking all our lives bringing them here!"

Dax had long ago used his dark gifts to brush up against Blade's innermost thoughts. There'd been little good to find, nothing other than a healthy dose of anger at the world, resentment for his lot in life, and few morals to guide his conscience.

"Who I bring here isn't your concern. Whether you like it or not, the women stay."

"I don't like it," Blade challenged, a sneer smearing his drink-ruined features. "You just brought us trouble we don't need."

"The only trouble you don't need is me on your bad side," Dax said. "You're here because it's what Jemmy wanted. But the longer he's dead, the more I wonder if I need to honor his dying wishes."

Blade's mud-colored eyes narrowed. For a moment, Dax thought the man might pull his knife. But Blade stayed his hand. He glanced at Robyn, taking in her sleek form, wealthy clothing, and worried look and then brought his gaze back to Dax. "I understand more than you think."

Dax didn't like the insinuation. "Go," he ordered. "Help Bones with the horses, and keep your opinions—and your hands—to yourself."

"Worried?" Blade dared to spread a wolfish grin on his face as he passed behind Robyn.

The Phantom in Dax wanted to bust free, to annihilate the insignificant being before him.

Gideon, leaning back against a far wall of the cave, watched him, watched Blade, and waited for all hell to break loose.

Dax took a step, intending to yank Blade back, but a hand atop his shoulder stilled him.

It was Randolph. The big, blond-haired man shook his head. Ever calm, knowing what lurked inside of his friend, he was often the voice of reason in Dax's ear.

"Don't do it," Randolph said quietly. "That's what he wants, you know. That's what Blade has always wanted—to bait the beast he suspects is in you. Right now, though, you got to tell me what you want done."

Dax calmed by slow degrees, able to keep a leash on the Phantom. He had to regain control and come up with a new plan for his men; now that he'd brought Robyn and her maid into this den of smugglers, he'd altered their course.

"As soon as the eye of the storm blows past, send John to Land's End," Dax said. "He's to give word that the lady and her maid are safe and will be returned as soon as possible. Tell him to talk only with Lady Archer, and if she isn't there, which I suspect she won't be, then with Lady A's butler, Harry. Tell him to make certain no one at the house calls an alarm. No one is to know we have the women with us. I also need John to ask after Lady Archer."

Randolph nodded. "Anything else?"

"Set Bones as watch for the incoming boats. Hopefully our crew is riding out this storm onboard the ship and not in the smallboats. As for the girl called Mattie, you'd better move her. If she wakes, I don't want her being witness to the men bringing in the cargo. And I'll need some water and anything you might have in your saddle packs. Robyn was hit."

"I saw," Randolph said, and lifted his left hand. Slung across his palm was a smooth belt of leather, a pack dangling from each end. "In the left, you'll find two packets—one of roots and one of herbs—and in the right is a skin of water. Mix a pinch of the herbs with three parts water then spoon the mixture into her mouth; it'll help calm her. Clean the wound, then crush the roots and let them lay directly over it. Wrap it all snug, but not too tight."

Dax nodded his thanks and took the packs. "I'll take her to my own area. She's in for a long night, I fear."

Dax knew he was, too. Robyn most likely wouldn't go willingly with him—especially not deeper into the caves—and the Phantom was eager to rise and was hungry to take charge.

Dax and Randolph moved toward the fire where John had laid the young girl down atop a bedroll. Robyn kneeled beside her, her back toward them. As though feeling their approach—and Dax's intent—Robyn got to her feet and turned about.

Her gaze fastened solely on him, as though he alone created and commanded her every fear. She drew in a breath—no doubt for courage—lifted her chin, and said, "Whoever was behind us hasn't followed. If you loan me two of your horses, I can take my friend and myself home. She needs a physician, dry clothing, and t-to be away from here."

She isn't the only one, Dax thought, noting how Robyn's sodden clothes clung to her form, the stain of blood on her cloak. Worry over her welfare knifing through him, he motioned for Randolph to gather up the maid.

"Wait," Robyn ordered, plucking at Randolph's sleeve. "What are you doing? Where are you taking her?"

"I won't harm her." Randolph lifted Mattie into his arms as though she weighed nothing, then headed off on a narrow stone pathway that threaded away from the main area of the cave.

Robyn took a step to follow, a cry of outrage on her lips, but Dax, coming up beside her, said softly against her ear, "Let them go. He'll watch over her. Now do us both a favor and don't fight me." Gently, he closed his fingers around her slim left wrist, attempting to draw her away from the fire and toward the slab of stone slanting upward to the ledge above.

Robyn instantly tried to snatch her hand away, but Dax wouldn't allow it. He couldn't. The men were watching, Blade especially. Rubbing down Sam's horse, Blade had a feral look in his eyes, his mind calculating how willing— or unwilling—the lady was to be here. If he could use Robyn as leverage against Dax, he would.

"This way," Dax murmured to Robyn, slinging the packs over his left shoulder. She tried to pull back, tried to dig in her heels, but Dax couldn't allow it. "Don't cause a stir, lass," he whispered, his lips near her ear. "Not now, not here."

Dax watched as Robyn's lashes lowered and she peered at the others from the corners of her eyes. She, too, was calculating, deciding in that brief instant whom to trust more—the others or him. Dax felt more than saw the slight squaring of her shoulders, the stiffening of her spine, and then watched as she lifted her lashes and looked directly into his eyes. He knew then that he'd won—but only for the moment.

He led her across to the marble-smooth incline of flat rock. At its base, he drew a flaming torch out of its holder with his free hand, then headed up the slick stone, warning Robyn to keep to its rougher-edged side nearest the wall. Once on the ledge he headed right, deep into the warren of walkways within the cave.

The torch's light flickered on walls wet from the earth's breath, casting freakish shadows that bounced and danced like wraiths. The air was cold and damp, smelling of earth and sea, rot and life.

"You're treating me as though I'm your captive," Robyn said. "I wish to leave."

"I know you do."

"So where are you taking me?"

"Someplace a bit warmer and drier."

"I find that difficult to believe. This place is hideous, nothing more than a hideout for thieves and smugglers, for men on the run, or on the prowl."

"Aye, it's that," Dax agreed. "A stone prison that can flood with seawater in a flash, houses bats on occasion, and is pathetic in all kinds of weather. But," he added, tossing a grim look at her over one shoulder, "it's home."

Robyn shivered, appalled.

Dax had been appalled, too—once upon a time. But

what had been unacceptable in his formative years had now become the norm.

Dax guided Robyn up the narrow incline that led to his private chamber, which was nothing more than a large hollow of stonework with a natural bench of rock for a bed and an opening far above in the opposite corner that made for a chimney flue. A small fire smoldered in the dip of rock directly beneath the flue, its warmth-giving glow banishing any cool moisture from the air.

Releasing his hold on Robyn's wrist, Dax shoved the torch into a natural indentation of the wall, and then moved to the fire. He stirred it with a stick, tossing in more wood from a nearby stack. The flames took hold, flaring with brightness, and coupled with the light of the torch cast the room in rich radiance. Satisfied he could keep her warm enough now, he turned.

"So what were you doing in those woods, lass?" he asked softly.

"What were *you?*" she countered.

Hoping to meet with your aunt, he wanted to say. *Trying to build a bridge back to you,* he wanted to add.

He said none of that, of course. He merely gazed at her, wishing he could share every truth about himself, wishing she would do the same.

But Robyn remained at the threshold of the chamber, exactly where Dax had left her. Her drenched hair hung in long skeins about her shoulders. The heavy wetness of her cloak and riding skirt looked to be weighing her down, and the stain of blood near her right shoulder had grown to a frighteningly large patch. Violet eyes wide, the fire and torchlight glittering in them, she watched Dax as if she had just had an epiphany about him.

"You're the one," she whispered, her words an accusation, not a question. "You're the man I met in London . . . the one who—who touched me, kissed me, the one I allowed to half undress me in that study."

"Aye."

"Why?"

"Because you asked me. Because—"

"*No,*" Robyn cut in, anger in her tone. "Why were you there? What was your intent?"

Dax blew out a breath, glancing down as he ran one hand through his wet hair. There was so much she didn't know. So much he couldn't tell her.

"Had you intended to rob the place?" Robyn demanded. "Is that it? Did I foil your plans when you found me in the study? And . . . and did you decide to—to toy me with after that, after I'd interrupted your night of thievery?"

Dax's head shot up. Ready to deny this, he stopped himself.

What else would she think? What else *could* she think? It was obvious she saw him as nothing more than a lowly thief and smuggler.

And he was that. God. He was exactly that.

"Yes," he lied, hating himself for it, hating the moment.

Robyn glared at him, her eyes showing an instant of deep pain, but she quickly shuttered that pain away, too proud to let him know how much his admission hurt. Voice sharp, she demanded, "Those things . . . those fiends that chased us in the mews, then vanished, what were they?"

"You don't want to know, lass."

"Yes. I do. Tell me."

He slanted a look at her. "Trouble, that's what they were."

"And you?" she asked, clearly remembering how the image of him had coaxed her out into the street. "Are you one of them?"

"No," he said. *I'm worse.*

"But I saw you—in the mews and later in the street— and you were just a shimmer of white."

"It was the moon. It played tricks."

She shook her head. "It was no trick. No play of light." She was trembling, favoring her injured right arm, her cheeks flushed in spite of her shivering. "There's something not right about you—you . . . *you are nothing mortal.*"

And then she did something totally unexpected. Before Dax could stop her, she snatched the torch from the wall, turned about and fled—not back the way they'd come, but deeper into the warren of snaking walkways.

Bloody hell, Dax thought.

He knew exactly what she'd find in the farthest reaches of the cave—and she wouldn't like it.

He gave her several minutes of running the fight out of her body . . . and then he followed, knowing he'd need a dose of his own dark magic to face what was to come.

Chapter Seven

Terrified, Robyn ran . . . around a corner, then a left-handed curve, and then fast and reckless along a path that narrowed considerably after a while. She didn't dare slow down, stop, or even think. All she knew was that the man she'd left behind frightened her beyond coherent thought. He was some being, some *thing* she couldn't—shouldn't—trust.

The narrow walkway she found herself in was dank and dark. She discerned a foul smell mixed with the scent of the ocean. The path was definitely a way out, but what lay between her and the outside, Robyn couldn't be certain.

Ignoring her fears of what lay before her, as well as the ache in her shoulder, she pressed forward. Going back wasn't an option. Neither was stopping.

The heavy torch she carried cast shadows on the wet walls. Frightful images, like a light show that had gone nightmarishly askew, loomed above and about her. And the smell . . . ! The stench grew worse as the passage narrowed even more. Robyn didn't have time to contemplate what she was heading into. She knew only that she could smell salty air amid the sharp stench. She plunged on, rounding yet another curve . . . where a waist-high wall of rock greeted her.

Robyn shoved the torch up, stood on the balls of her feet, and then peered into what appeared to be a huge inner area. It was pitch-dark inside, but from the other end of the area could be seen a pinpoint of what looked to be firelight. The fact that the flame of the torch flickered and danced told her there was fresh air coming through that far-off opening.

She narrowed her gaze, sharpening her senses as she focused on that distant spot of light. It was definitely an opening at the other end. Robyn could smell the scent of the sea clearly now, though the smell was laced with something utterly foul and menacing.

A way out is a way out, she reminded herself, placing the torch on the lip of rock and then hauling her body up and over it. Her movements caused a burning pain in her arm and fresh blood to flow. Once atop the lip of stone, she lay still for a fraction of a moment, sucking in a huge gulp of air that was both sweet and ugly.

Her skin tingled. The rock felt cool, too cool. Her arm hurt, she was dizzy, and she was hot inside. Every inch of her wanted to lie on that rock and hug it for dear life, but she couldn't. She had to keep moving.

Robyn swung her legs over the ledge and dropped down the few feet so that she was standing fully inside the putrid-smelling area. What was that awful smell?

Just as she turned to retrieve the torch, she felt something flutter alongside her left arm, heard a *squeak* and then felt a wave of combined movement ripple throughout the area. Dear God . . .

Bats.

She'd climbed down into a nesting of bats!

Robyn instantly stilled. The torch had yet to fully frighten the creatures only because she'd left it on the ledge. As for her own movements, she merely disturbed a few of them, but not enough to make them do more than flutter.

Robyn didn't move an inch. Instead, she gazed at the

glare of light coming from the opposite end of the cave. It was definitely firelight, and from that opening came the scent of water and the far-off voices of the men she and Dax had left near the mouth of the cave, Mattie with them.

Freedom was just a short distance away.

If she moved slowly enough, and if she left the torch behind, Robyn figured she just might make it to the opposite end.

She forced herself to move, bile rising in her throat. How many bats could inhabit one cave? A few? A thousand? She tried not to think about it.

Picking her way carefully, going slow inch by slow inch, she moved into the foul-smelling darkness, focusing only on the pinpoint of light that glared beyond.

She heard more whispers of movement as she gained the middle area. The air became oppressive then, filled with the sharp scent of bat droppings. It burned her nose, her throat. How many would it take to create such a stench? Robyn involuntarily gagged, wondering if she could get through this, could keep moving at a snail's pace and not lose her mind, her courage, or the contents of her stomach.

She yearned for some light. She wanted to haul in a sweet breath of air. She wanted to scream. But she couldn't call out, no matter how frightened she was. The man who'd kidnapped her—the haunting phantasm who'd kissed her senseless and then coaxed her from her bed with but a thought—was somewhere behind her, and before her, beyond the bats, were several of his friends.

Robyn inched forward, again . . . again . . . again. Every footstep felt like an eternity. She imagined stepping on a sleeping bat, but they hung upside down when they slumbered, didn't they? And they were sleeping now, weren't they?

Her mind played tricks on her, conjuring up any number of the foul creatures to slap into her face, tangle in her hair.

Robyn swallowed thickly, fearing she would vomit past the huge lump in her burning throat. Her eyes stung, tearing. Her limbs felt on fire. Her right arm, it seemed, *was* on fire.

There was only a short distance to go, the opening of the cave several feet above. Cool air, smelling of the sea and heavy rain, whispered past her. She'd have to climb to get to the opening.

Robyn reached high with both hands, not allowing herself to care that she was breaking apart the edges of her wound, or that more blood was flowing. She touched cool stone, pulled herself up, up . . .

"I wouldn't if I were you, lass."

Robyn heard the words so clearly it seemed they had been whispered directly into ear. She turned her face abruptly. Across the way, she could see the still-burning torch where she'd left it on the ledge . . . and nothing else. But she could hear him. He'd found her.

Robyn didn't pause to think. She whipped her face about, grasped the next highest rock, and hauled herself up with a too-quick motion. She got a view of the fire and the men they'd left behind earlier . . . and of the horses nearby. If Robyn hurried, she could get up and over the rock and scramble down to one of the horses. And if she were truly fortunate, she'd be able to find Mattie, get her astride, and then race fast for the mouth of the cave.

She clawed at the rocks, surprised, then panicking, as the stones tumbled out from under her grip. She thought she screamed, but couldn't be certain for her face was scraping against rock, and the bats, frightened into motion, were suddenly screeching and careening around her. Like dominoes that fell one after the other, the creatures took flight, dropping into the air, all of them seemingly headed her way.

Robyn ducked, covering her head, but they blasted against her, getting caught in her wet hair, the folds of her cloak. She beat them away, praying they wouldn't bite her. With a determination that surprised even herself, she hauled her body up the slanting of tumbling rock, intending to get free of the putrid cave. She swatted one bat away, catching its wet, boneless wing against her palm. She screamed, whisking it away from her. Another zoomed in to take its place.

"Get *off*!" she cried, heart hammering as a cloud of the creatures surrounded her. One landed on her neck. She thought she'd lose all nerve as she felt the tiny hairs of its body. She nearly gagged as she flicked the thing away from her. Her entire body convulsed as she climbed higher on the rocks.

"Lass. Don't."

His voice again, just a whisper in her head. Robyn was beyond listening. She climbed higher and higher, ignoring the fact that her body felt heavy and on fire and that her right arm was bleeding in earnest. She had only one thought, *to get out.*

Halfway up, she realized what he was trying to tell her. This opening out of the cave was a meager and dangerous one. Her hand gripped a stone, but the thing let loose beneath her grasp and a tiny avalanche came behind it. Robyn fell back and down, a tumble of loose stones coursing down on top of her as the bats screeched and whirred like a wind funnel above and around her.

The man materialized out of the madness, a shimmering essence that beat back the darkness and kept the bats at bay. He shoved the stones from her and then reached for Robyn's left hand, pulling her gently to her feet and then immediately against him so that she was *inside* of the shimmer of whiteness.

Robyn tried to fight him, but couldn't. He was too strong, too determined, and she was tired and terrified and . . . oh God . . . but she *wanted* to be flush against him. Inside the otherworldly light blazing from his body there were no bats, there was no stench. There was just him . . . and now her.

Robyn, unable to stop herself, pressed her open palms and her forehead against his chest . . . and simply breathed. He smelled of cedar and of the rain they'd ridden through. He smelled of man and might. She could feel a powerful energy in him, could almost hear its hum. She'd come through that energy when he'd hauled her to him, and for the briefest of moments she'd felt a bone-numbing cold, followed by the tiniest of zings everywhere her skin was exposed, as if a million little lightning bolts were zapping at her. Lifting her face, Robyn dared a peek up at him, fearing she'd see the face of a phantasm . . . but she didn't. She saw only his handsome features, the green weald of his eyes—eyes that held a flicker of power in them and something else. Desire?

He lowered his head so that their foreheads touched, his damp hair tangling with hers. Robyn thought he would kiss her, as he had that last time in the study, all soft and slow. But he didn't. Instead he, too, drew in a deep breath, as though he was fighting hard for control.

Wordlessly, he bent down and with effortless ease lifted her into his arms. One moment they were surrounded by a cloud of bats and the next they were back in his chamber of rock, with the firelight flickering and the torch once more in its holder. Robyn, blinking, felt fuzzy in the head—as if he'd whisked her back with a blurring speed . . . or had gone straight through rock. Impossible.

Or was it?

As he set her down on her feet and stepped away, Robyn felt again the arctic cold and whips of lightning, and then watched, amazed, as the tremulous light faded not from him but *into* him. She felt a scowl storm across her features as fear crawled up from her belly and bit deep.

"What just happened?" she demanded. "How did you get us from there to here?"

Dax felt a scowl of his own coming on, no matter that a part of him marveled, once again, at the fact that Robyn could perceive him when he went full Phantom. Her attempt at freedom had caused her to lose more blood and had made him shimmer into that bloody bat-infested area after her. There was only one thing he hated worse than his Curse and it was bats. And now here they stood wasting precious time. Robyn had been shot and was bleeding. He had to take care of her. Now.

"Your cloak," Dax said, ignoring her questions. "Take it off."

"*What?*"

"Remove it, lass."

"No," she flared. "If you think I am going to once more allow myself to be undressed—"

Bloody hell, Dax thought, cutting off her words with his movements. With just a few quick strokes he undid the enclosure of the cloak and then swooshed the thing up and off her shoulders, letting it drop in a sodden mass to the stone at her feet.

Robyn gasped, enraged.

Dax, however, felt a huge ball of anger curl in his gut at sight of what the low-life marauders in the woods had done. Her spencer had been ripped, the pristine blouse she wore beneath it savagely torn. Already a bruise was purpling the skin at the base of her neck.

Damn those men to hell. The Phantom lusted for their souls. He wished now he'd sent his arrows into their hearts, wished he'd snuffed the very life out of them.

Shakily, Robyn pulled the remnants of her blouse and jacket closed, her movements enough to ground Dax in what little shred of sanity he still possessed.

"I—I am fine, I assure you, so leave me be."

Dax's gaze moved to her right shoulder and the damage the ball of lead had done to her. A deep crimson stained the whole of her right arm. "I think not," he said, touching the ripped shoulder seams, gently pulling the material down and away from her. There was an ugly bullet graze, blood still coming out of it.

Robyn, following his gaze, peered at the torn flesh, her eyes widening at the sight of how much blood she'd lost—how much blood she was still losing.

She winced and glanced again at Dax, swallowing thickly as she did so. Gone were her bravery and her anger, and in their stead settled terror and thoughts of her own mortality. She was searching for reassurance now, even if she had to find it in a lowly thief that could turn phantom.

"I'll take care of you," Dax whispered.

Robyn said nothing, but allowed him to guide her to his rock bed, which was covered with furs.

"Flesh wounds can have the nastiest of bleeds," he said, deciding it was best if he just kept talking. He reached for Randolph's saddle packs, yanked out a piece of linen tucked inside the right pack, then made quick work of ripping the material into several strips. "Had a few myself." He nodded to a long-healed scar—one of many on his body—just beneath the hem of his shirt as he gently swiped away the mess of blood that had run down her arm.

Robyn chanced a glance at him, but seeing a peek of the lean, whipcord expanse of his muscled stomach and the trail of dark hairs that led down below the line of his trousers, she whipped her gaze back up to his. "H-How did you stop the bleeding?" she asked, clearly needing him to continue talking.

"Same way I'll stop yours: with pressure, some magic from Randolph's packs, and a clean binding."

She flinched. "Magic?"

"Roots and herbs, lass."

"Wh-Who is Randolph?" she asked.

Dax noted that she was trying hard not to faint as he swiped the material closer to her abrasion. "The blond-haired, blue-eyed brute. He's the truest of friends. And so is Bones. Sam, too. Sam's the one who was with us when we found you. Bones is the skinny fellow you saw near the fire."

"And the dark-eyed one who keeps to the shadows?"

Dax's gaze snapped up. He was quiet a moment as a whip of jealousy snapped in his gut. "That would be Gideon," he said, watching Robyn closely. "You'll want to keep clear of him, lass. He's someone you don't wish to tangle with."

She nodded, as if to say that dealing with one of his kind was more than enough for her. "Well, then . . . tell me about the others," she said as he tossed the bloody strip of cloth down to the stone and then opened both saddle packs. Clearly, she wanted to focus on anything other than her wound.

Dax pulled out the skin of water first, wetting yet another strip and cleaning away the worst of the blood. He tossed it away as well, then reached for the packets Randolph had told him about, finding the roots and crushing one in his palm.

"Sam was just young when I met him, barely nine at the time," Dax said, sprinkling the crushed root over her abrasion. "I was in the West Indies, browsing in some stalls near a wharf when he tried to pick my pocket." Reaching down, Dax lifted from the floor one of his own travel packs, dug inside of it, and pulled out a clean shirt of linen. He ripped it into strips. "He was just a scrawny orphan trying to feed his hunger. I tossed him some coins, thinking I'd seen the last of him."

"But you hadn't," Robyn guessed, watching as Dax wrapped one of the strips about her upper arm, then used a smaller one to secure it snugly, but not too tight.

"No," Dax admitted, shaking his head. "Like a stray cat you feed once, he kept turning up. Claimed I was his good luck in life. Said his mother had abandoned him on the quay and that he'd never met his father." Dax finished cleaning the rest of the blood from her arm. "So I kept feeding him, and one year turned into another."

Robyn watched as he opened a packet of herbs, took

out a pinch and then dropped it into a tin cup he pulled from the saddle pack. He added some water, swirled it in the tin, and then motioned for her to drink it. "It'll help calm you, lass," he said when she hesitated. "Will ease your pain."

Robyn took the cup. "And Bones?"

"Ah, Bones," Dax murmured, shaking his head, knowing Robyn needed him to keep talking. "He's been forgotten by the family he helped create and raise. His two sons set off to do better things than what they believed their father had ever done. His wife died a short time later. After a year of days and nights spent alone, he closed up his home and took to the sea. I met him in the West Indies, too . . . and like Sam he was searching for someone to trust and to share his hours. He's nearing fifty now, but you'd never know it."

"And so you took him in, along with Sam and—and the man you call Randolph?" Robyn asked, the tin poised before her lips.

"Aye," Dax said, motioning gently for her to drink the brew. "He'd give his life for mine. Just as Randolph would. And Gideon. I'd do the same for them."

Only then did Robyn finally drink the draught he'd mixed. She tipped the cup back, draining it, wincing as she swallowed.

Had Dax told her about the life he'd taken when he'd first learned of his full terrible strength, he knew Robyn wouldn't have drunk the potion. She'd have run for her life, just as her good sense had warned her to do when he'd found her in the forest, and just as she'd done a few minutes ago.

Among many things, one cost of the Phantom was a smuggled soul now and then—and Dax had taken far too many souls.

A long stretch of silence swelled between them. Dax gathered the dirtied strips of cloth, moved to toss them into the flames, then washed his hands with water from the flask. He returned to the rock bed, hunkered down, and drew the last of his clean shirts from his pack. Then he stood, handing the garment to Robyn.

"Take it," he said. "Your blouse and jacket are not only ruined, but their wetness will leave you chilled."

Robyn shook her head, looking from the garment to him. "No, I—"

"Don't argue. I'll turn my back," he said gently. "Just put it on, will you?"

As promised, for the next half hour Dax put his back to her. He made himself busy stoking the fire, then picked up her cloak and spread it over an outcropping of stone near enough to the flames so that it wouldn't smoke but would dry within an hour or so. From behind him he heard the sounds of Robyn shifting, of her wet clothes hitting the floor of the cave.

"All right," she finally said. "You can turn around now."

To his surprise, she'd not only taken off her blouse and jacket, but her riding skirt, boots, hose and undergarments as well. She'd put his shirt on and lay down atop the rock bed, pulling the fur up to her chest and tucking it beneath her arms.

The sight of Robyn in his makeshift bed nearly undid him. The edges of his shirtsleeves reached past her knuckles, the white of the material contrasting sharply with her dark hair and luminous, violet eyes. She looked a vision, a young, tantalizing beauty.

"Tell me true," Dax said, "how did you fare after I left you the other night?"

"What, you can't read my mind? You've invaded it enough since then, not to mention my dreams. You tell me."

"I don't know," he said honestly. And then, realizing the full of what she'd just said, asked, "You dreamt about me?"

Robyn attempted to glower at him, though in her drugged state the look was sultrier than she wanted, he guessed. "Hardly. It's more as if you barged into my dreams. Walked bodily into them."

Dax couldn't help but be intrigued. "I did, did I? And what happened?"

"Don't toy with me."

Dax wanted to playfully tease her, but knew better. "I'm not, lass. Tell me, what happened that night I left you?"

"Nothing good."

"So whatever happened after I left forced you to flee both the city and your home?"

"No. It was what happened *before* I met you that forced me to flee." Eyes turning glassy, she added, "Never mind all of that. I—I'm worried about my . . . friend. Her name is Mattie, and she's terrified of the dark. Will you check on her and let me know how she is?"

"I will," Dax murmured, glad she wasn't spilling all to the stranger she thought him to be, a smuggler at that. Robyn hadn't shared her courtesy title with him, or the fact that the girl was obviously her maid. Any thief worth his salt would hold the two for ransom. "I'll check on her soon," he said, "but I don't want to leave you just yet."

"I'm fine," Robyn insisted, the pupils of her eyes narrowing to just pinpoints. "In fact, whatever it was you put in that tin is making me feel . . . well, I—I feel much, much better."

High as a bird in the sky, Dax thought, wondering what type of concoction Randolph had instructed him to brew.

"Will you go, look in on Mattie and then—come back to me?" she asked, her voice dreamy, light.

Come back to her? If he had his way, he'd never leave her. Not ever. "Aye," Dax said, watching as Robyn relaxed, her long, dark lashes sweeping downward. A moment later she was asleep, caught up in the sticky web of whatever opiate Randolph's packets held.

Dax swiped up Robyn's garments from the stone, tossed her blouse and jacket into the flames, then spread out her skirt to dry near the fire, set her boots and hose to dry, too, and then headed out to find Randolph.

Several minutes later, he stood in Randolph's chamber— one much like his own, with a soft, cheery fire in a lip of stone—and watched in bewildered amazement the young, red-haired girl named Mattie. Sitting straight up and showing no signs of injury, she rolled dice carved out of bone as though she'd been born to do the deed.

"La," she cried, "but I be winnin' *that* roll, too! Y' be soft, Randy, sir. Pay up, I say!"

Randolph laughed, gladly tossing over a few coins from the pile in front of him. The pile in front of the maid, however, was larger. She happily raked in her winnings. It was only when she spied Dax that the smile fled from her lips. "Lawks," she gasped, jumping to her feet. "Have y' word 'bout m'lady?"

"She's fine," Dax said, "and asking about you."

"Oh, I be fine too. Randy . . . er, Mister Randolph here," she corrected herself, "brought me awake w' but a touch t' my cheek. And then he commenced t' teach me how to roll shaved dice. I never knew pieces of shaved bone could be such fun, or worth so much!" Her green gaze suddenly narrowing, she asked, "Yer certain m'lady be fine?"

"Very."

"Can I see her?"

"Soon," Dax promised. "She's resting now." His gaze flicked to Randolph. "She *will* wake up?"

Randolph nodded. "Close to dawn, I'd say."

"Dawn," Dax repeated—which meant she would sleep through the rise of his Phantom. Randolph was ever mindful of his dark legacy.

Dax told Mattie he'd send for her when Robyn came awake, then threaded his way out of the chamber. All was quiet in the main area of the cave. John had set out for Land's End, Bones to watch for the boats, and Sam and Blade were sitting near the fire, Blade nursing a bottle of drink. Sam nodded to him as Dax moved past. Blade only glared.

Gideon, Dax noted, was nowhere to be seen.

Robyn was still sleeping when Dax returned to his chamber. He slid down to the floor beside her, his back propped against the stone of his rock bed.

He had nothing to do now but wait.

Chapter Eight

Time inched by.

Dax thought about a lot of things as he sat watching the licking flames of the fire, listening to the sounds of Robyn's even breathing. He thought of the life he'd once known as a child, of the dark scourge that curled through him, of all the years he'd spent trying remember his past. . . .

Mostly, though, he thought about *her*.

It was late in the night when Robyn finally stirred. Near midnight, in fact. The hour Dax dreaded most. But he knew the fiends that chased him wouldn't materialize, not so deep within the caves. There was something about the thickness of the rock that shielded his presence from them. Jemmy had been the one to share that detail, had brought him here that snowy day he'd found Dax shot, his neck snapped. Dax was safe here, and he could keep Robyn safe here, at least from the faceless riders that wanted his soul—not from himself, though.

Dax glanced back, fighting the crick in his neck and wondering if Robyn had awakened from pain or just simply had come awake. He watched as she moaned a little, shifted atop the stone, then moved her weight off her right shoulder.

The movement brought her closer to him. Their faces were now on the same level. Dax could feel her breath on his cheek. She was still groggy, caught up in the web of half wakefulness, half slumber, her mouth pouty and pliant looking.

He shouldn't kiss her again, shouldn't taste what could never be his. . . .

He couldn't help himself.

Dax's mouth met Robyn's. His lips brushed against hers, light and tentative, a test, really, softer than the brush of a breeze.

Robyn, hesitant and sleepily shy at first, soon surprised Dax by opening to him like a flower offering its nectar to the heat of the sun. She tasted like heaven. Like home. Hit hard with longing, Dax shifted around, his right hand coming up to gently palm her face. Unable to stop himself, he lost count of the many times he slid his tongue inside her mouth, of how many times she met him with her own. Dax thought he might careen out of control, so warm and inviting was her mouth.

But this was wrong. She had no inkling of their past and "almost" future, didn't know that he was now a smuggler of goods—and souls, if unleashed. No longer the boy he'd once been, he was now a phantasm that could do her mortal danger.

Dax pulled back.

Robyn opened her eyes. Her pupils were still pinpoints, her brain still drugged.

Dax knew he should apologize, but he wasn't sorry at all to have stolen the kisses. Robyn said nothing. She merely settled back on the furs, turning her face away and staring up at the ceiling of rock above. Silence settled around them until, finally, she spoke.

"You haven't told me your name."

"You never asked."

"I . . . I'm asking now."

The heavy silence stretched between them as Dax thought of what name to give. His own? One of the many he'd been given throughout his life? "Dax," he said at last.

"Dax Dexter." He was a fool for sharing it with her . . . and yet that was who he was, wasn't it? Simply Dax . . . the luckless one with no future. Besides, she wasn't likely to be remembering any of this night.

The fire cracked and hissed, sparks shooting upward. "It's an odd name," Robyn whispered.

"Very," Dax agreed, thinking of how bitterly he'd balked when Sir Dysart had given it to him.

"Mine is Robyn. Sinclair."

I know, he wanted to murmur.

She turned fully toward him. "I—I believe that I've known you—even before our time in the study. It's true, isn't it?"

"You've never known the man I am, lass." His honesty scalded.

"No, not the man, but the boy," she breathed, her eyes drifting shut, Randolph's drug not yet finished with her. "I remember a lad . . . and a feather . . . I . . . I think I remember *you*, Dax Dexter."

He said nothing, stunned into silence as she fell back into the sticky net of a dream state. He sat, still and quiet, not wanting to move, not wanting to ruin this moment that would slip away all too soon.

She remembered him. God. On some level, deep in her subconscious, she remembered the boy he'd been, the feather he'd given her. Dax would have smiled but for the color washing from his skin, the Phantom within shimmering to the surface. The joy of the moment slid away, drowned in a cresting tide of evilness.

Dax jerked to his feet, feeling the change in him, feeling that sickening shot of cold that blasted outward from his gut and cramped his bowels. A grimace smeared his lips flat against his teeth as he felt the whip of cold jut up his spine and explode behind his eye sockets at the same time it blasted through his limbs. His hands gnarled into fists, his eyes slammed shut as acute spasms claimed every muscle and organ in his body . . . until . . . whiteness washed him, his Phantom radiating outward, a burn of piercing-cold energy hovering like a second skin over every inch of him. He felt no heat, no heart, only hunger.

The Phantom, fully awakened, dragged in a sharp breath, smelling *her*.

Dax's eyes flared open, blazing green through the phosphorescent glow as the beast in him pulled his gaze to Robyn. He could perceive every swish of blood through her veins, could hear the tiniest fissures of tissue beginning to knit together over her wound. And he could smell her, the wash of rain in her hair, the lavender she'd touched to her skin . . . the scent of his own self against her mouth.

He felt his green gaze slit hard as the Phantom shimmered in an arc over her body, wanting to plunder, to claim, and to never let her go. . . .

Robyn's body seemed to be floating. She no longer felt any pain, fear, or hotness. There were only images, dozens of them, snapping to life in her mind, the scenes flashing, nervy as a light show. Little by little, they gathered into form and shape.

She saw herself back in the past, as a young girl, riding her pony across the lands of her aunt's home. A forest surrounded her, and she imagined she could feel its coolness, could taste its earthy essence on the back of her tongue. She was riding out to find someone—someone who'd watched her from afar but whom she had yet to meet. She pressed forward, glancing up into the limbs of the trees, for that is where she'd find him, she somehow knew.

And find him she did. Sitting atop a limb, one leg stretched out in front of him, the other bent at the knee, the lad hovered four feet above her. A worn pack of crude arrows was slanted across his back with a tattered thong of leather, and in one fist he clutched a hand-fashioned bow. His eyes, Robyn noted instantly, were the color of indigo—rich, heady . . . as old as time. In a vivid tapestry of feeling, woven with threads of intense colors, Robyn watched as her younger self reacted to the lad on the tree bough. She wasn't frightened, but rather pleased, curious, and absolutely intrigued.

The scene shifted, sliding into a kaleidoscope of shape and hue that funneled itself into a whirling blur. Suddenly, she was standing toe-to-toe with the lad who was no longer a boy, but a man fully grown. It was night now, the moon's glow bathing him, hardening him. He was cold and she was cold, and somehow she knew that while there was pain in his eyes, there was dark intent in his soul. He reached for her—not her hand, but her heart. She ordered him gone, as if she had the power to do such a thing, then heard someone approach. She jerked toward the sound.

It was her cousin Alexander riding astride a huge mount and coming to her rescue. All blond hair and intensity, he came careening down the path, yelling for Robyn to run for home, yelling that Aunt Amy needed her.

There came gunfire then. Blue-tinged smoke filled the air, obliterating her cousin from view. By the time it cleared, the lad who'd dropped down out of the trees and became a man was gone . . . and Alexander, her beloved Sandy, lay on the earth before her, a dark spot of red staining his shirtfront.

"Sandy!"

Robyn came awake with a start, heart pounding as she bolted upright. She sucked in a breath, eyes wide as she glanced about. She wasn't in the woods of her youth, but in the bone-cold caves she'd never wanted to enter. And Sandy wasn't dead, she reminded herself. He was hale, hearty, and busy with championing the downtrodden in life. God willing, she'd see both him and his sister, Lily, again soon.

The fire had burned to embers. Only the torch remained lit, and even that was slowly losing its flame, its dying glare casting ghostly shadows on the stone walls. Robyn shivered, heart still racing, her mind all amuddle as to what she'd actually just experienced. Dreams, deathly dramas, and devastating desires all danced dully at the fringes of her brain, leaving her confused as she looked wildly about.

That's when she spied him.

Dax.

He sat across from her, on the floor, his back against

the rock of the opposite wall, his knees drawn up to his chest, a bottle of some liquid held tight in one fist.

He gazed at her. Steadily. Deeply. Silently. As though he'd been doing so for a long, long while.

Robyn shifted, passing a shaky left hand across her brow, not liking the intensity of his stare. She remembered only the frightening tail end of her many dreams—that, and the fact that he'd kissed her again. And had shared his name.

Forcing herself to meet his gaze, Robyn asked, "How long was I sleeping?" The huskiness of her voice and the rawness of her throat surprised her.

"Hours and hours."

Had he been hovering near her all that time, drinking, trying to numb his urge to . . . to *what*, she wondered? What was the reason for the pervasive blackness that now settled about him like a dark shroud? She felt as though there was another entity in the cave with them—his deeper self, the one she'd viewed that night in the fog-ridden garden and later outside her home. The essence of it shimmered dully, like a fire that had recently burned bright but had finally been tamped down.

"So you've been . . . watching over me the whole while?"

"No."

There was an edge to Dax's voice. He seemed but a shadow shape, hunkered down as he was against the gray stone, with his thick, black hair all atumble, stubble darkening the lower portion of his features. A golem, that's what he appeared, Robyn decided in that instant.

"Randolph sat with you for a time, while I . . ." He let his words trail off into the gloom, unfinished.

"While you what?"

"Got some air." He lifted the bottle. "And this."

Robyn shivered again, noticing how his brows drew downward, how he gripped the neck of the bottle with frightening force. Everything about him was granite hard, and beneath it all beat the ever-present sound of some *thing*, some fierceness in him struggling, as though he were denying it air, strangling it with his brute inner force and drowning it in alcohol.

Robyn wanted to glance away, but couldn't. The man was an elemental force, like the changing of the seasons that ripped autumn's glory from the trees—a force so fierce that nothing in his vicinity could turn away or remain unchanged—least of all *her.*

"Why do you look at me as you do?" Robyn asked, needing to break the silence between them, to shatter the snare in which he held her.

"How should a captor peer at his captive?" Dax countered, his hard voice cleaving through the gloom to batter against her. "For you are that. You told me so yourself. With longing, perhaps?" he asked cruelly. "Regret? I assure you, I could do that. Oh, aye . . . I could do that."

Robyn frowned at his words, wondering where the softness had gone—the softness he'd used when touching and kissing her in the study in London, even in these caves.

"I think you're drunk."

"If only I were," he muttered and took another long, deep draught of the liquid, swallowed, and then hissed out a breath through his teeth. "Care to talk about what you remember from the past hours?" he asked, nesting the bottle between his knees.

His mood, his drinking, his sheer presence frayed Robyn's already overwrought nerves.

"No."

Dax's head shifted in the gloom, lifting an inch, the last of the torch's light glinting in his green eyes. "So you remember nothing?"

"I remember you sharing your name," she said. *And I remember the color of your eyes in a dream . . . the taste of your mouth on mine.*

"Nothing else?"

She shook her head. Was that a flash of relief in his

eyes? Robyn couldn't be certain. It came too fast and was shuttered too swiftly.

"You talked in your sleep. Called out for someone."

A flutter of panic stirred in Robyn's breast. She thought of Falconer and Morely. Could she have uttered one of their names? Please God, she hoped not, knowing Morely would pay a thief's ransom to have her dragged bodily to him. But no, Robyn quickly decided, she'd dreamt of her cousin and possibly her aunt. *Or had she?* Perhaps, she thought, face paling, she'd cried out for *Dax*.

"Whose name did I call?"

"Sandy."

He said the word as if it were poison on his tongue, Robyn thought, watching as Dax tipped the bottle to his mouth and took another drink, as if to wash away a bitter taste. She heard the slosh of liquid as he drew the bottle down, his gaze never leaving her face. He didn't blink, didn't look away, and she saw again the flicker of something deep within him, the force like a lick of flame, heightening at times, burning low at others . . . but always, always there.

And whenever it flared, Robyn felt something lift inside of her, as if called awake, a wildness that whispered to her, making her skin tingle, her breath short, and her blood heat.

"You are in love with him?" Dax asked, blunt.

With his intimate query, that heat raced up Robyn's throat, spreading across her cheeks . . . and spreading lower, past her belly, to that place between her thighs where it settled and stayed and made her want to squirm. No man should affect her the way Dax did.

"So the answer is yes," he muttered, confusing her blush of discomfiture for that of a young woman in love.

He blew out a harsh breath of sound. That unholy light in his gaze flickered bright, burning through the darkness, searing into Robyn until, with what appeared to be a great force of will on Dax's part, the light dimmed once more.

Too late, though, for Robyn felt as if a spark had jumped from him to her, and she caught that spark in the depths of her soul. The wildness in her, all new and hungry, curled around it, like cupped hands keeping the tiniest flame alive. And every time she breathed, she fanned that flame higher.

Robyn inhaled sharply. Perhaps this was what he was fighting—only it was a thousand times worse for him.

"What is it you're trying to drink into oblivion, Dax?" she asked, needing to know, wondering if his turbulence had somehow just become hers.

"No," he muttered, his tone dark, forceful. "No changing the subject."

A wild whip of feeling slashed through Robyn. She wanted to argue. She wanted to have her question answered. She . . . simply *wanted*, like never before and as if she would never have enough.

Just as she was focused on her own want, so was Dax, it seemed, for he hammered her with questions.

"Have you allowed this Sandy of your dreams to taste you . . . as I have?"

No. Only you have tasted me, Dax.

"Has he put his tongue into your mouth, driving it deep until he got lost inside of you?"

Her heart fluttered. *Is that what you did . . . lost yourself inside of me?*

"Has he known you like no other?"

At that, Robyn balked. She wanted to say that Sandy was her *cousin*, for God's sake, that he was like a brother to her, but Dax's words, in their blatant crudity, were actually stirring that crazed, all-new wildness within her.

"I ought to loathe you," she whispered, damned if she would tell him anything about Sandy.

Something in him twisted, contorted, and she saw once more the signs that he fought hard to contain whatever evil thing it was he harbored within. His voice barely a whisper, he said, "Too late, lass. I loathe myself."

Without warning, Dax threw the bottle he held into the fire with one savage sweep, cleanly shattering it. The last of the embers flared, then sputtered and spit as errant glass skipped over the stone floor, skittering in all directions.

Robyn flinched as he moved toward her.

"Are you ready?" he asked.

Robyn inched back. Did he intend to do with her what he thought some other man already had?

He stood directly over her now, his body towering above like some warrior of old who'd come to raid. She could see clearly that he would indeed like nothing more than to take her, claim her, to erase any trace of whoever else might have touched her in the past. The mere thought of it both infuriated and enticed her.

"Well?" he demanded.

"Am I ready for what?"

Gaze shuttered, voice tight, Dax said, "To leave, of course. Your freedom . . . and your Sandy await."

He was going to let her go? Robyn could scarce believe it. She also couldn't believe her sudden hesitancy, or that she wasn't jumping up and dashing for the passageway.

But out there, beyond the caves, lay all the trouble she'd been fleeing, while here in this cavern, a wondrous wildness had sparked to life inside of her, fed by whatever force flickered in Dax's gaze. Even as he spoke, it widened and radiated outward to the very tips of her fingers and toes.

"Of course," Dax muttered, cutting into Robyn's thoughts, taunting her when she didn't immediately move, "if you'd rather, we could linger here. Just the two of us. Alone."

Oh, if only he knew how Robyn dared to imagine such a scenario. Just the thought of it made her melt inside. She was no longer the same person she had been when Dax had brought her into these caves. Robyn was a hungrier, more daring version of her former self, and this man was a sultry puzzle her body ached to unravel, to know, and to twine with. It was as if something in him called to her, making Robyn ache and want and need. He was power and fury and the darkest of desire.

Robyn's breath caught, her body tingled. If Dax knew what his suggestion was causing her to consider, he made no show of it.

"And you?" he continued in that low, dangerous tone. "Ah, *you* could reveal to me all that you've shared with this Sandy-of-your-dreams."

Robyn got to her feet. Dax didn't back away, and the movement merely served to align their bodies. Her breasts met his chest, her thighs with his. She wore only his shirt. Nothing more.

Dax's gaze held Robyn's as the heat of him, the hardness of him, tipped her blood through her veins and turned her body into living need. He enveloped her in a warlock's web of wanton eroticism, his eyes burning with green fire, his gaze on her face, her throat, the rise and fall of her chest beneath his shirt.

They were so close Robyn could hear the ragged draw of his breath, could smell the liquor on his tongue . . . and she could feel the firm, tight need of him straining against her belly.

He wanted her. Every sinew of his muscled body told Robyn it was true. She had but to say the word and Dax would tumble her down onto the furs, would hitch up his shirt and uncover the hot core of her that even now was tingling for his touch.

Robyn pressed her eyes shut, but instead of finding calm reason, she found only raw need and that wild want that would listen to nothing and no one. The pull, the opportunity, proved too much.

Lifting her lashes, she looked directly into Dax's haunting green eyes . . . and then pressed her hips fully against his.

His breath drew inward with a sharp sound. She'd turned the tables on him. He'd thought to frighten her with his words, never once believing she might actually give in to his suggestions. But he'd been wrong.

About her.

About this moment.

About how daring Robyn could be.

Throwing all caution aside, boldly fitting her body flush up against his, Robyn met Dax's gaze with a willful one of her own . . . and then pushed. Hard.

"This *is* what you want, isn't it?" Robyn asked, her voice sounding not her own, her mound of womanliness straining to surround his member.

She felt his hardness grow even more rigid, heard him suck in a breath and then let it out in one long, controlled hiss.

Robyn, emboldened by his reaction, laid her hands against Dax's chest. Her fingers fanned open, the rapid beat of his heart tattooing against each digit. Her legs were trembling, her boldness alarming even herself, but the wildness in her that had shimmered to life wouldn't allow her to turn back.

Rising up on tiptoe, she pressed more firmly against him, and then eased downward, stroking him with her body as she came to rest once again on the flat of her feet.

Dax's manhood bulged, his entire body shuddering with a violent need he tried hard to suppress.

"Lass," he rasped, "you don't know what you're about."

"Don't I?"

"Stop."

"Why?" Robyn asked, knowing his resolve was weakening, slipping away on a rising tide of passion. The knowledge of it was like a heap of gold in her hands. Shifting her hips again, feeling his need rock-hard and ready between them, she said, "I'm merely continuing what you began with your questions about others before you. Others who might have known me . . . touched me . . ." She moistened her lips with the tip of her tongue, clearly taunting him—and amazing her own self with her actions. "Don't you wish to know? For certain?"

Another shudder racked him. He drew his lids down low over his eyes, eyes that were now enflamed by need, by want, and by the ever-present demon deep within—an unknown force that actually stilled at her touch, amazed by it.

For the first time in her life, Robyn felt the true power of her femininity. Utilizing full use of it, she touched her forehead to Dax's chest. She watched as his nipples hardened beneath his shirt. She ran her fingers down and over them, then lower still, past his whipcord-lean waist, to the band of his trousers where, trembling, she slipped her index fingers between the material and his hot, smooth skin.

Dax's body convulsed.

Another moment, another touch, and he'd take her, Robyn knew.

"You're innocent," he said.

Yes, she thought, *but with you I don't want to be*.

"You don't know the half of what you're beginning," Dax warned as Robyn delved her fingers deeper.

"Then teach me."

Finally, suddenly, Robyn found her mark. Its tip was petal-soft and large, far larger than she'd imagined. Robyn stilled, a gasp catching in her throat—or was it Dax's gasp she heard?

"Bloody hell," he rasped. His hands shot up, capturing Robyn's wrists, curling about them. He gave a hard yank upward, forcing her to look at him as he did so. "Is this what one night in my presence has reduced you to?" he demanded hoarsely. "Do you think I want you as my *whore*?"

Stunned by that last word, Robyn couldn't answer. Shame burned up her throat, staining her cheeks, choking her. The brazen seductress she'd been but a moment ago vanished. The flame in her dimmed and the wildness that had fanned it fled.

"Do you?" Dax demanded.

"No." Robyn lurched back, hauling free of his touch. Immediately she wrapped her arms about her waist, turning her head to the side, shame engulfing her. What had she been *thinking*?

Just then, Randolph's voice came to them from the walkway beyond. "Dax?" he called.

Robyn peered beneath her lashes at Dax. He still stood facing her, his hands balled into white-knuckled fists at his sides, his green gaze hard on hers.

"What is it?" he asked the man, not taking his gaze off Robyn.

"There's news—it isn't good."

Dax's mouth formed a thin line. To Robyn, he said, "Stay here. Wait for me. Will you do that?"

Robyn nodded once, abruptly. She was terrified of his mood, *of him*, and she was afraid, blast it all, that she was going to cry. She'd all but thrown herself at this man, had *touched* him, and he'd treated her like a schoolgirl playing at being a lightskirt, the very thing her father had labeled her just a few days ago.

Robyn's face burned hotter. "Go," she rasped. "Just . . . *go*."

She felt him turn away from her, felt a shaft of cold air whisk against her with the movement. She listened to the sounds of Dax gathering up a coat, then heard his retreating footsteps, along with Randolph's, as the two of them threaded their way back to the mouth of the cave.

Only when Robyn was alone did she allow the tears to come, hot and heavy. She didn't know what frightened her more at that moment—Dax, or her own brazen self.

Chapter Nine

Details, Dax had once been told by Sir Dysart, were everything. Unfortunately, he knew precious few details about Robyn, the girl who had haunted his childhood, the woman he wanted in his future—the very same who had just offered her body to him like some . . . some *what*? A smuggler's backwater doxy, or a sacrificial lamb too trusting to know where he would inevitably lead her? What had possessed her to do such a thing? More to the point, what had *he* driven her to do?

Details. They were everything.

Dax's God-cursed Phantom had egged her on, he knew, with all that jealous rot about previous lovers. He had tried to drown the beast with a bottle of drink, but even now, with daylight soaking the world outside, the soul-smuggling fiend in him had been awake enough to put words in his mouth.

It had taken every bit of Dax's strength last night not to let the Phantom harm Robyn. When he'd shimmered over her sleeping form, he hadn't been certain what the monster in him intended. While he'd always wanted Robyn, the fierce hunger that had raged in him last night had been stronger than ever before, edgy, and dark as sin. He'd fought against it—hard, the hardest he'd ever fought—and in one blinding moment of clarity had been able to fetch Randolph to look after her.

And now this, Dax thought, tucking in his shirt and shrugging into his coat as he and Randolph threaded toward the mouth of the cave.

"What's happened?" he asked his friend.

"Soon as the storm lost its edge, John headed to Land's End with news of the lady, just like you ordered, Dax. He knew you didn't want any alarm sounded by her family, and no constable alerted."

"And?"

"Lady Archer still wasn't there. So John met with Harry, like you asked, who told him that Lady Archer hasn't been seen or heard of in days and was due home by now. Harry also said there's been trespassers spotted on her land. More than a few."

The men from yesterday, no doubt, Dax thought. Or their friends.

"Harry believes Lady Archer met with foul play," Randolph said. "He's asking for your help, and for a few extra men if you can spare them."

Dax would do anything for Robyn's aunt. He'd do everything.

"Whatever you need, Dax, I'm with you, as are several others of our crew. You know that."

Dax did know it, and he sent Randolph a grateful nod. "That will leave too few for what we'd planned here. I'll order the place cleared out and things shut down."

"The others won't like it."

"No," Dax agreed. "They won't."

He had known from the moment he'd regained full memory of his past that he would leave this life behind. He'd also known that he had risked much in corresponding with Amelia, and she even more.

God. Amy. What had happened? Dax felt in his gut that it wasn't good, and that her association with him was the cause of it.

He and Randolph were nearly to the opening of the cave now. Dax could hear the voices of the others as they lugged in their cache. To Randolph, he asked, "The girl, Mattie, is she still in your quarters?"

"Aye."

"Take her to Lady Robyn. Tell the two of them to stay put, then come back here. I have the feeling I'll need some help when I tell this crew we're finished here."

"It won't be easy," Randolph wagered.

Dax never once suspected it would be. Nothing in his life had ever been easy.

Robyn, having dressed and enfolded herself in her cloak, sat stiff and nervous on Dax's bed of rock. The torch spit and sputtered. The last of the embers in the fire pit had turned to cold ash long ago.

Robyn shivered, wishing Dax would return, and just as intensely dreading the moment of having to face him again. She saw a shaft of light on the floor of the cave then, coming from the opposite direction of the mouth of the cave. Looking up, she was greeted by the sight of Mattie bearing two steaming cups, the hulking form of Randolph following.

"Mattie," Robyn breathed, surging to her feet. The girl moved toward her, and Randolph headed back the way he'd come. "You're not hurt, are you?" Robyn asked, reaching out.

"Not a whit, m'lady," Mattie said, awkwardly balancing the old, battered cups as she met her lady's open embrace. "But whut o' *y'*?"

Miserable, Robyn thought, thinking of how she'd made a fool of herself with Dax. "I'm just glad to see you," she murmured instead.

The girl eased back. "Randy . . . er, Mist'r Randolph, he told me hows y' suffer'd a bullet graze." She offered up both cups. "One's tea, m'lady, the other be stew," she explained, then added, "Randy . . . er . . . Mist'r Randolph, he says y' shud eat somethin' afore we leave. Says we're t' stay put 'till he comes fer us."

Robyn could scarce believe how calm and right as rain her usually high-strung maid appeared. "So you . . . you weren't mistreated in any way?" she asked.

"Oh la, no, m'lady," the girl replied. "Randy . . . er, Mist'r Randolph," she corrected again, "he—he told me hows I wuz knock'd out clean and slept by a fire and when I start'd to come roun', he—he touched my cheek . . . and well, he talk'd w' me the whole night through, he did. Even taught me a game o' dice."

"Dice?"

Mattie nodded, red curls bobbing. "You knows how I hates the night, m'lady, but not last night, I swears. Went by ever so fast, it did." Mattie's brow puckered suddenly. "But I wuz worried 'bout y', m'lady. Mist'r Dax, he came t' let us know y' were all right. Randy . . . er, Mist'r Randolph, I mean, he brewed a tonic, he did, and then Mist'r Dax, he gave it t' y'. I knows, 'cuz Mist'r Randolph told me so. And Mist'r Dax? He cleaned yer wound, he did, and worried ov'r y' all the night through, ev'n drinkin' 'cuz o' his worry."

Robyn blinked, amazed at all she was hearing.

"And the whole while," Mattie continued, "I be thinkin' how glad I am that they found us, m'lady, and brought us here to this safe place."

"Safe?" Robyn echoed. *Hardly that*, she thought. It was dank and treacherous and . . . "I don't suppose you bothered to ask the man why he and the others are dwelling in these caves."

Mattie shook her head. "No, m'lady. I just figur'd they h' no place else t' go."

"Perhaps they're thieves. Or smugglers," Robyn pointed out. "Or even murderers hiding from the law."

Mattie's green eyes grew large. "Oh, no, m'lady, Randy . . . er, Mist'r Randolph, he be far too kindheart'd to be a—a thief, or a murder'r!"

Robyn took the mug of tea, obviously smuggled. She

sipped at the hot liquid, glad to have something to wash away the aftertaste of whatever Dax had brewed for her. As she drank the tea, she thought about what Mattie had said. Clearly, her maid was besotted with the man called Randolph, and Dax had obviously won her over as well . . . which meant that Mattie had yet to see the haunting image of Dax turning from man to phantasm. Robyn was glad. They both didn't need to be frightened, and if she could spare Mattie from all that she'd seen, then Robyn would do it.

So Dax had fussed over her while she'd slept? If that was true, why hadn't he demonstrated any of that caring sensibility when she'd come awake, crying out from nightmares? Where was the softness in him then? The man—or whatever he was—was a mass of contradictions. What was the truth about him? Did Robyn even want to know?

She got to her feet, leaving the tea behind. "We're leaving, Mattie. Now."

The girl gaped at her. "Now? But Randy . . . er, Mist'r Randolph says we're t' wait, m'lady, we're t'—"

Robyn wasn't listening. With her uninjured arm she yanked the dying torch from its holder, then headed out into the passageway, determined to deal with Dax Dexter and every threat he harbored on her own terms.

Mattie, sucking in a gasp at being left alone in the dark, quickly followed.

Dax headed down the slant of rock into the dome of the cave's opening. The area was a mass of men and mountains of cargo—casks of wine, barrels filled with spices, coffee, tea, corn and other grain, trunks of the finest fabrics, crates filled with furniture, heavy and well-tooled— all of it heading either north or west and none of it being logged in to any bookkeeper's ledgers or taxman's rolls. The men, shouldering the weight of their illegal cargo, paused at Dax's approach, his dark mood commanding their attention.

"Somethin' wrong, boss?" asked Bones.

"There's been a change of plans."

"Whut kinda change?"

"We're clearing out of here. Everything goes into the wagons and on the packhorses. Leave nothing behind, not even a footprint."

"But I thought only the food wuz t' be loaded," said Bones, "and the rest be tucked here fer—"

"You heard me," Dax said, dropping down off the lip of stone and landing firmly in his men's midst. "Every bit of it goes."

"That be a lot of cargo."

"There's room enough," Dax assured him, which there was. "Use all the wagons and take only the roads I've marked. Come first dark, you'll go in waves, with everyone gone by midnight." He glanced around at the men, speaking slowly, succinctly, taking care that they fully understood his instructions. "Four men to a wagon: two astride, two on board. For those heading north, stop only at the safe houses and staging posts I've indicated, nowhere else. Once you reach the drop-off point, you'll be paid the whole of what you were promised. You've each just earned yourself a tidy sum—and you're getting it far earlier than expected. Your work with me is done."

Bones blew out a breath of astonishment, while most of the men didn't seem to care much about anything other than their pay.

Blade, a burning fury in his one good eye, stepped toward Dax. "What the hell is this?"

"You heard me," Dax said. "You move the cargo, leaving no trace behind and causing no trouble along the way. Once you make the final stop, you get your due. It's that simple."

"And what about you? Aren't you coming?"

"Not this time. Gideon will lead the first wave north, but after that each group will be on its own."

"That wasn't the plan. There's more pay if we store things

here and move it slowly, through the clearinghouses. Besides, you were to be the front man for every load."

"I told you, the plans have changed. Now do as I say."

"The hell I will!"

"Then get out," Dax said. He didn't have time for this.
No time. Amy was missing and Robyn . . . God, but Robyn
was in danger as well, from the bulk of these men, and
most definitely from himself. He had to get her back to
Land's End, quarter her there, and set up sentries. There
were details to be taken care of, dozens, *countless* things to
set into motion.

"You can't do this," Blade growled.

"I just did."

Gideon came to stand behind Dax then, as did Randolph, Gideon holding nothing more than a look of dark
menace on his features, Randolph a flintlock pistol in
one fist.

Sweat broke out on Blade's hairline, but he kept his
good eye fixed on Dax all the same "You can't just put me
out, you hear? I want a vote!"

Dax looked about. "Anyone else want the same?" he
asked, meeting every man's gaze with his own. "If so, tell
me now."

Nobody moved. Nobody said a word.

Blade cussed at them all, and then, fast as a striking
snake, reached down, pulled a hidden knife, and flashed
the thing in the air. "When I'm through with you," he
muttered at Dax, "I'll have my name carved in your face.
Your eyes in my hand."

Dax remained perfectly still. Nodding to Randolph not
to be too hasty with the pistol, he kept his gaze trained on
Blade. "Put the knife away, Blade."

He shook his head, a lock of dirty hair falling over his
sweat-beaded brow. "I know what changed your mind," he
breathed. "It's that female you brought in here, the one
you been toying with all through the night while the rest
of us do the work!"

"Shut your mouth," Dax warned.

"That's it, isn't it? You brought her here against her will, then had your fun with her . . . and I'm thinking, maybe she liked it . . . maybe she ain't the lady she pretends to be."

"Enough."

"No, I'm gonna have my say, and you're gonna listen. I think you and that fancy skirt of yours found some fun and then hatched a plan. I think she's gonna run back to her family with a tale about how the rest of us took her, and you came along and saved her pretty little tail. Then you're gonna set the authorities after us, on the very roads you've plotted for us to take, and we're all gonna find a noose in the end, not only for the goods we smuggled, but for kidnapping that pretty piece and her maid. And you? Why, you'll get clean away, take the profit meant for us. I knew that witch was nothing but trouble."

Before Gideon or Randolph could stop him, Dax surged forward, slamming Blade to the ground, his insides roiling as his hands gripped the man's neck. "That woman," he breathed, "is a lady and—"

"And this lady can speak for her own self," came a very forceful female voice from behind.

Dax whipped his gaze about, seeing Robyn standing atop the lip of rock above. The folds of her cloak were tossed back, her hair a riot of loose, dark waves that cascaded about her shoulders and framed her gorgeous face. Her eyes were lit with a dangerous, violet light, one that told Dax she'd had enough of her stay here.

"I am no witch, sir," she said to Blade, her gaze cleaving him in two. "As for your assumption that anything happened between your leader and myself that could change the course of your plans, you are dead wrong. Now I suggest you put away your knife and your anger, and get to your feet because I wish to go home, and I won't be getting there so long as you waylay the man above you."

Dax didn't know whether to applaud Robyn or damn

her for not staying put in his chamber. She'd risked much—more than she realized—by presenting herself to the whole of his men and seeing the bulk of their smuggled goods. Why hadn't she stayed behind? Why did she always push things to a standoff?

"That's enough," Dax called. "Say no more. Look no more."

But Robyn didn't turn away, didn't back down.

Beneath him, Blade sneered. "Not only comely, but foolish, eh? And too good a piece for your thieving hands. No doubt there's someone willing to pay dearly to have her returned."

Dax had heard enough. He got to his feet, reached down, and yanked Blade up by his shirtfront, thrusting him back against a mountain of crates. Reaching into his coat pocket, Dax withdrew a purse filled with coin—more than the slime deserved—and slapped it against Blade's chest. "Hear me and hear me well," he said, green eyes blazing. "That's your payment in full. It's all you'll ever see from me. Now turn around and get out. And if you ever so much as show a toe of your body near that woman up there, I'll hunt you down and see you dead."

Blade snatched the purse from Dax's hand, opened it, and fingered through its contents. Satisfied, he shoved the pouch into his pocket, headed for his horse, then rode out to the mouth of the cave.

Silence reigned as the other men watched Blade leave. With a jerk of his right hand, Dax motioned to them, his patience worn thin. "Get this stuff loaded. All of it."

They moved.

Dax glared up at Robyn, noting how damnably beautiful yet vulnerable she appeared. Blade's words had shaken her—as did the view of all the smuggled goods surrounding them.

He moved toward her. "You can come down now. We're leaving."

"So soon?" she challenged, obviously in the mind to antagonize him.

Faith, but she could be a handful. Dax sent her a dark look of warning, not wanting the others to overhear anything of their conversation. The quicker he whisked Robyn out of here, the safer she'd be. "If you know what's best, lass, you'll still that tongue of yours."

A dangerous glint lit her violet eyes. "Too late," she shot back. "I've already seen and *done* more than is safe for me."

Her maid came up behind her then, skittering to a halt at the edge of the stone, her mouth dropping open at sight of all the cargo, of Dax's men moving it into the wagons.

"Oh, la, m'lady . . ." Dax heard the girl gasp. "Mist'r Randy, he never showed me all o' this!"

"Quiet, Mattie," Robyn said to her.

The girl nodded, and then, spying Randolph, hastened to hurry down off the rock toward him. Robyn followed, though at a slower pace, grudgingly picking her way down the slanting of rock, ignoring the covert gazes of his men, ignoring that she was totally out of her element.

Dax felt his insides roil. Irritable, he yelled for Randolph to saddle their mounts, told Bones, Monty, John, and Sam—the four men, besides Randolph, whom he trusted most in this motley crew—that they could stay on with him for a while longer if they chose, and that, in fact, he would need them. As for the others, he left them to Gideon's command, who set them to packing up the many crates of goods and contraband. The packhorses and wagons would be taken out through a large opening in the cave that gave way to a stretch of pebbled beach that ultimately led to an overgrown path that snaked inland. Gideon would now be the one to lead the first wave of them north.

Dax moved to meet Robyn as she came down off the incline. He reached out, intending to help her down the last few steps, but she ignored the hand he offered, dropping down from the final bit of stone on her own.

Dax let his arm fall back to his side. Robyn was in a rare mood. She thought she now knew a truth about him—and she did, a little anyway, but not the whole truth . . . yet even this newest piece of his ugly reality was abhorrent to her. He could see her revulsion written in every feature of her beautiful face . . . a face that had gone pale the minute she'd viewed the goods he'd arranged to smuggle into these caves.

How to tell her why he smuggled? Why they brought in staples for the poor in England's northern areas? *You see, lass, I'm Cursed, and well, first Jemmy and I—and now Gideon and I—have spent years trying to figure how to overcome it. And we thought perhaps atonement might do it. Thought perhaps it was some sin that brought the Curse on in the first place and so doing good might take the Curse away. So I'm smuggling in food and staples for the poor of England's north, and paying for it by smuggling in the luxuries the rich so enjoy but hate to pay a tax to receive.*

It was, alas, a conversation he and Robyn would never have, Dax knew.

"I told you to stay put," he said, his insides rubbed raw by the judgment he saw in her eyes. "Why couldn't you listen? I didn't want you to see any of this. I didn't—"

"Then why even bring me here?" Robyn cut in. Her voice, which had been so husky, so filled with a burgeoning desire not a half hour ago in his chamber, was now tinged with disgust.

"You know why. Because you'd been shot. I could hardly have left you to those men in the woods and the others who were racing to their aid."

"No, of course not. Far better to bring me here. To your den of smugglers."

Her distaste for him, for herself—and what she'd nearly allowed to happen between the two of them—was palpable. Dax felt the force of it slam against him. Though the storm of last night had cleared outside, Dax could see clearly that Robyn carried it in her eyes. Like a painter gone wild with brush and color, her gaze was filled with all the fury that nature had battered against the coast last night. But this fury was directed at herself . . . and at him.

She'd nearly lain with him, he could almost hear her thoughts shout, had nearly made love with him. . . . Clearly, the very notion now sickened her.

Dax pulled back, feeling the sting of her unspoken thoughts. Robyn—the love of his life, the best thing about his Cursed past, and the only hope of his impossible future—found him lacking. Found him to be, alas, everything she couldn't abide.

Hating the fear and loathing he saw in her eyes, Dax hauled back yet another step and then another. He pivoted around, shouting for Bones to help both Robyn and Mattie. "See to it they're ready to ride," he ground out. "We leave within the half hour."

Dax didn't linger to hear Robyn's reaction. He vaulted up and onto the incline that led to the belly of the caves and then sprinted up the rough-edged side of the rock, racing with a burst of speed he knew was caused by his own graceless knack with the female he left behind.

He'd wanted for so long to be with her, to spend time with her, and yet for a moment he'd been awaiting all of his adult life and a good many years of his childhood to experience, it had played out like a nightmare. Just like his past, he thought. Just like his God-cursed, soul-smuggling past.

He was running now, over treacherous, narrow walkways slick with moisture. And the darkness . . . It enveloped Dax, swallowing him deep, consuming him whole. He didn't care. He knew these luckless paths only too well. After Amelia had forced him to jump from her carriage, this hellish place had become his home. He'd hunkered down with thieves and smugglers, he and Jemmy hiding their Phantomness when they could, going off on their own when they couldn't. He'd lost what was left of his innocence here, as well as the good breeding and sense of pride his guardian had tried to impress upon him. He'd lost it all to these dark caves. Yet somewhere, within the tight spaces and bat-infested hollows, the young boy in him had dared to foolishly dream of one day breaking free of it all . . . of finding a way back to what he'd once been . . . of finding a way back to Robyn.

"Idiot," Dax muttered to himself, flying over the stone, banging against rock. "Fool, you!"

He stumbled into the cavern he and Robyn—his love, his life, his onetime betrothed—had so recently shared, and was stunned to find a blast of cool, wet air greeting him. Nothing remained of the fire. There was no light. No warmth. Not even her scent lingered in the air.

Dax thrust himself deeper inside the place, then dropped to his knees near the rock bed and its furs. Even the furs were cold, but they at least held her scent: flowers and rain . . . vital . . . all that was dear to him.

Dax breathed in Robyn's lingering scent as he leaned down.

He had one last thing to retrieve from these foul caves before he abandoned the place for good.

By feel and intuition, he found the crevice in the stone near the head of the bed, one he'd carved out when he'd been but a lad and had recently made use of when he'd returned here for the first time in years the other day.

He reached inside and withdrew a small, folded square of linen, the very one he'd carried with him since he was a boy. The material was old and worn, stained by years of travel. It was the contents of it that meant so much to Dax.

Inside was a ribbon, now dulled and frayed by time, but it had once been red as a valentine and had held Robyn's heart dangling from the end of it . . . a heart he still wore next to his own.

Tucking the linen into his pocket, Dax got to his feet, took a deep breath, and then left the chamber. He wouldn't be back. Even though the caves kept the relentless riders at bay, he'd never set foot in this foul place again. Hell would just have to come and get him.

BOOK THREE

The Besieged

Chapter Ten

They headed inland, leaving the Channel with its uneven, chalky cliffs and bone-cold caverns to their backs. Sight of the sea mews that wheeled inland to their nests in the craggy cliffs gave way to saddle-backed crows that dipped and soared in great numbers. A foursome of Dax's men rode out with Robyn and Dax: Bones and Sam setting a fast pace ahead, John and Monty bringing up the rear, all following Robyn's directions to her aunt's estate. Mattie rode with Randolph in his saddle, a silent Robyn with Dax.

Robyn was glad Dax didn't try to break her silence. She didn't want to talk—not about the future to which she was being led, and not about what had transpired between them. Tight-lipped, she kept her gaze trained forward, refusing to acknowledge Dax. She'd decided the minute she'd shared her aunt's name and direction that she'd neither speak to him nor allow him to further affect her in any way.

But as the path took a turn to the left in the grasslands and Dax's horse shook its huge black head and pranced sideways, Dax had to maneuver the reins more tightly. His arms closed in about Robyn, and her nipples, *her traitorous nipples*, pinched tight at the contact, bursting with feeling, while whispers of heat winged out to all portions of her body. Exasperated, Robyn shifted atop the saddle, but couldn't find comfort. There was no way to extricate herself from the man, his nearness, and that gaze of his that seared her soul.

"Easy," Dax murmured.

She whipped her head around ready to give him a sharp set-down, but realized too late he'd been addressing his horse, not her.

Taking advantage of the fact she'd nearly broken her stony silence, Dax glanced at her . . . and smiled. It was a devastating smile, drat him. The man—or warlock or whatever he was—was far too handsome for his own good. His eyes were a deep green in the morning's light, quite unlike the color Robyn remembered in the dark, torch-lit caves or that fog-washed night in the mews. Uncomfortably brilliant, they were, hinting of magic and power . . . of unearthly things not yet understood by her.

"For a moment there, I thought you might actually speak."

"A foolish notion," Robyn replied, then immediately wished she could snatch the words back. She wasn't going to respond to him, she reminded herself, wasn't going to react in any way.

"We've been riding for a long while, lass. Surely playing stiff as starch is wearing thin for you."

"Not at all."

She heard the *hmm* he murmured in reply, and knew that if she turned to look at him she'd see that smile still lingering on his lips.

Mattie and Randolph were far ahead and out of sight, but snatches of their conversation had drifted back to Robyn earlier. The two had been enjoying themselves, talking like gossipy fishwives, as familiar as a favored throw rug with each other. The realization didn't sit well with Robyn. She knew her maid was clearly taken with the man, but really, wasn't the girl just a tad bit uncomfortable?

Every bone in Robyn's body ached, she had a monstrous thirst, and her arm *hurt*.

But not as much as her pride. She'd been thinking a lot about those moments in the cave with Dax, when she'd all but plopped her virginity in his hands. Something had struck a fire in her, something from *him* had made her behave with rash and reckless abandon. Had that something simply visited her . . . or was it now a part of her?

Nothing inside Robyn seemed as it had before. She felt changed—or rather, as if she were changing, as if her mad dash into the South Downs of Sussex had become a different kind of journey altogether.

In the waning light of day, Robyn eventually began to notice landmarks from her youth. The first was the trunk of a dead birch tree into which Sandy had once carved all the cousins' initials; the second was the beginnings of a well-worn path she and Lily had taken the day they'd stolen a smoke from one of Harry's many decadently carved pipes. Robyn had gotten sick that day, inhaling too much of the exotic weed she'd pilfered from the pouch that her aunt's butler kept hidden in the kitchens. She and Lily had sunk down into the grass and willow herb, hoping to stop the dizziness in their heads.

She remembered all of that now, remembered it as though it were yesterday. For the first time since leaving the caves, she knew exactly where she was. She should have recognized the lay of the land long before now. That it had taken this long to notice something so intimately familiar was unsettling. For a place she'd thought she had burned into her brain in startling detail, a handful of hours in Dax's company had muddled it all in her mind, as though his very presence in her life had changed her perspective.

"From your directions, we're nearly there," Dax said.

Robyn didn't reply. She couldn't. Emotions were bleeding out of her. How was she to face a future she dreaded? And how, God help her, could she act as though nothing had changed? In the span of a few nights, Dax Dexter had opened Robyn's mind to a world she'd not known before. He had shown her all the passion she was capable of but had kept bottled deep inside of her until the moment he'd touched her. Because of Dax, Robyn had experienced hunger and heat . . . and had viewed a world filled with the unexplainable. Yesterday she'd have been glad to reach the safety of Land's End. Today, she wasn't so certain anyplace was safe. Time with Dax made her question what was real, what wasn't . . . and most disturbing of all, what she truly wanted and who she truly was.

They rounded a bend in the road and the grand archway of her aunt's estate sprang into view, its huge black iron gates flung open. But there was only the man called Bones standing in wait outside. Dax dismounted, talked lowly with him for a moment, and then swung back up onto the saddle.

"What?" Robyn demanded. "What's going on? Where is Mattie, and why is my aunt's keeper not at the gate?"

Dax nudged the horse into motion, his gaze straight ahead, his features inscrutable. "Mattie is at the house, as is the gatekeep, and nothing's wrong so far as my man knows."

Robyn craned her neck, watching as Bones closed the gates behind them and took position like a guard at watch as John and Monty, who had followed behind Robyn and Dax, headed in opposite directions around the perimeter of the gates. An unsettled feeling washed through her. She detected a slight tensing in Dax's body, as though he were preparing to spring into action if need be.

Heart hammering, Robyn turned and watched as the red brick walls of her aunt's manse came into view. It was an imposing structure with a huge tower at each corner, a parapet surrounding the upper front, and a cluster of fountains in the courtyard. There was no hint of any panic within the place, no sign of any scurrying to make haste for a lady who'd fled from Town only to be waylaid by a smuggler—who turned phantasm, by the way—and his lawless cohorts.

"It's like a ghost house," Robyn said.

Less than a quarter of the way down the graveled drive, Dax veered his mount to the left, moving directly onto the well-kept lawns, then skirted even them and headed for a line of trees darkening the borders of the main house.

"What are you doing?" she asked. "Just stop and let me down. I can get myself inside."

"What I'm doing is fulfilling my promise, and no, you won't be entering through the front door for all to see."

Once gaining the tree line and hidden from view, Dax slowed the animal to a walk and headed for the backside of the manse.

As they moved past the front of the main house, Robyn could see the great windows of the dining hall. She could see, too, the terrace of the ballroom, with its floor-to-ceiling windows and fashionable French doors. Beyond even that, she could see the back, left tower that housed her aunt's apartments and the rooms Robyn used while visiting, and further on, the stables that claimed a huge portion of the lands just behind the manse.

Dax drew the horse to a halt at the edge of the coppice.

Robyn followed his gaze.

In the distance, she saw the movement of activity as a carriage and its cattle were being stabled. Robyn could make out none other than Tom Coachman helping to oversee the livery hands. He'd not gone back to the city as she'd asked—either that or he'd been forced here.

Her gaze moved to the carriage, which she recognized immediately. Her heart kicked in agitation and dread. *Falconer,* she thought to herself, and instantly felt the heat of Dax's gaze on her.

"Are you all right?"

Robyn swallowed the fist of fear in her suddenly dry throat. She nodded.

"You're certain? There's nothing you want to talk about . . . nothing you're trying to run from?"

"There's nothing," Robyn lied. "I'm fine," she added. Robyn sensed he didn't like her answer, and she had to remind herself that Dax was someone—something—she couldn't, shouldn't trust.

He didn't pry further, though she knew he wanted to.

She wondered if he'd whisper into her mind and steal the thoughts from her—but he didn't, or at least she didn't sense that he had.

Instead, she felt a shift in him. A gathering of energy from deep within that he called forth. And suddenly, though it was bright day, she saw a rise of what appeared to be moon glow radiate up and off his body. She drew in a gasp as she watched it lift and widen and whisk around her, around the horse, in a hum of earthy energy. She felt the familiar licks of power where her skin was uncovered, felt the breath-stealing sear of wintry chill . . . and then she felt nothing at all but *Dax*, his hard, lean body beside her, his strong arms around her. But it wasn't just Dax with her, she sensed; there was something more, cocooned with them—something evil and hungry, something untamed.

She glanced up at him, at his eyes that had gone to a green gleam, and knew he was unleashing a small portion of whatever dark magic he possessed in order to get her inside.

"I take it whoever owns that carriage is someone you don't want to see."

Robyn said nothing, instinctively knowing that she shouldn't trust this dark magic of his, that whatever he'd let loose on a leash of his own could very well break free.

"No matter." He smiled—a slash of dark intensity across his too-handsome features. "*No one* will see you now."

With just pressure from his legs, the huge horse vaulted into motion, springing out of the coppice and onto the open lawns. If not for the sodden clumps of earth sent up behind them by its hooves, Robyn would have sworn the animal was racing not with its own power but Dax's. She was forced to hold on tight or tumble to the ground, the wet grass beneath them flying by as they shot across the open space. If anyone inside was watching, Robyn doubted they would view more than a white blur zooming over the land.

He took them to an area near the back, left tower wall, a space hidden from view . . . and only then did he tone down whatever it was that had radiated from him. The moonish glow and heady power dissipated until it was just a mist that coated Dax, tiny beads of moisture that his clothing and his skin absorbed, until it was no more, just a very faint hum Robyn could perceive deep, deep inside of him.

She blinked, pulling her gaze from him and realizing, finally, that he'd stopped near a hidden entrance, one that gave way to a case of narrow stairs leading to her aunt's private sitting rooms. It was a way in that only a handful of people knew about.

Robyn slanted a look at Dax as he swung his left leg up and over the back of the saddle, dropped down to the ground, then reached up to help her dismount. She jerked away from his touch, refusing his assistance, refusing to get down. She was unsettled—by his magic, by his intimate knowledge of Land's End, by Falconer's arrival, by the ache and burn in her injured arm . . . and drat it all, but something odd was happening here that Dax wasn't telling her, something more than just that he was like no other.

"Faith," he muttered, "are you going to let me help you or not?"

"Not," Robyn shot back, ready to jump down on her own, but he helped her anyway. They were hidden from the view from the stables, but could hear the voices of the livery hands at work.

Robyn stood but a hairbreadth away from Dax, the

breeze sending the scent of cedar, of *him*, swirling around her. She drew in a ragged breath, searched his handsome, unreadable features. "I want you to tell me," she said, lowly, succinctly, "how you know of this passageway. I want you to tell me why your man is standing guard at my aunt's gate as though he owns the place. And I want you to tell me, dammit, why no one about seems the least bit concerned as to where I might be!" Especially, she thought, since her father's coachman was here.

For the briefest instant, Robyn thought Dax might actually answer with some truths. She saw a shift of light—of feeling?—in those heady green eyes of his, saw a muscle twitch along his strong jaw line, darkened by a day's growth of beard. He was debating whether to share his secrets, Robyn was certain of it.

But there came a shout from the stables, followed by hearty laughter, and the moment was gone.

Dax made a motion to reach for the hidden latch of the door. "Go inside," he said. "You're here. It's what you wanted."

"Drat you! I should scream until somebody, somewhere, comes to my aid."

"I wouldn't do that were I you."

"Well, you aren't me," Robyn shot back, a recklessness building inside of her, that wildness that had come alive in her stirring once again. She stepped back against the cold stone of the tower wall. Bracing her palms flat against rock, she began moving alongside it. "My father's coachman is just beyond this wall," she warned. "If I scream loud enough he will hear, and he will come. Maybe *then* you'll be forced to give some truths."

"Don't do it, lass. I'd rather not have any attention focused on me."

Robyn blew out a snort. "Most smugglers and thieves wouldn't, and you're more than even that . . . far more, as you just illustrated."

His gaze narrowed for just an instant, as if her words

smarted. "Think about it, lass. Do you honestly want to cause a ruckus? I purposely sent your maid and Randolph ahead of us so the girl could help get you quietly into the house. In fact, she should be waiting beyond this door. Now I want you to go inside."

"And I want some answers. How do you even know about this private entrance? And what were you doing on my aunt's lands yesterday, and in that study in London days ago?"

Again, there was the slightest hesitation in him, as if he would just spill out his life's tale to her . . . but it passed as quickly as the last, and he said, "Mattie told Randolph last night about this passage. Though you think me a fiend, it was never my intent to ruin your reputation by keeping you in those caves. The fewer who know you didn't arrive here yesterday, the better."

"And?" she demanded.

"And what, lass?"

"Why were you on my aunt's lands yesterday? Why did you step into that study with me the other night—and how did you follow me home, lure me outdoors in nothing but my nightdress? And what is this power that spills out of you at will? *What are you?*"

Nothing but hard-edged silence from him.

"You're not going to tell me, are you?" Robyn was nearly to the point at which, if she took another step, she'd be in full view of the stables. She pivoted away from the wall, stepped into the clearing, and opened her mouth to yell.

She never got the chance.

With swift speed Dax came up behind her, clamped one gloved hand about her mouth, pressed his other flat against her belly, and drew her once again behind the tower wall.

"Let. Go." Robyn tried to pry his hands from her.

Dax whirled her about, and then moved her straight back . . . until she was flush against the hidden door, the whole of his long, lean body pressed tight against her.

"You want me to let go? Then promise to be quiet."

"No promises," she muttered beneath his hand.

"Ah, now that's a pity, lass," he said, his forehead touching hers, his heat melding with her own, "for I'm not letting go until you do. Now will you keep that lovely mouth of yours closed and go inside?"

Seconds slid into a full minute before Robyn, angry, nodded. Once. Abruptly.

"Good choice," Dax said as he eased his hand away from her mouth.

Robyn, furious, immediately pressed her palms against his chest in an effort to push him away. "Perhaps I'm no more trustworthy than a thief and smuggler myself." With that, she called out.

Had Dax not been fast enough, Robyn's yell might have carried all the way to the stables, but he swallowed the sound into his own mouth as he brought his lips down on hers in a hard, hungry kiss.

Robyn tried to yank away, but it was the kind of kiss that sucked the air from her lungs, made her head dizzy and her knees weak and . . . *oh* . . . his tongue tasted the inside of her mouth and she was lost, utterly lost. She could not fight this man, not when he did such delicious things to her. A leap of excitement surged in her belly, pushing a ragged sigh up into her throat, and Dax, devastatingly handsome, dangerous Dax swallowed her sigh just as easily as he had her scream.

From the first moment she had met him, every time Dax had touched her, kissed her, he'd made Robyn realize how very female she was. She felt again—as she had in that cool study in London and the even cooler caves—a wild sensuality stir to life inside of her and recognized it for the dangerous sensation it was. The last time Dax had unlocked such a wealth of hidden feeling in her, Robyn had all but insisted he take her virginity.

There came more noise from the direction of the stables. Hearing the sounds, Dax ended the kiss, abruptly pulling back. Mouth pulled into a tight line, he reached his right hand beside her, unlatched the hidden handle of the door with a quick thrust, then popped the thing open. "Go. Inside," he said, his tone and his mood suddenly dark.

Robyn, ignoring the command, stared up at him. She could feel the cool air from the tower staircase stealing against her, could smell the mustiness of an area little used. Once again Dax had driven her to a frenzied height of wanting—only to back away.

"Why?" she whispered. "Why do you do this to me?"

"Because I want to get you inside with none the wiser, because—"

"No." She looked up at him, tortured. "Why do you kiss me as—as though I am the most precious thing you've ever found . . . only to cease the magic you've begun?"

She felt him haul in a breath. "Magic?"

Robyn nodded. "Yes. Magic." And it was as though Dax had been transported somewhere else, somewhere far and away, by her choice of words. And that wildness in her that only he could breathe to life, sparked full-bodied into motion, and she thought to herself that she didn't care if he was thief or spell-spinning smuggler, she wanted him. She wanted more of how he made her feel.

But the voices drifting to them from the stables proved an irritation, distracting Dax. Whatever small headway Robyn had made in piercing through to his true self was instantly gone. When Dax returned his attention to her, he had that fierce glint in his green eyes, the same he'd had that night he'd shimmered like a phantom in the foggy mews. "Go inside," he said again, and then spun away, getting quickly astride his mount and turning the animal about.

The creak of the saddle leather beneath him made Robyn think of all the miles they'd ridden together, made her remember the heat of her body tucked against his.

"So this is it?" she asked, a tightness in her voice. "You touch me, you kiss me, you show me there exist things in this life I've had no inkling of—such as beings like you, who take my breath away—and then you just leave?"

She thought she saw a shadow begin to creep over his features, into his eyes.

He glanced away. Drew a breath. "Go back to your life, lass. Back to the Sandy-of-your-dreams. You'll be safer there."

"Of course I would be safer with him. Sandy is my cousin, for godsake."

When he looked at her again, the shadow was all she saw. "Go inside," was all he said.

With that, he nudged the huge horse into motion, making fast for the way they'd just come . . . leaving Robyn alone.

She stood there, the coolness of the tower stairs at her back, a breeze from the wood line at her front. She listened to the sounds of Dax riding off until she heard nothing of him at all, and then she hung her head, amazed to feel as if he'd just taken a piece of her with him.

Long moments later, Mattie came tiptoeing down the stairwell and poked her head outside the door. "La, m'lady," the girl breathed. "Be Mist'r Dax gone?"

Robyn lifted her face, opening her eyes and gazing at the spot where Dax had just been.

"Yes, Mattie. He's gone."

Mattie motioned Robyn inside. "There be trouble, m'lady. Yer father and that oily groom-t'-be of yers sent Mist'r Falcon'r t' fetch y' back home. He be pacin' downstairs, waitin' t' speak t' y' and thinkin' y' have a headache." Mattie started up the steep, winding staircase. "Only yer aunt's butler and 'er cook knows y' didn't come here last night, and o' course, Tom Coachman and Benjamin who were told t' turn back by Mist'r Falcon'r. Everyone else? They be thinkin' y' took t' yer bed and I spent the night at yer side."

Robyn wanted to close her eyes in dread but did not dare, considering the steep narrowness of the stairs. Falconer had forced her father's coachman and footman back here?

Mattie continued chattering and pulling her along. "Now don't go gettin' all afeared, m'lady. Randy . . . er, Mist'r Randolph, that is . . . took care o' things. Why, right now there be a hot bath being prepar'd and in yer rooms is some clean linen t' bandage that arm o' yers. Randy . . . er, Mist'r Randolph . . . he insist'd that yer arm be tend'd to, and Harry, he be the one who sent word t' Cook t' take care of y' right quick."

Robyn grew dizzier as they headed higher up into the tower and Mattie wore on with her explanations. All Robyn really wanted to do was race back down the steps and chase after Dax.

But he was gone, back to whatever world he inhabited, and she was alone now, left to face the mess of her life, compliments of an uncaring father.

Mattie paused at the topmost step, finally looking back and noticing the strained features of her mistress. "La, m'lady, yer not gonna faint on me, are y'?"

"No, Mattie, I am not going to faint." She was going to cry. Leaning her uninjured arm against the stone, Robyn did what her mother had always taught her to do whenever she was scared or sad . . . she breathed. But all she could taste, all she could smell, was *Dax* . . .

"Come, m'lady," Mattie urged softly.

Robyn moved.

True to Mattie's word there was a bath being prepared, and Cook, who had worked for her aunt far longer than any other servant save Harry, was in her chambers with clean bandages and an antiseptic Aunt Amy had discovered while traveling in Scotland. The stuff was called "tincture of iodine." It stung Robyn's wound and stained her skin. While the old woman fussed over her, Robyn learned that Falconer had arrived with an associate whom he addressed only as Drago.

"Mr. Falconer claims the earl bade him come take you back to London, my lady."

Doom. "And my aunt?" Robyn asked, knowing that Aunt Amy, of all people, would know best how to get rid of Falconer and undo this sham of a betrothal with Lord Morely.

"Not in residence, my lady."

Doom and doom and more doom, Robyn thought as dread settled thick in her stomach.

"Had her Ladyship known of your visit," Cook was saying, "she'd have doubtless made every effort to be here. But you know how your aunt can be, my lady. She comes and goes, with none knowing when she'll return."

Yes, Robyn knew.

"What should be said to your caller, my lady? Are you in residence?"

Robyn debated hiding from Falconer, but didn't want to cause more of a stir in the household than she already had. She would face the man on her own and be done with it. What could he do to her? He could hardly drag her from the premises. At least, she hoped he couldn't.

"I'll meet with him," Robyn answered.

Chapter Eleven

Restless, Dax stood alone within a thick line of birch trees on Amy's lands, watching as the setting sun slanted black shadows across the bright bark, the last of its rays a rich gold but holding little warmth. Soon, there would be no light at all . . . there would be only darkness, followed by midnight—the thought of which increased Dax's inner disquiet.

All day, he had been fighting the evil within. Ever since those moments alone with Robyn in the caves he'd felt a shift inside himself, a change of sorts. It was as if he'd passed a point of being able to control his Phantom during the day. Though there were hours left until midnight, he could sense the sickening rise of power coming on, could feel his insides bracing for the transformation.

It was why he'd left Robyn alone at the hidden tower entrance earlier. He hadn't liked doing it, hadn't wanted to leave her like that. He'd wanted to see with his own eyes the moment she took the stairs and the door shut behind her, but he had not dared linger, not with the way he was feeling. When Robyn had talked of magic, with her voice near breathless, Dax had thought he might weep. Her words had whisked him back to those moments when he'd first met her and Amy in the cottage, before he'd lost all innocence. She'd made him remember that once upon a time, far too long ago, he had been worthy not only of her hand in marriage, but of her heart in keeping.

But the beast in him, that cold and heartless creature, had wanted to lash out at all of the emotion washing through him. Choked by feeling, chased by the fiend unfurling inside, Dax had forced himself to ride away.

He'd spent the next few hours scouring as much of Land's End as possible, searching for anything that might have told him what had become of Amy—and for any sign of the marauders that had attacked Robyn and her maid. If he'd found those men, unleashing the Phantom would have been pure pleasure. He'd found nothing, though.

Now, as the purpled shadows of the woodland hid him from view, he watched as Harry, the servant Amelia Archer trusted most, headed toward him. The old man moved carefully through the gathering dusk, mindful of the roots and uneven ground at his feet. Dax had sent word to him via John and it had been Harry who'd suggested the time and place of their meeting.

Dax stepped into the old man's line of view, though he was careful to keep the color of his eyes couched by shadows.

"Praise be . . ." Harry breathed.

At sight of him, Dax's mind winged back to that disastrous day when Harry had uttered the one word that made all the difference in his life: riders. It had been Harry who'd served as trusted outrider of the carriage that brought a young Robyn into Dax's life, and it had been Harry who had warned Sir Dysart of the riders trailing Dax. He swallowed past the lump of feeling in his throat as Harry came to stand before him. "I didn't think I'd ever see you again."

The older man, skin thinned with age, his hair just wisps of white that lifted in the breeze, grew misty at the sight of Dax. "Nor I you, Your Gr—" he started to say with a bow, but Dax stilled his words and his actions with the lift of one hand.

"Harry, do not. Please. I am simply . . . Dax. Though little of that luckless lad you met so long ago remains in me."

"Forgive me, but there is nothing simple about you," the old man breathed, his gaze sparking with a nostalgic light. Clearly, he was seeing a titled son and not the Cursed thief and smuggler Dax had become. "By the grace of angels, but you've the stance of your father . . . the very look of your mother. Tall and handsome, you are, and every bit a mix of your parents." A crisp and folded handkerchief in hand, Harry pressed the cloth to the outer edge of one eye. "If only Lady Archer could be here right now. She never once lost faith. She always believed you lived, that someday, somehow, you would find your way back to where you belong."

Emotion unraveled in Dax with Harry's words—and immediately the beast in him bit hard. "What's happened to her?" he said, not knowing how much longer he had before the Phantom fully emerged and overrode the man.

"I fear nothing good, but I have no proof of that"

"Your instincts are all we have, Harry. Tell me what you know and what you believe. Tell me everything."

"Lady A headed to London over a fortnight ago, saying only that she might have a lead as to the true identity of your age-old nemesis and that she would send a messenger with word of her progress. I received but one message: that she had indeed found a clue and intended to be here to meet with you. I've heard nothing since. The men I sent out returned yesterday with no news—she wasn't at her town house, and there were no carriage accidents reported, no trouble sighted along the roads. Lady A would not have missed meeting with you. Had she been able, she'd have been here."

"Aye, she would have been here," Dax agreed, his gut wrenching not only from the coming transformation but also with worry for Amelia. He raked one hand through his hair, fearing the worst. "Do you think the lowlife marauders who attacked Lady Robyn and her maid were lying in wait for Amy on her return?"

Harry considered the notion. "It's possible. Lady A believes that the enemy of your past—the very one who saw your father hanged for treason—desires not only to get to you but to silence her as well."

Dax wished he'd had the opportunity to make Ned and Bart talk, or at least the time to send a mind-sway in their direction, but his first concern had been for Robyn. Now, if he hoped to learn anything from them, he'd have to pick up a trail. "What a tangle," he muttered. "I take it Amy had no knowledge of her niece's visit."

"None at all. Given the threat she believes still exists to your life, she'd not have wanted Lady Robyn anywhere near here."

Dax had figured as much. Something—or someone—had forced Robyn to flee to Sussex. Dax shuttered his gaze as the beast in him rippled with icy heat.

"Besides, the Earl of Chelsea long ago forbade Lady A from visiting his daughter. He blames Lady A for the death of his wife."

Dax pulled his attention back to Harry. "Lady Robyn's mother is dead?"

"Gone since January last."

Something bled inside of him. His heart. For Robyn. "And was Amy responsible, as Chelsea believes?"

"No," Harry said. "But that didn't stop Lord Chelsea from casting blame. The problem was that he never understood—or even tried to understand—the women in her Ladyship's family . . . or his daughter's legacy."

"What legacy?"

"That of helping . . . and healing. That's what the countess was about the day she died—helping another."

Dax absorbed the information even as the fiend in him snapped at the ache swelling in his heart. "Tell me about this visitor at Land's End," he said, feeling chased by time. "I saw a carriage being stabled earlier. Who arrived here?"

"A man named Falconer. He's traveling with an associate whom he addresses only as Drago."

"Friends of Amy's?"

Harry shook his head. "To my knowledge, Mr. Falconer and Lady A have never met. He announced himself as being a representative of one Lord Reginald Morely. He claimed Lady Robyn's father bade him to come and take her back to London with him."

"And you believe it?"

"I know very little of Lady Robyn's life in Town. As for Lord Chelsea, he could have sent the devil's own to fetch his daughter. Lady A has often said one can never be certain which way the winds are blowing with Chelsea and his only child."

Dax filed this information away for later. Gad, but he knew so damnably little about Robyn and her life. He ached to slay every one of her dragons, but he had a few of his own to murder first. "Harry, will you grant me a favor?"

"Of course."

"Will you make certain Lady Robyn and Mr. Falconer are kept as far away from each other as possible? If she desires otherwise, she'll no doubt let you know immediately."

Harry nodded, and then said that he was glad it had been Dax who came upon Robyn and her maid yesterday and that he'd brought them safely to Land's End.

Ah, but I almost didn't, Dax thought, remembering the taste of Robyn's mouth in the dark, the shape of her breasts beneath his shirt, the feel of her hand around his stiff arousal.

Harry was still talking, saying something about Lady Robyn having inherited some healing magic.

At that, Dax went perfectly still, his mind yet again lurching back to the day he'd first met Robyn, as Harry said that he'd looked at Dax and had seen a lad without home or family . . . and then he'd looked at Robyn and saw a heart huge enough to make none of that matter.

Dax lowered his head. When he spoke, his voice was just a whisper. "You saw all of that, did you?"

"I did. And though her father wished otherwise, Lady Robyn never forgot her first betrothal, to you."

Dax blew out a breath he hadn't realized he was holding. "She doesn't know of our past, Harry. She doesn't remember me. And I'm going to keep it that way."

"But—"

Dax brought his head up, sharp. "No." The golden light of day was fading fast, the shadows becoming deeper, swallowing the woodland. "This is the way it has to be. Whoever ruined my family may very well have taken Amy. I've come back to avenge my parents, Harry. As I told you, I'm nothing like the boy you remember."

"No, you're more," Harry insisted. "Your father was a great man, and from the first moment I saw you I knew you were destined to follow in his steps, no matter how long it took."

"But I haven't followed his path."

"You will, and as I stand before you now, I swear it would be my greatest honor to help you start along that path, to help you right all the wrongs."

Dax shook his head. "There *is* no righting anything, Harry . . . there's just—there's only me wanting vengeance." He felt as he had on that icy day when the Curse had claimed him. Then, as now, Dax knew that he was on the cusp of tragedy. "What is to come promises to be dark indeed. No one within my circle is safe—not you, certainly not Amy . . . and now, God help me, not even Lady Robyn."

"I'll face this foe with you."

Emotion swelled inside of Dax, irritating the beast. "No, Harry. I won't have your blood on my hands. Besides, I need you here at Land's End, helping protect Lady Robyn and available in case there is word from Amy."

"Then here is where I'll be."

"I've posted my men at watch around the property. No one will be getting in—or out—without your say-so. Come morning, I'll head back to the city where I'll try to pick up Amy's trail. I'll leave a few men behind to keep watch and to be here should you or Lady Robyn have need of them."

"I have alerted the constable here, and have sent word to the city about Lady Archer's disappearance. I know they will do all they can to locate her Ladyship, but . . ." Harry let his words trail off.

Dax knew what the old man was thinking: that the fiend from Dax's past was someone, some *thing* the authorities would not be able to subdue. "I'll do what I can, everything I can, to find Amy and bring her home, Harry."

"I believe you. May God go with you, Your—" Harry stopped short again of addressing Dax formally. Instead, he said simply: "There is food inside, a place for you to sleep for the night."

Dax nodded his thanks. He'd take the food but not the bed. The Phantom was too stirred by the coming darkness and he knew he had little time left; his control was sliding away just as surely as the daylight.

As if sensing the strangeness in Dax, the growing need in him to be alone, Harry said, "The cottage where you first met Lady Robyn . . . you are welcome to it, Your Grace."

Dax flinched. "Harry, any title due me went to the Crown the day my father was hanged."

"Forgive me, but I must give you the respect and honor due you."

Respect? Honor? Dearest Christ, if the old man only knew of half the things that had transpired in his life, he'd not use such a reverent tone. "You don't know the low roads I've taken, Harry, the things I've seen, have done—"

"Due only to circumstance, I'm certain."

Dax shifted, the restlessness in him a funneling cloud now. He narrowed his gaze, watching as shadow ate shadow and the sun's light slid down and down. He felt a snap of frigid cold deep within, followed by flaming heat. His eyes burned from the inside out. He glanced at Harry, wondering if the Phantom had finally won.

"You should go now, Harry." *Or I should.*

The old man took a step back, but then held motionless, as if he realized he was in the presence of some fierce force and that any fast movement could bring certain death. "For years," he said quietly, "Lady Archer and I searched the whole of Sussex for any sign of you. Once, a year to the day of your disappearance, I swore to her that I'd spotted you. It was along the coast, early in the morning and dark still. Your whole face was aglow and you looked right at me. Your eyes, which were once so blue, were green . . . as green as they are now. You didn't harm me then. I'd like to believe you won't be doing so now."

"Then you don't know me at all," Dax said, and he headed away, fast, his insides curling as the Curse came to life.

It was late in the evening by the time Robyn—fed, bathed, and dressed in a gown of midnight blue brocade with long, fitted undersleeves that kept her warm and hid her bandage—sat on the cushioned stool of her vanity as Mattie arranged her hair into a loose chignon at the nape of her neck, leaving a few tendrils to curl about her features.

"I can get someone else to help me finish dressing, Mattie. You should be resting. You suffered a nasty blow to your head."

"Oh, la, I be fine, m'lady. It be only a small bump and only hurts when I push on it, so I decided I be pushin' no more at it. I had a short nap, I did, and Cook, she fussed ov'r me most of the day."

Robyn couldn't help noticing how much energy Mattie possessed. It was as if their night in the caves had given the girl a renewed spirit. The man called Randolph had clearly done more than sweep Mattie up off the ground—he'd swept her off her feet.

A glance in the looking glass told Robyn the night had changed her, too. She saw an image familiar in some ways, but unfamiliar in many other ways. Her irises seemed a shade more violet. And her eyes sparkled with an inner light, as though Dax had set to flame a spark inside of her—one that had lain dormant but was now ready to burn bright. Her lips appeared fuller, as if Dax's mouth had coaxed them into the shape they were meant to be. And her skin held a glow of its own, an inner radiance that would not be contained.

"La, m'lady," Mattie breathed, meeting Robyn's gaze in the glass, "y' look as though y' been to the very stars and back."

"Maybe I have," she whispered, remembering the moment Dax had pulled her right through his radiance and later had tangled his tongue with hers. "Maybe I have, Mattie."

Twenty minutes later Robyn descended the great staircase leading to the main hall of Land's End. A glance out the windows of her apartment earlier, and again in the hall just as the sun had set, had revealed two of Dax's men in the distance: Sam and John, keeping watch on the manse. Robyn didn't doubt that Bones was still posted at the gate, and that the others were somewhere on her aunt's lands.

All of which told her Dax might not be far away . . . which meant he wasn't leaving, at least not yet. The thought made the blood push fast through her veins and that whisper of wildness in her shimmer to life again. With too many questions and no answers, she picked up her pace, anxious to get through her meeting with Falconer.

She could hear voices drift to her from the front parlor, where Falconer and his man had been led hours ago. One was Harry's voice, no doubt offering refreshment. Robyn moved toward the sounds. A voice from behind, however, stilled her in midstep.

"Ah, Lady Robyn . . . at long last. I thought perhaps you had abandoned me to that parlor until the end of time."

Robyn turned slowly about, a cold shiver running up her spine at sight of the dark-haired, gray-eyed man who stood just beyond her. Falconer.

"The thought had crossed my mind."

"Come now, I can't be put off that easily, my lady. I must say, I went to an awful amount of trouble to get here, not to mention the bother of a time I had trying to ferret out where you'd gone off to in the first place."

"How *did* you find me?"

"Oh, it wasn't I who did the calculations, but my associate, Drago. He surmised that a frightened bird would most likely take flight to a familiar nest. Fortunately, he was correct. We realized how close we were to finding you when we stopped your father's coach as it was heading back to Town."

Robyn could only guess what ugly scene must have taken place along the road. She remembered well the man called Drago, with his feral-looking eyes and boxer's broken-nosed features. He'd joined Falconer that first night she'd learned of her father's disastrous game of hazard with Lord Morely. Drago frightened Robyn nearly as much as Falconer and the specter of Morely.

Bluntly, she said, "I don't like that you forced Tom Coachman and Benjamin to return here, or that you followed me."

"And your father doesn't like that you left London without so much as a by-your-leave."

"I've a mind of my own, Mr. Falconer. You'd do well to remember that. I do what I please, when and how it pleases me."

"Which is precisely why Lord Morely and your father deemed I should come fetch you."

Damn her father and his lack of luck at the gaming table. "Bear in mind, sir, *I* have not deemed it to be so."

"Fortunately the earl and I have already settled things."

Smiling coolly, Falconer moved toward her with a slow, easy gait, stopping but a pace away.

Robyn watched, wordlessly, as he lifted his right hand, showing her a packet of papers.

"I was enjoying yet one more hour in that sitting room when I remembered a certain something I'd left in the carriage," Falconer said, tapping the packet against the heel of his gloved left palm. "Have you any idea what this bundle represents, my lady?"

"I've no doubt you'll tell me in full, ugly detail."

"It represents a beginning and an end. Your father was not pleased when you fled the city—not with you, and certainly not with the servants you enlisted to aid you in your mad dash."

She knew where this conversation was heading. She knew, but could do nothing to stop it.

"The bundle contains several missives, all written in your father's hand and sealed with his wax. Three are for the servants who aided you. They will be put off without so much as a farthing, my lady, and certainly no recommendation, should you choose to continue to be difficult. The earl has instructed me to present each of them with notice of termination and to inform all parties that he intends to lodge a complaint for their involvement in your hasty flight from home and the use of cattle and carriage not their own."

How cruel her father could be. How utterly heartless.

"Also contained herein is a copy of the notices your father dashed off to the papers, announcing your betrothal to Lord Morely," Falconer continued, his tone giving no hint of remorse for the news he was imparting. "By now, the morning's papers will have a full account of your plans to wed. The banns will be called beginning this Sunday. All of which brings me to the brightest bit of gold in this packet, which is a letter intended for a holy order in the northernmost wilds of Yorkshire, my lady. Deny Lord Morely, and you'll find that not only will your father be ruined financially and the servants who aided you cast off into a perilous future, but you, my lady, will find yourself among the cloistered."

Fury surged inside her. How dare this nothing of a man think she would bow to threats. She was about to tell him what he could do with his packet of bloody papers when Harry—stiff-limbed, big-hearted, wonderfully wise Harry—moved into the hall and saved her from the moment, saying there was an issue with the staff that only she could settle, which of course there wasn't.

Falconer, not fooled, gave Robyn another cool smile. "I take it that's my cue to go back to the parlor and await your good graces," he said lowly to her. "You can offer my man and me lodging for the night, or we can find it elsewhere. Either way, plan to leave with us at first light. Your father and your fiancé are eager for your return."

Robyn, fuming, said nothing as Falconer headed once again for the sitting room. Damn him, but she'd let the two men cool their heels for another few hours, and only then would she see to it they had rooms—in the tower farthest from her own.

Only after Falconer had gone the length of the long hall and disappeared into the parlor did Robyn speak.

"I don't suppose, Harry, that you know where my aunt is."

"No, Lady Robyn, unfortunately I do not."

Robyn regarded him closely, knowing very well Harry was one of Aunt Amy's closest confidantes. The man had been in her aunt's service for all of Robyn's life and half of his. He knew about the females of her family, of their abilities to heal and to comfort—and he'd kept tight-lipped about all of it.

"I thought as much," Robyn said, not so much irritated by her lack of information but rather by the hunger now eating at her. It was the same hunger she'd experienced in the caves—the hunger for Dax, for more of how he made her feel. It bit at her belly, kicked her heart to a faster pace. "Very well then, tell me this instead, Harry: Where is he?"

The old man brought his watery blue gaze to her. "My lady?"

"Dax Dexter," Robyn said, knowing that she couldn't stay away from Dax, not even after he'd so blatantly rejected her advances in the caves. He was connected to her aunt in some way . . . and now, after their time together, Robyn felt connected to him—felt that the flame of unbridled heat that burned bright in him had somehow jumped to *her*.

"I know you know where he is, Harry, where he intends to sleep," she went on. "I also know you're the one who aided him in getting me inside this house with as few people knowing my whereabouts as possible. You allowed him to post one of his men at the front gate and gave clearance for the rest of them to prowl the borders."

The old man denied none of it.

"All of which indicates to me that you trust him, Harry . . . and if you trust him, then perhaps I should do the same. So tell me," Robyn said, her voice going soft as she thought of Dax, of her need of him, "where I can find him, or else I'll spend the rest of the night searching."

Harry told her.

Chapter Twelve

Dax sensed Robyn's approach long before the pale glow of her lantern filtered through the aged slats of the abandoned cottage. The shafts of light shifted across the gritty floorboards like an unfolding fan as she moved along the length of the building, heading for the door.

Even though the black dome of night echoed with the ever-present wind and the loud wash of the Channel below, Dax could clearly hear her. He heard her breathing, which was fast, like her heartbeat . . . he heard her footfalls, which were but the barest of whispers through sparse grass and across loose stone, damp dirt . . . he heard even the sound of her fist curling in soft fabric as she lifted her skirts to hurry her pace.

That she had followed him here, to this lone patch of his past where he intended to ride out the midnight, away from the others, away from *her*, irritated the man, but excited the Phantom. The man wanted to leave, to use his Curse to shimmer away before she found him, but the beast was determined that he stay.

Dax heard the click of the latch as it was slowly lifted, watched as the door came open an inch.

The light of her lantern edged back the blackness of the room. She took a cautious step inside.

"Dax?"

Just a smudge of a shadow in the far corner of the room, he kept silent. Best to let her believe she'd wasted her time in climbing to this wind-tortured lip of land. Let her turn around and leave. Please. God. Let her go and be safe and—

Too bad for him, *for her*, that the bloody Phantom was roused. The beast in him forced movement.

As he stepped to the edge of the lantern's light, Dax felt like nothing he'd ever known. This wasn't the same as in the woods earlier today with Harry when the Phantom radiated outward, but more as if the soul-smuggling fiend in him had burrowed right down into his bones and needed no phosphorescent glow to herald its presence. Arctic cold snapped through Dax's muscles, while hell's own heat boiled in every organ.

He smelled Robyn's fear and her sex and the wind in her hair. He tasted the heady wildness that sang through her veins and the salt of the sea on her skin. He heard the fast *swish, swish, swish* of blood through her heart, sensed the iron strength of her will, and while the man in him cherished her above all things, the Phantom in him had only one thought: *prey*.

He stepped into the light. Smiled. Ice and heat. And then moved.

Before Robyn could turn, before she could flee, Dax reached for her, his right hand curling around the back of her neck. "No," he rasped. "You're not leaving. Not yet." His fingers pushed through the soft strands of her hair. "You came here for a reason. Tell me why."

The lantern's glow cast a ring of light about her delicate features, her violet eyes dark as midnight, her lips a luscious dusky rose. "You," she said, her answer coming as swift as the footsteps that had led her inside. "Whether you are man, sorcerer, or haunting phantasm . . . I—I came to find you."

The fiend in him grinned. "You found me."

Without a sound, Dax pulled Robyn to him, so that she

was flush against him, her breasts to his chest, the hardness of him snug in the vee of her thighs. Her lantern, swinging with the movement, tipped its light to the ceiling and back. The smoke of it scented the air.

Dax dug his fingers deeper into Robyn's hair, his gaze on her lips, his thoughts on her soul.

"I'm going to taste you," he said. "I'm going to take you," he warned.

Robyn didn't balk; she didn't do anything at all . . . but breathe.

Dipping his head, Dax took in that breath. He drew it deep as his mouth covered hers. Her lips opened to him. Her tongue met his. She tasted of forest and sea, of fresh night and fantasy. She tasted, damn it all, of Phantom-carved cravings. Was that what this moment was—a mindsway fashioned by his Phantom? Is that why Robyn had brazenly followed him here, was letting him hold her, kiss her . . . because she could do no less?

But even as these dark thoughts battered his brain, Dax couldn't stop himself from taking what he could from her. He brought both hands to her face. Her cheeks were cool, her mouth a hot brand against his. He kissed her, long and deep, as he thought about all that he'd done to her in that study in London so many nights ago, and all that he wanted to do to her still. There were those dimples, down low on her back, that he intended to explore with his tongue . . . and her nipples, luscious and pink, that would need their own special attention . . . and there was the heat of her, the creamy heart of her that he ached to pierce with his hardness.

For now, though, he had her face in his hands, her body against his, and a wild whip of abandon racing through her blood. She'd let him do anything, Dax realized—she'd beg him to do everything. That's what the Curse did best, Dax thought, a brief bit of sanity beating against him.

It was that flare of feeling that made him let go—of her hair, her body, her lips.

And it was her history, too, that made him release her. There was power in the path of her ancestors, a timeless knowledge in her very blood. Robyn had yet to realize her full potential, Dax knew—but still, whatever mix of gifts from her heritage had been stirred into her soul was a potent brew, enough to make the Phantom recede.

Hauling in a breath, Dax lifted his head and stepped back.

Robyn should have turned and raced for safety then, but she didn't. Instead, she stayed. She even dared to lift her chin and meet the icy fire of his gaze.

"Are you all right?" he breathed.

A nod. "I'm always all right."

She'd said the same words to him the first night he'd found her again, yet Dax knew that she wasn't all right. She was new to the passion that sparked between them. He could hear her heart slamming hard in her chest, could see the flush in her face, could smell the scent of her excitement. And he could feel her heat, hotter than his own. Yet when she spoke, there was resolve in her tone.

"I'm glad that you and your men are still here," she said, surprising him. "And no matter what just happened between us, I . . . I *am* glad that I've found you."

"Oh?" Her words were calm, cool, her steadiness like the wash of a warm tide pooling about Dax, dousing his fires, melting the ice in him, sinking him back into sanity.

"Yes. I didn't like the way you left me earlier today, and I have some questions I'm hoping you will answer."

Her calmness was exactly what Dax needed to ground himself, to beat back the beast—for now, anyway.

"All right." He nodded. "We'll talk." *And then you'll leave and you'll be safe*, he thought. Though Dax could utilize pieces of his Phantom at will and at any time, after midnight the Phantom claimed *him*, leaving little of his own will to surface.

He reached out, took the lantern from her grasp, and

motioned her deeper inside the room to the single table with its two chairs. He shut the door as she took a seat, this time throwing the bolt. Out in the night, Dax heard his horse stir, rising from its bed of grass amid bushes of wild thyme. Like its master, the animal felt the approach of midnight.

Robyn, eyeing the pile of arrows Dax had heaped atop the scarred table—and his heavy bow and leather packet filled with even more arrows propped against one leg of it—glanced up as Dax pushed aside a few of the arrows and set the lantern down. She was wearing her hooded cloak. She loosened the strings of it. Her eyes were a deep shade of violet, darker than Dax had ever seen them, and her mouth was but a lush moue in her beautiful face. She kept her spine straight, not touching the chair back behind her, her chin tilted slightly upward as though she had come for an intense purpose and was drawing on every ounce of strength she possessed. She obviously had something to say but couldn't quite decide on the words.

Resolutely, Dax sat down in the chair opposite her, eager to get this business over with—eager for her to be far away before his Phantom surged free. "You shouldn't have come here alone, lass. These woods aren't safe, as well you know."

Robyn glanced briefly at the arrows, his bow. "It appears not many places are." Her gaze shifted back to Dax. "You've seen to it my aunt's home is surrounded and well guarded. Who is it you think will be getting in—or even out?"

"You, for one. Obviously my men aren't as vigilant in their watch as they should be."

"On the contrary, Randolph tried to stop me—even after I informed him that I've seen you at your . . . worst. It was my aunt's butler who told him to let me go, and it was he who directed me here."

"Harry." Dax shook his head, wondering if the old man was attempting to play matchmaker. What Harry didn't realize was that he might as well have given Robyn a map to hell itself. "The old man is getting far too soft in his dotage, I'm afraid."

"So you know him."

"I know of him."

Robyn skewered Dax with a direct look. "Why are you here? More to the point, what do you know about my aunt that you're not telling me?"

Bloody hell. Dax settled back in the chair, his weight causing the old thing to creak and groan. He wanted to groan himself.

"I don't know much about your aunt," he said honestly. "As for my men keeping watch on the place, I decided it would be best given the fact you and your maid were accosted yesterday—and given the fact that I let a few of my arrows fly. Revenge, y'know, can be a nasty business."

"No, I don't know," Robyn said. "I know nothing of revenge. I am, however, beginning to believe that any and all of what you do has the potential of turning nasty."

"It does," he said. *It will,* he thought.

"And my aunt?" she demanded. "Are your men standing guard because you believe something has happened to her? And are you here, in this cottage, because you think more trouble will come?"

Dax shifted in his chair. To answer in the affirmative would be to admit that there was indeed trouble afoot—and from there he'd have to explain how he'd come to know Amy and how her disappearance was all tangled up in the blackness of his past and the precariousness of his future. In truth, to say anything at all right now would be to draw Robyn even further into his coil.

"Oh, never mind," she said, cutting into his thoughts. "I didn't actually believe you'd give me an answer. I know my aunt very well, and like every other female in my family Aunt Amy is probably determined to face whatever trouble she's in on her own. So given that fact, here is what I really want to say: If Harry trusts you—and I can see that he does—then I've decided I should trust you, too."

She stopped a moment, breathless, and then in a rush, said, "And I do, Dax. I do trust you. From the moment we met, you've helped me: at the soiree, in the woods, in the caves. Even though a part of who you are—*what* you are—terrifies me . . . I trust you."

Of all the words Dax had heard Robyn say since he'd found her again, those meant the most to him. And frightened him more than he realized possible. For Robyn to place her trust in him, to possibly come to care for him, would be to leave her prey not only to the Phantom but also to his every enemy.

"You obviously know my aunt or you wouldn't have such intimate knowledge of the lay of these lands, or even of this cottage," Robyn continued, "and you certainly wouldn't be on such close terms with Harry. I know something is wrong, and you've an inkling of what that something is. I sensed it in Harry's behavior and I sense it now in you—all of which leads me to believe that my aunt is indeed in trouble and you are in fact here to help." Wind whined against the boards of the cottage. The Channel, far below, rolled and surged, ever restless, victim to the wind that sent it curling against the rocky shore, slapping it into spray. "I come from a long line of females who have been no stranger to danger: my mother's mother and her mother and hers and hers . . . and my own, of course, and her sister, Amelia, Lady Archer, my aunt . . . and your . . . ?"

Godmother and godsend and everything good, Dax wanted to say, but didn't.

"Acquaintance," he said instead, and the word fell flat off his tongue, felt wrong as he remembered the wild carriage ride he'd shared with Amy, how she had gathered him hard to her by his coat collar mere seconds after Sir Dysart had been shot, how she had willed him to be brave, to save himself. Her intensity had helped sustain him in the moments that followed, moments that had become hours, days, weeks, *years*. He'd been buoyed through it all by Amy's firm resolution that he should survive—that, and the memory and the promise of Robyn.

Dax watched as Robyn bowed her head, drawing in a long breath, as though gathering the courage to continue. It was then he realized that she'd come here to say far more than what she'd just shared.

He yearned to make it easy for her, wanted to pave the way for her to say whatever it was that weighed so heavily on her mind she'd journeyed to this cold cabin on the hilltop in search of him.

When she didn't speak, he whispered, "Robyn," and he saw her shift at the sound of her given name on his lips— the first time he'd spoken it aloud. "Why are *you* here?" he asked gently. "Why did you come looking for me?"

There was a long stretch of silence, and then, very slowly, she lifted her face, her violet eyes luminous. "Because I couldn't stay away—because I need . . ."

When she didn't finish, he asked, "Need what, lass? What is it you need?"

"You. I need you, Dax, and more of what you've made me feel. In the study. In the caves. And I can sense that you need me, too. Perhaps in ways I can't even understand."

Lord. God.

Numbed wordless, Dax watched as Robyn stripped off her gloves, finger by finger, and than laid them on the chair's seat near her left knee. Next, she slowly drew the cloak off her shoulders, allowing the heavy material to ripple downward to the seat of the chair. Like the lick of an ocean wave bathed in midnight, the material pooled about her hips, then fell free of her thighs, revealing to him the treasure of her curves encased in a gown of midnight blue brocade.

She was gorgeous and comely and more than Dax dared dream about, but even when he blinked she was still there before him, peeling off her layers. He sucked in a hard breath, felt his blood quicken, his loins tighten.

"What are you doing, lass?" he whispered, trying desperately to keep his voice steady.

Robyn stood, shrugging away from the cloak and the chair, leaving both behind. Her eyes darkened to the color of a starless midnight. Inexorably she moved toward him, saying softly, breathlessly, "I am offering myself to you—again—and am hoping you won't deny me this time."

She smelled of lavender and lovely dreams. She smelled, God help him, of the past Dax could all but taste on the back of his tongue, and of the future he feared he might never have with her.

"Ah, lass," he whispered hoarsely, "only think what you are saying."

If Robyn heard him at all, she made no show if it. Wordlessly, she lowered herself to her knees before him and placed her hands, palms open, atop his thighs. "Please," she whispered, face tipped up, her hands and her body trembling. "Tell me you won't deny me this time . . . won't deny *us*."

Dax nearly melted at the contact. He sucked in another hard breath, held it this time, and then let it out slowly. "You know I must."

"No. I don't." Robyn splayed her fingers, boldly yet gently caressing the hard muscles of his thighs. "I had thought a man such as yourself wouldn't care what brought me here, that you—"

"Would take advantage of you?" Dax cut in, placing his hands over hers, stilling them. "That the fiend in me would gladly rob you of your innocence . . . that the thief and smuggler in me wouldn't count the cost to you? Is that what you thought?"

A shiver rippled through her at the harshness of his tone. In the glow of the lantern's light, Dax could perceive the threat of tears gathering in her eyes.

"No," she whispered. "I—I had thought you would help me. That somehow, someway, you'd help rid me of this wildness that wants to consume me . . . that you would understand my need . . . and—and that you would not judge me."

Beneath his hands, she turned her palms up and gently curled her fingers about his.

Dax looked down. Her skin was soft against his, like the touch of a whisper. His hands were browned by the sun, roughened by reins and work. Every bit of him wanted to know the touch of her hands on his naked skin, wanted to meld with her and be absorbed into her body. But this wasn't right. He didn't want her to come to him out of a desperation fueled by his Phantom—and that was exactly what this was, wasn't it?

Bloody hell, but he didn't know. Frustrated and frowning, he returned his gaze to hers. "Contrary to what you might think of me, lass, I'm not one to take a woman's maidenhead and then simply walk away. Though the life I've led hasn't exactly been sainted, I'm not without a conscience." *Not yet, at least.*

"I—I don't think that. If so, I wouldn't be here."

"You're here because you're feeling reckless," he said. *You're here because of the Curse,* he thought.

"No." She shook her head, insistent. "I'm here because I—I don't want to be anywhere else."

"Ah, lass . . ." Reaching down, he gently threaded his fingers through her soft hair, guiding her head and her body upward. He should be the voice of reason right now. Better yet, he should have put her out the door the moment she'd arrived—but he wasn't and he hadn't, and now God help him, the Phantom was hungry for her and the man was enchanted, enflamed.

Robyn found his mouth, her lips opening and closing against his. All clear thought vanished as the force of his need and the touch of her mouth swept him away. His own arms trembling, he caressed his way down her back, over the curve of her buttocks, and then lifted her, guiding Robyn to turn just so as he placed her on his lap. She leaned back into the cradle of his right arm, the lantern's light painting her in warmth.

Dax lifted his left hand and traced his fingers across the curve of her jaw, marveling at the softness of her skin even as he kissed her, full and deep. Robyn wrapped her arms about his neck, her fingers doing their own exploring. She delved deep into his hair, sifting through the silky strands, then massaging lower to the corded muscles of the back of his neck. Dax felt a trail of goose bumps tingle down his spine. Did she realize the sway she alone held over him?

He decided in the next instant that she must, for she strained against him, turning slightly so that her breasts met his chest. His whole body convulsed with delight while the Phantom in him stretched, ever reaching for her.

Wanting to please Robyn as much as she pleased him, Dax dropped his left hand lower, smoothing a path over the long column of her throat, then lower to her breasts, her nipples peaking beneath the fabric of her bodice. He lightly ran his open palm across them, and then settled it over her right breast, cupping her, kneading gently. Robyn sighed against his mouth. Dax swallowed the breath, taking it deep within him, reveling in the feel of it, of her, as he slanted his mouth over hers and drove his tongue hungrily against her own.

He lowered his left hand, skirting the area where her thighs met, and moved lower, to her long legs and the hem of her gown. He raised it slowly, smoothing his palm up and over her stockinged calf, and higher, past the garter that was tied above her knee, and higher still, to the damp inner curve of her thighs. He could feel the heat of her, the honeyed wetness. She was ready for him, her body intuitively preparing itself for that moment when he slid himself inside of her and joined them for all time—for that is what this night would mean for him: the joining of them forever.

Moving his fingers, he touched her, *there*.

Robyn let loose a tiny gasp. Dax kissed it away, his fingers easing between her plump, soft folds, finding the wetness of her, the nub of her. He stroked and teased until again Robyn gasped and again Dax swallowed the sound into his own body. Gently he caressed her, taking care to go slow and steady, to take her to heights she'd only imagined. Her legs parted slightly, and his fingers grew slick with her wetness. Dax kissed her tenderly, deeply, then dropped his fingers down a space and entered her, pushing inside.

She sucked in a breath of astonishment and he knew then that he'd taken her past the point of no return. She wanted this, wanted him, as much as he wanted her.

Cradling her more gently in the crook of his right arm, Dax pressed Robyn down with another long, slow kiss, and all the while let his fingers show her what pleasure awaited them and what he wanted to do to her with another firmer, harder, part of his body.

He wanted to undress and view every part of her; he wanted to taste her, wanted to watch as her womanhood swelled and his fingers dipped inside of her. He wanted to make love to her in a fine bedchamber lit with the soft glow of candles, and he wanted to take her down into a mattress so thick the two of them would be swallowed into its middle.

But all Dax had with Robyn was here and now—just these stolen moments in this cold cabin weathered by salt and by sun, the Phantom growing stronger with every passing second, and the midnight close at hand. . . .

He wanted more. He wanted so much more.

Determined to make the most of this moment, Dax set every one of his senses to focus solely on Robyn. Gorgeous in the glow of the lantern, she smiled, shyly at first, as his gaze devoured her and his hand pleased her with the pressure of his palm, the gentle probing of his fingers. With slow, deliberate strokes he swept her into a mindless frenzy where her back arched slightly, her limbs shuddered, and her breath came past her lips in tiny, hard pants.

Dax felt his own need rock hard between their bodies, but it didn't matter because she was breathless and beautiful and she was lacing her arms about his neck and blowing the loveliest of sighs into his right ear. He loved her like this, all soft and dreamy. *His.* He wanted to tell her so. Wanted to say so many things.

But suddenly, it was as if a wall of invisible energy had slammed into the cottage. A wave of intensity blew against Dax and Robyn, lifting the ends of his hair, the hem of her skirts. The lantern burst apart, its flame blown into nothingness. Blackness blanketed them.

Nearly midnight. He had a mere sixty seconds before the riders arrived, before he turned Phantom . . . before all hell broke loose.

Dax, furious at himself for losing sense of time, quickly pulled away from Robyn and in a flash helped her upright, getting to his feet as well.

He gathered up her cloak, drew it around her, and in the darkness reached for her, his right hand molding itself to the warmth at the back of her neck as he dragged her toward him. He kissed her long and deep one last time, as if to capture the taste of her for all time. With his lips pressed against hers, he murmured, "I'm sorry, lass. God . . . I'm sorry."

"Why? What's happening?"

Dax dragged his mouth to her ear, and whispered: *"They're here."*

Instantly Robyn's skin chilled, her body stilled. She knew, without asking, what he meant.

"There is only one way to defeat them: a sharp object through the left eye. Remember that, Robyn. Tell me you will."

"Y-Yes, of course."

"And whatever happens, promise me you'll do what you must to save yourself. Even if it means hurting me."

"What? No." She shook her head. "I won't. I—"

"Robyn. Listen to me. You know what's coming—but

what you don't know is what's coming *within me.* I can't control my actions. I need you to promise me."

Robyn, a firm resolve in her eyes, reached up to cup Dax's face in the palms of her trembling hands. "Only if you promise me that we'll continue this."

A growl formed deep in his throat. "I promise. Someday. We will."

With that, Dax pulled away from her mouth and her body, her warmth and her sweetness. Knowing he'd just let go of his one lifeline to sanity, he swiped up his bow, slung his quiver of arrows across his back, and faced not the door, but the eastern wall, shielding Robyn with his body.

Dax slammed his eyes shut, touched the heart talisman he wore about his neck—Robyn's heart, the one she'd gifted him with so many years ago—and listened with his Phantom senses.

Now, he thought and opened his eyes.

The hooded rider and its destrier sliced through the weathered wood of the cottage in a raging blaze of energy. Rider and beast weren't even halfway through the wall when Dax moved, fast. Just as the animal's hooves landed on the floorboards in a scrape of sound, Dax let one of his arrows fly—a swift, hard hit to the area where the rider's left eye socket should be. Both rider and beast exploded in a blinding ball of energy that shattered into a shower of dust.

Another came immediately after that, focused solely on Robyn. Dax, bow at the ready, sent rider and beast into oblivion.

He didn't wait for more to appear; he quickly spun about, driving Robyn straight back against the wall just as he felt the Curse begin to curl up and out of him. The familiar sickening shot of cold sliced through him as the color washed from his skin and the evilness in him began to rise to the surface.

"Dax! Talk to me. You're frightening me. I don't understand what's happening. I don't—"

Dax stopped Robyn's words with just a tug. He pulled

her through the rise of arctic-cold energy, past the odd glimmer of light emanating from his skin, and brought her body flush against his own. For the briefest of moments, Dax could feel Robyn's heart and her heat—and then he could feel nothing at all as he took her right *through* the wall . . . out into the night and the wind and a wild world circled by soul seekers.

A half dozen in all, the fiends and their mounts gleamed in the pitch-dark night, silent sentinels filled with a deadly purpose, each huge warhorse clawing at the earth, blowing frost from its nostrils. It was the Curse that commanded the creatures . . . the Curse that put each rider on the path of harvesting souls. The high-pitched hum of their combined energy was like a continuous screech cutting through the night. The scent of that energy hung thick in the air. It tasted like something tart and foreign on the back of the tongue. Dax knew it well; it was the taste of dark magic. The riders had formed a half circle around this side of the cottage, as though expecting Dax to make his way outside once the first riders appeared.

If Dax thought he could shimmer beyond their reach, he would have, but the gifts of his Curse weren't that generous. He could move himself and anything within the field of energy surrounding him from one point to another, but only short distances at a time. In order to get Robyn to safety—back to Amy's manse with its thick stone towers—he'd have to shimmer her there space by space. Unless, of course, he went full Phantom and used the darkest of his powers and became a Soul Smuggler, which he wouldn't do. Couldn't. Not with Robyn so near.

He was left with the one choice he'd made night after night since that stinging cold day he'd been captured by the Curse: fight the fiends that surrounded him, fight the beast that dwelled within him, and try not to take an innocent soul in the process.

All of these thoughts snapped through Dax's mind in less than a second, the same amount of time in which Dax felt himself being pushed down and out of the way by the Phantom as it rose higher and higher. It wanted to snuff him out completely, conscience and all.

The scent of Robyn swamped him, making the beast in him hungry and the man in him worry over how to protect her. Dax loosened his hold and positioned Robyn behind him, praying hard that he would be able to save her and not steal her soul.

"Why don't they move?" she asked, nearly having to shout to be heard above the loud screech of energy. Her fingers curled tight into the back of his shirt. "Why don't they attack?"

They will, one by one, he started to say, but his body was no longer his own. The evilness had crested; the Phantom was in charge now, and it grinned at the riders, eager to do battle, which was the only good thing about the moment. As long as the Phantom was kept busy with the riders, it would not be intent on Robyn, would not be craving her heart or her heat . . . or her soul.

The fiends took that grin as their cue. As one, they jerked at their reins, rousing the warhorses into an air-clawing frenzy.

"Dax."

Dax felt Robyn's fear—huge, suffocating fear—and yet she didn't cower, she didn't run. God. He wished she could simply race free of this nightmare. He hated that she was terrified, and he was furious that she was in harm's way.

Unable to help her in any other way, Dax began to fashion a mind-sway with his Phantom, hoping that this time it would work. If he could do nothing else for her, he would lessen the terror of the moments to come. Weaving calm with his dark magic, he began to move it through the thickly charged atmosphere toward Robyn . . . but he never got the chance to whisper it against her skin.

The first rider charged. Though instead of coming dead on, the fiend rode a circle about them. There was no attempt to engage Dax in fight, as there usually was. Instead, the creature's sole intent was Robyn as it drew the circle tighter and tighter.

Dax realized then that the riders had discerned Robyn was his Achilles' heel. They were determined to have her . . . and doubtless wanted to use her in order to get to him. And then? They would suck the soul right out of her. . . .

Like hell, Dax thought just as the creature reached down and out, intending to swipe Robyn up and off the ground. It got a fistful of her cloak . . . and nothing more. Dax didn't allow it.

Fury exploding inside of him, he willingly merged with the Phantom and then reached deep for the darkest power of his Curse.

Untold energy flared hot and bright inside of him. Dax felt it sear his organs and sizzle through every muscle until it beat out of him in a humming wave of sheer power. The glow of him bit back the darkness, his eyes a blaze of beryl fire.

And then he heard it—heard Robyn's sharp inhalation of breath—and he saw her face go ashen and her eyes fill with dread, when all he'd meant to do was protect her.

"Oh, God," he heard her gasp. "You *are* one of them."

"No. I'm worse."

Chapter Thirteen

Robyn stumbled back, her feet tangling in the folds of her cloak, which had fallen to the ground. "*How* much worse?" she demanded, kicking free of the garment and inching away from him.

"You don't want to know."

Oh, but she did. Her very life depended upon it. She knew that now. She knew she'd not be leaving this cold, windy cliff top on her own. If the ghostly riders didn't kill her, the beast that had claimed Dax surely would. And she knew it was indeed a beast inside him because she felt, suddenly, the mind-sway Dax had fashioned for her, the one he'd woven to help her cope with this wild night. She'd brushed against it when whirling away from the rider that had torn her cloak from her shoulders. Like a whisper of cool silk against the skin of her neck, her face, it felt nothing at all like the highly charged air swarming with the riders' combined energy.

It was instead smooth and welcome and all things wonderful, and so she'd stepped into it, allowing the magic to soak into her skin, to put calm where there was chaos. She didn't fight it this time, but welcomed it. And in the span of seconds in which she'd seen the change in Dax to this very moment, she felt more than just Dax's mind-sway slip inside of her. She picked up on the vast desolation he carried inside of him, the huge battle he daily fought against this . . . *thing* that inhabited him. Just as her mother had always tried to tell her, Robyn now understood there were indeed truths hidden in the world: magic, mystery . . . and evil. There was evilness hidden inside Dax. He fought to keep it contained, but it was there—and now it was *here*, in front of her.

The wind whipped Dax's hair into wild disarray. The glow radiating from his body burned hotter than the sun, whiter than the moon. He was no one Robyn knew—not the man who had taken her to great heights of passion only a short time ago, not even the phantasm that had lured her from her bed out onto the street. He was far more than that; he was all power and fury and dark, dark intent. Robyn could sense the steel in him, the savage intensity. And she could feel his voracious hunger . . . for her soul, for her very life.

Gone was the attentive, would-be lover who so recently had held her in his arms and touched her in places no other man had known. His lips, which only moments ago had been so soft and yet searing against her skin, were now pressed into a firm, hard line, and his eyes went from burning with an intense beryl fire to being as dark as a forest filled with driving rain. The latent demon Dax harbored and had kept hidden from her was now unraveling within him.

Robyn didn't take her gaze off him, not even when she spied from the corners of her eyes another rider breaking rank and charging their way. It was the mind-sway Dax had spun for her that kept Robyn from dropping in a dead faint. It kept her coolheaded and plotting a route of escape. In the span of a heartbeat, she planned that she would lunge away when the rider reached this . . . *being* Dax had become, and then she would run and not stop and—

The haunting phantasm on horseback didn't ride straight for Dax. It came for *her*, swooping low and reaching out with one long, ghostly arm, spindly fingers raking at her neck. Robyn screamed at the searing cold contact, jerking back, her feet tangling in the cloak again. This time she fell, down and back, catching herself smack on her wrists, as above her she watched Dax transform yet again.

By the murderous intent in Dax's blazing green eyes, the rider might just as well have cleaved Robyn's body in two. With lightning speed and inhuman strength, the beast that was Dax grabbed at the phantasm's reins, hauled both rider and animal directly to him and slammed them into the vortex of power that emanated from him. The colliding energies annihilated the phantasm and its mount, exploding them into a ball of blinding bright light that sent a shower of sparks shooting in all directions. The remaining riders surged into motion, two of them charging Dax, the third routing wide to the left.

Dax—or whatever he was—reacted in a bold flurry of pulsating power. Licks of energy beat out of him, arcing in the air, turning the grass to smoke. He bit back the night with his eerie brilliance, a force as unstoppable as the wind, as fierce as a firestorm. Muscles bulging, he reached behind him with both arms and drew two arrows from his pack. One in each fist, he shot them through the air like javelins, piercing the faceless fiends, sending them and their horses to dust.

Robyn scrambled back, digging her heels through sand and dirt and the tangle of her cloak, trying desperately to get up, to get away, but the third and final rider thundered at her from the side. With a screech of energy, it dropped to the ground, reaching for her.

Robyn screamed, skittering around, kicking out with one foot as the rider lunged for her throat. *"Dax!"* His name tore up and out of her before Robyn could think it through. She hadn't meant to pull the beast's attention back to her, didn't want that pulsating energy directed her way.

At the sound of Robyn's cry, he turned, saw her dilemma, and reacted instantly. Violent rage whipped across his features as he reached for yet another arrow. Robyn saw no more of him after that. One moment she was thrust back on the ground, her skull slamming hard against dirt as she felt the clawing hand of the rider curling about her throat—and the next moment she heard a wild screech as the fiend was lifted bodily from her, an arrow's shaft slammed into it. Whips of bright white light snapped above and around her, ending in a shower of dusty brilliance that never touched her.

Robyn lifted her eyes to . . . Dax.

He was above her.

He was all around her.

He was the air in her lungs, the stars in her night. He was man and he was might. He was energy and he was silence, here but not here, . . . evil and elemental. All beauty and all beast.

"What . . . ?" she began, and then realized, suddenly, what was happening as Dax, her cloak in one fist, lowered himself down and over her body so that she was *inside* of the energy that coated him. "No," she moaned, feeling the ice-cold heat of him slide under her skin. "No, no, no . . ."

"Don't fight it. Don't fight me," he commanded.

And she couldn't. She honestly couldn't. She didn't want to. She just wanted to drift with him . . . to mold to him . . . *to meld with him.* It felt as if her skin were sliding away from her bones, as though her heart would soon burst through her ribs and give itself wholly to his hands. He was calling forth her soul. She knew it, and yet she couldn't care. There was a frightening harmony in the beating of their hearts, and she knew this was the end. She would follow those ghostly riders into a harsh netherworld, and there would be no return for her.

Bit by bit, he was smothering her, sucking at her soul. She felt the shimmer of it, dislodged now, finally free. Like a scent released, it rose . . . and rose . . . and—

"Dax." Robyn pressed her lips to his ear, her voice just a rasp of sound. She was weak. Too weak. Sickeningly weak. "Hear me. Help me. Dax. I need you. *Please.*"

It was as if a burst of sanity cleared Dax's head and his heart. Robyn knew he had heard her, for the evilness that gripped her receded just a bit, enough so that her soul whispered back and down, like a feather floating to earth. She caught it and held fast as sweet air filled her lungs, and even though the energy that surrounded her blazed like a bonfire, Robyn felt safe—safer than she'd been, at least.

Instead of stealing her soul, he shimmered her— *shimmered them*—back to Land's End in a whirl of energy that made Robyn's head go light and her body weightless. She knew that if not for Dax's arms around her she would have spun off into the night. But Dax kept her anchored to him, the hum of his immense power throbbing all around her. It seemed as if he moved them on the same path as light. Like a moonbeam, they passed miles in a mere moment, through night and air, forest and stone . . . right into the room she'd known since childhood.

It all happened with lightning speed, yet Robyn felt drugged and dreamy—as if the world had shifted while she and Dax remained still, just the two of them tucked together in a timeless nook of space. She could feel the beat of his heart, the heat of his skin, the rough growth of stubble on his jaw. Instead of the hard ground beneath her, there was the soft mattress she knew so well. There was the room where she'd spent the bulk of her youth, and there was pitch darkness and there was light . . . and always, always, there was Dax.

Stretched out on top of Robyn, his arms bent at the elbows and holding his weight, he stared down at her as the intense buzz of sound began to dissipate. The scent of lavender and fresh linens permeated the tang of energy, telling Robyn that whatever creature Dax had become, he was somehow managing to tone down some of its vast power.

She drew in a shaky breath, wondering if more riders would come charging into the apartment.

"You're safe now," he said, doubtless reading her thoughts. Not Dax's voice, but close.

"How do you know?"

"The stone, it's a barrier they cannot penetrate."

"But you just did—*we* just did."

"Because I am a Soul Smuggler, not a soul seeker. There is little that can stop me."

Robyn, so very thankful he hadn't harmed her, that he'd fought hard and kept the beast from consuming her, gathered her daring and reached up with both hands to frame his face. "No. You're not a Soul Smuggler. *You're Dax.*" She said the words clearly, succinctly, hoping Dax could hear her, that the beast within him would fully recede.

A shudder rippled through his taut body as man fought beast, and Robyn knew it was Dax's will that won out when he turned his face into her left palm and brushed his lips across the inside of her wrist, still tender from her fall. His gentleness took her breath away, igniting a wild hope inside of her.

Closing her eyes to the colorless veneer that was his skin, Robyn drew her hands down, to his shirtfront, and lower to its hem. Hands trembling, she tugged and pulled and pushed past the barrier, seeking Dax's warmth, wanting to find once again all that she'd experienced with him in the cottage. "Come back to me, Dax," she whispered. Robyn explored the tight, corded muscles of his abdomen. "Don't leave me." She drew her hands higher, over the smooth, sculpted details of his chest—and then discovered the ornament that dangled from a cord looped about his neck: a hammered, heart-shaped piece of silver that matched her own. She'd know it anywhere, it was that precious to her.

"What's the matter? You don't like what you've found?" It wasn't Dax's voice she heard, but twisted evilness that tunneled its voice up and out of Dax's body.

Robyn went perfectly still, her mind winging back to that horrid moment when the boy of her dreams—the lad who had held her future—found his death in a runaway carriage. She'd given him her heart that very day . . . she'd given him *this* heart, the one gifted to her by her mother and her aunt. The one that was part of a trio.

"Where did you get this?"

He didn't answer. Wouldn't. Not at first. And Robyn knew, she *knew*, he wanted her to believe the worst—and she did.

"Tell me," she demanded, curling her fist around the hammered silver. "Where? *How?*"

"Stolen." That green gaze of his once again shuttered to the color of darkened forest rain. "From a luckless lad."

"You *fiend.*" The words came out of her like a moan. She thought of the boy she'd met and lost—and missed even now—and felt her heart shatter all over again. "Tell me you didn't harm him." Robyn yanked at the cord, wanting to tear it from his neck. "Tell me, damn you, that you didn't take his soul."

"I am a Soul Smuggler. It's what I do." Muscles rippled as he leaned down toward her. "It's what I'll do to you."

Robyn, her mind filled with horror and heartache, hauled back, trying to scoot out from under him, the mattress making her clumsy as her elbows and heels sank deep into its thickness, her blasted cloak twisting about her shoes. He wavered in her vision, the sight of him smeared by her tears. It was Dax's face she saw, but the Phantom's heartlessness that crushed her.

"Get out," she said. "Leave Dax's body. *Now.*"

She heard the rise of energy again, harsher this time as Dax's body arced over hers, the beast bristling at her tone, her order. Tiny whips of power lashed at her, stinging wherever her skin was exposed. Robyn pressed her eyes shut, afraid the pulsating energy would snap the sight from them. The scent of his dark magic whisked up her nostrils, the taste of it tart as it slid down into her throat.

She felt the wash of arctic cold as he came closer, closer. She felt her soul tremble, as if called to, as if caressed. Even though her instinct for survival demanded that she fight, Robyn suddenly didn't have the strength. Her thoughts slid to the boy she'd met once and lost forever, to her mother who'd betrothed her to him, and to Dax, who suddenly reminded her of both.

Perhaps, once her soul lifted away as it ached to do, Robyn would be reunited with them—with her mother who left her too soon, with the boy who never left her heart . . . and with Dax. Where did he go when the Phantom emerged and the hunger for souls took root? Would she go there, too?

Enough. Her voice and yet . . . not.

Robyn sensed the sudden stillness in Dax's body, the fast whip of motion as the Phantom turned its attention from her to . . . something else. She snapped her eyes open, following his gaze with a twist of her head. There. In the far corner of her room, near the wardrobe, could be seen a flickering shadow on the stone wall. No, not a shadow, but light, Robyn realized. It was light that flickered as something, *someone*, walked toward them from a far distance, as if through a huge, great hall, as though the stone was no longer a wall but a passageway into that airy, ancient space. Nearer and nearer still, with singular purpose . . . until the small, distant shape took form: female, familiar, beloved.

"*Mama.*" Emotion bled out of Robyn as a terrible fragility gripped her, the tears in her eyes becoming a stream of wetness. Her mother. Here. Somehow. *Here.*

The Countess of Chelsea drew closer, until her size grew proportionate to the room . . . until, it seemed, the very room gave way to that ancient hall, expanding to allow another time, another place to lay itself over the present. There was torchlight and coolness and the scent of something precious in the air, as if time upon time upon time held a scent and it was *this*—harmony at its fullest, a perfect blend of every possibility in the universe. It was all revealed, like the fine webbing of a spider's silk, sensed only when light reflects in its wetness or when a body moves through it . . . and that moving body was her mother—ageless, a face of sheer beauty—heading with swift sureness straight for Dax who reared up and back, getting to his feet, the Phantom flaring hot and bright. His gaze slanted hard to a green gleam as he gave a hiss of power . . . and then shimmered into nothingness as the ancient hall spilled into the space where he'd been a mere second before.

Robyn scrambled up to a sitting position, stunned as she watched the form of her mother begin to move past. It was as if two opposing planes had scraped against each other, melded, and then become one, and in that swift span of time—as Robyn felt her mother's presence just as surely as she did the beat of her own heart—the countess deliberately brushed against the foot of the bed, dragging the tangle of Robyn's cloak to the floor.

Robyn lunged forward, intending to catch her mother's attention, her sleeve, *anything*, but she wasn't fast enough. There could be heard a scrape of energy, like the hulls of two ships butting off one from the other, followed by a distant *boom*, and then . . . silence. The whole became two halves once more. There was only Robyn, flat on her belly near the end of the bed—and her mother, never pausing, never losing her intense concentration, looking neither left nor right, but walking dead ahead . . . right through the opposite stone wall. Just as she did so, the ancient hall contracted into a mere funnel of torchlight and then nothing at all as the cool rush of air and the tang of time whispered away. Robyn, her lungs gone dry from the sudden absence of oxygen, her mind unable to push beyond the thought of heaving in a full breath, succumbed to the blackness that claimed her.

She came awake to a stir of fresh air across her face, the slant of candlelight against her closed eyelids. "Dax?"

"Gone, my lady."

Harry's voice. Robyn opened her eyes. The old man stood in the doorway, a hoop of yellow light from the fat candle in his left fist softening the lines of worry around his mouth. There was no softening the sharp concern in his watery blue gaze, though.

Robyn pushed herself up, ignoring the dizziness that swamped her. "Gone?" she asked, fearing the worst as the events of the night came back to her in a sudden rush. "Where? When?"

"To London. Hours ago, though I just now learned of it." Before she could ask why, Harry added, "To search for Lady A. You were correct, my lady, to be concerned about your aunt. I should have told you when you first asked, but she was always one to protect you. I felt it my duty to do the same."

"I know that, Harry. I would never doubt your judgment. Just please, tell me what's happened to her."

"I'm not certain. I only know she was at her town house in the city and was to have returned home by now. She had mentioned being close to solving a mystery from the past. I fear she has met with foul play, and now . . . Dax . . . and a few of his men have gone in search of any clue to her whereabouts."

Robyn digested the information. She had known her aunt was in trouble; she'd known it the moment she'd arrived at Land's End to find her gone. And she had known from the moment in the cabin with Dax, that he and Aunt Amy were in some way connected. "You talked with Dax? Before he left?"

"No. Not since last evening. It was Randolph who just now told me of their plans to leave before dawn. He said Dax rode out earlier. He also said Dax left orders for you to be secreted in a safe place—a place not even he knows about."

Robyn looked up, sharp. "What?"

"Dax was very specific in his request, Lady Robyn. He

wants you taken to a place he knows nothing about, a place far removed from Land's End, from whatever trouble has found your aunt . . . and from Misters Falconer and Drago. He left Sam, John, and Monty to see to your safety. Even now supplies are being packed, a carriage readied." He motioned to his right hand in which he held a valise. He set it near the door. "Bandages and antiseptic for your arm," he explained.

Robyn looked down at the valise. *Dax had thought of her.* Even through the haze of his Phantom, Dax had fought his way to the surface long enough to make plans for her safety, including clean dressings for her wound.

Into the silence, Harry asked, "Are you all right, my lady?"

Overwhelmed, Robyn sat motionless. "Yes. No. I—" She pressed one hand over her eyes, drew in a breath, blew it out. No. She wasn't all right. She was falling apart. "I saw my mother tonight, Harry." She dropped her hand to her lap and looked up at him. "Here. In this room."

That Harry didn't tell her it was impossible, that he merely stood still waiting to hear the rest of the tale, told Robyn that perhaps she wasn't bound for Bedlam.

"Wherever she is, I—I believe she tried to move out of it, or through it, or at least beyond it for a moment because she thought I was in danger. She wanted to help me. I know she did. Look. There." Robyn motioned to her cloak on the floor. "She brushed it off the bed, purposely, as if to tell me something. As if . . ."

". . . as if there's something about the cloak that she wants you to know," Harry finished for her, moving inside the room at Robyn's nod.

They headed for the tangled mass of fabric, Robyn kneeling to swipe it up from the floor as Harry held the candle close, its light flicking odd shadows around them and giving his white wisps of hair a ghostly sheen. They each saw the rent in the fabric at the same time, along the lined, quilted collar. Had it been torn as her mother passed by, sending it to the floor—or before that, perhaps by the Phantom as he'd dragged Robyn into the hollow of Dax's arms? "It's just as you said, Harry. There *is* something here." Robyn began ripping out threads until she had the whole of the thickly quilted collar pulled apart . . . and there, folded like a fan deep in the collar, was an oilskin, and inside of it a key.

"It looks to be a map," Robyn said, smoothing the oilskin over her lap. Cut into the shape of a ragged square, it depicted in crude outline the lay of northern London Town at the bottom, and near the top a series of lines and dashes, with the words *bridge* and *barrow*, and at the very top the word *ROSE* spelled out across the whole of the material. "What do you think it all means?"

"I don't know. I've never seen the map. But the key, if I'm not mistaken, is to the wardrobe, there."

Robyn followed Harry's gaze to the huge cedar wardrobe and the two drawers of its massive base. The key was a perfect fit. In the top drawer were her mother's things—lace and kerchiefs and a cashmere shawl, all smelling of the countess, of wildflowers unfurling in morning's hush. Robyn felt the burn of tears, of loneliness. Oh, how she missed her mother—that scent. She swallowed hard, past the hurt, and pulled open the bottom drawer. More memories, this time in the shape of gloves—kidskin, silk, satin, and more—and beneath them a heavy pelisse with four frog closures and plushy fur trim . . . and inside of it a strongbox. Robyn glanced at Harry. The old man's blue eyes were keen on her as the candle's light danced between them.

Robyn had kissed a phantom this night, had been attacked by specters, and had watched her mother—whom she'd buried over a year ago—walk through her room. Whatever the strongbox held wouldn't surprise her, she told herself. Nothing could surprise her this night. Nothing.

She lifted the lid.

There, on a bed of banknotes, lay a half-dozen hearts of hammered silver—all similar to the one she wore on a ribbon about her neck, to the one Dax wore. Similar . . . and yet flawed. They weren't ancient pieces. There was a precision to them that smacked of man's touch.

"Replicas," Robyn said.

"To the very pieces your mother and aunt intended for you," Harry replied, and when she looked up at him, her brows lifting, he added with a smile, "I know at least that much. Lady A always told me that you've a heart for healing and for magic, and that the silver was part of that magic."

Robyn pressed her eyes shut, remembering and remembering. . . . "Aunt Amy once told me that the silver would be my life and my purpose. I was so young, though, I eventually forgot her words. But I remember them now, Harry." She opened her eyes. "I remember her sharing the ancient silver with me, and showing me the replicas, telling me that they had been fashioned by a Lord Thomas Ballinger." Robyn began to dig through the piles of banknotes. She found a small velvet pouch at the bottom of the strongbox. Inside of it was a ring and several brooches—but nothing else. "It isn't here."

"My lady?"

"The third heart. It isn't here. I have one that I wear . . . I gave one as a gift when I was just a girl . . . and the third one—*it isn't here.* Why hide the key and the map in the cloak if the third piece of silver isn't here?"

Harry leaned forward, frowning, thinking, and then in a hushed voice said, "Ah, my lady, but that is precisely why the key and the map were hidden in the cloak. Because what is here"—he pointed to the contents of the strongbox—"and what is there"—to the map—"will most likely lead one to the third piece of ancient silver."

Robyn sat back on her heels, stunned, but nodding in agreement. She locked her gaze with Harry's. "Which means the attack on Mattie and me in the woods wasn't a random act of thievery." Dread dribbled down Robyn's spine. "Those men wanted the cloak, and whoever hired them wants the silver—and may even have Aunt Amy." Her thoughts winged back to the cabin where the soul seekers had come, where Dax, as Phantom, had fought to protect her. She'd thought the specters had lunged for her throat . . . but perhaps it had been the hammered silver they sought.

"Dax needs to know about this," Harry was saying as he hauled himself up with one hand clutching the wardrobe. "I'll send a runner after them. I'll—"

"No," Robyn cut in. "I'll go."

The old man shook his head, clearly appalled at the idea. "Though I risk my position, I must tell you no. His Gr—er, Dax, was very clear in the orders he left, Lady Robyn. I'm to get you packed and whisked to a safe, secret place—and then I am to wait here for word from either Lady A or . . . Dax."

There were things he wasn't telling her, Robyn knew. Things about Dax and her aunt, even herself. She loved the old man for his stalwart loyalty, and she loved him for checking on her tonight with a candle in his fist and his heart in his throat because he knew about Dax's dark legacy—or at least he knew a little of it—and even so, he'd told Robyn earlier where to find Dax and had held firm to the faith that Dax wouldn't harm her.

It was because of that love that Robyn let a small white lie lift to life between them. "You promise you'll send word to me the moment you learn anything?"

"Of course, my lady."

"Very well, then. Send a runner after Dax." She handed him the map, but kept the strongbox.

Harry pocketed the oilskin, then moved to light a single lamp for her before leaving. "I've already roused your maid," he said. "She'll be in soon to pack what you need. I'll send Sam up for your trunks. He'll lead you out through Lady A's private entrance; that way you'll avoid Misters Falconer and Drago."

Once again, Robyn had almost forgotten about Falconer and his threats. Almost. "He won't be pleased to find me gone, Harry."

"I can deal with him, my lady."

"Yes." She smiled. "You can." Harry could handle anyone. "It's my father's servants I'm worried about."

"Your maid is to go with you. Tom Coachman and Benjamin can remain at Land's End. You know your aunt will find work for them if need be."

Robyn felt her throat clog with emotion. "Thank you, Harry. And thank you, too, for . . . listening to me talk about my mother."

"I'm glad to know she is watching over you."

Robyn caught the glimmer of tears in his eyes as the old man hurried out of the apartment. She watched until the glow of his candle faded away, and then glanced down at the things she'd discovered. She spilled the contents of the pouch into one hand. The ring was gold, heavy and huge, with a cherry red ruby in its center flanked by two shields with elaborate markings upon them. Two lions, each raised on hindquarters, were etched into the gold as though holding up both the shields and the ruby. It was obviously a signet ring, the shields denoting a family crest. But whose? And why had Aunt Amy added it to the strongbox with the silver and banknotes?

Robyn had no idea but was determined to find out. She slipped everything back into the pouch, scooped up the banknotes, then tucked everything inside the valise. She packed a few things—a very few—on top of the bandages and antiseptic, quickly changed from her gown to a riding habit, and headed for her aunt's apartments and the hidden entrance.

She had to hurry. Dax was doubtless miles away by now.

Chapter Fourteen

He felt her—her passion, her purpose—long before he could hear her in the far distance. She was the wind that whispered through spring's green. She was the heat of the sun and the harmony of the earth. She was all of this and more as she followed him, her heart a strong, thrilling beat, the horse beneath her eating ground with its long strides. She'd saddled the animal herself. He knew that instantly. Knew, too, that she'd fairly flown over lesser roads, taking shortcuts she'd known since girlhood, even chancing wide fields and wild land, risking the animal's limbs and her own neck to try and catch up to him.

Dax knew all of this and marveled that he'd ever assumed she would go willingly to some undisclosed place with Monty as coachman and Sam and John as guard. She was made of stronger stuff than that—it was in her heritage, in her very blood to meet every obstacle head-on. He knew that now. It had been stupid and foolish of him to believe she would simply forget the night in the cabin, the riders that had come, the Phantom that had tried to steal her soul and was alive in him still. That wasn't her way. Not at all.

The dark magic in him had never truly toned down since midnight. He wasn't outwardly radiating his Phantom, but he wasn't normal, not by far—which was why he didn't backtrack to Robyn, but let her come to him. Besides, he could perceive another in her wake: Sam, tracking her. Obviously they'd noted her absence back at Land's End and had sent him after her. If there was trouble for Robyn, Sam was close enough to help.

The odds that Dax would be able to tamp down his Phantom before Robyn reached him were slim, though. Something had shifted—in him, around him—*something*. It was becoming more and more difficult to separate man from Phantom.

At long last he heard her approach—the hoofbeats of a single horse, coming at a fast clip. Dax wasn't surprised when the other men tensed. Until now, he, Randolph, and Bones had met only with a fast-moving Royal Mail coach and a stage or two carrying passengers into the heart of the South Downs. At the pace Robyn had set, she wouldn't be slowing any too easily. It wouldn't help her to find three riders strung across the roadway, so Dax motioned them off the road. Wheeling his big black horse around, managing the animal into the thicket, he asked Randolph and Bones to stay put for a while . . . just as she came around the bend in a thunder of hooves—louder, faster than was safe.

"Faith," Dax muttered, seeing nothing for a split second but a blur whiz past. Dax charged after her, the wind funnel of dirt kicked up by her horse smacking his face, smarting his eyes. He'd have shouted her name, but knew his voice would be drowned in the clatter of hooves, whipped away by the wind. Instead, he whispered it, letting his Phantom move it on magic to curl and settle inside the shell of her ear: *Robyn*.

Just a breath of her name, and he was gaining on her.

In the space of three gallops, he was beside her.

Standing up in his stirrups, Dax reached out his right arm, grasped the left rein of her mount and eased upward. The animal let out a whinny, rolling a startled gaze toward him.

"Whoa!"

"Dax."

Robyn turned her face to his, and in that scant second when she first realized it was truly him beside her, Dax's heart squeezed. Time seemed to still as he looked into her violet eyes and saw a flash of happiness. She was glad to see him—no matter all that had happened between them last night, there was an instant of happiness sprung to life in her at the sight of him.

"Aye, it's me," he said, wanting nothing more than to drag her from her saddle and onto his own so that he could touch every part of her, make certain the fiend in him hadn't harmed her. "Help me slow this animal," he said, voice rough with emotion, "before you find yourself tossed headfirst over its ears."

She nodded, trying, but the roan was nervy, wild, so Dax once again pulled up on the rein. The animal blew out a breath, tried to jerk its head to the side, then gave up the fight, calming by degrees.

Finally in pace, the animals slowed their wicked speed—and Dax could drink his fill of Robyn. God, she was gorgeous, more beautiful than anything he'd ever seen or known, or ever would. She'd inherited every bit of her mother's grace. He knew that now. He'd seen with his own eyes the Countess of Chelsea as she'd moved like a vision through Robyn's room last night. The Curse in him had curled tight at the sight, the beast hissing as if burned by angel fire, but the man in him had been spellbound, blessed to get a glimpse of the one who had given Robyn life, had molded her into the spirited woman Dax had fallen in love with all over again.

Dax hadn't wanted to leave Robyn. Not alone. Not after she'd witnessed her mother's ghost moving through walls, willing to face down a Phantom. To stay, though, would have meant to take Robyn's soul . . . and so he'd shimmered into nothingness, only to materialize outside, in the darkest depths of the night. He'd clawed his way to a sane moment, found Randolph, and told him to send Harry to look after Robyn, to arrange for Sam and John and Monty to whisk her away to safety. He'd shimmered back to the cottage, gathered his things, then had ridden hard away, intending to keep well clear of any unsuspecting souls until the Phantom had simmered down to just a low boil. But its power echoed through him even now.

"Robyn. Last night . . ." He wanted to ask how she'd fared when he left, if he'd hurt her, if seeing her mother had been too much after all that had happened, but the evilness in him wouldn't allow the words to form. The cold, heartless creature bit hard at the emotion washing through him.

"Dax, it wasn't you. I know that." Her voice was breathy, the apples of her cheeks speckled with mud from her mad dash. "I'm all right. Truly." She was breathing hard still, her chest rising and falling. Her eyes were a dark, dusky violet in the day's bright light.

Brave, beautiful, and his betrothed, he thought—or at least she had been, once. Dax forced himself to focus. To say what needed to be said. "You shouldn't have followed me. It was a foolish thing to do. It's dangerous for you to be here. *I'm* dangerous."

"If that were so, Dax, I never would have survived the night . . . but I did, and I'm here, and I know you're heading to Town in search of my aunt. I know because Harry told me. I can help you find her."

"Robyn—"

"It's true. I can."

"You're going back. Now." Her reins still held tight in one gloved hand, Dax made a motion to turn the animals about.

"No. Wait."

Robyn covered his hand with hers, and he felt her— through kidskin and thick leather, he felt her heat and her heart. Dax looked up, instantly caught in the depths of her gaze. He waited, listening.

"Last night, my mother . . . she led me to a box that she, or possibly my aunt, had hidden. You saw her, Dax. I know you did. She was in that room with us, and the Phantom was irritated by her presence—which tells me that whatever dwells within you isn't omnipotent. It has a weakness, Dax, my mother proved that to us."

She let go of him, reached for the small valise she'd lashed to the saddle, dug inside of it, and pulled forth a small drawstring pouch, spilling its contents into her left palm—a tumble of silver hearts, brooches of the same . . . and a ring—a ring he knew well.

The sun's light flashed in its ruby, kicked starbursts to life in its gold. All the while Dax could hear a voice in his head, distant but dear: his father, telling the boy he'd once been that one day the ring would belong to him. He felt caught in a warping of time as he recalled that day with his father, sun streaming through a tall window, his mother seated near him, smiling—and this moment, the day's sun hot on his neck, bright on the brim of Robyn's riding hat, as he listened to her words. As she told him of a trio of talismans hammered into hearts, and how he wore one and she another, but that the third was . . . missing, perhaps. Of how the miscreants who'd attacked her and her maid had wanted the cloak she wore, and that that's where she and Harry had found an oilcloth with a map sketched on it and a key, which led her to a strongbox filled with silver replicas of the talismans. Of how she knew the name of the person who had fashioned the replicas and that perhaps this man knew something or might be able to lead them to something, and of how she believed it all might be connected: the silver, her aunt's disappearance, her mother's appearance, the oilcloth with its map markings . . . all of it.

"The man is in London," Robyn continued, unaware of Dax's chaotic thoughts. "He still lives. We can find him and ask him all he knows about the pieces, and—and about the marks on the oilcloth, which Harry gave to one of your men. I can get an audience with him, Dax, I *know*

I can, for his is a name I've heard not only my aunt mention, but my father as well. My name alone will assure me a moment of his time, and that's all I'll need."

But surely if Amy had thought the creator of the silver pieces could have aided in solving any mystery, she'd have sought the man out by now, Dax thought. Then again, perhaps she had . . . and that was why she was missing.

The beast in him shimmered, not liking thoughts of hearth and home and a family long gone from him dancing through his head, not liking the emotion that was beginning to build in his heart and bunch tight.

"Dax, are you listening to me? I know where to find this man."

"I hear you," he said darkly, the evil in him rising, widening, elbowing aside any good, "and the answer is no."

"What do you mean, *no*?"

He had to fight to get the words out. "You're not going to London. You're not getting involved in this."

"I already *am* involved. I was accosted while wearing that cloak, the very same given to me by my aunt . . . and *she* is missing."

"Which is why I'm taking you back."

He started to lean forward, but Robyn pulled up on the leads before he could reach them, her roan prancing sideways at her quick motion. "I'm going with you, Dax."

Dax sensed a snap of cold deep inside his body, and a flare of green sparked in his gaze. "What, last night wasn't hideous enough for you?" The Phantom wanted to cease with the talk and simply smother her in dark magic. "You'll have it. In fact, I can promise you'll have it every night, precisely at midnight, unless of course by some act of God we can manage to squeeze ourselves into a handy slab of rock. That won't matter, though, because if the riders don't murder you, the Phantom in me will."

He'd expected her to turn away. She didn't. "You go through that every night?" She took his silence as a yes. "Oh, Dax." And her voice was a soft caress that soothed.

"Dammit, Robyn, I don't want your pity. I want you far away from me. I want you safe."

"I won't abandon you."

"Consider it self-preservation."

She shook her head. "I'd rather face those riders and whatever is inside you than the man my father has sent to fetch me." A beat of silence, and then, "His name is Falconer. He works for a Lord Reginald Morely. Both men, I'm learning, are very good with threats. I don't doubt they'll carry through with each and every one of them."

Dax went stone still, the Curse in him coiling tight at the thought of someone—anyone—threatening Robyn. The beast in him claimed her as his own, to do with as he wished, while the man in him cherished her above all other things. B'god but he'd snap the life from them. "Is Falconer the one who found us in the study?" At her nod, he promised, "I'll deal with him, and this Morely, and every bloody threat they pose to you."

"Are you going to storm all my castles at once?"

"If that's what it takes to see you safe, then yes."

Her gaze drank him in. "And what about you, Dax?" she whispered. "Who will see you safe?"

The question jarred him. Not since his mentor had anyone truly worried over him. "I'm not your concern."

"No?" Robyn looked down, the brim of her hat hiding her expression. "I wonder." She stirred the hearts in her palm with one gloved fingertip. "Perhaps all of this was meant to be, Dax. You. Me. My aunt. My mother. Have you thought of that?"

Yes. No. He didn't know. The only thing he knew for certain was that Robyn had been a part of his every thought since that moment all those years ago when he'd first met her in the cottage. "It's a cruel fate, then. I don't want to drag you any further into my hell, Robyn."

"You're not dragging me. I come willing."

"I can't allow it. You're going back to Land's End."

She snapped her palm shut, lifted her face, and said

calmly, "No. I'm not." And he saw her mother in her at that moment, and her aunt, and a long march of women from whom she'd descended, and he loved them all and he loved her most—for her tenacity, for being so true.

Just then, Randolph and Bones rounded the bend and came to a halt alongside Dax. "My lady," said Randolph, sketching a quick bow from the seat of his saddle.

"Hello, Randolph. Bones." Robyn smiled, her tone light, as if she'd just met with them while out for a morning's ride.

Bones dragged the hat from his head, nodded in respect, then quickly glanced at Dax. "We be headin' back?" he asked.

"Yes," Dax said, the man in him beating down the evil. Not for long, though; he could never hold the Curse down for long.

Randolph shot Bones a look, as if to say *pay up.*

"No," Robyn quickly replied.

And it was Bones's turn to smile.

In the end, Dax let Robyn have her way and her will because she was so damned determined, and because he loved that about her . . . and because, blast it all, the beast in him loved it more. She gave him the pouch with its hearts and its brooches and his father's ring, and he tucked it into his saddle packs before the weight of his father's ring crushed the boy that still dwelled within him.

The rest of the day melted away into a trail of miles, mud, and dust, and though they stopped a few times, Dax kept a swift pace. If his guess was correct, Falconer and his man had set out in hot pursuit of Robyn once they'd realized she'd fled from Land's End. The question was, how long had it been before they'd realized it—an hour, a few hours? The men could be as close as the last turn in the road. Had Dax interacted with them, he could have used his dark gifts to track their location, but as it was, he was as blind to their location as any other mortal.

Dax had no intention of stopping at any inn—not with the riders that came each midnight or the evil that crawled beneath his skin. Add to that the fact that Robyn was far too beautiful and her clothing too fine for anyone in a common room not to remember her and relay the information to anyone asking, and there existed a need for Dax to make use of the life he once lived at Jemmy's side.

Just as the edge of the earth began to swallow the sun, Dax led the way to a livery stable at the easternmost side of a village they wouldn't have to pass through until morning. With the area deserted, chances were strong that no one had seen their approach. The place was roomy, clean, and best of all was built of stone, thick slabs taken from the nearby fields and pieced together with precision. There would be no rush of the riders this night; they wouldn't be able to sense Dax—or Robyn—beyond the rock.

The owner's name was Sims. He'd been one of many to join Jemmy in his illegal ventures, though unlike the others he'd harbored visions of respectability. Eventually, he'd taken his earnings and bought himself a stable and some horses, setting himself up as a businessman. In the years since, he'd married, started a family. Dax had always liked him. More than that, he trusted him.

It took only a few shared words for Sims to remember Dax, and though he had no extra space in the small home he shared with his wife and four children, he offered Dax the use of his stables for the night. "There's room in the hayloft," he said, "and in the tack room beyond the stalls."

Dax thanked the man, reaching into his saddle pack to pay him for his generosity.

Sims shook his head. "I won't be taking your money, Dax. Though you were just a boy when last I saw you, you saved my neck more than a few times. Use whatever you need for your horses. You're in luck, as there are more than a few empty stalls this night, and my wife, Meg, and her sister have spent the day making meat pies. I can bring enough for sharing. Some ale, too."

True to his word, Sims returned within an hour, his oldest son, Thomas, with him. Between them they brought the promised food and drink, plus a bucket of warm water, soap, and clean but threadbare linen for washing.

"For the lady," said Sims, nodding to the water and soap. "She doesn't have the stamp of one accustomed to the wear of the road."

Dax thanked him. He knew the many miles Robyn had ridden since before dawn, and the fast pace she'd set for herself in catching up to him had taken a toll.

Lowering his voice, Dax said, "There may be some who come behind us, questioning after her whereabouts."

"They'll get nothing from me other than I never laid eyes on her—or you and your men. Only Meg, me, and our boy know you're here."

Dax watched as the tall, lanky youth dished out the food, receiving a warm smile from Robyn for his troubles. The boy blushed. The Phantom radiated its displeasure. Dax felt his lips curl, his hands ball into fists . . . but he sucked in a breath, fighting it, always fighting for control. "He resembles the you I remember," he said to Sims.

The older man smiled "He's a far sight better than I was at his age. He hasn't known a dishonest day in his life, and God willing never will. Meg and me, we work hard, determined none of our own will ever know the feel of an empty belly or what it's like to live with no home and little hope, like we did all those years ago with Jemmy." After a moment, he asked, "Where is he, by the way? Do you know?"

Oh yes. Dax knew. "Dead."

Sims was quiet for a second, and then nodded, as if to say, *What other end could come for one of Jemmy's ilk?* "I only hope it was quick."

It had been, very; the Soul Smuggler in him had made certain of that. Dax didn't say the words. He said nothing at all.

"Those were lean years with Jemmy," Sims said into the quiet, "but they gave me a strong thirst for a better life.

And I found it." He looked over at Dax. "What about you? You ready to settle down, take a wife, create a child or two of your own?"

Though the fiend in him snarled at the idea, the man in him fastened his gaze on Robyn as she took a bite of meat pie. She savored the mouthful as though it were the most succulent thing she'd ever tasted and then beamed a smile up at Thomas, who blushed some more. Dax saw the flash of her even, white teeth as she told the boy to give her compliments to his mother, and then she engaged him in conversation about his life, his siblings, his work at the stable with his father.

"I do yearn for a wife," Dax said softly, watching Robyn, his gaze turning dark with want, "a home of our own, and children to fill it."

"So why the wait?"

He shook his head, dragging his gaze to his old friend. "It's a long story. Complicated."

"If I remember, most things with you always were. For what it's worth, Dax, from the minute Jemmy brought you into camp, I knew you didn't belong. I hoped then, as I do now, that one day soon you would find where it is you do belong." He clasped his hand atop Dax's shoulder, gave it a friendly squeeze, and then said good night. "I'll see you off in the morning," he promised, and called to his son, telling him it was time to head home.

Maybe it was the touch that prompted Dax, or perhaps it was the talk of friendship and shared pain. Whatever it was, it stirred the man in Dax and pulled him up and out of the boiling bite of his Phantom.

"There's something more I need."

Sims paused, motioning for Thomas to go outside ahead of him. "I'm listening."

Dax turned his back to the others, his voice dropping to a low whisper. "I need to send the lady back the way she came. I need some fast horses, a sturdy carriage. Most of all I need a seasoned driver with a deadly aim."

Sims nodded, considering the request. "The cattle I've got right here and you're more than welcome to borrow them for as long as you need. I can get you a carriage . . . but as for the driver? I'd do it myself, but these days I never leave my family alone through the night. All I can do is point you in the direction of a man I trust."

"Where?"

"Back room of the inn. He rolls dice there every night."

"You're certain he can shoot?"

"Better than even Jemmy."

It was the assurance Dax needed. He shook the man's hand and then watched as he headed outside to his son. Turning, Dax found Robyn's gaze on him, tight.

He wondered how much she'd overheard, but then he knew. He could read it in the shadows of her eyes, the hitch of her breath, and he wondered if she had any idea at all about the war he fought every day, just to stay sane.

"Shall I take the first watch?" Randolph asked, getting to his feet.

Dax shook his head, his gaze never leaving Robyn. "I'll take care of it. You and Bones can bed down in the tack room. Lady Robyn will have the loft."

Only when she and Dax were alone did Robyn speak.

"You made a promise to me in the cabin last night. Do you remember it?"

Oh, yes. He remembered. Every second of every moment he'd ever spent near her was etched into his mind.

But he steeled himself. To the memories and to the magic that was this woman who had haunted his dreams and his daylight for as long as he could remember. He steeled himself, needing to be firm, emotionless.

"You don't belong with me, Robyn."

"So you keep saying."

"It isn't *safe.*"

"I've already told you, I'd rather face the perils of the beast in you than the ruthlessness of Falconer."

"I never said I was sending you back to him."

"Wherever you send me, he'll find me." Slowly, she rose to her feet. "No matter who you hire to spirit me away from here, *from you*, I'll find my way back," she said, "and then I'll help you find my aunt, and then I'll help you face whatever is inside of you . . . and then . . ."

He waited, silent and listening, but she didn't finish.

She simply turned away and headed for the ladder and the loft above.

Dax let her go.

He couldn't keep her with him. *He couldn't*. To do so would be to put her life in further jeopardy . . . would leave her prey to his own love and lust for her. Far better just to cut their ties now, to send her to some safe space.

A long while later, Dax stood in the shadows outside the stables, his Phantom focused on signs of anyone hovering about. There were none. The night was bright from a fat moon and was quiet, save for the sounds of male laughter and voices from the common room of the inn Dax hadn't bothered to locate. As he'd held watch in the shadows, he'd tumbled over and over in his mind the idea of putting Robyn into a carriage with a driver he didn't know, then trusting the fellow to get her safely back to Land's End, to Harry and his men. The more he thought about it, the more he decided it was a course of action he couldn't take. Now that he had Robyn with him he didn't want to let her out of his sight. He was afraid of trusting her welfare to the driver of a fast-moving carriage, to anyone but himself. Yet, that was his problem: *He* was her greatest threat. The man in him wanted her heart, the fiend in him craved her soul—and neither one wanted to let go.

Dax leaned back against the rough stone of the stable wall and blew out a breath of agitation.

He'd trust her to Randolph, he decided, whether the fiend in him liked it or not and whether or not Robyn would like it. Randolph could get her back to Harry, who in turn would see that she was taken somewhere safe. Dax

would make use of the carriage and cattle Sims had offered and have Randolph take Robyn out of here before
first light. He'd get everything ready himself. He'd do it
before the Phantom rose, and then he'd ride far and fast
from here so that when the Phantom hungered for
Robyn, he'd be nowhere near her. He'd fight the bloody
Curse in him with everything he had. He'd rip out his
own heart if that's what it took to keep her safe.

His decision made, Dax took one last look around the
area and then headed inside. Midnight wasn't far off—an
hour, maybe less.

A lone lantern, hanging from a hook near the door,
burned a soft light that lit only the entranceway of the stables. Dax could hear the snores of his men coming from
the far end of the building. Directly above him, there came
no sound at all.

Knowing he wouldn't see Robyn again after tonight,
Dax tipped his head back, ready to gather the gifts of his
dark Curse in order to peer past wood and nails and see
her. He wanted to make certain she'd found a comfortable spot in which to sleep. He wanted to gaze at her one
last time, to burn her image on the back of his eyelids so
that he'd never forget the sight of her, no matter how
many years his Curse kept him in existence.

But he couldn't do it, couldn't use his dark gifts for his
last look at her. He wanted to view her as a man would,
not as a fiend, so he grabbed the lantern from its hook
and climbed the ladder.

As soon as he reached the loft floor, he knew he'd made
a mistake.

The space held a sweet, earthy scent laced with a whisper of the night's air. There were a few sheaves of hay here
and there, but mostly loose straw. Robyn, fully awake, sat
on a small stool. Nearby was a small opening in the stone
with wooden panels that swung inward. She'd opened the
panels several inches, allowing beams of moon glow to
stream inside. Her dark hair all aglimmer, she looked to

be spun from a fairy tale, a beauty of such magic and rich radiance that she seemed not of this world.

She'd shed her jacket and boots, had washed the dust of the road from her, and wore only her chemisette and riding skirt, her trim, stocking-clad ankles showing in full, generous view. Near her feet was the small valise she'd strapped to her saddle, out of which spilled several rolls of bandages.

As though she felt the heat of him, Robyn turned.

The sight of her face framed by her unbound hair nearly took Dax's breath away. He wanted to run his fingers through the glossy tresses, wanted to wind a strand around his wrist, making himself a prisoner to her as he gently drew her body flush against his own. Her eyes were rich pools of violet, the color reminding him of that moment when daylight surrenders in a slow, easy glide into the vastness of what will soon become midnight's light-devouring depths.

Watching her watch him made Dax suddenly wonder if he were that midnight . . . and she the daylight his blackness would soon devour.

BOOK FOUR

The Beloved

Chapter Fifteen

"I came to check on you," Dax said as their gazes met and held. "To make certain you're safe. Asleep." *To look at you one last time.*

Robyn smiled, as if she'd been expecting him—or had wished him into being . . . here, now, with her. "I'm safe, but not asleep. Sleep would only hurry the dawn and I don't want that, not tonight." She motioned to the moonlight washing inside through the opening of the loft, a pale tract of phosphorescence. "You don't mind that I opened the doors, do you? The dust and scent of the hay was sharp. Since it's not yet midnight I thought it would be all right."

Gad, but she'd managed to open every door within him, why not the upper ones of this old livery stable? Besides, the riders couldn't sense anyone or anything surrounded by stone.

"It should be fine," he said. As long as neither of them stuck out a limb, as long as no light showed from the loft, they shouldn't have a problem with the riders or be found by anyone who might have trailed her. So thinking, Dax turned down the wick of the lantern, extinguishing its glow, and then set the thing on the timbers.

Darkness swallowed him while Robyn remained lit by the moon, her eyes violet splendor in the silvery sheen, her hair luminous in the shimmering light. He felt entranced, as though she were woven of nothing but his heart's deepest desires. He imagined he could see a look of longing in her gaze, a longing as deep and as keen as the one aching in his chest.

As soon as the thought entered his head, Dax banished it. The best thing for Robyn, the safest thing was that she not learn to care for him, that he not allow her to get too close. So long as she remained emotionally and physically distant from him, she had a chance to survive—something his parents hadn't been able to do, nor Sir Dysart, and perhaps not even Amy.

Steeling his insides, grinding down hard on his wandering thoughts, Dax made a motion to climb down the ladder. "If you don't need anything, I'll go below and—"

"But I do. Need something."

The pull of her voice, the heat of her words caused Dax to hold perfectly still. He watched as Robyn nudged the rolls of bandages at her feet with one stocking-clad toe.

"I've been avoiding the task of changing my dressing, not quite certain I can manage it on my own. I'd wanted to ask for help earlier, but I . . . I feared you would only scold me again for following you."

Faith, he thought, chiding himself for not thinking of her every comfort. "Of course I'll change the bandage." He climbed the last rungs of the ladder, leaving the unlit lantern behind. As he moved toward Robyn he told himself he'd simply see to her wound, make sure she was comfortable, and then leave.

But as soon as he came beside her, as soon as he stepped into the white slant of the moon's glow, Dax felt undone. Dazed. As though he'd left safety behind and had entered a space where magic and memory mixed to create a heady brew that would soon drown him.

He watched as Robyn leaned down and lifted a roll of bandages, her movement sending the scent of her into his body. She smelled faintly of the day's heat, the night's coolness, and that sweet, heady essence that was all her own. Dax felt his head grow light. He felt his heart squeeze and his testicles tighten. He felt at once lost and as if he'd just found home. Lord, but she was his every thought, his every emotion, and it was killing him not to tell her of their past, not to tell her that she was once his betrothed, that she was his first love and his last . . . that she was his everything. God, how he wanted her, *needed* her.

He clenched his jaw, the Curse in him uncoiling, the Phantom hungering for her soul. "There's soap below. And water," he muttered, looking for an avenue of escape, if only for a moment—time enough to calm his racing heart, his rising passion. To try to tame the fierceness of the Phantom. "I'll go get them."

"They're already here." Robyn motioned to her left. There, on the timbers, sat the pail of water, as well as the soap and one of the washrags Sims and his son had brought.

Robyn had hauled it all up the ladder, he supposed. The stool, too. Wanting to make certain she hadn't opened the wound, and wanting to make certain it didn't fester into something nasty, he hunkered down, dragging the pail toward him, sloshing droplets over the rim. Before he could reach the soap and linen, Robyn did, placing both beside the pail.

"You seem . . . agitated," she said.

Cursed is more like it, he wanted to say. *And wildly aroused by the mere sight of you,* he wanted to add.

But he didn't utter any of those words because suddenly all he could feel was the snap of frigid cold deep within, followed by the familiar flare of heat as the Phantom grew. It didn't like the emotional surges raging in Dax, didn't like all the want and need and love and lust boiling inside of him. Dax could feel the Phantom rise, moving muscle, pushing against his skin. His fingers felt large and clumsy as he tried to work the fine material of Robyn's sleeve up and over the bandage's bulk.

"You're not safe around me."

"Shh," she whispered. And then, "Here . . . I'll pull my arm out of the sleeve and—"

He fully intended to stop her, but with an abandon that both excited and worried him she shrugged free of the sleeve . . . and then all he saw was the loveliest shoulder, a space of white that clung to the curve of the most magnificent breast and a nipple that was pearl-hard and purely gorgeous. She wore no corset, just a petticoat with a bodice that did little to conceal her lushness. Dax's breath left his lungs in a rush.

"Robyn." He intended to remind her that she wasn't safe from his Phantom, to warn her that he was hard and heavy with need for her and she was so bloody gorgeous he couldn't think clearly, but she silenced him with just a look, nodded toward the bandage on her arm, then leaned down to dip the washrag in the water.

As if with her nod she'd laced the air with a spell that could soothe the beast in him, Dax moved to her unspoken command. He eased forward, placing his weight on the balls of his feet, his elbows on his knees. Carefully, he peeled off the layers of linen, trying hard to focus his thoughts on the wound and not the woman.

Impossible.

Her skin was incredibly soft. He remembered well the sight of her half-clothed body. He'd viewed nearly every inch of her while in his caves, had touched the same while in the cottage. He knew the turn of her hips, the line of her trim waist, the slight curve of her belly, the enticing silk of her inner thighs. . . . Knowing what was still hidden from view enflamed him.

He tossed aside the old bandages and took the washrag that Robyn instantly offered. His gaze met and held with hers for a fraction of a second, their fingers touching, the wetness of hers further inciting him.

Tamping down his arousal, Dax took the rag and carefully cleansed her wound. The skin was mending. She'd not opened the wound during her mad dash from Land's End or the climb into the loft, thank God. Once it was cleaned, he gently dabbed at the bruised site, then folded the cloth and worked it around the injured skin, taking care to clean away any trace of anything that could lead to infection. Satisfied, he took the roll of linen she handed him, tore off a strip, then dabbed the area dry.

By the time he was finished Robyn had the small bottle of antiseptic in her hand. Passing it to him, she held valiantly still as he applied it, and though he knew it must sting, she didn't flinch as the liquid penetrated the deepest valleys of her abrasion.

Dabbing away the traces that bled down her arm, Dax glanced up, expecting to find Robyn's face a mask of pain.

But she wasn't grimacing.

Instead, her gaze was fixed on him, her thoughts clearly not on her wound. There was passion written on her features—in the way her mouth parted slightly, her dusky-rose lips ready to kiss and be kissed; in the lift of her chin; in the sparkles of interest he could see in the depths of her eyes.

Dax hauled his gaze from hers. In a hurry now, knowing the moment was fast spiraling out of control, he wrapped a new bandage about her arm, tying it firmly, but not too tight, telling himself that he'd simply gather the old bandages, get to his feet, and *get out*. As he washed his hands and dried them, he told himself he'd tell her goodnight and then he'd go and she'd be safe and he'd stay clear of her through dawn, and then Randolph would deliver her to Harry and . . .

Foolish hopes—Dax knew this in the next instant when he made a motion to move away and Robyn reached out, her right hand touching his shoulder. Like lightning lacing the length of him, he felt the force of her touch burrow deep down inside to the very root of his being, where it exploded in a hot burst of violent need.

Dax drew in a shuddering breath, fighting the pull, fighting the thousand different ways Robyn enticed him. It was dangerous to stay, dangerous to linger so near to her.

She smelled too good and her body was far too inviting. To stay would be to ravish her, to claim her, to finally make her his own even as the fiend in him smuggled her soul.

If Robyn had an inkling of any of this, she seemed not to care, for in the next breath she peeled off the chemisette altogether.

"Faith," Dax said, fighting to keep his breathing at a normal pace, "don't do this, Robyn, don't—"

"Hush," she murmured softly. "For a surly smuggler of goods and souls, you talk far too much at times." Casting him a slow, tremulous smile, she slid off the stool to her cloak, taking his hands in hers as she did so, urging him to join her.

Dax swallowed thickly. He wanted to pull away. He *should* pull away. One of them, at least, should keep their wits about them.

These were his thoughts as Robyn drew him down beside her. One minute he was making a motion to stand, and in the next she'd managed to stay him, to draw him into the sphere of her moonlit paradise. Suddenly, he was awash in the moon's glow.

"Robyn, do you even realize what you are doing? No doubt it's my Phantom that makes you act this way."

"Not the Phantom, but the man. *You* make me feel this way, Dax." Before he could stop her, she shifted, breathed, and he felt her breasts meet his chest, her thighs his. "Touch me," she whispered. "Teach me what you like . . . and what I'll like. Teach me as you began to do in the cabin, and in your caves before that, and the study before that . . . only this time, Dax, don't stop. Not for anything."

He intended to pull away but she brushed her lips against his, light as a whisper, and her breath was suddenly against his cheek, feathery and soft, filled with yearning, and it fanned to life every need he'd ever had for her, every dream he'd ever dreamt of her. Any thought of retreat, any hope of disengaging himself long enough to grab for his sanity died as her words burrowed into his brain. Suddenly it seemed his erection was a league high and three fields wide. How he wanted her—had *always* wanted her.

"Dearest Christ," Dax whispered. He hauled in a breath, pressing his eyes shut. *"You don't even know what I am."*

"I do." Robyn framed his face with her hands. Soft. Gentle. "You're Dax."

"No." He wasn't. He was more than that and less than that and God but he could no longer separate the man from the monster. "I'm Cursed, and I'm careless with souls, and I cannot be trusted."

"I trust you. You helped me that night in the study . . . and you saved me that day in the woods, and in the caves, and last night at the cottage."

A ragged sound tore up and out of him. "Last night I nearly sucked the soul from you. Tonight will be no different."

"I won't believe that. *You* didn't hurt me, Dax. Whatever is inside of you wanted to, but not you."

His eyes flared open. "It's not yet midnight. There's still time—for me to go, or you . . . *one of us."*

"I'm not going anywhere. I'm right where I want to be."

"Dammit, Robyn." Dax took hold of her wrists, forced her hands from his face. "I'm a danger to you. I always will be." He jerked away from her, surging to his feet. He would have paced away, but she sat up, catching him at the knee with one hand. He looked back and down. Her face was pure beauty, bathed in night's radiance, her eyes sparkling in the moonlight.

"I trust you, Dax. Before midnight, after midnight. I trust you."

God, she was mad—to touch him, to trust him, to *stay.* Couldn't she see the coming transformation in him, couldn't she feel it? He was burning inside. Arctic cold and the heat of Hades alternated in him, one after the other, over and over, making his gut clench and his every muscle scream.

He couldn't head for the ladder or shimmer away because the fiend in him damn well didn't want to. All it wanted was Robyn, her body, her soul, her everything.

Dax put his back to her, blowing out breaths as he brought his hands in front of him so that she couldn't see him ball them tight into fists, fighting, ever fighting. He watched as the color washed from his skin, as his Phantom radiated outward until a burn of piercing cold energy hovered over him like second skin, whiter than the moon's glow. He felt the age-old absence of heart and heat, felt the gnawing hunger that made him thirst for souls . . . and he felt *her.*

"Dax," she was saying. "Tell me you'll stay."

He felt the smile curve his mouth. Felt the Curse in him uncurl and become content. He felt all of this as he moved to the opening of the loft, braced his hands on either side, and stared one last time at the moon that had dared to touch what was his.

"Aye, I'll stay," he said, and he heard the soft breath she'd been holding slide out of her . . . just as he heard the blood swish through her veins and the creamy heat of her build and pool between her thighs—all of this just as he shut the doors, cutting off the moonlight and the night and the chance for her screams to carry on the wind, and then he turned back to her, smiled, and said, "I'll stay until dawn, in fact."

Robyn, seeing the whiteness that was his face, got to her feet. For the barest moment he thought she would flee—or at least try to—but she didn't. She stayed where she was, strong, unafraid, *willing* him to come to her. And though the Curse in him was harder and darker than ever before, he felt somehow tamed by her presence, leashed.

He moved toward her, testing this new bind on him, marveling at it, at her. He purposely brushed against her breasts as he moved, smiling at the catch in her breath, the way her lips parted as his energy licked at her. Not pausing, he pressed his left hand flat against her belly and walked her backward into a corner of the loft where the roof slanted and the stone was thickest, kicking straw as he went, until a pile of it was heaped there. A few more kicks and he had the hay spread into a bed of sorts.

Her eyes held his, challenging him, begging him—he wasn't certain which; all he knew for certain was his own raging need. He brought his hand up, caressing her cheek, painting her with trails of white energy. She didn't pull back, but instead leaned into his touch, her gaze locked to the green of his. And then he smiled because he knew he was going to have her, and she smiled because—he didn't know why, he only knew that her smile made the lust leap in his veins, and so he tumbled them down onto the hay, thinking he'd take the lead, thinking he'd take her . . . but Robyn surprised him.

She shimmied over and atop him until they were breasts to chest, nose to nose, and while a moment ago he'd felt dominant he now felt . . . different. As if Robyn could master the beast in him, as if she alone could direct the Phantom.

She settled down and into him, passing through the wintry chill of his Phantom, through the sharp slice of energy that coated him, and he felt his world tip as she came inside the whiteness and suddenly there was no day or night for him—there was only Robyn. In his arms. At long last. And that's when it happened. For the first time since he was a lad of twelve, Dax felt himself move into the spaces left vacant by his Phantom, felt himself coexist with the Curse, one not more dominant than the other.

His erection became engorged as it pressed against that spot between her legs, that place he'd longed to be for far too many years. Raw need unfurled inside him, rolling along every nerve ending, and while last night the fiend in him had been intent on stealing her soul, his only thought now was to touch her, to stroke her . . . to please her in every way he could, as man, as Phantom, as both.

Dax drew Robyn's face down to his, his mouth to her mouth, his tongue tangling with hers. She tasted slightly of the magic she'd just moved through, but mostly she tasted of the night and of nectar so sweet it stole his heart. He was thick with need, heavy from it, from countless years of wanting her, of dreaming about her, coming to a head. His hands, sliding down her back, couldn't get enough of her. He explored the soft roundness of her buttocks, the firmness of her thighs, the sweet curves of her hips before finding the enclosures of her skirt and helping her shimmy out of the soft velvet. She gasped as Dax rucked up her petticoat only to smooth his hands over her naked backside . . . and then lower, to her garters tied just above her knees. He tugged once, twice, untying the garters as Robyn, breathless, drew one leg up, shivering, as Dax slowly drew the silk stocking down and down and down. He drew off the other stocking in the same manner, leaving Robyn with her knees drawn up, her sweet body straddling him. There came no shame, not even when he cupped her bottom and anchored her to him, his erection thick and hot between them, straining against his breeches. Instinctively, she slid herself against the hard thickness, her woman's core spreading and molding to its shape, beckoning him.

A low growl escaped him as Dax kneaded her bottom, then drew his hands higher, sliding them beneath the bodice of her petticoat, working forward to her breasts. He cupped them, glorying in their weight, the full, feminine softness, the way her nipples hardened at his touch.

Breaking the contact of their lips, he moved his mouth lower, then lower still, raking his teeth over one nipple, capturing it between his lips. Material and all, he suckled her. Robyn's back arched. Her knees tightened against his hips. Nipple flowering in his mouth, she ran her fingers through his hair, drawing him to her, her lips raining soft kisses across his brow, shattering him.

And then she was exploring him through the fabric of his shirt, running her palms down his chest and then hungrily making her way back up, this time taking the material with her, allowing the air and her gaze to touch his flesh.

He watched as her lips parted on a breath, as her chest rose, as her fingers swirled over his skin. A muscle in his chest jumped at her touch, as she traced her fingers over the scar where he'd shot himself as a boy—a shot that for anyone else would have been mortal—and then to the hammered heart of silver she'd gifted him with so many years ago. The cord on which he'd looped it was old but still strong. He watched as Robyn slid one finger beneath the cord, lifted it, and stared hard at the silver talisman that dangled there.

"I'll take it off," he said, remembering how Robyn had reacted last night at the sight of it. "I'll give it over to your keeping. Whatever you'd like."

"No. Leave it." She pressed a kiss to the silver, where the halves of the heart met, and then laid it over the spot where Dax's heart beat, where his skin puckered with scarring. "Let it be between us."

It was the only thing he'd allow there, he thought, as she continued with her exploration, whispering her fingers over his ribs and the flat expanse of his stomach, to the line of hair that ran beneath his breeches. Her gaze, it seemed, was ravenous to view every inch of him. She saw his many scars, the leanness carved by a hard life, yet she didn't pull away. She touched first one tattered line of skin and then another, brushing her fingers over them as if she could bring health and healing to his every ill—and Lord, but it felt as if she had. Beneath her touch, all the years and all the tears he'd spent without her, all the pain and all the loneliness whispered away into nothingness.

Gently, tenderly, she stroked him, and wherever her fingers touched, her lips soon followed. She kissed each muscle in his abdomen, kissed her way up the ladder of his ribs, kissed his scars and the silver, and then moved her mouth upward, to the base of his throat to his chin, rough with stubble . . . to his mouth.

Here, she stilled, hovering above him, her hair like dark silk about them as everything inside of him—good and bad, man and Phantom—quivered to perfect stillness, marveling at the moment, at the precious, beloved woman he held.

He stared into her eyes, wondering if she could read in his face, could hear in his every heartbeat how dear she was to him, how very much he loved her.

"Dax," she whispered, and her voice was so throaty it nearly made him come, "I want you inside of me. I want all of you. In me. Please."

Her plea unhinged him, made his shaft grow thicker still. He'd waited years for this, to have the slight weight of her body on his, to hear these words . . . but she didn't know that. Lord, there was so much she didn't know. He was wrong not to have told her about their shared past by now. And he was wrong to be with her right now, like this, knowing that she wanted him to make love to her. He couldn't promise her a future . . . so how could he take the one thing from her that a future husband would expect?

"Dax," she murmured, pulling his mind back to her, reminding him, with a kiss and with her tongue, what his nearness was doing to her. "Tell me you'll love me. Tell me you won't stop this time."

Faith. There was so much he should tell her—*would* tell her, he decided. But not now. Not this night. Right or wrong, tonight he would give her only what she wanted.

Whether he was being fiendish or selfish, he would do what she asked.

"I'll love you, Robyn." *I'll always love you.*

From now until the sun rose, Dax told himself he would be her midnight, where there was only flesh and feeling and sweet release for her. And she would be his daylight, a shining brightness that would burn bright within him, would sustain him through the long slant of eternity that lay before him.

Though what he desired most was to bury his hardness deep inside of her, Dax wanted to be certain he brought her pleasure first. He let his right hand travel downward to where her hottest parts burned, rubbing the heel of his palm against the nub of her. At his touch, he felt her shift, felt the breath come out of her, and knew that with but a little patience, he could make her first time a memorable one. It was what he wanted above all else—above even his own driving need. Fitting her to one side of him, his left arm looped about her neck, he cradled her there, then turned her face to his and kissed her deeply, fully, as the fingers of his right hand sought out her softest folds.

Robyn gasped, overcome by the sensations he strummed to life within her. Dax swallowed the sound, mating his mouth to hers. Below, between her thighs, she was wet and ready for him, a rich, fertile field created to be tended by him. His fingers delved inside—as they had in the cabin—entering her and playing her like some tender, beloved instrument, fracturing her senses, leaving her weak limbed and panting for breath. He could feel her passion mount, could sense it in her trembling limbs, in the way her mouth opened more fully for him, in the way her tongue tangled with his and her breasts strained against him.

Dax took her higher still. He nipped her lips gently with his teeth, drew his fingers outward and upward, finding in her heated folds that nub of flesh that throbbed. She moaned as he touched it, caressed it. She sobbed as he twirled around the swollen, sensitive bud with one finger, dipping inside of her with another. Her moan became a tiny gasp, laced with wonder, then a full-throated sigh.

He felt her turn to liquid heat, felt the hot, sweet core of her grow slick with want. "Let go, love," he murmured against her mouth, encouraging her to lose all reason.

"No," she rasped, writhing against him, "I want you *inside* me, Dax."

He had to catch his breath at her words, had to stop himself from spilling his seed right then. He growled against her mouth and murmured, "Aye, I know . . . and I want to be. . . . God, I want to be."

"So do it." She rubbed against him. Hard.

Dax moved his mouth to her cheek, sucking in a breath. "Just let me touch you, love. Let me do this for you."

Robyn dragged his hand from between her thighs. *"No,"* she said again, voice ragged. "I want you inside me for the first time." And she sat up, abrupt, and peeled off her petticoat, her breasts jutting out as she reached high with her arms and then tossed the material aside, her hair falling back down around her shoulders in dark waves. She sank back down to him, her nakedness an incredible enticement, her skin unbelievably soft . . . and then her hands were at his trousers, opening them, sliding inside of them . . . and then his hard shaft was in her grasp, pulsating, wanting to pump and to push and to cream every inch of her.

Dax fought for control, but Robyn snatched it away as she boldly stroked him, as she learned the hard, long length of him, as she explored the petal softness of him . . . as she massaged a bead of wetness from the tip of him.

"God. Robyn. You're driving me over the edge."

"So go. Fall. Just whatever you do, take me with you. Promise me."

"Robyn—"

"Promise me."

"Aye," he said, yielding, unable to take anymore. With a growl, he pulled away, sat up long enough to tug off his boots and hose, then stood, impatient, yanking off his trousers, his shirt.

When he dropped back down onto the hay, she was ready for him, ready to give and to take . . . to become one. He took charge this time, pressing her back and down, drawing her slowly into the glow of his Phantom once again, but this time stopping at various parts of her body and letting the tiny whips of energy lick at her until she moaned with delight. And then he drew her in fully, spreading her thighs wide, rubbing himself against her, thick and hard, over and over, thrilling her, until she ran with honeyed wetness and the nub of her was so tight and so hard he thought she'd burst. With deep, devouring kisses, he slid his arms beneath her, filled his hands with the cheeks of her bottom and then pulled her up . . . and pushed inside of her, one long, powerful thrust that took the air from her lungs and made her gasp. He knew that it burned her, knew the moment she felt a pinch of pain, so he kissed her and stroked her and held himself still when all he wanted was to take and to claim and to own.

But it was Robyn who moved, who began to take, to claim. She opened to him, wider, put her hands on his buttocks and pulled him close as she pushed her hips to meet him and soon Dax was lost in the rhythm that she created and he matched, in the feel of her hot tightness swallowing him whole, in the kisses she pressed to his cheek . . . in the ones he gave back.

And then he felt it. Felt Robyn's lithe, beautiful body go taut as she strained against him . . . and then there was no straining at all, just Robyn falling deep, deep down into the hay, dragging him with her and blowing a soft, sweet cry into his mouth as she shuddered to a climax and her insides convulsed around him over and over. Only then did Dax reach for his own release. It came immediately— hard, fast, a shattering explosion of intense feeling that rocked both man and Phantom and made the energy surrounding him snap and flare bright as he pumped himself into her and filled her with his seed, with life, and she held him fast.

She was his now. For good or bad. His.

Chapter Sixteen

Cocooned within Dax's Phantom glow, skin to skin with him, Robyn closed her eyes and drank it all in: the man, his dark magic, the millions of ways he had moved her. She didn't want to forget a moment of this night and so, piece by piece, like tiny treasures, she placed into the folds of her memory the many things about him that pleased her. Such as the feel of his touch—like that of gold, shimmering, yet not with beauty, but warmth; the smell of his skin—all male, tinged with a touch of cedar and a tang of energy, and purely, totally Dax; the taste of his kisses—like exotic island spices that intoxicated.

As she tucked away each nuance of him, Robyn marveled anew at the sensuality he'd brought to life in her. Every nerve ending still vibrated with delight while echoes of his heated touch continued to roll through her. She was suddenly a silken and capable creature, a being of wisdom and energy she had long suspected that she would one day meet—and now she had, because of Dax.

Robyn didn't count the burn or the stinging soreness he'd left in his wake. She didn't worry that she'd just lain with a man who harbored a fiend within. She didn't care that she'd given him not only her virginity but also her future and her heart and—oh . . . everything a woman could give to a man. None of it signified. Nothing mattered, other than the fact that she felt wholly alive for the first time in her life. Felt, in fact, as though she could control her own destiny.

What had begun days ago in that dark, cool study in London had become something else—something more, something vital. Robyn had not just allowed Dax into her body, but into her heart. For an infinite moment this night he'd danced with her there, and she had shared with him all the colors she contained, letting him paint her with his own, until they were awash in a sea of radiant hues that streamed in unending ribbons around her, drowning her in beauty and light, in a symphony of shades, edged with emotions so raw, so beautiful, she'd wanted to weep with joy.

No matter what the future held, Robyn would have no regrets. Allowing Dax to make love to her, allowing herself to love *him*, had been as natural as taking in air.

Her only regret was that she knew he intended to send her away, to secrete her in some safe place while he charged off into the unknown to find her aunt, and to do whatever else it was a man who harbored a soul-stealing fiend inside him did.

But that moment was hours away, and until then, Robyn decided, she would take what she could. She would enjoy the man and these few stolen hours with him. She would learn what she could about him, discover his every detail.

So thinking, Robyn let her fingers sift through Dax's hair, loving its length, amazed by its baby-fine texture. It was surprisingly soft for a man who was all strength and might. But that was Dax—he held surprises. He was a man woven of mystery. He held magic that could move her, grace that gave her pause . . . and kisses that made her melt.

When he shifted, rolling onto his back, she let him go,

wanting to see the part of him that had been inside of her, that had brought her to such ecstasy. Though no longer so huge and thick, the sight of him still brought a catch to her breath. She scooted closer, her curls slick with their lovemaking. He responded to her movement, her wetness. Robyn smiled, beginning to learn how very much she could sway this man, this smuggler, this soul taker who had walked into her life with such swift ease.

She wanted to know about the man. She wanted to know about his past . . . his hopes . . . his dreams. Robyn yearned to know as much about his mind as she'd just learned about his body.

Pressing a kiss to his throat, Robyn whispered, "Tell me."

He drew in a breath, palming her neck, massaging her. "Tell you what?"

"Everything. All you are willing to share about yourself."

"I doubt you'll like what you hear."

"Allow me to decide."

He let his hand glide down the length of her back, cupped her bottom, tugged her close. "I've already told you—I'm Cursed and careless with souls. What more do you need to know?"

She smothered a gasp as he brought her against him, tightly, hips to hips. "I need to know about . . . you," Robyn answered honestly, as soon as she could find her voice. "About the boy you were, how you became the man you are."

He blew out a small, mirthless laugh as he kissed her temple. "Oh, is that all?"

"Yes," she said. "That's all."

A long moment of silence slid past—time in which she began to wonder if she'd pushed him too far, had asked for too much.

But then he began to speak, and oh, he didn't sound as if she'd pushed or prodded too much. He sounded glad—as if sharing his story with her, sharing *anything* with her, had forever been the greatest goal of his life. And so Robyn held very still and very quiet, listening, letting him share however much or however little of his past that he would.

He told her that his life, as he knew it now, had begun when he was just a lad and an accident—a shot from a gun—had left him with no memory of anything other than the fact that his name was Dax. He told her that a man named Jemmy—a man like him, Cursed with a Phantom inside that rose every midnight to battle soul seekers and to steal the souls of others—had taken him in, that Jemmy and his band of men had lived on the wrong side of the law, thieving mostly, smuggling at times, using the caves and a network of tunnels as a safe house through the years.

"It was Jemmy who taught me how to steal, to smuggle, to shoot an arrow straight to its mark . . . and to deal with the fiend inside and with the others that rose each night," Dax said. "By the time I was six and ten, Jemmy—all of us—were in deep trouble. We were constantly on the move, never staying long in one place. We returned to the caves a lot through the years, but eventually even those were crawling with Revenue officers looking for us. Jemmy, deciding we'd be safer taking to the open seas, headed us for the docks of Portsmouth, where we boarded an Indiaman bound for the West Indies.

"I lost myself on that voyage. The evil in me couldn't be contained, though both Jemmy and I had thought we'd leave our Cursed selves behind once we reached open water. We didn't. Even the riders kept coming.

"Days before we dropped anchor, Jemmy drew me aside. He smelled of rot and bloat and a decay that was borne deep in his belly, and I realized then that he was eating himself alive—all because he was tired of the Curse and wanted an end to it. I'll never forget what he said, though I've wished countless times since then that I'd not heard the words at all. He said he knew of only one way for him to be released from the Curse." Dax pressed his eyes shut, drawing in a deep, unsteady breath. "He meant that the Phantom in me could defeat the one in him. That night, it did."

Silence welled between them. Robyn would have comforted Dax if she knew how, if she thought he wanted her to, but he had gone still as death and so she remained as she was. Waiting.

Long moments later, Dax said, "Before that night, Jemmy told me to claim his musket, his pistol, his arrows, every weapon he had in his packs, and to take charge. He told me how, too. Said I was to bribe the captain with a pouch of gold—one he thrust into my hands—and have the captain vouch that he, Jemmy, had left the ship hours before anyone else and had gone ahead to purchase a stronghold for us. The captain was to tie Jemmy's body into a roll of blankets, weight it with ballast, and toss it overboard long after everyone else had gone ashore. Meanwhile, I was to take Jemmy's other horde of gold, buy property, take up residence, and act as though Jemmy still lived and was calling the orders."

"Did you?" she asked in a whisper.

"Aye. I bought the strongest fortress the man's gold could purchase, set myself up in the highest reaches of it, and then wondered what the devil I was going to do next.

"Jemmy, though, had been plotting all of this long before we'd ever taken to the seas. He'd made contacts in those final weeks before we left England, painting a line between there and the islands. Before the week was out, people came calling—men in government, men who owned plantations—and every one of them desired to do business with Jemmy.

"I played the part of his negotiator, made deals that caused my stomach to churn, then pulled back and watched as the funds poured in. Jemmy's men, who'd once welcomed me but had since come to despise me due to Jemmy's favoritism, were only too eager to get involved, and every moment of every day I had to watch my back lest one of them put a knife in it. Our stronghold became a clearinghouse for all manner of stolen goods, with governments offering the ships to transport it—ships that would glide into hidden coves where no taxes could be counted. I'd taken Jemmy's place, but on a grander, more intricate scale. I was but seventeen."

Robyn pressed deeper into the hay, seeking comfort from the hard truth of Dax's tale. "How long did you stay there, living such an existence?"

"Until a little over a year ago . . . until memories started calling me back to England."

"What kind of memories?"

He cast a glance at her from beneath his lashes. "Good ones," was all he would say, and then turned his gaze to the rafters above.

Robyn shifted uneasily, a whisper of cool air assaulting her body. "What is this . . . curse that has claimed you?"

"You really want to know?"

Robyn nodded.

"The Curse," he began in a low voice, "is a power unlike anything—cold at times, hot at others, always dark . . . *infinite*. It rises from within, making me yearn to roam, to take, to conquer. From the stroke of midnight to the break of dawn, I am Phantom. Jemmy and I, and later Gideon and I, would talk for hours about the Curse, wondering what brought it into our lives, what sin we might have committed to manifest it, what act of selflessness might make it disappear. All we know for certain is that the more we use our dark gifts, the closer we come to being wholly evil, to stealing more souls—and to eventually losing our own. Nothing of this earth can defeat me. Not a shot of lead, the blade of a knife . . . or even the carnage of a crashed carriage," Dax said, his voice thick with emotion. "Only the relentless riders that trail me every midnight and whose goal is to harvest my soul pose a threat to me—them, or another Phantom. Until I learn what—or who—is the catalyst that will bring me back to the living or make me truly dead, I will know no peace. Jemmy had no peace. It is why he made such elaborate arrangements for me to succeed after he was gone—it gave him something to focus on. And at the end, it is why he succumbed to the Phantom in me. Now Gideon, and me, and others like us are the ones who can find no peace.

"I've done things I'm not proud of and, as Phantom, have gone beyond the boundaries of anything human. . . ." He turned his gaze to her again, pain in his eyes. "And tonight, both the Phantom and the man have enticed you to feel things you should not have felt, to do things you should not have done."

"Dax, never say that."

"You deserve a future. What happened here tonight was—"

"Exactly what I wanted," Robyn cut in. "I regret nothing."

He was still, quiet, and then: "That you remain alive, that the fiend in me hasn't tried to smother you, suck the soul from you, amazes me."

"Whatever is inside of you has a weakness—my mother proved that to us last night. Perhaps this is a new beginning for you."

He shook his head, the green gleam of his gaze brighter than even the whiteness of his Phantom. "No," he said, voice pitched low, "this is more like a pause of sorts. Somehow you've calmed both Phantom and man, but one of them will soon crowd out the other."

The calm before the storm. That is what he meant, Robyn knew.

"I just wish . . . I wish that I could help you, Dax. At the cottage, when those haunting phantasms—those soul seekers—came at me, I caught a glimpse inside of you, of what you face every moment, and the weight of it nearly shattered me. I don't know how you do it, how you manage one day to the next."

"I manage," he said, "by thinking of good." He reached up and gently smoothed a strand of hair from her brow with the back of one hand, and then he leaned over and kissed her gently, the barest of brushes.

Robyn knew then that no matter what tomorrow might bring, being with Dax, here, now, was perfectly right.

"Will you stay with me for a while longer?" she whispered against his lips.

He nodded, his mouth on hers. "Just tell me what you want, what you need."

"You. *Only you.*"

Drawing her body atop his, Dax once again made use of his Phantom, his hands, his tongue, and his lips to bring her to dizzying heights . . . and before the night drained into dawn, he had taken her to that thrilling place where only touch and sensation existed. There he danced inside of her, causing all her colors to bloom and to bleed with his own until she was soaked in a beauty so bright it dazzled her. Rolling her over, fitting her body beneath his, Dax sank deep inside, filling her with himself, with every drop of molten emotion he contained. Her senses scattered as Dax touched her *there*, drawing out her pleasure long after his own had been found. The dance continued until, with a ragged whisper that contained his name, Robyn's shudders ceased and her world stopped tipping as she floated back down into the hay, the scent of Dax filling her mind, the hot seed of him filling her body, Phantom and man holding her tight.

It was dawn when Robyn awoke, alone, atop the scratchy hay, her cloak covering her like a blanket. "Dax?" she called, voice just a whisper.

A long moment slid past, and then, "Here."

Robyn could sense, in that single word, in his tone, that something had changed—in him.

Slowly, she rolled over, wondering what she would find, remembering only too well how frightening he'd been that morning in the caves.

He stood a few feet away, near the opening that led to the stables below. There wasn't a bottle in his fist, thank goodness; he'd not had the urge to drink his beast into oblivion while she'd slept, at least. He was fully dressed, the glow of his Phantom just a pale, mistlike shimmer about him, his eyes a darker green. In the seep of dusky light coming through the panels, she could see that his features were hard, unreadable. Her heart fell.

"What's wrong, Dax?" She couldn't manage her voice above a whisper.

"Nothing."

"Liar."

"Very well. Everything. Everything is wrong. This day, last night, what I have to do, what I want to do . . . it's all wrong, every goddamned thing is wrong, Robyn." He lifted his hands—his paleness haunting—and put one glove on and then the other. "The Phantom has usually receded by now. But not today, and I'm thinking tomorrow will be no different. In fact, I wager it will be worse."

Robyn's mouth went dry, her heart hollow. "Whatever happens, Dax, we'll deal with it, we'll manage—"

"We? No. There *is* no we, Robyn. There can't be, because the fiend that is me doesn't allow that kind of thing. Nothing . . . no one . . . is safe around me."

"But last night—"

"Was a mistake that I won't allow you to repeat."

Robyn closed her eyes, hoping to find the colors he'd created within her, the heat with which he'd seared her senses, the tenderness in which he and his Phantom had wrapped her. But she saw nothing, felt nothing other than a cool void of black. She opened her eyes.

"You're sending me away, aren't you?" She tugged at the cloak, wrapping it tight around her as she sat up. "You've found a driver and a carriage, and—and you're sending me away."

"You knew last night that was my plan."

Yes, and I don't like it, Robyn thought, feeling suddenly mulish and selfish. She didn't want to leave. She wanted only the night and Dax inside of her again. She wanted to dance, damn him. Until she died, she wanted to dance with this man.

That's when it hit her—*she loved him.* Her smuggler of souls had smuggled the love right out of her, and she was the only party to pay a duty, a tax so steep she wondered if she could afford the cost: no colors, no dancing . . . only gray, dingy dawns. That is what her future would hold without him.

"I was afraid this would happen," Dax said into the stillness.

That her love for him would bloom in the blood of her virginity? Ah, no, Robyn wanted to point out. It hadn't been when he'd taken her maidenhead that she'd fallen helplessly in love with him. *That* had happened days ago, she realized now . . . in the caves, when he'd kissed her even more deeply than he had in the study . . . when he'd watched over her, tended her wound, when he'd tried to drown the Phantom in him in order to protect her.

"You were afraid *what* would happen?" Robyn demanded, still whispering—God, but he'd smuggled not only the love from her but her breath as well—and wondered if he was using his dark magic to read her thoughts, and if so, whether he'd chide her for falling in love with him. She tugged the cloak closer.

"I feared that come dawn when I looked at you, I wouldn't be able to let you go any more than I was able to do so last night."

"You mean you didn't—"

"No. I didn't. If anyone is going to take you anywhere, it will be me. Unfortunately, where I'm headed is no place you ought to be."

Robyn resisted the urge to move, to blink, or even breathe, afraid that if she did he would change his mind. He obviously wasn't happy with his decision. In fact, he looked as if he'd just thrown caution to the wind for the first and only time in his life.

And mounting in his green gaze was that storm-tossed look Robyn recognized and feared—the one that had overcome him when he'd turned Soul Smuggler the other night at the cottage.

Though he'd been a tender lover last night, though her own magic had made the Phantom in him subdued and sensuous, Dax was now a mix of man and beast, of magic and might—all of it clashing, each piece of the mixture straining to have ultimate rule.

In spite of all of that, Robyn was glad—glad he was taking her with him. There was no place else she wanted to be.

"Thank you for having a change of heart, Dax."

He scowled. "Every instinct tells me to get you to a safe place, just as every urge tells me not to let you out of my sight. I can't do both, Robyn. So I'm going to take you with me because that's what the Phantom wants and that's what the Phantom will get. But you'll do only as I say, when I say, and if I need you to be apart from me, then that's how it will be. Do you understand?"

Robyn nodded, mute. These were hardly the words she'd hoped to hear after the night they'd just shared. Still, they were enough. He wasn't sending her back to Land's End, back to Falconer. He wasn't cutting her out of his life. That was all that mattered. "I understand," she murmured, reaching for her wrinkled petticoat and dragging it under her cloak, intending somehow to get the thing on without allowing her nakedness to show.

"Do you? I wonder."

Again, Robyn nodded. Again, she wondered at the storm

whipping up inside of him. She began to struggle—with the mass of material and the ribbon of her petticoat—beneath the tent of her cloak.

"Sam arrived in the night," Dax said.

"Oh?"

"Yes."

"And?" she prompted.

Silence. An awful silence, and then, "Why didn't you tell me, Robyn? Why didn't you tell me that Falconer can cart you off to god-knows-where and leave you there if you refuse to return to London with him . . . and why the hell didn't you tell me that you are to *wed* Morley, that your father has blessed the union, that the goddamned banns have been cried?"

Why? Yes, why would be good to know, it would be wonderful to know. Robyn tugged tight on the ribbon that seemed determined to disobey her, then reached over to scrape up her skirt from the floor.

Her attempt at modesty irritated Dax nearly as much as this mess with Morely and Falconer and his own inability to send her packing aboard a swift coach driven by anyone other than himself.

With something that sounded distinctly like an animal growl, Dax paced off the distance between them, ripped the cloak away, and then took her by the hands, drawing Robyn to an upright position.

"Stop," he commanded. "Stop acting like I haven't seen every part of you, haven't kissed every inch of you. Stop not sharing what you *should* be sharing—that a man who terrifies you has your father's backing to claim you as his wife or lock you away forever."

Toes and nose to him Robyn felt dizzy. "Morely and his watchdogs are my worry, not yours."

"Robyn. *Anything* that worries you becomes a target of mine."

"I can take care of this, Dax."

"Too late."

Oh damn, and damn again, she thought. How she hated this dawn and this moment. She wanted the night back. She wanted her tender lover to return and replace this harder, colder version of the man who now stood so close she could feel his magic and his murderous anger radiating from him.

"Along with Sam came John, Monty, your aunt's horses, and one of her carriages—a whole bloody party arrived on our heels last night," Dax said. "It appears Falconer and his man set out immediately to find you when they realized you'd slipped away from Land's End."

Robyn felt the color drain from her face.

"They passed by here as you slept. Sam and the others only stopped because I led them here."

Robyn went perfectly still as Dax moved his hands to the ribbon at the bodice of her petticoat, skimming over the tips of her breasts as he did so. Robyn felt her nipples, her belly, tighten.

He undid the hasty, lopsided bow she'd made, then created a new bow, a perfect one.

Robyn swallowed, loving the feel of his hands on her, the scent of him. "I want you to know that I . . . that Morely means nothing to me . . . that last night with you . . . it meant *everything* to me."

Dax smoothed his fingers atop the bow, then placed his hands on Robyn's shoulders—warm hands, masterful hands, intoxicatingly beautiful hands. He touched his forehead to hers, sparkles of his energy flicking against her skin, a soft lock of his hair brushing her temple. He wanted to kiss her, she *knew* that, but instead he took a deep breath and pulled away, turned, and headed for the ladder. "Get ready. We leave soon, and there's someone waiting for you. It seems your maid is as reckless as her mistress."

Mattie, *here?*

With that Dax was gone, climbing down through the opening in the timbers, his dark head disappearing . . .

just as the night had disappeared: swiftly, far, far too swiftly.

Robyn hugged her arms about her waist. She missed the night . . . and the dance—most especially the dance.

BOOK FIVE

The Betrayed

Chapter Seventeen

The London that Dax drew Robyn into was worlds away from the one she had known all of her life. This London was shabby and scarred, with filth in the gutters and too many families crowded into small spaces. It had narrow lanes and dingy boardinghouses, and was exactly the type of area her mother and her aunt would have bravely ventured into during one of their many outings to help others.

That thought helped Robyn step out of the carriage into the cool dusk . . . into Dax's keeping. He stood on the uneven pavement, one hand held out for her, his eyes as green as the woodlands they'd left behind, his mood just as untamed. In the miles since they'd left Sims and his livery stables, Dax had evolved into a harder, darker version of himself. A push-pull of war waged within as Phantom and man battled, each determined to override the other. He didn't want her with him, Robyn knew, and he just as fiercely didn't want to be without her.

As he drew her down the steps, Robyn sensed the vibration of his Phantom energy, felt the low hum of its power as it coursed through him. He was something wholly new—not just a man harboring Phantom magic, but a man melded with that magic, all might and little mercy. The shimmer of his Phantom coated him like a thin smear of star shine across the heavens, lifting from his skin in tiny pulse beats.

Robyn drew in a breath, hoping it would help calm her, but she managed only to get a lungful of the smells surrounding her: the tang of Dax's magic, the cedar that clung to his coat, and the Thames that wasn't far off. There was the scent of bloated fish in the air, wood wet and moldy, and the burn of coal smoke. She tried hard to acclimate herself to this strange place, to the man in front of her.

A few street sellers with their basket-laden donkeys had yet to head back to the countryside surrounding the city and could be heard hawking the last of their day's wares. A grizzled old man was dismantling his spinning wheel and grinder at one corner of the street. Nearby, a heavy-set, ruddy-cheeked woman with a large straw basket hefted against her hip and a young boy standing flush against her wrinkled skirts offered matches for sale. Only a few fistfuls of pointed, homemade splints of wood that had been dipped in sulfur remained in her basket.

Once firmly planted on the pavement, Robyn looked up at the building looming in front of them, with its series of sagging lines and weathered wood—wood that would be little protection against the relentless riders come midnight.

"Coo, m'lady," murmured Mattie, hovering on the top step of the carriage, "it be far frum whut y' be accustom'd to. Mayhap y' shudn't be stayin' here."

"Mattie," Dax cut in, though gently. "We talked about this. You know what has to happen now. The only reason I allowed you to join us is because you agreed to do as I ask."

"And still do," Mattie replied. "Yer plan be a good one, fer certain-sure." Casting Robyn a hope-filled smile—one bracketed with an apologetic look in her eyes—the girl ducked back inside the carriage, taking the seat she'd just vacated as Dax put up the steps and latched the door.

"*What* plan?" Robyn glanced up at him. "Why isn't Mattie coming with us?"

"I'll answer. Soon. Just not here." Robyn felt Dax's gloved hand close more solidly over her own as he led her away from the carriage and instructed Bones, seated atop the box, to head for the nearest stables and quarter the horses and the carriage there. To Randolph, still astride and waiting behind the carriage, he said, "You know what to do."

Randolph nodded.

As the carriage moved off, with Randolph, Sam, John, and Monty riding astride behind it, Dax led Robyn not into the wooden boardinghouse in front of them, but down the street and into an even narrower, obviously older, lane.

There were no gaslights. Given the height of the buildings and the lack of space between them, there was no place for any light from the dying day to squeeze through, either. There were only shadows and growing pockets of pure black.

As Dax drew Robyn into the dimness, she realized suddenly that he had planned all of this—their arrival at this time of day, Mattie's confusion over where Robyn would truly be housed, even the fact that the carriage wouldn't fit within the narrow confines of the lane. He had wanted to bring her here with as few people as possible any the wiser.

Halfway into the lane, as shadows hugged them tight, Dax leaned his head down to hers, and whispered against her ear. "There. Across the way. That's where we'll stay." Beyond his shoulder, Robyn spied the structure: brick, three stories tall, with only two of the bottom windows holding any signs of life in the faint lamp glow coming through thin drapes. "It isn't much, but it's far from prying eyes and a place to keep you hidden while we decide how best to locate your aunt."

Yes, hide, Robyn thought. She needed to do that now— needed to hide from her father, from Morely, from Falconer and Drago. How ironic that the moment she tasted freedom she had to relinquish it. She thought all of this just as Dax slid one arm around her, pulled her against him, through the arctic-cold of his energy . . . and shimmered them off the street.

For a scant second, she was weightless, lighter than air. It was as if Dax had stepped off the edge of the world and plunged them into a sphere of existence where space could not be measured. There was nothing but the two of them, body against body, his breath in her ear, his arms around her. Robyn clung to him, holding tight as Dax moved them through night and over pavement, through air and brick . . . and into a flat housed on the uppermost floor.

She would have staggered back a step the moment her feet touched solid floor, but Dax's hold was too sure, his focus on her unwavering. Once again, she marveled at his dark gifts, realizing the frightening magic of him. She felt the heart talisman grow warm against her skin.

"You shouldn't do that, Dax," Robyn scolded when she finally caught her breath. "You told me yourself, the more you use your gifts the more you put yourself at risk for stealing souls—and for losing your own."

"There are a great many things I should not do," he said darkly, and his energy flared bright in the darkness, sizzling.

Robyn decided not to respond. She let him move away into the blackness. Given the outside appearance of the building she had expected a dank place, but it wasn't stale air she breathed in. It was the scent of good polish lovingly rubbed onto precious furniture, of drapes and rugs recently aired. She waited as Dax lit a light and then drank in the sight as the flat bloomed into view. Everything in the room seemed to her a clue about the man, for surely this was a place of retreat for him, a haven he'd come to at least once in his life.

A small, circular table claimed one corner of the room, covered with Flemish linen and flanked by two straight-back chairs. A Welsh rug had been thrown over the large sofa to protect its cushions, and against the opposite wall was a three-tiered bookshelf, filled with much-thumbed volumes. The central living quarters were small but cozy, and in a mezzanine above was a bedchamber that held a bird's-eye view of the lower room. It had a tiny, round window that would, on a clear night, be filled with the moon's glow, Robyn decided—just like the loft at the livery stables.

The bed beneath the window was huge, taking up nearly all of the mezzanine. There was an old wardrobe there and a bedside stand with a washbasin and pitcher.

In the main room, the mantel above the fireplace held an array of candles burned down to various degrees, and a table in front of the sofa was littered with sheets of vellum, all written upon in bold, decisive handwriting.

"Have you come here often in your life?" Robyn asked.

"No." Dax shed his gloves and then moved to gather up the sheets. "I was here for a time as a child, and returned days ago when I first arrived from the West Indies."

Robyn watched as he quickly scooped up the papers. There were dozens upon dozens of sheets. "Yours?" she asked, wondering how a man raised by thieves could have learned to write or even read.

Silence slanted between them and she knew Dax was debating whether to answer, and if so how much—or how little—he should share.

Finally, he said, "The writings are from my guardian. He kept a journal of our years together. After his death, a—a mutual friend kept the notes safe for me." Dax turned away, tucking the pages into a volume he'd plucked from the shelf. He closed the book and shoved it tight between several others.

He'd had a guardian?

That bit of truth sank deep into Robyn, not meshing with the tale he'd shared with her in the loft. But she didn't press, didn't ask about this "guardian," or how Dax came to know the man, or even be parted from him. She didn't dare. The Phantom in him was a hard shimmer now, the man in him just as fierce. It was as though having brought her to the flat left Dax vulnerable in some way—laid him bare, *revealed*. For a man who once dwelled in dark caves, who kept his thoughts to himself, she guessed how difficult it must be for him to allow her this much of his existence.

Glancing once at the book with the journal of Dax's years tucked inside of it, marking it in her memory, Robyn turned her attention back to him. She watched as he moved to the hearth, hunkered down, and began to lay a fire on the grate. He took his time layering the kindling he took from a deep-bellied kettle; it was clear his mind was on other things.

Robyn studied him—the strength in his every move, the way his wavy hair curled at the ends, skimming his coat collar.

Rising briefly, he took flint and a sulfur-dipped stick off the mantel, hunkered back down, and then struck the match, holding the burning tip of it to the kindling until the wood took the flame. Firelight soon flickered against his features, growing brighter.

Silent, Dax added a larger piece of wood and watched as this, too, began to burn—slowly at first, until the wood crackled and spit, hissing as it became ringed with flame.

With but a tiny spark, he created a blaze—that is what he's thinking, Robyn knew, and guessed he was likening the licking flames to their moment in the loft and to his decision to bring her with him to London . . . to every choice he'd ever made concerning her.

"It will be all right," she whispered.

He stared into the fire. "What will?"

"You. Me. The two of us, here, together. It . . . everything will be all right, Dax."

A full moment slid by, the silence between them broken only by the snap and hiss of the fire. Elbows on his knees, Dax threaded his hands together and bowed his head, a wave of hair falling forward, shuttering his profile from her view.

Quietly, he said, "I need to go out. I don't know when I'll return. I want you to stay here. Bones will be outside your door and Sam nearby on the street below. Whatever you need—food, whatever—tell Bones, and Sam will get it for you."

Robyn felt panic stir inside of her. "To do what? I want to go with you, Dax. I—"

"Robyn." That was all he said, and she knew, with that one word, he was both asking and warning her. He got to his feet, raking the hair back from his face, then turned fully toward her, half of him coated in firelight, the other half a shadow-smudged Phantom. Light and dark, that is what he was, man and monster.

Robyn hugged her arms about her waist. "Are Mattie and Randolph going with you?"

He nodded. "And Monty and John."

"What about the riders?"

"They won't bother you here."

"It's you I am worried about, Dax."

"Don't be. I can handle them."

"Yes. Of course you can, and no doubt all by your bloody lone self." Her panic twisted into anger; she was angry that he was leaving, and she was angry that while he'd brought her here to this haven of his past, he still wasn't telling her everything.

Robyn stared at Dax hard, ready to argue with him, wanting to push him into revealing whatever it was he was keeping from her—but one look in his eyes, at the green gleam that flickered with the might of the Phantom and the anguish of the man, and every bit of that anger slid out of her. Instead of pushing at him, she wanted to pull him close and hold him tight.

"You *will* come back?"

"I will," he answered. "And if you have need of me before then, all you have to do is think of me and I'll come to you immediately."

She drew in a breath. Nodded. And then he was gone, the scent of cedar and a lick of energy whispering against her as he shimmered away.

That night passed, as did two more, and still no Dax. Randolph brought Mattie to the flat on the third night, leaving her alone with Robyn for a few hours. The young maid was enjoying her newfound freedom, Robyn realized. Dax had arranged for Mattie to have her own rented rooms from which the girl headed out to learn whatever tidbits she could from the network of domestics in the city. But there had been no headway in the mystery of her aunt's disappearance. None of Aunt Amy's staff in the city knew any more about her whereabouts than those at Land's End, and the authorities had uncovered no clues. Robyn also learned that her father hadn't let word of Robyn's flight to Sussex spread—not even as news leaked of her aunt's disappearance. *So much for fatherly concern*, she thought sadly.

"Not even yer cousins knew, m'lady," Robyn said. "Mist'r Dax, he be askin' me who y' wud want t' know about yer situation. I tol' him Miss Lily and Mast'r Sandy. He insisted I get word of y' to Miss Lily through her maid. I let 'er know y' be safe but hidin' and Miss Lily, she sent word back that Mast'r Sandy suspect'd yer father wasn't being truthful and that he be takin' up with others t' try and find y' and yer aunt."

"Thank you, Mattie." Robyn wondered who Sandy had "taken up with" and could only imagine to what lengths Sandy would go if he thought she was being held somewhere against her will. "Can you do something more for me?" At her maid's nod, she pressed a folded sheet of vellum into her hand. "It's a message for Lord Thomas Ballinger, asking him to meet with me. Whoever delivers it should wait for an answer."

The girl glanced down at the note.

"What is it, Mattie?"

"Mist'r Dax, he be wantin' t' be inform'd of all I do and everyone I talk t'. I be sharin' this w' him first, and w' Randy, er, Mist'r Randolph, yes?"

Of course Dax would want to know all—would want to know everything. "Yes, of course, Mattie."

By the time Mattie left the flat, off to ferret out whatever information Dax wanted her to pull from the world of domestics, Robyn realized that her maid was enjoying the adventure of her life. And from the look in Randolph's eyes as he followed Mattie out the door, he was enjoying his time with her as well.

Robyn debated following after them or just leaving on her own. But something in her, something stirred to life by Dax, didn't want to leave. She had seen his dark gifts, had experienced them firsthand. If anyone could pick up her aunt's trail—no matter how cold—it would be Dax.

Sam and Bones saw to her every need and made certain Robyn was well fed, venturing out to bring her bread fresh from the bakery, full meals from a local chophouse, wine, cheese—whatever she desired. They brought her glasses for the wine, plus linen and silverware, soap, even a footbath. They did not, however, bring her news of Dax, or any clue as to what he had set out to accomplish.

Late in the evening of her fourth night alone, Robyn sank down into a steaming bath, determined to wash away her thoughts of Dax, but soon realized that keeping him out of her mind was going to be impossible; every place she touched held a memory of him.

By the time she toweled the wetness from her body and stood near the fire to dry her hair, a wild heat was beginning to build—inside her and between her thighs. Her breaths grew shallow. She wore only the heart talisman looped about her neck and a knee-length shift that was nearly transparent in the fire's light. Beneath it her nipples were tight and hard, her breasts full and aching for Dax's hands . . . for his palms to slide over them, for his mouth and his teeth to mark them.

Combing her fingers down through her hair, she dropped them lower, over her sensitive breasts, down over her belly, and lower still, to that place only Dax had touched, to that space he'd tasted and teased and eventually pleased. Eyes closed, she touched herself, thinking of him, needing him, remembering how he'd kissed her that first time in the study, of how he had stroked his hands down her naked back. . . .

"I'm no longer the man who found you alone in that room. I am now fiercer and far more terrible and I want you just as much—if not *more*—than he ever did."

Robyn's eyes flared open as Dax shimmered into the flat directly in front of her, his right hand covering hers, pressing hard, firm, his Phantom like a bright shimmer that sucked her in.

"Dax." Energy snapped and flared, devouring her so that she was *inside* of his shimmer. The heart talisman dangling between her breasts became like a hot brand against the sensitive skin there.

"I felt your need," Dax said, and his gaze slid over her body in a slow slide that made her insides smoke.

Robyn felt heat steal up her neck, her cheeks.

"Do not blush," he murmured, his hand nudging hers away, his fingers exploring her through the thin shift. "I like that you are wet for me, that you think of me when you stroke yourself."

He pressed one finger inside of her, material and all.

Robyn's breath caught.

Another finger . . . and then . . . .*pressure*, wonderful, mind-numbing pressure, all while he palmed the nub of her, making her weak and wanton. Bowing his head, he opened his mouth over one nipple and sucked. Robyn nearly came right there with the firelight in her face and Dax's fingers inside of her, his mouth on her breast. She gripped him by the shoulders and realized her hands were trembling. No, they were shaking, *she* was shaking, she wanted him so badly.

"You—you could sense my need?"

He turned his face, looking up at her, his mouth, teeth, and tongue still working her nipple. "Maybe I fed it," he said around the hard pearl of her.

And she felt his energy burn bright and snap at her with tiny whips as he suddenly pulled away, long enough to shrug out of his greatcoat. He tossed the heavy thing to a chair in the far corner. His jacket followed, and then he peeled off his shirt, letting it fall to his feet, the possessiveness of his gaze startling as he took in this new view of her in the shift. With a heady grin, he dropped to his knees, put his hands on her legs, and began to hike up her hem even as he tongued her through the material.

"Lord, but you're beautiful."

She *felt* beautiful . . . and desirous and daring and, oh, so many things. She felt powerful and precious, excited and drowsy—and *hunted*, she realized dully.

"Dax."

Was he more Phantom than man? She wanted to ask, but his gaze became a green gleam that pinned her, that made her nipples go harder still and her belly pinch as keen desire tipped through her. And then he grinned and she was lost, to the Phantom and the man and everything in between. He got to his feet, the fire behind him crackling and snapping, an out-of-control flame that matched the lust she could see pumping through him.

"I should be afraid," she whispered.

"But you aren't, are you?"

"No," she gasped and shook her head, her mind swamped by her need of him, her body overwhelmed by how much she desired him. That wildness he'd stoked to life in her in the caves so many days ago burned hotter than the sun. She wanted him to take from her and to give to her; she wanted his heat and his hardness. She wanted to consume and to be consumed.

"Let me give you what you want," he said, as if reading her mind. "What the both of us want."

Yes. *Please.* Before she could utter the words, he turned her around and suddenly her belly was against the back of the sofa. Dax, behind her, was lifting her shift, murmuring words she couldn't hear or even understand, and then he was kissing a hot trail down her spine to the dimples of her lower back where he stopped, lingering there—as if kissing her dimples was the one thing in this world he'd wanted to do more than anything else—thrilling her with his tongue and his mouth as his fingers slid inside of her once more.

Robyn thought she would go mad with need, her bottom lifting up and back. Dax gave a low laugh, thrilling her, and then he eased upward, his hands between them, working open his trousers . . . and then he was free, thick and hard and heavy, the head of him jutting into the cheeks of her bottom, and she moved and he moved and then he pushed himself inside of her, all of him, and she died a tiny death as he pumped himself into her, her breasts in his hands, his mouth at her neck as she came and came again, the talisman a hot heart between her breasts.

Long minutes later, his face buried in her hair, his arms tight about her, Dax shimmered them up into the mezzanine, where he laid her down across the bed, covered her body with his, and took her one more time into bliss.

After that night, Robyn no longer slept alone. Though Dax continued to venture out, he always returned just before midnight, when the Phantom was a wild beast in his chest and the man hungered ravenously for her. It was as if he wanted to relive their time in Sims's livery stable over and over again, as if he trusted that the magic of Robyn could subdue and seduce the beast within him. He'd shimmer them into the bed in the mezzanine where he'd drive himself deep inside of her, and then he'd shimmer them to the rug in front of the hearth, where he'd stroke her until she was once more achy with need . . . and then he would move over her and in her and all the world and her every care would whirl away.

One day blurred into the next, and each evening Robyn

would slice some cheese, set out two glasses and a bottle of wine, and wrap the day's loaf of bread in linen warmed by the fire. She would light a candle—just one—and place it between the glasses on the table in front of the sofa, and then she would sit down and wait for her phantom lover, for news of his progress in finding Aunt Amy, for his touch that drove Robyn wild.

Dax was using his magic with more and more frequency, shimmering in and out of the loft, focusing on conversations lanes away, sliding inside her thoughts when she least expected. He was edgy and dark, the Phantom a demanding lover. While she believed in him absolutely when he told her he was getting closer to discovering what had happened to her aunt, she didn't know how much longer she could tolerate being tucked away in the flat. She needed to be actively involved in the search. She also feared that Dax was getting closer to some other truths as well—about his past, about his future, none of it good.

Robyn decided, deep into her second week in the loft, that she'd had enough. She would be going with him the next time he ventured out. The candle had burned low. The fire in the grate was but a pale, golden glow, its one fat log sizzling with heat. But Dax didn't return as he usually did, and it was well past midnight when Robyn, sitting on the sofa waiting for him, finally fell into a fitful sleep, her dreams a confusing riot of images. She dreamt of Falconer and of a faceless Morely, of Sandy and her aunt. At the last, it was Dax's face filling her dreams.

She dreamt the sound of him in the hallway, the exact timbre of his voice—quiet, wonderfully deep—as he told Bones to get some rest. Dreamt even the scent of his magic as he shimmered inside the flat.

She heard the rustle of his greatcoat as he drew it from his body. Heard him move to stir the fire and throw a new log atop it. Burning bark snapped and spit. The poker clanged once as it was replaced on its iron hook. And then there was nothing but the sound of his breathing . . . and, suddenly, the feel of his body near to hers.

"Robyn."

She didn't want to open her eyes, didn't want to end this dream. "Hmm," she murmured, shifting slightly.

"It's late. You should be in bed."

She felt the touch of something—his hand. Yes. Open palmed. Brushing against her cheek. First cool and then rough and warm, always pulsating with his energy. The pad of his thumb brushed against the bow of her mouth. She touched it with the tip of her tongue and realized that this was no dream.

She opened her eyes to see Dax leaning over her, so close she had a view only of his eyes, the color of beryl fire. "Dax . . . where have you been?"

"Everywhere," he said. Then he shrugged and added, "Nowhere." He gazed at her long and deep. He ran the back of his knuckles lightly across her chin.

Robyn felt dread begin to pool in her belly. "Oh, God, you've learned something. Tell me."

"Relax," he soothed. "I don't have bad news . . . but I don't have much news either. Your aunt was in the city as recently as a fortnight ago. With Mattie's help, my men and I learned from Lord Ballinger's domestics that Amy met with him briefly. No one has seen her since. Following that meeting, Ballinger departed Town. He's expected back tomorrow."

"Lord Ballinger? Dax, I told you I could get an audience with him, that I wanted to help you find my aunt. You don't need Mattie talking to the man's servants when I can go directly to his front door."

"And put you in perfect view for Morely to track?"

"Yes, if that's what it takes," she said, her anger flaring. "He might know where my aunt is."

"I won't allow you to become bait for Morely or his men," Dax said, iron in his tone. "We do this my way."

Robyn, agitated, pulled away and watched as Dax settled

onto the cushions beside her. It was only then that she noticed what she should have noticed the moment he'd awakened her. *"You cut your hair."*

He nodded, rubbing his hand against his jaw. "And had a shave."

"But . . . *why?*"

A flash of feeling flickered in his green gaze, snapping with a hard, unreadable light. "Because it was time," he said simply, a grim undertone to the words, as though something monumental had taken place in the last several days—something he'd wanted, yet didn't want. "You don't like it?" Her answer, it seemed, was important to him.

"Yes, I—I like it." But it would take time to get used to this "new" Dax. Gone were the longish strands she'd tangled trembling fingers into just last night. In their stead was a riot of close-cropped waves that gleamed rich black in the firelight. And he had purchased new clothes—fine clothing, of a cut, thread, and color of a man-about-town. Even his Phantom held a different glow, more muted, as if the Curse had settled into his skin. He was a mass of contradictions: chilling and lethal when threatened, heartshatteringly tender when least expected.

And he was being tender now as he reached out, took her by the hand, and drew her body toward him. She went willingly, quietly, and nestled against him as he stretched out on the sofa and she did the same. Toes to toes, they lay there in the warmth and golden-rich glow, Robyn's left ear pressed against Dax's chest, the fingertips of their right hands touching. Just as she drifted into sleep, Robyn felt Dax shift, felt him brush his lips against her brow, in a kiss as light as a feather.

A feather that became a wing for her dreams.

And dream she did—wild, crazed images that came one after the other. She dreamt of her childhood bed at Aunt Amy's home, and of a young boy, blue-eyed and with a white plume in his fancy hat, asking her about hearts and magic.

And then she dreamt of Sandy, riding to her rescue, the

hooves beneath him sounding like thunder. She wanted to yell to him that she was fine, that she had found both her past and her future. But when she turned, she saw only smoke from a gun's blast . . . and then crimson—a river of it—as Sandy toppled from his mount, a gaping hole in his chest. When she screamed, it was her aunt's voice she heard, crying out for both Robyn and Sandy.

Robyn jerked awake with a start.

She was in the flat, on the sofa, Dax sprawled alongside her, his skin a pale glow of magic. He was sound asleep, one strong arm stretched above him, his other arm cradling the spot she'd just vacated.

Heart hammering, Robyn eased up and off the sofa, away from him, not certain she wouldn't be violently ill from her dreams. *Dreams?* No. *Not* dreams, but memories . . . and a *warning of what was to come?* Confusion swarming her, she went to the window where she parted the curtains and pressed her forehead against the pane, looking out at the London Dax had brought her to.

Robyn sucked in a cool breath of air, blew it out, and watched as her breath condensed on the glass, bringing into view the press of a lone fingerprint there. She placed her own atop it, amazed to find something revealed in the heat from her mouth. Life was like that—layers existed, unseen, until one breathed them into focus. It was what her mother and aunt had always wanted her to learn.

Robyn let the curtains fall back into place, turned away from the window, and then moved to the sofa—to Dax.

She sat down, looked at the man she had come to love, *and breathed.*

Chapter Eighteen

A moment later, Robyn watched as Dax came awake.

"I—I wish you would tell me," she murmured. "I wish . . ."

"What?" he whispered. "What do you wish, Robyn?"

She blew out a breath, hoping beyond hope to perceive the layers of him.

"To know about all of you," she finally admitted. "To know about more than just the stealer of souls you've been or the boy thief you once were." Unable to help herself, she glanced at the bookshelf, at the volume into which Dax had tucked his guardian's notes.

He followed her gaze. "You could have read the papers anytime. You were certainly alone here for long enough."

She shook her head. "I wouldn't do that—not without your say-so."

A moment slid past.

"I say so now. Read it. All. Every word."

"Dax . . ."

"I want you to, Robyn. I *need* you to." In a whisper so soft she had to strain to hear, he added, "*You* need to."

Robyn watched as he got to his feet, moved to the bookshelf. Sliding the huge volume from its perch, he opened it, removed the notes, and then returned to Robyn's side, handing them to her.

Carefully, she took the pages—dozens upon dozens of them. They felt heavy in her hands. Could it be she held just a journal, and not the weight of Dax's world?

She laid the sheets on her lap, looking up at him.

"You're certain," she said.

"I am." With that, he moved to the hearth where he stirred and stoked the fire and then bent down to light a slim stick of kindling. Standing, he touched its burning tip to each of the candles atop the mantel until the flat was ablaze with light.

Robyn realized then that he must have done this very thing when he'd first returned to England. She could imagine him alone in this flat, light surrounding him, as he read through what his guardian had written. Clearly, whatever the journal held was something Dax did not want kept to the darkness.

She sat back and began to read.

As the burning wood in the grate crackled and spit, as the pages sifted through Robyn's fingers and her mind devoured every word, Dax remained quiet. Eventually, he uncorked a bottle of wine, pouring them each a glass. Robyn barely noticed, too engrossed in the weaving of words, in the story of his early years.

Every now and then she would glance up at him, sometimes with a smile, sometimes in wonder . . . and sometimes with a look so sad she knew it tore at his heart. He didn't interrupt her. He said nothing at all. He only watched, and waited . . . waited for Robyn to put all the pieces of the puzzle together.

Every page detailed Dax's early years, though never was his name written in the passages. She realized that he'd been taken away from his father at an early age. From the time he was five years old until he was twelve, Dax had been under the protection of a guardian, a man Dax's father had obviously trusted . . . and one who had clearly loved Dax and wanted only the best for him.

She learned of Dax's many "firsts," of his milestones in

life, and of his devotion to his studies. He'd had a propensity for numbers and for languages. Dates were noted, and there were vivid descriptions of all the places Dax and his guardian had lived, which were many—Paris, Venice, Rome . . . *even Sussex.*

The notes began when Dax was five years old, and continued until he was twelve . . .

Until, Robyn thought, *that moment when Jemmy found him in the woods.*

In the South Downs. Of Sussex.

When he was twelve.

Dear Lord, she thought, one singular notion taking root in her mind—one that involved Dax, herself, and their earliest years.

The last entry, unlike the others, had been hastily scrawled. Dax's guardian had written of freezing rain, of a cold cottage, that they awaited Dax's godmother to come and lead them to safety, to a home where Dax was to have met his future.

That was it. The boy's story ended there.

Robyn placed the pages on the cushion beside her. Throat suddenly dry, she reached for the wine, barely tasting the liquid as she swallowed it past the lump in her throat.

She lifted her gaze to Dax, not surprised to find his own fastened on her. How long had she been reading—an hour, two hours? She didn't know. She felt as though she'd just unlocked a treasure chest, one teeming with truths. And now, as she looked at Dax and he at her, she was seeing him clearly, wholly, for the very first time.

My God, she thought, her mind tumbling back in time, remembering snippets of what her aunt had said to her . . . remembering bits of her own past . . . until, piece by fuzzy piece, the past came into view.

"The—the accident you spoke of that night in the loft, Dax . . . it involved your guardian, didn't it?"

"Yes."

"And my aunt. She was there, wasn't she?"

Again, he answered in the affirmative.

"And you . . . you had been to Land's End earlier that morning, hadn't you? To that cottage, near the cliffs."

He nodded.

Robyn set down the glass, her mind spinning, her entire body beginning to tremble. "It's you. You're the one," she whispered, tears gathering in her eyes, emotion tightening her throat. *"My first betrothed."*

Amazement, elation, and a thousand other emotions swept through Robyn. She got to her feet, her gaze still locked with his. And then she moved toward him, as though drawn to a distant, dazzling place on her horizon— one that had been forever out of her reach, but no longer.

Dax straightened, watching her, trying to guess her mood as he placed both the bottle and his glass on the mantel. "You're disappointed."

"No." The word came past her lips in a breathless rush of feeling. She stopped an inch away, lifted trembling hands, and gently touched either side of his face as she gazed deep into his eyes.

"Robyn. What are you doing?"

"I am looking at *you.*"

"Do not. God. Robyn. All you'll see is a fiend and a thief and a smuggler of—"

"No," she whispered, running her right thumb along the crescent-shaped scar beneath his left eye. "Not that."

"Then what?" he demanded. "A man who didn't tell you the truth? A fiend so hungry for you that he'd take you wherever he could, would suck the soul out of you?"

"I see *you,* Dax."

Her words undid him, Robyn realized, as did the moment with all its truths and heartrending realizations. He pulled back, away from her touch, his eyes wet with tears. He pivoted, putting his back to her, not wanting Robyn to see him cry. She knew then he had wanted to come to her as a man worthy of her attentions—as the favored son he had once been and not the soul-stealing Phantom he'd become. He had wanted her to learn the truth of their betrothal at a moment when all was right in their worlds. Not here—not like this.

But the truth was out, and Robyn realized Dax wasn't so certain he could live with the naked emotions he'd just viewed in her eyes. All of her life, Robyn had painted a bright, lovely memory of her first betrothed. Even after it was thought he'd died, she still wondered what kind of man he would have become. Now, instead of the white knight she'd conjured in her mind, she had before her a man cursed. A man perhaps not worthy of her. That is what Dax was thinking, she knew.

"Dax. Don't turn away."

He hauled in a labored breath, and she perceived, in the shaking of his limbs, in the way he held himself out of her reach, all of the thoughts teeming in his brain. She knew he wondered how to explain the volley of feelings searing through him. Knew he was questioning how to tell her that he'd waited years for this moment, only to find himself shattered by it.

A loud rap sounded on the door, startling them both.

Robyn dashed away her tears, thinking Dax would move to the door.

He didn't.

He remained where he was, shoulders lifting with every deep breath, as if he was steeling himself, reaching deep within to draw forth some armor of old.

Robyn forced herself to move; it could be one of Dax's men with news about her aunt, or Mattie with word from Ballinger.

A man, well over six feet tall and built with the girth of a giant, loomed in the hallway. He barely took note of Robyn, clearly believing her to be some hired domestic and not worth his time. "I am Lord Thomas Ballinger," he said, his voice booming loud in her ears. "I have come at the behest of one Marquis of Sommerset, son to the Duke of Denville."

Robyn blinked, her mind tripping over the lofty titles. She was about to say there was no marquis present, no son of a duke, but Dax spoke before she had a chance, his voice clearer, stronger than she'd ever known it to be.

"I am he."

Robyn gaped at Dax, watching as he turned to face Lord Ballinger. What she saw swept the breath from her lungs. Dax was no longer her Phantom, the smuggler, or even the attentive lover she'd known, but much, much more than that. He seemed to stand a head taller and a mountain stronger than just a mere second ago, having found within him that mantle of protection he'd sought: his birthright—the truth of *who* and *what* he was.

A fierce pride shot out of his piercing green eyes. The autocratic cast of his handsome, hard-as-granite features was impossible to deny. He looked every inch a man born to privilege—one snatched from it and then tossed in with a rough, unholy lot. He appeared, Robyn thought, like a warrior returned home who would lay claim to all that was his. Why hadn't she seen it before?

And *she* had been his, from the moment of her christening, Robyn reminded herself, trying hard not to tremble at the transformation she saw before her. But no matter how much she thought she'd learned about Dax this day, Robyn feared that her true education concerning this man, her lover, her *betrothed*, was about to begin in earnest.

Lord Ballinger, not realizing Robyn was the daughter of the Earl of Chelsea or the niece of Lady Amelia Archer, swept past her, his focus completely on Dax. Robyn let him go, deciding it was best to keep her mouth shut.

"B'god," Ballinger declared in his great, booming voice, "but you've the mannerisms of your father through and through. I had thought, when I read your missive, that someone was playing a very cruel trick. I came here myself, intending to face whatever fiend made use of your name and your seal."

"As you can see, it is me, in the flesh," Dax answered. "And make no mistake, I am indeed a fiend."

Ballinger's dark eyes seared into him. "We thought you were dead."

"For a good many years, so did I. But I've returned and intend to deal with all those who wronged my family." Dax glared at the man. "Will I be starting with you, Ballinger?"

Robyn stiffened, glad enough to be invisible to the two men. There wasn't an ounce of tenderness to be seen in Dax. His eyes gleamed with grim purpose, his features hard as stone.

Lord Ballinger faltered, finally losing his bravado. "I deserved that, I s'pose. God knows I'd wonder the same, were I you. But hear me, and hear me well, I had *nothing* to do with what happened to your family."

"No?" Clearly, Dax didn't believe him. "What about my father, Ballinger? Where were you when he was hanged for treason against the Crown? Were you begging before the House of Lords to stay his execution . . . or did you watch as my father, stripped of his title and all of his possessions, dangled from a noose he didn't deserve?"

Perspiration beaded on Ballinger's beefy brow. "Of course I didn't watch your father die."

"But neither did you cry out his innocence, did you? Damn you for being such a coward!"

"You don't understand. The evidence against him was staggering, there—there was no changing the tide of sentiment against him."

"Who created this 'evidence'?" Dax thundered, causing Robyn to jerk at his savage tone. "Tell me, or I'll see to it *you* dangle from a noose, one wrought by my own hands."

The huge giant of a man shuddered. "I—I don't know. I swear to you I don't!"

Dax whipped away from the man, strode to the circular table at the side of the room, and tore open one of the saddle packs he'd brought up to the flat days before. From it he withdrew the map Robyn had found and Sam had delivered to him, and several of the heart replicas. Moving back toward Ballinger, he put all on the table before the sofa. "Does any of this stir your memory?"

The older man paled. "Where—where did you get those?"

"Where do you think?"

"Lady Archer?"

"Yes. These were in her possession. What *wasn't* there, Ballinger, was the original talisman."

Truly ill at ease, the man took a kerchief from his pocket and pressed a path across his forehead with it in quick, jerky movements. "That hasn't been seen since—"

"The day my mother was murdered?" Dax cut in, a savageness in his tone. "Since the moment I was pulled from the carnage of my mother's carriage and whisked away from my father, forever?"

"Yes," the man breathed.

Dax glared at him, years of pain and anger pouring out of his gaze. "What do you know of the talisman? Why is it so valuable? Why, b'god, would someone commit murder to possess it?"

"I swear to you, I don't know." Ballinger heaved in a labored breath. "I know only that it was a gift to your mother from Lady Archer, that it was part of a trio."

"You were paid to create replicas of the talisman. Why? Were you planning to steal the original from my mother, perhaps? Replace it with a fake?"

"Of course not! Don't be absurd. Your father commissioned me to create the replicas. I was but a younger son at that time, having not yet come into my title. I—I dabbled in that sort of thing and your father knew it."

"Why even create them? For what purpose?"

"As bait," Ballinger said. "To lure and capture the one person in the world bent on destroying your family."

"Who?"

"I don't know! Nor did your father." Ballinger shook his head, pinned beneath Dax's hard stare. "I can see you don't trust a word I am saying, but I never intended any harm for your father. I admired him, I swear it. Though there were many who despised him. Your father had more than a few enemies—but he always suspected the person bent on ruining him was someone he'd never met . . . was someone only your mother knew."

"And you have no inkling who that might be?" Dax demanded.

"No, I don't." Ballinger was sweating in earnest. "There is a man who still lives. H-His name is Tisdale. He was your father's solicitor. He's an old man now, paralyzed. I—I went to see him, in Stevenage, and fetched him from there yesterday. At an inn, on the way back to London, we learned that Tisdale's cottage and an adjoining barn were devoured by flames in an explosion. He would have been dead if not for the fact I went to get him.

"Amelia Archer came to me days ago," Ballinger continued, "asking the same questions you ask now. She intended to speak with Tisdale, and then I think she meant to go *here*." Ballinger jabbed a beefy finger at the crude map. "This oilskin depicts the area where you were born, in the Cotswolds. It is believed that your father hid the talisman shortly after your mother was murdered, and that he'd created this oilskin map so that one day *you* could claim it, if indeed you still lived." Ballinger paused, his face a mask of pained anxiety.

"Go on," Dax said. "Tell me everything you know."

The behemoth of a man looked truly ill. "It is a sad tale, I fear. Your father . . . he spent a fortune and years of his life searching for you, but it was as if you had vanished into air. Not even the men he hired—and there were many—could ferret out a clue as to what became of you. Eventually, he—he was brought up on charges of treason against the Crown. He was charged with having republican sympathies. Given the fact your mother was French, and all the monies he funneled to her family in France, it—it was not such a difficult thing to believe. He was hanged, declaring his innocence to the end. That's all I know. I told Lady Archer as much when last I saw her. But then she started questioning me about Tisdale and if perhaps the man could have created the evidence against your father. That's when I decided to go see him myself."

"And?"

"And the man is old, feeble, and paralyzed . . . but he can tap out a yes or no answer, and when I asked if he'd fabricated proof that led to your father's hanging, he answered *yes*. When I asked if he had been forced to do so, he answered *yes* again. So I brought him back to the city with me. I intend to have him questioned by the authorities this very day."

Dax drew in a hard breath, nodded. "And Amy?" he demanded.

Ballinger shook his head. "I—I don't know where she is. I truly believe she intended to question Tisdale . . . and I also believe she intended to head back to your father's home in the Cotswolds. She and I agreed that if your father wanted something hidden, he'd doubtless hide it there. I think she intended to search the grounds once more, in hopes of finding the talisman and luring your father's true nemesis into the open. She said she believed someone still lived who wanted what Denville once had, and who was still searching for you."

Dax said nothing, his gaze shadowed, his Phantom fully absorbed into his skin, as if he had sucked it all inside where it was boiling at a hot simmer that would soon spew out of him.

"What *did* happen to you?" Ballinger asked. "Where have you been all of these years?"

Dax snapped his gaze to the older man, his eyes a green gleam. "To hell and back."

Ballinger sucked in a breath, his jowls shuddering with the movement.

Dax motioned to the door. "Go," he ordered. "Watch over Tisdale, see that he is questioned by the authorities, tell them that whatever answers he can give will most likely help lead them to Lady Archer . . . and if you are asked about me, *by anyone*, you know nothing. You have not seen me. I do not exist. You understand that?"

The older man mopped once more at his brow, nodding profusely. "Yes, I—I understand." He stared hard at Dax, his own face tortured. "Whatever you have in mind, I hope you will remember that with the testimony Tisdale is about to give, your—your father's name could be cleared and you, young man, could find yourself ascending to the titles your father once held. Please . . . do nothing foolish or—or hotheaded."

A lone muscle twitched along Dax's strong jaw. He said nothing, promised nothing.

Ballinger, for all his height and girth, shuddered anew at the specter Dax presented. "God be with you," he muttered, then exited the flat with haste, not even glancing in Robyn's direction.

She moved to close the door behind him, swallowing thickly as she turned to face Dax—or rather, *not* Dax. Her mind was in a whirl, her brain tumbling with countless questions. He was the son of a duke, a marquis in his own right, and he'd *known* of Lord Ballinger?

"Say nothing," Dax warned, even before she had a chance to speak. "Ask me nothing. Not now."

Struck mute, Robyn could only nod.

Dax sank down onto the sofa, placed his elbows on his knees and his chin to the steeple of his fingers beneath it, and glowered down at the oilskin map. The demon he harbored was in his gaze. He was seeing his past, Robyn guessed, seeing it . . . and living the pain anew.

Long minutes ticked past. One of the candles on the mantel guttered, as did another, and then another. The room, that so recently had been lit with such brightness, that had been a place where nothing need hide, became filled with tall, eerie shadows that flickered against the walls.

Robyn wondered if Dax intended to sit there all day. She wouldn't interrupt him. If it was time he needed, or silence, then that is what he would have.

Robyn's heart ached—for Dax and for all he had lost—and it ached for herself and for all she had never known but *should* have known and shared with this man since the day of their betrothal.

At long last, Dax stirred. He got to his feet, took up the map and the heart replicas and tucked all back into his packs, and then put away his mentor's notes.

"Gather your things," he said.

"Dax, what—"

"Just do as I say, Robyn."

She did. Hurrying up into the mezzanine, she grabbed some clothing, bandages, a small satchel. By the time she came down the steps Dax was snuffing out the last of the candles. He grabbed a few handfuls of sand from a bucket near the hearth and threw them on the fire, smothering the flames.

Robyn watched as the room became almost completely dark, only a seep of the gray day outside coming through the drapes. She pressed her eyes shut, already missing the things she and Dax had shared in the flat.

Nothing, it seemed, could remain the same.

"You are to stay in the city, but not here," he said. "I'll find somewhere else where you'll be safe."

Robyn's eyes flew open. *"No."* The word was command, not a plea. "I won't stay. I'm going with you, Dax."

She felt him shift in the semidarkness, felt the force of his edgy anger. "Do not defy me, Robyn."

"Nor you me," she shot back, and then, knowing he intended to head out the door, his decision made, she caught his hand with hers, ignoring the flare of energy coming from him, and held fast. "Do not push me away when I've only just found you, Dax."

He stilled, but said nothing.

Terrified he would leave her and she would never see him again, Robyn said, "From the cradle, those who loved me most decided my life should be joined with yours. I know that now—perhaps I even knew it when you found me in that study and were so willing to play the part of my lover. It was you, Dax, who once gave me a feather to give wing to my dreams . . . and it was you who once let me put my heart into your hand." Squeezing her fingers around him, she rasped, "It's still there, Dax. *You will always hold my heart.*"

Robyn thought she heard Dax catch his breath. She thought, in fact, she heard him moan.

But still he said nothing.

Robyn blew out a breath. "I'll only follow you. You know it's true."

"Dearest Christ . . . You don't know what evil lies in wait for me."

"However frightening it is, let me face it with you."

He jerked away. "Someone, somewhere, murdered my mother and ruined my father. I intend to find the fiend . . . I intend to destroy this person."

"No matter where you're going, no matter *what* you intend, I want to go with you." She put her forehead to his chest. "Don't leave me behind, Dax, not when we've just found each other."

She felt a breath shudder out of him . . . and then he wrapped one strong arm about her, turned his face into her hair, and held her tight.

She knew then he wouldn't leave her behind.

Within an hour, they headed out of the city just as they had entered it, with Dax's men riding as guard and Dax leading the way. Once again, Robyn found herself within the confines of the carriage, but this time there was no Mattie to keep her company.

Black thunderclouds ate away the gray day, and soon

the lands they raced across were battered by driving rain and a wind gone wild. Streaks of lightning flashed in the distance as thunder boomed and rolled.

Robyn held tight, forcing herself not to lose her courage or lessen her conviction that she wasn't hindering Dax in joining him. Surely they could get farther, *faster*, if she too rode astride. But he had insisted on taking the carriage, and she had kept quiet, thankful that she was allowed to join him at all.

Every clap of thunder seemed to her to shout one word: doom. Robyn couldn't shake the sensation of being followed, of being *hunted*. She felt as if they were the perfect prey of some unholy beast recently unleashed—a beast not even her phantom lover could defeat.

Chapter Nineteen

Robyn, nerves frayed, doubted she could tolerate one more second inside the carriage. She was sick of the smells of wet horse, of damp cushions, of smoldering coal in the brazier at her feet . . . of rain, of mud, of *fear*. London was miles behind, rainstorms behind. Though they had stopped at an inn and lingered over a deal table in a private dining room earlier that morning—a luxury, given their pace—Robyn still felt ready to climb the carriage walls.

Making a decision, she rose to her feet, holding herself steady against the constant swaying as she rapped sharply on the trapdoor.

Bones lifted the thing, shouting down at her, "M'lady?"

"I wish to stop," she yelled.

"Stop?" he echoed, confused. "But Dax said—"

"I've had enough, Bones. Please!"

"Say n' more, m'lady."

Robyn, wrung out, dropped back down onto the cushions as Bones brought the team to a halt and called ahead for Dax.

He came riding back within a few minutes, thrusting open the carriage door. "Are you all right?"

"No." Robyn ignored the blast of wind and rain that

swirled inside. "I want to ride with you, Dax. I—I'm frightened. We're being followed, I can feel it."

Dax frowned, his face beneath the brim of his hat streaming with water and droplets of mud. He wore his greatcoat, and that, too, was streaming wet and mud splattered. Sharp needles of rain, whipped into chaos by the wind, sliced against him as his huge horse blew out powerful breaths of air.

"We are being trailed," he admitted, "and have been for a while now. We're nearly to the borders of my childhood home. Randolph rode ahead. He says there is a cottage near—what's left of it, anyway. I plan to stop there and hole up inside the thing while our followers come into view."

Dax had *known* they were being followed?

Every day since leaving the flat had been a miserable one, Robyn decided. "Let me ride with you," she said again, but knew he wouldn't—not in this weather. "Or come inside with me." She knew she sounded desperate, but couldn't care.

Dax's rain-smeared features, so harsh and hard after riding too many miles to count, softened somewhat. "All right," he finally said. He turned his head, shouting to Monty, who rode directly behind the carriage, asking him to lead his horse. To Bones, he called out to mind the ruts, that the rain had ruined the road up ahead. With that, he dropped down off his saddle, landing neatly inside the door. The carriage bounced with his weight, then righted itself. As Monty took quick control of Dax's mount, Dax rapped on the door above, giving Bones the signal to once again move the team.

Robyn held his gaze as he sat down across from her. "Thank you. I know you'd rather be out there with your men."

"Is that what you think?" He shook his head. "Here is nice, Robyn. In fact, I like being here. With you."

Robyn felt her heart warm, and some of her fear fell away even though thunder cracked overhead and rain slammed in sheets against the carriage. It appeared they were entering the very center of yet another storm.

"Who's following us?" she asked.

He didn't hesitate in sharing all he knew with her. "Falconer. With at least six men, the bulk of them a motley crew. Sam's doubled back a number of times. He says the band of them is closing in and has been throughout the night."

Robyn winced. Morely was going to this much trouble to retrieve her? It made no sense. She felt sick at the thought of Dax having to deal not only with the nemesis of his past, but Morely's henchmen as well.

"I shouldn't have come," she whispered. "Only look what I have brought in my wake. . . ."

"Perhaps."

"What do you mean?"

"They've been trailing us for a while, Robyn. A group of men on horseback could have overtaken us at any time— especially now with the road ravaged by the rain and Bones having to slow the cattle."

"I don't understand."

"Think about it. It's almost as if they're watching . . . waiting for us to lead them somewhere."

A sense of horror filled her. "Are you saying that Morely and his men might possibly be involved with your past?"

"I don't know. Anything's possible." Dax shook his head, a haunted look in his eyes. "Whatever Falconer's purpose, I intend to meet him head-on—and to make it perfectly clear that you won't be dragged back to Morely or your father."

Fear filled her belly. "Dax, promise you will do nothing rash . . . that you won't put yourself in harm's way because of me."

He met her gaze from beneath the brim of his hat. His green eyes were shadowed, filled with the press of the past and the unfolding of the future, but even though a storm more volatile than the one outside was brewing within him, Dax turned his mouth to a small, reassuring smile. "I'll take care."

It was what she needed to hear.

Robyn watched as Dax removed his wide-brimmed hat and shook the water from it. He dropped it to the floor, near the brazier Bones had lit to keep Robyn warm. Next, he shed his gloves and greatcoat, doing his best to shake them out as well. Draping them across the cushions beside him, he sat back, reaching up with his hands to smooth back his wet, short-cropped hair.

Robyn was glad enough to simply watch him, his movements. There was no shimmer of the Phantom visible; it was as if his body had absorbed it totally, as if man and monster had meshed and were now one. Robyn guessed the Curse was coiling tight within him and she feared when it would explode outward. He'd pushed them beyond limits to reach the Cotswolds. Robyn could sense in him his determination to find her aunt, and for the lost boy inside of him to make sense of his past. He'd been alone for so long, had faced so many impossible situations, and yet there was still a wealth of tenderness in him.

Robyn felt a rush of emotion pour through her. In the soft light of the brazier, his face was more handsome and more dear to her than ever before.

"Do you realize, Dax Dexter, that I don't even know your true name? In spite of all we've shared, all the days we've had together, I don't even know what to call you."

"Robyn . . ." he breathed. "Don't, lass."

"Don't what?"

"Look at me like that."

"I can't help the way I look at you," she whispered, and thought, *No secrets, no longer.* "Won't you share your true name with me?"

"You know what it is. Only think back—back to your first betrothal."

She shook her head. "I knew you only as the 'dearest son' of my aunt's 'dearest friends.' That is how every sentence ever uttered about you began. I was never told your true name." She leaned forward. "I'd like to hear it now . . . from you."

He stiffened, hesitating, perhaps remembering the boy he'd been, with a new name for every country he passed through. He drew in a breath, let it out.

"Broderick," he whispered at last. "Broderick William Arthur Charles Mallabourne."

No simple name for this man, but a host of them— doubtless garnered from his father and grandfathers before him. Wonderment filled her.

"*Broderick,*" Robyn murmured, testing the feel of it on her tongue, the weight of it in her heart. She removed her gloves, leaned forward, and took his rain-cold hands in hers. "And who *are* you, Broderick William Arthur Charles Mallabourne?"

"Robyn—"

"Tell me. I need to know. I *want* to know."

Dax brought her hand to his lips, placing a kiss against the inner side of her wrist, his mouth warm and soft on her skin. Voice low, steady, filled with both pride and pain, he said, "I am the son of the Duke and Duchess of Denville, and one day was to have inherited the title, Marquis of Sommerset."

Green eyes beginning to fill with tears, he said, "My mother died when I was five. My father, knowing her death had been no random act of thievery, guessed that my own life was in danger. He called upon a close friend—Sir Dysart Carlyle—whom he begged to take me abroad, tutor me, and keep me safe. Sir Dysart did just that. For years. You've read his tale . . . you know the ending."

"But I don't know all of the beginning. What of my aunt?" she asked softly, knowing now was the time to learn all truths.

"Amy is my godmother. She was my mother's bosom friend and remained the most stalwart supporter of my father. He asked her to help keep me hidden . . . keep me safe. She, Sir Dysart, and my father laid the plans that would see me secreted in far-off places for many, many years. Your aunt became my guardian's closest confidante as the two of them decided where and when I would be transported. They purposely kept my father ignorant of my locations.

"The duke, you see, feared he might one day be tortured and forced to tell all. He and Amy believed someone wanted me dead. He had no clue where I was, no idea of the countless cities and villages Sir Dysart and I dwelled within, or of the many false names I was given for every country we visited. He was only given word of my safety and nothing more—and all of this came to him from Amy. That is why my guardian kept a journal of my early years. It is, alas, a journal my father never viewed."

Robyn laced her fingers with Dax's, knowing how difficult the telling of his tale must be for him. "And your mother?" she asked, sensing Dax needed to talk of the woman he'd lost too soon.

"What Ballinger said was true: The talisman was dear to my mother. She always kept it near her, just as she always kept me near to her. There was a carriage accident when I was five. My mother's footman later swore she was hauled from the wreckage, and that the talisman would have been cut from her body by the thieves who'd caused the accident had the man not stopped them. The culprits fled, leaving my mother's corpse and the talisman behind. They left the scar on my face as well. . . .

"I was with her in that carriage. I tried to protect her. I threw my body atop hers, and that's when the knife came, carving the skin from beneath my eye. When I looked up . . . my mother was dead, my face ruined."

Robyn reached up, touching the scar beneath his eye, lovingly brushing her finger along it, wanting to soothe his every pain. "*Dax.* How very brave your mother must have thought you to be when, young as you were, you tried to protect her."

"But I couldn't save her," he rasped, turning his face and pressing it against her hand, losing himself in her touch. "I *didn't* save her. And then my father saw to it I was hidden away . . . and years later Sir Dysart was murdered while trying to tame the team of yet another carriage and I was no more able to save him than I was my mother. I decided then that if I became no one and nothing, then Amy would live and my father would live.

"So I did what Amy yelled for me to do. I jumped from that runaway carriage. After that, I hit my head and accidentally shot myself in the chest, and my memories vanished and the Curse uncurled inside of me and then Jemmy found me and, well, you know the rest. Years passed, years of thievery and soul smuggling, the Phantom always forcing its will, while all the while I tried to remember the life I'd once had. It wasn't until January of last year that my memories returned—all of them, like a flood.

"But even before that, Robyn, you were the one bright spot in my world; the essence of you was always with me," he whispered. "And always I dreamt—of the parents I'd lost, of *you*, our betrothal, and of the life we might one day share. The memory of what you were to me, what you represented, was forever in my mind, Robyn, and you have always, *always* been the hope for my future. You still are."

Tenderness engulfed her. "Oh, Dax," she murmured, "*Broderick.*"

He kissed her, full on the mouth, a kiss so deep, so filled with feeling it lifted her heart and poured joy through her. He was all that was dear and sweet and good in life. He was her yesterday and her tomorrow, her beginning and her end. He was her love—first, last . . . *forever.*

The carriage suddenly bounced, a bone-jarring thud that jostled them apart, away from each other.

Robyn would have fallen to the floor had Dax not caught hold of her. He drew her to the cushion beside him, steadying her, and then guided her right hand up to the bootstrap to their left, telling her to hold tight.

The carriage slammed hard down into a sinkhole in the road and then heaved up and out, causing Robyn's teeth to snap together. The taste of blood bloomed in her mouth. "What's happening?" she gasped.

"Nothing good, I fear." He was already on his feet, bracing himself, rapping sharply against the trapdoor. Long seconds later the door was whipped open.

"We got visitors," Bones shouted down. "Chargin' right at us from behind. The bridge ahead be washed out, the stream overflowin'."

Dax lowered his head. He glanced once at Robyn, then looked up and yelled, "There should be a cottage nearby."

"We be headin' for it—Randolph says there be a good chance we can make it."

"You can handle the team alone?"

Bones shouted that he could, and then added, "But we be facin' a rough ride."

Dax let the trapdoor slam back into place and then fell to the cushions beside Robyn as the carriage pitched sharply, the crazed movement sending them crashing from one side of the panels to the other. The brazier tipped and spilled, hot coals skittering across the floor, one glowing nugget sliding into the material of Robyn's hems.

"Robyn. Your skirts."

Dax stomped on the coals with one boot, kicking them away from her as Robyn scrambled to get her feet up, shaking out her skirts. The lump of coal clattered to the floor, leaving a burn hole near the hem of her riding skirt. She beat at it with one of his gloves that she snatched from the seat until there was nothing but a black-ringed circle.

Dax, seeing that the brazier still held a bellyful of hot coals, hauled himself to his feet, grabbed tight to the bootstrap with one hand, and reached for the handle of the door. Dragging the brazier near it, he opened the thing and kicked hard, sending it out into the night, far off to the side of the road, an arch of cinders flaring briefly behind it.

Darkness swallowed them as he slammed the door

shut. A wicked turn of the carriage thrust him forward into the corner of the cushions beside Robyn. Pivoting around, he pressed his back into it, held tight to the bootstrap with his left hand and then stretched out one long leg, hooking his foot against the opposite seat for leverage.

Through the inky blackness, he reached for Robyn, drawing her body tight against his, holding her fast with his right arm. She pressed her face against his shirtfront, wet from the rain that had pelted against him when he'd opened the door.

"Dax," Robyn gasped, her entire body trembling, "your Phantom . . . I—I didn't feel it just now, as you pulled me to you."

"I know. I'd have taken us out of here before now if I could have."

"You mean you can't—"

"No. Something's happening inside me—something is forcing a dark calm within, one that deepens the farther north we go. I've felt it for days now."

Robyn could feel the heart talisman beneath his wet shirt. Like her own, it gave off heat. She reached for it, drawing it outside of his shirt.

"I feel that, too," he said.

With her other hand, she dug for her own. "Mine is warm as well." And she held both talismans tight in each fist.

"Take it," he said. "I want you to wear it. Ever since you gifted me with it, I've felt it has protected me. I want to know you're protected now, as much as possible."

Robyn shook her head, unwilling to take the very thing from him that her mother and aunt had known would protect him. And she couldn't hide her fear from him, either.

"It's all right," Dax whispered, his mouth slanting against her forehead as he kissed her there. "Everything will be all right, Robyn."

But she could feel the mad thudding of his heart, could hear in the catch of his voice that he was frightened. Doubtless he was remembering those horrid moments when he'd lost his mother and later his guardian. He knew firsthand the carnage of a carriage tipped to its side, a team gone wild . . . the hideous sounds of wood splintering, of harnessed animals unable to dash away from their deaths.

Robyn clung to him, pressing her eyes shut. He cushioned her every time the carriage bounced and rocked, held her tight during each wild turn, and she knew as he held her, as he soothed her with hoarse whispers, that he would give his own life to save her. Every thump of his heart seemed to say *not again, never again.* He would not lose her as he had his mother, Sir Dysart, and Amy.

Robyn lifted her face. In the darkness, she felt the rough stubble as he rubbed his cheek against hers—and then she felt the sting of salt in the cut on her lip . . . the salt of his tears.

The carriage rammed down into a final rut, mud sucking at the wheels. With a last thrust that threw them hard into the corner, the conveyance ground to a halt, listing to one side. Even before she could think clearly, Dax was guiding her upright, asking if she was all right.

"Y-Yes," she gasped, hearing shouts outside above the din of the elements . . . and in the distance, a single gunshot.

"Bloody hell," Dax muttered. "They've given a warning shot."

From above, Bones whipped open the trapdoor, shouting down. "Stuck tight," he yelled. "The cattle can't budge us—and we got visitors."

"I heard," Dax yelled. "How far is the cottage?"

"A way and a bit, but the land be flooded!"

"Unhitch the team," Dax ordered, and Bones immediately dropped the door back in place.

Dax groped for his coat, found it, and then shrugged into the thing. To Robyn, he said, "I've got to help them. You stay in the carriage. Once we get the team free, I'll get my own horse and come for you. You open this door to no one but me. No one, do you hear?"

Robyn was trembling uncontrollably now. Falconer and his men had *fired* on them. "Oh, God, Dax," she gasped. "It's *me* they're after. I—I should just go willingly, so that you and the others can—"

"No."

Though but a single word, it passed Dax's lips with the force of a thousand storms, paralyzing Robyn. Even though only moments ago they'd been locked together in fear, holding each other close, Dax had since forced that fear deep down inside of him. He was reaching now for the soul-stealing fiend willing to face the devil itself for what he wanted . . . and he wanted *her*.

Intense, commanding, he said, "Stay here. Stay safe."

He shoved open the carriage door just as a bolt of lightning ripped across the belly of the sky. In that one savage burst of bluish-white light, Robyn saw Dax's face. Not even that wild blaze could penetrate the dark pools of green that were his eyes. Robyn felt the Phantom churning inside him, hard and relentless, a funneling fury that would soon erupt. As he turned away and dropped down out of the oddly tilting carriage, Robyn knew he'd fight to the end to keep her safe.

She heard another shot fired from somewhere behind them, heard Dax shouting to his men, and then felt the carriage rock as the first of its team was unlashed. Thunder continued to crack overhead, streaks of lightning sizzled brightly, one after the other, causing a crazed light show to play against the carriage windows . . . and then she heard her own name, shouted into the wild wind from far behind.

"Robbie!"

Robyn snapped her head up. Only her aunt and cousins called her Robbie. She knew that voice, had heard it all her life.

"Sandy," she gasped aloud.

So *this* was the group Sandy had "taken up with" to try to find her? She wished now that she had told Lily all about Morely and his men. She wished she had been able to go to Sandy the very moment she'd learned about her father's disastrous game of chance with Lord Morely. What lies had Morely spun, what false sense of chivalry had he concocted to make her cousin come charging after her even while Falconer and his men fired on their carriage? Furious to think Sandy had been tricked, terrified over his safety, Robyn lunged for the door. She couldn't stay inside the carriage, not when her cousin was obviously racing for her, his back to Falconer and his band of gun-toting henchmen.

She entered into a wild night.

Stinging needles of rain pelted her. The ground beneath was awash in water—angry water, rushing hard. And the wind! Great gusts of it whipped around her.

Another series of lightning bursts lit the land, illuminating the lone cottage on a hill far away . . . *impossibly* far.

Robyn looked to her right, behind her.

From a distance could be seen a lone rider—Sandy—and a number of riders behind him, dark shapes moving fast toward her, pistols and shotguns in their fists.

Heart thudding, Robyn turned from the sight and ran. Though Dax had told her to stay put, she knew she couldn't, shouldn't. The men following Sandy were clearly ready to deal a swift death to anyone who stood in the way of their ultimate goal, and *she* was that goal.

She needed to lead them away from Dax and the others so they'd have enough time to free the team, mount up, and get away.

Hoping Dax would forgive her, praying that he and his men would be safe, she ran straight into the eerily lit night.

Frigid water sucked at the hems of her skirts and cloak, filling her boots. She stumbled, righted herself, and then pressed on, glancing back.

Sandy had veered off from the men behind him. Seeing her silhouette in a flash of lightning, he urged his horse into the rising waters. But the nervy animal balked at the high water. Sandy struggled, trying to calm the beast, but it was no use. He dropped down off his saddle, leaving the animal behind, calling out to Robyn once again.

She shoved the sodden hair from her eyes. *Oh, God, oh God,* she thought. The moment was like the nightmare she'd had in the caves and then again in the flat: Sandy, charging to her rescue . . . Sandy, shot, awash in—in not *water,* but his own blood. . . .

"No," Robyn cried. "Turn back!"

She noted that Dax was now astride his own mount and racing toward her . . . and one of Falconer's men from behind Sandy lifted his gun, aimed, and fired.

In spite of the rain and the distance, the shot hit a mark, though not the intended one. Sandy, eyes widening, jerked forward, the lethal lead slamming into the back of his left thigh just as a bolt of lightning lit the sky, daggering its way to the ground.

Robyn, horrified, watched as Sandy twitched from the hit and fell face-first into the rushing waters. He rolled once, hideously limp, and then was swept away, his body tossed about, sucked under.

Robyn pivoted, trying desperately not to lose sight of him.

She saw nothing more than black water. She thrust through it, realizing she was heading directly for the swollen stream, into deeper, angrier water. The force of it had sucked Sandy down and was now drawing his listless form parallel to the bank.

"Sandy!"

Nothing. Only the wind, the rain, and her worst fear come to pass.

The horror overtook Robyn, filled her, numbed her. She couldn't believe this was happening—*had* happened.

Falconer's men, breaking formation, led their horses in a swift circle around the highest of the water and then veered straight for Dax and his men. She could see Monty, Bones, and John working to unhitch the last of the carriage team, while Sam, a double-barreled gun in his fist, aimed and fired, affording them cover. But Falconer and his men kept coming.

Monty undid the last of the hitches, helped Bones to mount the horse, sans saddle, and tossed up the leads to him. John raced for the bench of the carriage, yanked out the blunderbuss stored there, and then tossed it to Bones, who caught it with a sure grip. Both John and Monty headed for their own mounts then, intending to climb astride, but a duo of Falconer's men fired. One shot. Another.

Monty fell. Then John.

Robyn felt bile rise in her throat at the horrific sight. The acidic stuff burned as full nausea claimed her. Water rushed about, slamming into her, knocking her sideways. She caught herself with both hands, lifted her upper body above the swift tumult, then swayed crazily.

Bones was shouting at the murdering fiends, the butt of his blunderbuss tight against his shoulder as he aimed. Robyn saw fire burst forth, and then watched, dead inside, as one of Falconer's men toppled to the ground.

She saw Falconer take the lead, heard him yell—and realized, suddenly, what his command meant: He wanted Dax. He wanted him dead.

That's what all of this was about, Robyn realized—not her and Morely and a marriage contrived by her father . . . but *Dax.* Dax and his past.

Robyn gasped, the force of the water knocking her down into murky blackness. She sucked in a mouthful of air, and then saw nothing at all.

Chapter Twenty

Dax's blood chilled to ice as he saw Robyn swallowed by the swirling water. No, *no*! He'd have used his dark magic to make a desert of the area, to annihilate the men who charged them, to move with swift speed and snatch Robyn up from the ground, to *save* her. . . . But he couldn't. His Phantom eluded him, flickering hot and then cold, here and then not here, as unpredictable as the lightning that flashed against the blackness above. It was as if being near the place of his birth, with the trio of talismans so close together, was a leash to his beast. With no quicker way to aid Robyn, Dax urged his mount into a run. The huge beast shot forward, barely skimming the flooded ground, leaving a froth of black water in its wake.

Dax kept his eyes trained on the spot where he'd last seen Robyn, hoping, praying to catch sight of her again. *Please, God. Let her live, let her live, let her live!*

Nothing. Just black water and dark land and this all-consuming fear tearing up from his belly, eating him alive. For too many years he had believed his Curse to be the worst thing in his world. He'd been wrong.

Watching as Robyn drowned, losing her—that was true torture.

He slowed as he reached the area where he'd last seen

her, and then hauled on the reins, his horse sending up
a geyser of water as it stopped, then pranced in a circle,
tossing its head, blowing steam, feeling Dax's fear. There
was nothing. Not here. Not around him. Nothing—

No . . . there was *something*. Just downstream. Dax caught
sight of a flutter of movement. A shadow. And then a
shape. Above the waterline.

"Robyn!" He shouted her name, his throat raw from the
fear eating at him, his body paralyzed with worry. And she
heard. Dear God, she heard.

Fighting the current that dragged against her, Robyn
managed to get her head above the water, her shoulders,
her chest . . . her arms. With huge effort, she planted both
knees firmly beneath her, and then turned into the sound
of Dax's yell, coughing water from her lungs. "Here," she
managed to call, faint but alive.

She'd have staggered to a stand if possible, would have
held steady for him. He knew that. But the water was a
wicked force. With one slight movement she lost all bal-
ance and went down again, this time onto her back, arms
flailing.

Dax, leaning forward as shots were fired at him from behind, pressed his thighs against his horse. He whispered
words of encouragement as the animal responded to his
lead, bravely heading into deeper water, but he couldn't
keep the animal here long, and he knew it—knew that if
he did they'd all be swept away.

With Falconer and his men bearing down on him, Dax
raced for Robyn. His heart in his throat, his body rising
up in the stirrups, leaning half out of the saddle, his left
hand managing the reins, his right swooping down—low,
strong, sure—Dax caught hold of her . . . and then he
pulled, upward and inward.

Robyn came onto the saddle in front of him, coughing
and dripping wet, her hems like lead weight, but she was
alive and responding and Dax could care about nothing
else. He had to press his eyes shut for a moment as she

leaned into him, one cheek against his chest. And when she gripped one small hand over the arm that snaked about her waist, holding her tight, and she gave a little squeeze of thanks, Dax thought he would weep. He slanted his mouth against her sodden hair, kissed her . . . and breathed.

From behind came another volley of shots, most sputtering into nothingness in the downpour. Bones and the others were following Dax's lead, while Falconer and his henchmen were moving in whatever direction would serve their purpose of seeing Dax dead.

Another blaze of lightning snapped as Dax veered to the left, away from the deeper water, and then right again when he saw that the land there sloped downward and was more flooded than the area behind. Ahead of them now was nothing but a narrow span of the swollen stream . . . and beyond that lay higher ground—much higher, none of it flooded.

"I need you to hold tight—we have to jump it."

"Dax. It's too *far.*"

But Robyn was already shifting in the saddle, getting a solid seat, and beneath them the horse, as cunning as it was fast, was gathering its muscles.

"We'll make it," Dax said, wanting to reassure her. *We will.*

He used his heels, something he rarely did—and the animal knew what to do. Blowing out great puffs, the huge horse moved, surged, eating up the water-soaked land . . . and then launched itself into the air.

They came down hard on the other side of the flooded stream, the horse's hindquarters landing deep in a black swirl of water. Well trained, the animal didn't panic but was all brawn and bravery as it clawed at the ground in front of it, chest heaving as it worked its way up the rocky bank, scattering rock and mud in its wake, Dax and Robyn keeping their weight forward and low.

There was no flooding at the top of the bank and no threat from Falconer and his men, at least not yet. Dax glanced back, seeing Bones make the jump, but Sam, coming behind, could not; his mount wasn't bold enough. The water and the rain and the shots of gunfire made the animal skittish. Sam hauled back, trying to calm the beast as he moved it out of the worst of the rushing water.

Dax shouted to him. "Robyn's cousin—he was shot, swept downstream! Go! Find him!"

Sam gave a wave that he understood and headed downstream in search of Sandy.

Randolph, bringing up the rear, met with trouble just as he hit the highest water and a shot rammed into his horse. The animal went down, forcing Randolph to throw himself clear of its weight. He landed in the rushing water. As strong as he was he couldn't fight the swift current, and Dax watched helplessly as the man rolled and thrashed, desperately trying to grab on to something solid before he was sucked away.

"I'll get 'im," Bones yelled, racing alongside the stream, his gaze not leaving Randolph. Once far enough ahead, he vaulted off the saddleless horse and went skidding down the rocky bank, grinding to a halt just downstream of Randolph. Feet planted wide against the press of water, he reached out with the only thing he had—his blunderbuss—yelling for his friend to grab hold.

Randolph flung out one arm, his gloved fingers clawing for the butt of the gun. He grabbed it, held tight. It was enough. With the leverage, Randolph rolled free of the fiercest rush of the water and crawled his way up and onto the bank. Bones scrambled to his side, helped him up, and then half dragged him up the steep bank.

Dax, seeing Falconer and the others closing in, headed to catch the bay Bones had ridden. Coming abreast of the nervy carriage horse, he shouldered it in with his own mount and then reached out, seizing its mane, getting the animal under control.

Bones, with Randolph at his side, ran toward them. "Those bastards got Monty and John!"

"I saw," Dax said, still holding tight to Robyn with one arm. He motioned for Bones to get astride.

"I be damned if they be getting' the rest of us! I say we make a stand, face 'em as one, eh?"

"With what?" Randolph yelled into the wind. "We've got your blunderbuss and little else. My own gun and powder were strapped to my horse! Even if we flee, we won't have a lead for long."

Randolph was right, Dax knew. All they had was one carriage horse and his own mount. Two people astride Bones's unsaddled bay wouldn't get very far, very fast—especially with one as large and as muscled as Randolph. As for weapons, they were left only with what Bones held: Dax's pistol, his powder horn, and the bow and pack of arrows he always carried strapped to his saddle.

Given the odds against them, they were easy targets.

Unless, of course, Dax made himself a lone target—and afforded the rest of them a long enough chance to escape.

Making his decision, Dax eased his arm away from Robyn, slid down off the saddle.

Robyn whipped her frightened gaze to his. "Don't you dare," she said, shaking her head as he grabbed the packet of arrows, strung it across his back, and then reached for his bow.

"*I'll* stay," Randolph shouted, knowing his friend's mind. "Leave me your gun, and—"

"No," Dax cut in. "Don't argue—there's no time. This is my fight. You get on that saddle and you ride, and you don't stop, not for anything."

Randolph, a grave look in his blue eyes, did as his friend ordered.

Dax looked up at Robyn . . . at his love, his life, his everything, and seared the sight of her—right now, right here—into his memory.

And then he took the cord with its heart talisman from around his neck.

"*No,*" Robyn yelled, suddenly understanding the sacrifice

he was about to make. "I won't leave you, Dax. I won't. Don't do this to me, to us." Struggling against Randolph's hold, she threw herself to the side, reaching out for Dax.

He caught her with both hands to her face, looping the heart talisman over her head, returning what she had given to him so many years ago. For what he planned, there would be no hope for him. He knew that now— knew he had no hope and no future, no nothing . . . but he wouldn't tell her that; he needed her to leave, to go . . . to be safe.

Rain pummeled them, wind whipping a heavy lock of her hair against her mouth. Eyes locked with hers, Dax kissed her hard, hair and all. Against her lips, he rasped "I love you. I've always loved you. I'll always love you."

With that, he pulled back, slapped one hand against his horse's rump, and yelled to Randolph, "Go! Now!"

Randolph dug in his heels and the animal shot forward, Bones following.

"Dax!" Robyn screamed, but the sound was drowned by the wind . . . and followed by gunfire. Falconer and his men were now crossing the swollen stream bed.

Dax whipped around, glad Robyn was on her way, glad she would get free of this mess. That fact alone helped him to face the coming moments.

Reaching back with his right hand, pulling an arrow from his pack, Dax knelt on the wet ground, fit the end of the arrow against the bowstring, then lifted, aimed . . . and released. He hit one of Falconer's men in the shoulder, toppling him down into the rushing stream. That left four others, all now on the same side of the water as Dax. Two headed up the bank directly beneath him, and two scattered wide, one to each side.

Wanting to give them no target, Dax threw himself down onto his belly. The rain came in hard, stinging sheets, the wind was wild, and though both made it nearly impossible to distinguish what was what, the elements also stood in Dax's favor. Guns misfired in such conditions.

Even shots that did fire didn't always hit their mark. His arrows, though, could.

In a flicker of lightning, Dax spied movement to his left. He spun toward it, bow up and at the ready.

It was a rider, racing straight for him.

He waited, blood thundering in his temples. He intended to unseat the man and then somehow get atop his horse and ride free.

Seconds ticked off, filled with the sound of rain, thunder, and the smashing of hooves against mud and water.

Five more feet.

Three.

One.

Dax rose, pulled back, and let the arrow fly. He saw its tip flash in a rip of lightning and then watched as it hit its mark.

The horse, suddenly riderless, skidded atop the wet, rocky ground, not knowing how to behave without firm guidance. Dax shot to his feet but had to let go of his bow to grab the lead from the horse's halter as it whipped in the wind. He seized it and held tight while the animal fought him. Remembering every trick Jemmy had taught him, Dax reined in the horse, grabbed for the saddle horn, then swung himself up and over the animal's back. Before long he had full reins. In another moment or two he could take control, could be flying after Robyn, Randolph, and Bones.

He hauled about, intending to race away . . . and then it hit: a shot of lead against his right shoulder, digging through his leather arrow pack, the force of it thrusting him forward. Dax, eyes widening, hauled in a harsh breath, sucking it through clenched teeth. He tried to keep control of the horse, but it slowed, began to buck.

Damn . . . damn!

Dax was thrown into the air, then slammed down hard on his injured shoulder. He felt something inside explode and he knew he was damned. This night would be his doom.

A savage energy burst from deep within, sending wintry

cold rolling throughout him, freezing his blood, stabbing sharp needles of icy pain into his brain. His wound stopped bleeding, stopped hurting. He felt nothing but frigid cold . . . and then heat—hot, searing heat, the devil's own. It flamed through him, and where muscle had frozen hard as marble, the heat melted away the cold and put motion where there had been none. Spasm after spasm whipped through him, arching his spine, contorting his limbs, his face smearing into a grimace. Just when he thought he could take no more, just when the pain was a vicious scream in his brain . . . it stopped, all of it, the cold and the heat and the wicked hurt.

Dax snapped his eyes open and knew instantly they burned in the night with a green gleam.

He could see as if it were daylight and not a rain-ravaged night.

And he could hear. Everything.

Once again the gifts of his Curse were upon him.

. . . And once again, he could hear hooves—a thunder of hooves.

The riders, he thought, *they are coming . . . for me.* And for the first and only time in his life he damn well wanted to cheer them on. Soon, Dax knew, he would have a horse he could ride. And he'd have a legion of followers. Ghostly ones.

Dead or alive, Phantom or man, Dax was going to give Falconer and his men what they deserved.

He made a motion to get up, but suddenly a fiend was beside him. Looking up, he stared into a face from his past.

"Blade."

In a flicker of lightning, Dax saw the tip of Blade's knife gleam bright.

A second later, he felt its piercing cut deep inside his left eye.

Robyn clung to Dax's saddle horn as Randolph gave the animal its head, letting the huge, brave beast fly along a twisting, turning path. They shot through driving rain, thunder rumbling, lightning flashing.

Just as they saw a hint of the open road ahead, Falconer came charging from behind, two of his men in tow.

Bones, yelling for Randolph to keep going, veered sharply to the left, one of Falconer's men following in dogged pursuit.

Randolph steered Dax's horse toward the road, but this area of the Cotswolds was rocky and uneven, and like a ghost materializing amid the slant of gray rain, a huge, bulky stone suddenly loomed before them. Cursing, Randolph eased up on the reins, guiding the horse to the left and around it. In that split second of slowing, Falconer and his man gained on them and came abreast on either side.

Falconer, eyes cold and emotionless, ordered Randolph to hold up, while from their other side another man reached out and caught the horse's bridle, bringing the animal to a cruel halt.

Robyn would have been thrown from the saddle if Randolph hadn't held tight to her—but in saving her from being tossed to the ground, he lost his chance to reach for Dax's pistol.

Falconer's man swiped it from its holster, aiming at Robyn as he pulled back on the hammer.

"Do nothing foolish," he warned.

"Blade!" Randolph breathed, stunned to see him. "Don't do this, man," he said, reduced to begging for their lives. "Don't—"

"Save your breath, *friend*. I cut my ties with you and all the others that day in the caves. Ran into a bit of luck, though, when I stumbled on to Falconer's men that morning. They were in a mind to learn about Dax. And me? I was just the one to give them all the details, join up with them, and help hunt him down."

"Where is he?" Robyn demanded. "Where is Dax?"

Blade, fixing his gaze on her, hooked a fist to one thigh,

pushing back his coat and exposing the long-handled knife sheathed there. "Gone. That's what he is."

No. She wouldn't believe it. Could not. "You *lie*. He's not dead. There is nothing you or Falconer or any man could do to kill him."

"Oh, he's dead, all right. Took my blade right through the eye, he did . . . just before them demons from hell came for him."

Soul seekers. Midnight. Oh. God. Robyn felt her body go slack and a horrid rushing sound begin in her ears as she remembered Dax telling her that nothing of this earth could harm him . . . nothing but a soul seeker or another Phantom.

"That's enough, Blade," Falconer said, a dangerous impatience threading his tone. He came side to side with Dax's mount, his dark gaze taking in Robyn—her sodden hair, clothes . . . the talismans about her neck. He reached out, caught her around the waist, and dragged her from Dax's saddle onto his own. Blade, gun trained on Randolph, warned him with the gesture to put up no fight.

"Here ends your flight, Lady Robyn. Lord Morely and your aunt await your arrival."

His words barely penetrated the grief whirling through her. Her aunt, here, in the Cotswolds? With Morely? "I don't believe you," Robyn said struggling against his hold. "I believe nothing either of you say."

"Lady Archer has been in Lord Morely's care for some time now—in fact, since the day you arrived at Land's End to find her gone. Should you not come willingly, I doubt Morely will be merciful with her. You are the only reason he has kept your aunt alive. If you want her dead, keep fighting me."

Robyn instantly stilled.

To Randolph, he warned, "If you value your life—and the lady's—you won't try anything." He motioned for Randolph to move forward. "Head for the road."

Randolph glanced at Robyn, willing, she knew, to fight to the death for her.

"Go," she whispered brokenly. She wouldn't risk her aunt's life, or his.

Randolph moved.

Blade followed.

Robyn, held tight by Falconer, turned her head, looking back, hoping beyond hope to see some sign of Bones or Dax. *Oh, God, Dax* . . . A snap of lightning whipped at the belly of the sky and then lost itself in the night. And it seemed to Robyn there was no life behind them, nothing . . . and a pain unlike any she'd ever known erupted deep inside.

Falconer brought them to a manor house—huge, sprawling, and under construction, though it appeared as if no work had taken place there in a number of weeks. Through the rain, a pale, yellow glow could be seen spilling out of nearly every window. At the base of the front steps, a lone, stone-faced man with a gun in his grip stood sentinel.

Falconer stopped before him. "Get Morely. Tell him I have Lady Robyn, and am taking her to the stones." He swung to the ground, dragging Robyn off the saddle with him. She tried to yank away, but his hold was vicious. With his free hand, he took a length of rope from his saddle and tossed it to Blade. "Tie his hands," he ordered, motioning to Randolph, "then take him inside, along with the saddle packs."

Falconer headed away from the house, yanking Robyn along beside him.

Wind-driven rain washed into her, sheet after sheet, cold and piercing. If not for the fact that Randolph and Aunt Amy were being held captive—and something else, a secret *something* beginning to reveal itself inside her— Robyn would have fought Falconer. She'd have lashed out at him until he'd had no other choice but to pull his gun on her. She no longer cared what happened to her, for she was dead inside. The light had been snuffed out of her the moment she'd learned Dax had been killed. But to fight Falconer now would put Randolph at further risk, and Aunt Amy as well. And this *feeling* inside, a sense she'd inherited from her mother and aunt and every woman before her, needed time to manifest itself.

Steeling her nerves, tamping down her grief, Robyn allowed Falconer to haul her away from the manse to a stone structure that showed briefly amid fitful snaps of lightning. *A barrow*, Robyn thought, following Falconer inside, remembering the oilskin map she'd found in her cloak, with its words and crude markings.

Constructed of large stones, the barrow was as tall as a man and as wide as three . . . and inside it was a hollowed void. Cold. Dank. Dark—utterly dark.

Earth smell swallowed her. Subtle energy beat beneath her feet, its ancient tempo calling to something deep, deep inside of her.

This was hallowed ground, Robyn knew. A place preserved through the mists and march of time. Against her chest, the heart talismans burned—hers and Dax's. She touched them briefly and felt the earth shimmer in response.

"Why did you bring me here?" she asked, wondering what Falconer knew—about her, about the talismans, about Dax.

He didn't get a chance to answer. Another man came into the barrow, taller, stronger, more intense: Morely.

"Welcome, my dear. No, no, don't turn. Just move, if you please." Morely pressed one hand against the small of Robyn's back, open palmed, and thrust her forward, so that she was dead center in the middle of the barrow. "There. That's where you belong. And to answer your question, *this* is why you are here—for you to simply be, that's all—for you to stand here."

"I—I don't understand. What does my presence have to do with anything?"

"Ah, no doubt your lovely, mysterious aunt will be able to explain all; we'll visit her in a moment. Until then, my dear, just stand here, yes? Simply be present in this place."

The wind blew rain through seep holes in the stone. Snaps of lightning leaked inward, turning the barrow to licks of brilliance here, there, then gone . . . again and again, over and over.

Robyn turned quickly, wanting to see the face of the man who had ruined her father at the gaming table, had sent his watchdog to trail her, had sent killers after Dax.

In one brief instant of flaring light, she saw him: hair a shocking white, skin milky and translucent, eyes a strange blue with deep red pupils. As emotionless as the skin of his face was without color. Half Phantom, Robyn thought . . . but no, he was not even that, for there was no shimmer of power in him, no infinite depths of energy beating inside of him. He was neither man nor Phantom, but something in between—a being Cursed and caught, wanting entry into one world . . . but dying in this.

He smiled, watching her watch him, and it was a ghastly sight.

"Do I frighten you, Lady Robyn?"

She turned her face away from him. "No."

He laughed—just a grunt of air through his lips, really— and then he was silent.

The talismans became hotter. Sizzled. Warming her skin through layers of material. The energy beneath her feet lifted, widened.

And her secret—the *sense* about her that she'd been gifted with at birth—grew by leaps, by bounds, an energy all its own, feeding itself, multiplying. Robyn breathed, drinking it in, marveling at her own self being revealed . . . for *she* was the secret she'd discovered, a being of incredible possibilities, a conduit through which the energy of the earth could flow.

And Morely knew. Somehow, he knew. That's why she

was here, Robyn guessed, to capture whatever energy lifted out of the earth.

"Tell me," Morely whispered, "tell me what you *feel* . . . what you *see*."

Robyn wanted to lie, wanted to say she felt nothing but his heartlessness and the barrow's hallowedness, but suddenly a wealth of images bloomed around her and she gave a small cry of alarm, unable to help herself.

"Everything," she gasped, terrified. "I see . . . feel . . . everything."

"Excellent," Morely breathed, and he stayed where he was, blocking the only way out of the barrow.

Chapter Twenty-one

Life and death and all things in between spun crazily around Robyn, from one chunk of stone to another. Time seemed to warp and fold as happenings played out on piece after piece of stone—her life and the lives of others, even Morely's.

She watched as a younger Morely, with color in his skin and feeling still in his heart, paid in blood to coax a Curse from the French soil. She watched as he died during a massacre following the fall of Robespierre . . . and then rose from the red-soaked ground, caught between two worlds, his thoughts forever on a woman he could never have.

Robyn winced, moving beyond the disturbing truth of Morely . . . and then she felt the presence of her mother, Dax's mother, and others, countless others—all murdered by soul-seeking Phantoms. Robyn realized then that what she had thought to be truth—that her mother had been run down by a carriage, that other women in her family had died of this or that—weren't truths at all, but mind-sways woven through the thoughts of mortals, fashioned by Phantoms wanting to shield their presence. All through her family's history, the women had been taken because of what they could do, because of the gifts they possessed.

And she would be no different, Robyn knew, for she saw her own final moment . . . one of smothering darkness and hot, hot flames.

Her breathing went shallow, her lungs thick, until she moved beyond even that. . . .

Until she saw *him*—Dax, but not Dax—a blinding pulse of whiteness in the rain-dark night, his Phantom aura fully realized.

He was at the bank of the stream where she and Bones and Randolph had left him, but the sight of the flooded area and the dark night were the only familiar things about the scene. Around him lay the litter of Morely's men. All of them downed, swiftly no doubt. And beyond them, like a swath of white flame, was a circle of soul seekers, their combined energies a vivid brilliance and vibrating screech in the air as they readied to charge Dax.

He was a being Robyn did not recognize. His left eye was a swirl of blackness, nothingness upon nothingness, while his right eye was a green gleam.

All else about him—everything about him—was a ghostly shimmer, the color of moon glow and madness.

It would be futile for the soul seekers to challenge him. They would not win. Dax would destroy them—one by one or all at once, it made no difference to him, though he preferred that they choose to follow him, Robyn knew. And in her mind she saw them doing just that, and her heart did a slow slide into despair for she knew Dax was lost to her.

She clutched one hand to the talismans about her neck, as if doing so would heal him of his Curse . . . as if doing so would ground her in some way, would ground *him*.

But it didn't. Instead, it was as if she'd physically touched him.

Dax lifted his head. Like an arrow sent true to its target, he honed in on her, knew exactly where she was, and why . . . and he reached for her, telling her he would soon race for her. Hard. Fast. Unrelenting.

Robyn felt the force of his mental touch. Felt the expectations of his physical desires. This night, the soul-stealing Phantom would have her.

This couldn't be the way of it, the end of it.

Robyn, wanting to change the outcome of the visions she saw, pressed her eyes shut tight. She focused her thoughts far beyond what was happening around her, remembered every second of every hour that she and Dax had shared . . . and mixed the memories with every hope she'd ever harbored of the life they might one day have had.

And then . . . *nothing*.

Robyn snapped her eyes open. No visions. No Dax. No lightning. Not a thing. Even the wind had died down. She heard only rain. And the breaths of Morely standing behind her, heavy, through his mouth.

"What just happened?" she whispered, shaken. "Why bring me here?"

"Surely you can feel it—how your presence stirs the energy here, thinning the barrier between this realm and another," he said, taking her by the arm. She caught his scent as he dragged her back outside. He smelled of wet wool and moldy dreams.

Robyn was a sodden, frightened mess as he drew her up the stairs and into the manse. She stumbled into the foyer, hearing the echoes of their footsteps in the huge space, seeing workmen's tools collected in a corner . . . and light, a blaze of light. The place was filled with it. Candles smoked in fixtures along the walls and in whatever other vessels would hold them. Some were set dangerously close to wall hangings, others placed in odd spots on the floor, the collective light causing hideous shadows to dance against the high ceiling and dusty flooring.

"This way," Morely said.

He dragged Robyn from the front foyer into a long hall filled with oil lamps and more candles, thrusting open a set of doors at the end.

The light of the foyer and hall paled in comparison to the brightness of the room within. The unfurnished area was filled with a stunning luminescence—from candles and lanterns and a roaring fire in the hearth—all of it magnified several times over as it was reflected in the tall, drapeless windows.

"Robbie!" Amelia Archer was seated in the only chair of the room, near the windows, a bound Randolph kneeling beside her.

Robyn, blinking against the brightness as Morely thrust her into the room, cried out at the sight of her aunt.

Usually flawless in her attire, Amelia appeared worn and wrinkled, her day gown of light blue poplin torn at the hems, her rich black hair with its few hints of gray escaping its many pins. She wore no jacket, gloves, or hat. And no shoes.

"Auntie." Emotion overwhelmed Robyn as she ran to Amelia's side. "What's happened . . ." She knelt down, pushed up the hem of her aunt's gown and saw that Amelia's left ankle was swollen several times its natural size. Purpled an ugly blue-black, there were angry streaks of red radiating up her skin from the misshapen joint.

"The bone is broken, I'm afraid."

"How?"

"Morely and his wretched cane. He found me digging into the dark corners of his life and didn't like it." Amelia reached for Robyn's hand, gripping it tightly. "I'd have run from here days ago, had I been able," she whispered. "Whatever happens, Robbie, if you can get free, *go*, do you hear? Even if it means leaving me behind."

Robyn shook her head. "No, I won't do that." She couldn't help the sobs that came, the trembling as Amelia drew her into a warm hug. She pressed her face against her aunt's neck and held tight, not certain she wouldn't shatter into a thousand pieces.

"Robbie. Sweetheart. They haven't hurt you, have they?"

Robyn dragged in a ragged breath and again shook her

head. "Not me. *Sandy*. And Dax . . . and all his men, all
but Randolph." In a rush of words, she told her aunt
everything that had happened since she and Dax had begun their search.

Amelia, listening quietly, running soothing strokes up
and down Robyn's arms, glared at Morely. "I can only pray
the authorities listen to Ballinger and understand what
Tisdale knows. Denville committed no treason against the
Crown. It was you, Morely, who created false evidence to
see him hanged. I know that now. You were forever trying
to ruin Denville . . . and all because Simonne chose him
over you. You never understood that she did not love you,
that she was never yours."

"But she should have been . . . *would have been*, if not for
Denville."

"He did nothing but care for her while you, vile creature that you are, caused her death."

"Not me," he shot back, "but the soulless creatures determined to have all our hearts. If you are going to damn me,
Amelia, know your facts. I intended only to steal the talisman. *Nothing* more. I never meant for her to be harmed."

"You did more than harm her. You killed her and ruined the lives of her husband and son."

"*Enough.* No more, do you hear?"

"And now look at you," Amelia went on. "Colorless.
Heartless. You're just a shell: not dead, yet not alive, not
fully. And all because you made a blood pact with an old
seeress who drenched her life in sorcery—a pact that you
believed would bring you Simonne. But it didn't, did it?
You followed a path others took, Morely. Robyn's mother
and I met too many like you—men and women who sold
their souls in the hopes of claiming something or someone
they would never have. All of them Cursed in the end."

"I said enough, Amelia. You know *nothing*."

"I know everything! Simonne came to Robyn's mother
and me for help. She knew of the Curse you'd called out

of the ground. That's why the Countess of Chelsea gave Simonne one of the talismans—as protection for her and for her son. You wagered your soul to the devil, Morely, but not even hell wanted you. Haven't you realized yet that you are the one who fed the Curse . . . and in the end were fed to it?"

To Robyn, Amelia said, "He became half man, half Phantom, but with the strength of neither. He told me himself that the cost to restore him fully to life is the soul of his firstborn son—a son who will inherit his Curse."

Robyn felt her stomach go hollow.

"Say no more," Morely blasted, body jerking at the cold truth of Amelia's words. He ran one hand over his face, drew in a deep breath, and then fixed his sights on Robyn.

"Do you even know where you are? Have you any clue as to where you've been brought, and why I've filled this place with light?"

Robyn, terrified of him, yet at the same time trying to understand what he was and what he'd sired, shook her head.

"This was once known as Morning's Rose . . . and I am certain it holds the third of the trio of heart talismans, two of which you now wear. It is the house Denville built for his wife, the one he intended for his son. But he was forced to pass the property to Amelia or see it lost to his son forever . . . and it is now part of your dowry, compliments of your aunt."

"That much is true," Amelia said. "Denville and I both hoped Dax had survived the carriage accident, that we would somehow find him and bring him home. But years went by, and the evidence against Denville mounted. He knew he might very well be hanged, and so he saw to it that Morning's Rose was passed to me. His instructions were that I keep it maintained for Dax should he ever return. In the event that he did not, it was to become part of your dowry." Voice going quiet, Amelia said, "Last January, when your mother died, Robbie, it put into motion a series of events . . . events that have led all of us here, to this moment."

Robyn felt a tremor of emotion whisk through her, felt as if she was at the edge of a truth she already knew. "What do you mean?"

"Dax had no memory of his life until the moment of your mother's death. He contacted me, Robbie, and shared with me how the pieces of his past returned to him. I believe your mother, once she passed to the other side, sought Dax and helped him to remember his past." Amelia stroked a wet strand of hair from Robyn's face. "I know all of this sounds fantastical, and that it must be overwhelming for you. But from what you just told me, my sweet, I know that you've seen your mother for yourself . . . and have felt the stirrings of your own capabilities."

Robyn, tears in her eyes, nodded, knowing it was because of her time with Dax these past weeks that she had come to recognize what was inside of her. She motioned to Morely, as if to ask, *How did we come to be here with him?*

Amelia seemed to read Robyn's mind. "When Dax boarded a ship to return, I brought in workers to restore the estate. That's when Morely turned his eye my way. He is determined to have all of the talismans. He has long suspected that Denville hid one of them somewhere within Morning's Rose."

Robyn jerked her gaze to Morely, finally understanding why he'd lured her father to a hazard table, why she'd been attacked while wearing the cloak . . . and even why Falconer had sought out Sandy and lured him to the Cotswolds. Every bit of what Morely had done had been because he wanted the talismans. She closed her eyes, drawing in a too-shallow breath as she remembered the sight of Sandy being shot, of him tumbling into the water.

"You have always been an important link to my survival,

my dear," Morely said. "You were gifted at birth with the breath of life I need and betrothed on the day of your christening to the one person in this world—and the next—who can destroy me."

Robyn opened her eyes. "What are you talking about?"

Amelia put one arm around her. "He's talking of your legacy, Robbie. It's why he took you into the barrow. It's why he won't harm you now."

Remembering the terror of all she'd seen and felt while inside of the barrow, Robyn pulled away from her aunt and got to her feet. Afraid and overwhelmed, she felt the heart talismans burn hot, right through her wet clothing. Agitated, she shrugged out of her drenched cloak, letting it puddle at her feet, her gaze never leaving Morely.

"It's just as I've always told you," Amelia said, her voice calm. "You hold your magic within your heart. You are all that is good. It is as simple and as complex as that. There is no possible way the goodness in you can aid anything evil. Just the opposite. What is good can be saved by you, Robbie. And what is evil can be destroyed."

To Morely, Amelia said, "You were a fool twice. The first was when you made your pact with the seeress . . . and the second is now in believing my niece holds the key to your salvation. She doesn't. Look at her and you will see your doom. Touch her, and you will taste it."

Fury flared in him. "Shut. Up. Amelia." With a flick of one hand, he motioned for Blade to dump the contents of Dax's saddle packs, determined to find the oilskin that would lead him to the final talisman Denville had tucked away somewhere within Morning's Rose.

Robyn looked at the contents of Dax's packs littering the floor between her and Morely. She saw the oilskin . . . and also saw a sight that tore at her heart: a lone, red ribbon lying atop a frayed and soiled piece of linen. It was the very ribbon she'd given to Dax all those years ago when they had first met in that cold cottage in Sussex.

It was the ribbon upon which she'd threaded a heart talisman.

Robyn's stomach clenched, remembering the sight of Dax, the taste of him, the *feel* of him. If she couldn't save him, she could at least attempt to save her aunt and Randolph . . . and maybe even a part of Morely, whether he deserved it or not.

Slowly, she lifted her gaze to him. "You don't need the oilskin. I know where it is. The talisman. I can lead you to it."

Morely's mouth spread into a smile, one that didn't reach his inhuman eyes. "Yes," he breathed, nodding. "Yes, I think you would know."

"I'll lead you there, but only if you allow my aunt and Randolph to go free."

"No," Amelia said. "Don't do this, Robbie."

"I saw what I have to do. You'll be all right, Aunt Amy."

"It's you I am worried about."

"I know," Robyn whispered. "And I love you for that."

Morely grabbed Robyn and headed for the door. Motioning to Amelia and Randolph, he yelled to Falconer, "Get them out of here." To Robyn, he snarled, "Where to?"

"Upstairs . . . on the third floor . . . in the rooms that once were Simonne's."

He grabbed hold of her by one arm, thrusting her hard toward the door.

They went the length of the hall before Robyn heard it—gunfire, in the distance. Morely, hearing the sound as well, dragged her into the nearest room, one that was unlit. In the darkness they could see a sweep of land . . . and riders, with torches. Morely's men were firing at them.

"Damn their interference," Morely muttered, and then turned his attention on her. "Tell me. What did you see while inside of the barrow?"

Robyn held her gaze steady with his. "Your doom," she whispered, and she looked beyond him, to the flicker of torchlight in the distance . . . and beyond even that . . . to Dax.

He wasn't shimmering his way to her, but charging through the night atop a huge warhorse not of this realm. He wasn't shimmering, because he was leading a legion of the hooded riders—now his riders, his minions—to the lone manor with its hallowed barrow and ancient talismans . . . and to her.

He was coming for her, Robyn knew. He would destroy Falconer and Blade and Morely, especially Morely. No one and nothing would be able to stop him. He would reach them, and they would die.

"No," Morely rasped, as if he could hear her thoughts, and jerked her away from the window, heading back to the hall.

Hearing more gunfire, Morely began kicking over the candles and lamps as they made their way to the stairs. Once in the gallery above, he shoved over more of the lights. Soon, flame danced and smoke swelled.

"What are you doing?" Robyn cried.

"Giving myself cover for when I leave here. Now lead me to the talisman."

He shoved her hard forward, and by instinct alone Robyn led them deeper down the hall that was lined by smoking lanterns, and then into a series of rooms at the right, the silver hearts burning hotter as she went.

They entered into a sitting room and then the bed-chamber beyond it. The area was cold and dark, lit only by the glare from the hall, but Robyn could make out the hearth with its mass of stones—and that is where she'd find the talisman, she knew. Of the many images that blasted by her in the barrow, she remembered vividly the one of Dax's mother, here, in front of the hearth. With trembling hands, Robyn felt along the upper stonework, felt the indent of a rose outline and then, pushing, felt the stone give way. She plunged one hand inside the opening, groped there, and feeling something soft, yet hard, pulled

free a small pouch, the hearts about her neck fairly burning her now.

Morely quickly plucked the pouch from her hand. "Finally," he said, opening it and upturning it all in one swift
motion. The third talisman tumbled into his left palm.

Robyn drew in a breath, for it seemed the very air rippled, clear and crisp—as if an earthly energy had shimmered upward from the heart and pushed all elements
from its path. She touched her hand to the talismans at
her chest, curled her fingers around them, and held tight.
Yes. *There* . . . she felt an arc of responding energy from
the pair and from her own body as well, a subtle vibration
that held the earth's harmony . . . pure, sure, strong.

Morely, watching her, held perfectly still. "It's happening. You feel it." He glanced around them, just his eyes
moving in the white freakishness that was his face.

"What is? *What's* happening?"

He snapped his palm shut around the talisman. "We
have to hurry."

"So go," she gasped, smoke curling into the room, burning her throat. "Take the talismans and go. Th-There's still
time."

He gave her an oily smile. "You care so much for me,
then?"

"Hardly. I just don't want Dax to suffer at your hands
any more than he already has."

"Ah, my dear, but he does have to suffer, just a bit more,
and then I'll be done with him. You see, what your aunt
said was true: The cost to restore me fully to life is the soul
of my firstborn son . . . and he is that, you know."

Morely took her roughly by the arm, dragging her back
the way they'd come. The gallery was choked with smoke
now, flames eating at the walls, the floor. Robyn, gagging
on smoke, her eyes tearing, tripped over her wet skirts,
falling forward.

"Stay on your feet!"

"There's nowhere to go!"

He hauled Robyn upright, whirled about, and dragged her to the farthest end of the gallery, thrusting her back against the wall, her skirts dangerously near a duo of lanterns. Morely nearly toppled a small table with yet another blazing lantern. "Call them."

"Who?"

"Why do you think Simonne betrothed you to her son, to *our* son?"

"I don't know!" Robyn yelled, her throat scorched, her brain starved for fresh air.

"Because you and all the women of your family were born with the ability to touch the talismans, to *use* them . . . and whoever does that can control the soul seekers. *Now call them.*" Face inches from Robyn's, Morely took her right hand and shoved it over the heart talismans dangling about her neck, and then took her left hand and pressed it to the talisman in his palm. "Call. Them."

And she did, God help her, she did it—she gripped the talismans and mentally summoned those hideous fiends because she wanted them away from Dax, because she wanted him to be free of their relentless menace once and for all.

She heard the high-pitched hum of their energy first—a sound like the screech of animals—and then she saw them, beasts and riders materializing in a blaze of raging energy, right through the flames, and she watched as Morely's eyes went wide with excitement, with anticipation, and she knew what he intended: for the soul seekers to take Dax's soul the minute he arrived. But Morely didn't know about Dax . . . that he'd turned full Phantom at the stream . . . that he would shimmer himself here in a matter of a heartbeat once he knew Robyn had called the seekers.

Let Morely learn on his own, Robyn thought, and gripped the talismans tight. She felt a shudder rip through her, felt the flames and the heat and the smoke seemingly fall back as the gallery gave way to another place, another time, just as when her mother had come to her in the tower.

But while there had been the scent of something precious in the air the night the Countess of Chelsea had walked through the room, as if the convergence of planes had been harmony itself, Robyn smelled nothing precious now. This wasn't harmony waiting for the fiends, but all that was dark and disturbing, eternally evil. Robyn sent them through to it.

Though it was the Curse that commanded the seekers, that put them on the path of harvesting souls every midnight, it was Robyn who could end them. She knew that now. With the talismans, with the time she'd spent in the barrow, she held the energy that would send the foul fiends back to the hell that had spawned them.

Morely cried out as first one seeker and then another and another charged from the flames . . . straight into the depths of darkness. *"No,"* he yelled as the last one was sucked away and the gallery expanded once more into full view, the flames and the smoke harsher now, and nearer. "Fool! What have you done?" He pulled his hand from hers, the talisman glowing bright in his palm.

"I just saved your soul," she cried.

"But he doesn't want his soul," Dax said, shimmering into view. "He wants to be fully Phantom. That's why he set the house aflame, because he intended to leave here not as man but as Phantom, something nothing can kill."

"And I will," Morely said.

Dax's energy was a hard shimmer that neither the flames nor smoke could penetrate. His right eye was a green gleam, his left a swirl of blackness, while whips of energy burst in fitful snaps just inches from his skin. "Tell her, Morely," he said. "Tell Robyn your true plan—for me to come after her, for the seekers to snatch my soul . . . and for you to become full Phantom."

"Even with the seekers gone, I will still have what I want," Morely growled.

"Oh? How so?"

"Because of Robyn. Because she is your first love and your last, because you will do nothing to harm her . . . and you'll do anything to save her."

"The man in me would have. But the man in me no longer exists."

Robyn saw the telltale signs of the Phantom gathering its energy, ready to suck the soul from Morely.

"Dax. Do not."

"Give me one reason why I should spare his miserable life."

"Because if you kill him, your own soul will be forfeit. It is the cost of the Curse. It is why your mother betrothed you to me." Robyn had witnessed the truth of the past while inside the barrow. She knew now what she had to do.

But Morely saved her the trouble as, in a rash move, he lunged for her, toppling the small table and lantern beside him. The lamp tipped into him, shattering. Oil spewed out, coating Morely's left side, catching flame, and igniting with a *whoosh* of sound. Robyn shrank back into the corner, watching in horror as Morely was engulfed in fire.

He dropped the talisman as he tried to beat out the flames, his colorless face a mask of pain, his red pupils becoming pinpoints. Agonized seconds later he threw himself against the window, *through* it, into the rain . . . and then tumbled through the air, three floors down to his death.

Robyn, her throat raw with smoke and choked by fear, whipped her gaze to Dax, fearing the Phantom would now pounce.

"Breathe," he said.

And Robyn remembered that first night they had met, as children, and she'd told him, whenever he was afraid, to just breathe. . . .

Robyn did as he said, gulping fresh air from the window, and then she slid to the floor and lunged forward, snatching up the third talisman, clutching it to the duo dangling from her neck. The action took her far from the window and the exit it offered, but she wouldn't leave the talisman behind.

Robyn began to quake uncontrollably as she felt the press of heated flames, as she remembered the vision she'd had while in the barrow—one of smothering darkness and hot, hot flame.

Dax, the fiend that he'd become, was that darkness, she knew. His gaze was on her, hard, relentless. He would come to her, would lay her flat, and then he would cover her, claim her . . . and she would be no more. The only good thing about it would be that she would die in his arms.

No. Her mind, her very will, balked at that sad scenario. She wanted to live, with him, for years and years. Robyn gripped the talismans tight. She would not die like this. She refused.

Flame erupted between them, Dax's gaze never leaving her. He moved directly through the fire, reaching for her . . . and that's when she saw it: Dax's Phantom and his human self parting, the flames eating at the Phantom, holding it tight in the hotness . . . while the man stepped free. His left eye, pierced by Blade's knife when Dax had turned full Phantom at the flooded stream bank, was now healed and healthy, while the bullet wound he took as a man moments before that now bled freely.

"Dax." She looked up at him . . . at the cuts and burns on his sun-bronzed skin . . . at the blood blooming at his shoulder . . . at his blue eyes. *Blue.* As blue as the moment when she had first met him.

"Aye, it's me, love."

His voice sounded a league away, but his arms—oh, sweet Lord—she felt his arms wrap around her, hold her tight, and then draw her upward.

Robyn, blinking through the blinding smoke, through her tears, wrapped herself about him. "Oh, God, Dax . . . it *is* you."

"And only me," he murmured, gathering her close,

sidestepping a little at the force of her coming so hard into his embrace. "I'm here, Robyn. I'll *always* be here."

She believed him. She clung to him.

He kicked in the nearest door, stumbling inside of the room as a volley of fire swooshed down the hall. They landed in a heap on the floor, Robyn on top of him, their legs tangling, Dax slamming the door shut with his booted feet.

Darkness swallowed them. Cool, clean air laced about them.

Trembling, Robyn sucked in a breath, burrowing her face against his shirtfront. He smelled of smoke and mud, rain and leather. He smelled of *life*.

And blood.

"Dax. Your shoulder."

"Grazed only. There's no lead in me."

She wanted to fuss over him, but he wouldn't allow it.

"I—I thought you were lost to me," she whispered.

"For a while, I thought so, too. But I'm here now, and have no intention of leaving your side ever again."

"Oh, Dax . . ." And she trembled, the horror of it all still too stark in her mind.

In the cool, blessed darkness, Dax sought her lips, kissing her, drinking her breath and her fears into his mouth. "It's all right," he murmured, not breaking their contact. "Everything's going to be all right. I've got you."

She nodded, crying, kissing him, her body and her mind slowly calming.

Gently, he said, "We need to move, love. We need to get out of here." And with a final kiss that promised her a lifetime of pleasure, he helped her to her feet, took her by the hand, and led her away from the smoking door to the window.

He motioned for her to turn her head away, and then with one booted foot smashed out several leaded panes and the wood as well. He cleared away the broken shards of glass, the splintered pieces of wood, then climbed onto the sill, threw one leg over it, and drew Robyn onto his lap.

"We'll have to climb down."

"Dax. You've been shot. You can't hold me and climb at the same time."

"I can." He grinned. "I will. Now that I have you, I'm not letting go." He scooped her against him with one strong arm and began the descent down a sturdy trellis with the other.

Fresh air hit her face . . . and rain, a steady pour of it. Far below, she saw her aunt, with Randolph and Bones on either side of her. Near them, on horseback, was an even dearer sight—Sam, with an injured but alive Sandy in the saddle behind him. Robyn felt her tears mingle with the raindrops. The night that had been so filled with horrors was now one of blessings. There were other people gathered on the lawn, with one man standing out among them. Lord Ballinger. So it had been Ballinger and his men riding up the drive with torches. Spying them, Ballinger shouted some orders, but Randolph and Bones were already on the move to help Dax and his lady.

"I've been thinking," Dax said, a bit too chattily for Robyn's comfort.

"Concentrate, or you'll slip," she scolded.

"I've been thinking about us," Dax went on, "and our betrothal."

She clung to him, rain plastering her hair to her skull, her clothes to her skin. "What about our betrothal?"

"I think it's gone on too long."

"Oh?"

"Aye." He nuzzled her wet neck. Nipped her earlobe. "I think I've waited long enough. It's time I married you." He paused, ignoring the shouts from below, the cold rain, his bleeding shoulder. "If you'll have me. Cursed though I may still be."

"Yes," she said, without hesitation. "To everything. To anything."

And she kissed him, full on the mouth, her hands framing his face, the heart talisman a warm tingle against his cheek and her palm, the other two caught between their hearts—and it felt right, felt good . . . felt magical.

BOOK SIX

The Bride

Epilogue

Robyn and Dax were married at Land's End at the height of the Summer Season, on a day that was breezy, sun smeared, with puffy clouds in the sky and the scent and roar of the sea in the air.

The manse overflowed with guests, among them Randolph with a beaming and newly beringed Mattie on one strong arm, and a grinning Bones and Sam as well. Sandy and Lily were there, as were all of Robyn's other cousins, and Aunt Amy, of course, who presided like a queen over the festivities, her ankle on the mend.

All charges of treason against Denville had been dissolved once it was learned Morely had forced Tisdale to create evidence against Denville. Had Morely not thrown himself to his death, he would have been subject to execution for bearing false witness against a peer.

The only family member not in attendance at the wedding was Robyn's father, whom Robyn had forgiven and who was now under the care of a private physician in Brighton—his grief over his wife's death being treated with something other than drink. Robyn looked forward to the day when her father would laugh with her again, when they could talk of the woman they'd both loved and had lost.

With the earl's good wishes, it was Sandy who gave her over to Dax, to Broderick.

Champagne flowed. Cook's delicacies, heaped atop table after table, were devoured with gusto, and as the sun set and the musicians Aunt Amy had hired tuned their instruments, Dax—*Broderick*—took hold of Robyn and didn't let go.

They danced and danced, and hours later, just before the final set, Robyn drew Dax out onto the terrace, and then down a flight of stairs to the back of the manse.

Eyes heady, filled with longing, Dax willingly followed.

"What are you doing, my love?" He paused on the last step to pull her close, to kiss her deep.

"Come," she murmured, slipping out of his hold, then guiding him down onto the grass and around the tower, where a carriage waited.

He halted abruptly at sight of it.

"Robyn . . ."

Gently, she took his gloved hands in hers, lifting both to her lips. "I want you to know that not all carriages will take you to disaster. I want you to know that you are not a bad omen, but a man who is a harbinger of good things . . . *very* good things."

"Robyn," he said again, hesitating.

"I know of a certain cottage I'd like to visit once again with you, only this time, I've made certain there's a very comfortable bed there." She met his gaze, asking the words he'd asked of her that first night together in the study: "Do you trust me?"

All the years of pain and separation he'd endured, all the loneliness, fell away. "With my life."

"Then come with me," she coaxed, "into the carriage . . . into our future."

His blue eyes heavy lidded with passion, Dax grinned—and then he swept Robyn up into his arms, holding her tight and kissing her soundly as he carried her to the carriage.

MELANIE JACKSON

A Curious Affair

Recent widow Jillian Marsh wasn't planning on killing herself that March night, but she hadn't ruled it out, either. It had rained for the last seventeen days—days in which her jaws were locked together and she was unable to speak. And ever since she'd been hit by lightning last October, the cats in town had been talking to her. Which meant she was insane, right?

But that night something changed. The cat Atherton appeared with something very interesting to say, and since Jillian could hardly go to the town's new lawman with a feline eyewitness, it was up to her to find out if there was indeed trouble afoot—or if this conspiracy and her newfound and unwanted attraction to Sheriff Murphy were all part of an endless hallucination.

ISBN 13: 978-0-505-52738-7

New York Times Bestselling Author

Marjorie M. Liu

Lannes Hannelore is one of a dying race born to protect mankind against demonic forces. And while those who look upon him see a beautiful man, this illusion is nothing but a prison. His existence is one of pure isolation, hiding in plain sight, with brief solace found in simple pleasures: stretching his wings on a stormy night, long late drives on empty highways, the deep soul of sad songs. But when Lannes finds a young woman covered in blood—desperate and alone, with no memory or past—he will be drawn into a mystery that makes him question all he knows. And though it goes against his nature and everything he fears, Lannes will risk his heart, his secrets, and his very soul, in order to save someone who could be the love of his life…or the end of it.

A Dirk & Steele Romance

THE Wild Road

AVAILABLE AUGUST 2008!

ISBN 13: 978-0-8439-5939-0

To order a book or to request a catalog call:
1-800-481-9191
This book is also available at your local bookstore, or you can check out our Web site **www.dorchesterpub.com** where you can look up your favorite authors, read excerpts, or glance at our discussion forum to see what people have to say about your favorite books.

CHRISTINE FEEHAN

Savannah Dubrinski was a mistress of illusion, a world-famous magician capable of mesmerizing millions. But there was one—Gregori, the Dark One—who held her in terrifying thrall. With a dark magic all his own, Gregori—the implacable hunter, the legendary healer, the most powerful of Carpathian males—whispered in Savannah's mind that he was her destiny. That she had been born to save his immortal soul. And now, here in New Orleans, the hour had finally come to claim her. To make her completely his. In a ritual as old as time . . . and as inescapable as eternity.

DARK MAGIC

ISBN 13: 978-0-8439-6056-3

Sandra Schwab

Sweet passion...

After a magical mishap that turned her uncle's house blue, Miss Amelia Bourne was stripped of her powers and sent to London in order to be introduced into polite society—and to find a suitable husband. Handsome, rakish Sebastian "Fox" Stapleton was all that and more. He was her true love. Wasn't he?

or the bitter taste of deceit?

At Rawdon Park, the country estate of the Stapletons, Amy began to wonder. It seemed that one sip of punch had changed her life forever—that this love, this lust, was nothing but an illusion. She and Fox were pawns in some mysterious game, and black magic had followed them out of Town. Without her powers, would she be strong enough to battle those dark forces and win? And would she be able to claim her heart's true desire?

Bewitched

ISBN 13: 978-0-505-52723-3

◻ **YES!**

Sign me up for the Love Spell Book Club and send my FREE BOOKS! If I choose to stay in the club, I will pay only $8.50* each month, a savings of $6.48!

NAME: _____

ADDRESS: _____

TELEPHONE: _____

EMAIL: _____

◻ I want to pay by credit card.

◻ **VISA**   ◻ MasterCard.   ◻ DISCOVER

ACCOUNT #: _____

EXPIRATION DATE: _____

SIGNATURE: _____

Mail this page along with $2.00 shipping and handling to:
**Love Spell Book Club
PO Box 6640
Wayne, PA 19087**
Or fax (must include credit card information) to:
610-995-9274
You can also sign up online at **www.dorchesterpub.com**.
*Plus $2.00 for shipping. Offer open to residents of the U.S. and Canada only. Canadian residents please call 1-800-481-9191 for pricing information.
If under 18, a parent or guardian must sign. Terms, prices and conditions subject to change. Subscription subject to acceptance. Dorchester Publishing reserves the right to reject any order or cancel any subscription.